THE
KING'S
CHOSEN

HIDDEN ENEMIES

THE
KING'S CHOSEN

HIDDEN ENEMIES
BOOK 2

L. WAITHMAN

GREENLEAF
BOOK GROUP PRESS

Published by Greenleaf Book Group Press
Austin, Texas
www.gbgpress.com

Distributed by Greenleaf Book Group

For ordering information or special discounts for bulk purchases, please contact Greenleaf Book Group at PO Box 91869, Austin, TX 78709, 512.891.6100.

Design and composition by Greenleaf Book Group
Cover design by Greenleaf Book Group
Cover illustration by Carrie-Sue Kay
Map design by Carrie-Sue Kay

Publisher's Cataloging-in-Publication data is available.

Print ISBN: 978-1-62634-984-1

eBook ISBN: 978-1-62634-985-8

Part of the Tree Neutral® program, which offsets the number of trees consumed in the production and printing of this book by taking proactive steps, such as planting trees in direct proportion to the number of trees used: www.treeneutral.com

Printed in the United States of America on acid-free paper

22 23 24 25 26 27 28 29   10 9 8 7 6 5 4 3 2 1

First Edition

To my husband James, for turning a kayak adventure on the Murray River into a lifetime together. And to my children Max, Matt, and Maddie who graciously accepted their lives being turned upside down when I started to write Lucas's story, but who have shown nothing but support.

LORD HAMMOND'S CASTLE

KING ITAN'S CASTLE

BLACK LOG INN

LORD ARON'S CASTLE

MONASTERY

BLACKSMITH'S FORGE

KILLEAND'S CASTLE

MELOC'S CASTLE

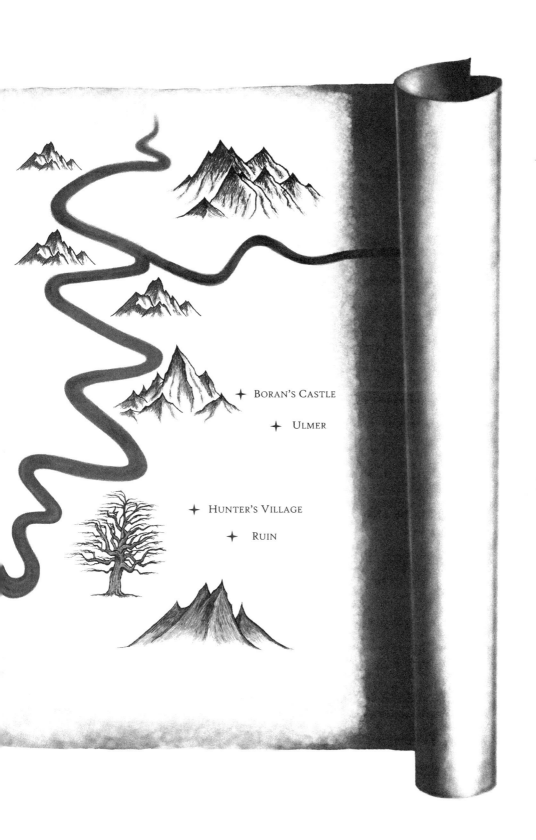

BORAN'S CASTLE

ULMER

HUNTER'S VILLAGE

RUIN

CHAPTER 1

Lucas opened his eyes. Where he was or what had just happened was an absolute mystery to him. Water splashed against stones, and he heard the gentle snorting of horses nearby. He was lying on a bed of pebbles on a riverbank, his wet clothing clinging to his skin. His head rested on a bedroll. Could it be his? He looked to his left and saw Officer Verron sitting next to him, gazing out over the river. The officer's long mustache, which curved upward to his sideburns, made him recognizable even from afar.

The river. Yes, now he remembered—he had been trying to cross it.

Several soldiers stood some distance away, their eyes on him.

"I see you're awake," Verron said, turning his head to look at him. He gave him a long stern stare. "Give me one good reason," he said, "why I should not be arresting you right now, and having you dragged back to the king behind a horse, for abandoning our overnight camp the way you did."

"I'm sorry, sir," answered Lucas, attempting to sit up, "but I don't think I have one."

"I understand that the skirmish with the hunters may have affected you," Verron continued, "but we should have spoken if something was troubling you. I did not expect you to desert."

Lucas shook his head. "I did not intend to. I honestly don't know what drew me to the river, in the dead of night."

Verron's eyes softened. "Could you have been dreaming?"

"Quite possibly, sir," answered Lucas, although he did not believe he was at the time. He touched the side of his neck and felt a small lump where he'd pulled out the poisoned dart just seconds before everything had gone dark around him.

"That looks like a bee sting," said Verron. "Might be the reason you lost consciousness and fell off your horse."

Lucas nodded. It was easier than trying to explain that he was stopped from crossing the river by someone whose presence he had felt when it was too late to do anything about.

Officer Verron stood up. "We need to get back to camp," he said. "I left half the troops behind to go after you, and I sent the other half out to search. I will need to think on what to do with you."

Lucas rose as well and followed Verron's lead. He felt the eyes of the soldiers on him as he took the reins of his horse. He could tell by the expressions on their faces that they were confused, but surely they did not believe he had tried to desert? After the extent to which he had risked his personal safety for them the day before, to protect them, it made no sense.

Was the fight with the hunters not enough to prove his loyalty?

They had almost made it back to camp when Zera suddenly stepped out from behind a tree. Her hair poked out in messy tufts here and there, and she was still wearing her battle armor—and the dark circles under her eyes revealed that she had slept little. As the only other chosen at the temporary camp, it was clear to Lucas that she felt the full burden of protecting him. Officer Verron's horse spooked a little, and Zera backed up until the officer regained control over his horse. Zera flashed Lucas a nervous look before addressing Verron. "I am here to warn you, sir," she said hastily. "The messenger you sent last night, to the main camp at Lord Aron's castle, requesting the king's presence here, and assistance . . ."

"What about him?" asked Verron.

"He must have met General Finton on the road, sir. The general then came to the camp, demanding to know why half our company was not present. He knows that you went after Lucas in the night."

"And? That's the truth. I don't see why you've stopped us on the road to tell me this."

"The general is convinced Lucas deserted, sir."

"Did someone tell him that?"

"No, sir," answered Zera.

"But he believes that?"

"Yes, sir."

Lucas was not surprised that Finton was thinking the worst of him. The general had never hidden his dislike of him. He saw him as the cause for his son Eli's loss of leadership over the elite borns and had tried to discredit him in the eyes of others at every opportunity.

Verron nodded. "Get yourself back to camp," he said. "Don't let anyone see you do so. I don't need any more of my soldiers accused of desertion." He turned in his saddle and looked at Lucas. "And I need you to keep quiet. Do not say a word—I will handle this."

As soon as they rode into camp, General Finton approached him, carefully avoiding the smoldering fires and stepping over bedrolls that cluttered the ground, left by the soldiers that had gone to search for Lucas in the night and had not yet returned. Finton's pace and demeanor—and the formally dressed soldiers flanking him—made it obvious that he was on a mission, and that he'd been anxiously awaiting their return.

"Well, well," he said, "I would never have thought, when I woke up this morning, that I would have dealings with a deserter." His piercing eyes made Lucas cringe, but he tried to return the general's stare as casually as possible.

"General Finton," said Officer Verron. "I am pleased to see you here. How did you know we required assistance?"

"I encountered your messenger early this morning," Finton answered, without taking his eyes off Lucas. "Had quite a tale to tell regarding your encounter with hunters yesterday, so I came to offer a helping hand, but now it looks like I have to deal with another matter altogether."

"I appreciate you coming," said Verron, ignoring the general's gesture towards Lucas. "We have several wounded to take back to the king's camp at Lord Aron's castle, and a large group of hunters still traverses the woods. I lost five of my men during the attack, and they still require burial."

"Then we best not delay the inevitable," replied Finton, turning to two of his soldiers to give the order. "Arrest him!"

As the two soldiers approached him, Lucas saw that Zera had made it back into camp and was standing some distance away, watching some of Finton's soldiers, who convened by a large oak tree. Lucas watched as a magpie flew towards the tree and settled on one of its branches. Seeing the bird was not a good sign. In times past, it had meant death was near.

But Finton surely wouldn't see him killed?

As Lucas took a closer look at the men, he could see that one of them held a rope in his hands—his heart beat faster when he saw the hangman's knot at the end of the rope, and he instinctively tightened his grip on the reins. Officer Verron shook his head at Lucas—a signal that he not do anything rash.

Though it was hard to resist the urge to turn his horse and bolt, Lucas complied when told to get down from his horse. The two soldiers then gripped him firmly by the arms and led him to the tree, where the rope was then thrown over a branch. They were moving quickly, and Lucas knew their urgency could signal only one thing.

"May I ask what the meaning of this is?" asked Verron, dismounting faster than Lucas had ever seen him do. His voice sounded strained, and full of alarm.

"What does it look like, Officer?" Finton responded. "The boy deserted in the night, and you know full well what the penalty for that is."

"I don't know what you've been told," Verron answered, "but Lucas is no deserter. He was the first to go after some hunters that returned in the night, and, in his hurry to act, he failed to wake us before getting on his horse to chase them down. That was the boy's only mistake and the only one for which he should be held accountable. Do you not think I would have placed him under arrest myself if he'd tried to desert?"

"Your fondness for the boy has not gone unnoticed, Verron," answered Finton. "So, no, it would not surprise me if you would allow him to get away with it."

Verron broadened his shoulders. "We were attacked by the largest group of hunters I've ever come across," he said loudly, "and I don't believe there is a soldier who will contest that, if not for Lucas, the majority of us would likely be dead."

In the silence that followed, Finton glanced over his shoulder and caught Lucas's eye. Lucas's heart hammered in his chest. He hoped Finton was rethinking his decision, but then one of the two soldiers began to tie his hands behind his back, and Finton did nothing to call them off. It was Verron who stepped forward.

"Do not interfere!" said Finton, putting a hand on the officer's chest to block him. "I'm no fool. You would not have left half your company behind if hunters had come back in the night. I will take your word for it that he saved lives, and that is why I am willing to do this quickly, without further suffering."

"You cannot do this," protested Verron, trying to get past him. "He's a chosen, and you don't have the authority. He must seek audience from the king."

Finton's face turned red. "I will have you stripped of your position if you take another step," he shouted, turning around to rejoin his men, who waited under the tree.

"You were not here, sir," called Verron after him. "If you believe that a crime was committed, then it should be decided by trial."

At this, Finton only stormed away with more urgency, dismissing Verron with a wave of his hand. Lucas heard the harsh, ascending call of the magpie nearby and knew he was in danger. He felt the coarse bristles of the rope as it scraped along his face and settled around his neck. He looked at the face of the soldier who was adjusting the tightness of the rope around his neck. Lucas knew this soldier. He had been there during the attack on the treasury wagon, as had some of the other soldiers who stood at hand. He could sense they took no pleasure in carrying out the order, and they carefully avoided eye contact. Still held firmly by his arms, Lucas knew there was no way for him to get out of this, until the sound of swords being drawn from their scabbards made him look back in Verron's direction. Finton had heard it as well and turned around, his face filling with dread. Every soldier standing behind Verron had pulled their sword.

"You cannot be serious," Finton called out. "You're willing to risk your life and that of your men for *him*?"

"He risked his life for us yesterday." Verron's voice was steady. "We owe it to him, and I cannot stand by and watch as you destroy one of my best soldiers on a whim."

"On a whim! It is *your* personal attachment to the boy that is clouding your judgment," scolded Finton. "A grave crime has indeed been committed, and the punishment *will* be carried out." With that said, he gave a nod to the soldiers standing by Lucas, who then gripped the rope.

Lucas saw a look of horror wash over Verron's face, and he felt the rope pull tight around his neck. Just as his body lifted from the ground and he struggled to breathe, an arrow swished by. It narrowly missed the soldiers holding the rope, but it had startled them, and they let go in their surprise.

When his heels touched the ground again, Lucas saw Zera reloading her bow and noticed Verron had given her a nod to do so.

"That was just a warning," Verron told the soldiers. "Touch that rope again, and the next one will not miss its target." When the men made no move to continue with the order, Verron returned his attention to Finton. "Have the rest of your men stand down as well, General." Verron motioned to Finton's soldiers, only a handful of which had pulled their swords in defense but lowered them when they realized that their comrades had not.

Faced with the prospect of his soldiers either turning against him or being killed in the process of carrying out Lucas's sentencing, Finton had no other choice but to stand down. "The king should be arriving at the end of the day, if my messenger made it safely and in time," continued Verron, before Finton could say anything else. "I will ask that he determine what happened here."

Finton stood motionless, his body tense and his eyes glaring, but then he slowly nodded. "I am willing to wait until nightfall," he said. "If the king is not here by then, the boy will hang as a deserter, and you and your men better not stand in my way." He then turned back to his soldiers. "Stand down," he said, "and secure the boy to the tree for now."

Verron waited until the rope was removed from Lucas's neck before he had his men stand down. He then ordered them to dig the graves for the dead.

Lucas wasn't sure if the poison that had been in the dart was still affecting him or whether his body simply needed to rest. He felt

7

exhausted and allowed himself to doze while Verron's soldiers were busy digging graves around him. He was hungry and thirsty, as Finton had not permitted anyone near him for hours. He felt an itch on his nose and, since his hands were tied behind his back, bent his head to his shoulder to scratch it. The movement caused one of Finton's soldiers to turn and look at him with suspicion.

"Just an itch," said Lucas to put the soldier at ease. He sat up straight again and noticed Zera had stepped out of the grave she was digging. She had her black trousers tucked inside her laced boots and a belt held her white chosen shirt in place, but the sleeves were stained with the dark forest soil. Her battle armor and tunic lay discarded in a pile on the ground. He could tell Zera was anxious to take some form of action, but Finton had him well guarded by the soldiers that were most loyal to him. There would be no way of getting close without bloodshed. She glanced up at the branch above him, where the magpie was still sitting, and then looked towards the creek where Finton stood with his back turned—talking to one of his officers. She grabbed a water skin before walking over to Verron, who was digging a grave near Lucas.

The officer had removed his jacket and was wiping droplets of sweat from his face with the sleeve of his white shirt.

"Sir," said Zera and held the water vessel, made from animal skin, out to him.

"Thank you," said Verron and put the spade down to take a break.

"Sir?" asked Zera while the officer drank. "What if the king doesn't come? The general will be hanging Lucas, and we can't let that happen."

Lucas was relying on the king's evening appearance, but hearing Zera's question suddenly diminished that hope. He couldn't help but look up at the magpie.

"Keep your voice down," Verron hushed. He finished drinking and handed Zera the water skin back. "I am not going to let him hang

Lucas, but we need to keep our distance from both of them. Any wrong move on our part will likely see Lucas killed. I want to keep the general at ease and give him the impression that he's in control. I'll think of something that will get all of us out of this mess." He picked the spade up again and made a subtle gesture with his head for Zera to leave—the general was coming their way.

For most of the day, Finton had been keeping a watchful eye from a distance, but now he sat himself down on a large boulder, only a few feet from Lucas.

"Time is running out for you," said Finton. "The king should have been here by now."

Lucas looked at the shadow of the tree. It was getting longer, indicating evening was drawing near. "He may still come," he replied. "There's at least an hour of light left."

"There is," said Finton, "but even if he gets here in time, you should not be getting your hopes up that the king will see circumstances any differently than I do."

"I did not try to desert, sir," said Lucas. He stretched his legs and tried to flex the muscles in his arms. They had gone stiff from being held in one place, and he felt a strong desire to move them. The tree bark was digging into his back, and he tried to blow at an insect that was crawling on his face. His only consolation was that it could be worse—he could be swinging from the tree instead of being tied against it.

"You abandoned camp," said Finton. "Without your superior's consent, in the darkest hour of the night. You did not stop when called out to do so. That is deserting."

Lucas turned his head away. There was nothing he could say to make the general change his mind. Finton had wanted to see him gone from the moment the king first laid eyes on him, and even more so when he had defeated his son, Eli, during the chosen test.

Lucas was slowly resigning himself to the fact that the king might not be coming. He watched the soldiers finish the burials and saw Verron cross the stream to go up the hill where he and Zera had encountered the hunters the previous night.

It was at that moment they heard the sound of approaching hooves pounding the forest floor.

Lucas used his seeing mind to look past the tree he was tied to and observed King Itan riding into camp. With his back straight and his chin with its brown stubbly beard held up, the king looked confident and tranquil as his body followed the rhythm of his horse in canter. Egon, wearing all black underneath a maroon vest, rode by his side, and the king's guard was right behind them. The sight brought Lucas relief. He didn't think the king would want to see him dead, not since he had saved his life and prevented the poisoning of Lord Hammond at a banquet, whose death would have stopped a new alliance with the lord's family. Egon, on the other hand, Lucas was less happy to see. Even though Egon had once been a chosen himself, the king's guard officer, with his long black hair tied in a ponytail, held a reputation of cruelty, and the fear of being punished by him kept the chosen in line.

Lucas saw the king dismount and address one of Verron's soldiers. The soldier pointed up the hill, after which the king immediately walked to the stream. He stepped into the water with his high black leather boots and waded across with Egon close behind.

Finton had left his seat to go and meet the king, but didn't reach him in time. The king's guard horses had blocked his path, and by the time they had moved out of the way, the king was crossing the stream.

The general's face was red with anger when he returned, his stride significant and purposeful. "You will be coming with me," he said. He pulled a dagger from his belt and kneeled beside Lucas to cut the rope from the tree.

"Where are we going?" asked Lucas. He saw Zera jump to her feet from the log she had been sitting on and put her hand on the pommel of her sword.

"Up the hill," answered Finton. "I would like to hear what outrageous lies Verron is about to tell the king. And I don't trust you further than I can throw you, so you are coming with me."

"Can I have some water first, sir?" asked Lucas when Finton grabbed him under his armpit and pulled him to his feet. "I'm very thirsty."

"No," answered Finton. "You certainly may not. Whether you will be given a drink or not will be up to the king. Now let's go."

Lucas could hear the king and Egon on the trail ahead of him when he had climbed halfway. He used his mind and could see Verron waiting for them, not far from where he and Zera had encountered the hunters.

"It's good to see you survived the attack, Officer Verron," said the king.

"I believe we were lucky, sire," answered Verron. "And perhaps there was a little bit of skill involved as well."

"And is this where the two chosen encountered the hunters?" asked the king. "I wanted to see it for myself."

"A little higher up," answered Verron and proceeded to lead the way after the king asked him to. When they reached the correct spot and came to a stop, Lucas continued to use his mind to see the king and Egon looking around and assessing the area, taking notice of the trampled bushes and eroded soil.

With one foot higher than the other, the king stood on the sloping ground and had his thumbs tucked over his belt as he surveyed the area.

Lucas watched the king's every move, hoping to see some sort of sign that Itan was pleased with the result. Perhaps then he would be more forgiving. As much as Lucas had honed his power to observe from afar, the mind of another was off limits, impossible for him to enter. He knew this, because he had tried.

"I hear Lucas took several hunters out all on his own?" asked the king. It was exactly what Lucas needed to hear.

"He did."

"They had the upper hand, being on higher ground," said Egon. "He should not have survived this, and yet we were told he is not even injured?"

"No, he wasn't," answered Verron, "but I did have an incident with him later which may have been influenced by what happened here on this hill."

The king and Egon both peered over their shoulders as Lucas climbed the last few steps to reach them, and Finton shoved past him, knocking him off balance momentarily. Egon rested his eyes briefly on Lucas, and Verron stared with a furrowed brow after he got back on the path.

"Was that necessary, Finton?" asked the king. "I am sure the boy would have stepped aside if you had told him to do so."

Finton was leaning forward with his arm resting on one knee. "No harm intended, sire," he answered, breathing heavily. "I didn't realize how steep this slope was."

"Very well," said the king and directed his attention to Lucas. "You may go down, now, and return to your troop as we discuss what has transpired. And what steps will be required next."

Lucas hesitated, not sure what to do, before shifting down the path.

"Stay here," snapped Finton, turning around to stare at him. "Certainly, sire, you do not mean to allow Lucas to return unescorted? The very reason I have brought him up here with me is because he cannot be trusted. And especially after the night's events, you—"

"Do not contradict my order, General," said the king. "I don't need the boy here."

"I understand, sire, but I wish to keep an eye on him," said Finton.

"What for?" asked Egon, his tone terse.

"When you hear Verron's explanation of what happened," answered Finton, "I am sure you'll understand."

Itan shook his head. "I don't think so," he said. "Lucas is a chosen and, as such, he has no business listening to what his superiors have to say, especially not if it involves him directly."

"Go back down, Lucas," said Egon sternly, "and wait by the stream. You'll be called upon when needed."

Lucas gave a quick nod and turned around. As soon as he was out of sight, he heard the king ask Verron to continue with his story, and Lucas could not help but stop to listen and used his mind to watch them.

"What reason did he give for leaving?" asked Egon after Verron told them how he had caught up with Lucas by the river. He had turned to an ax stuck in a tree trunk next to him and reached for the handle to pull it free. Egon was strong, but Lucas could tell it required effort to release it from the tree, and he hated to think what would have happened if it had not missed its intended target. He had pushed Zera out of the way when the ax came flying through the air, and it had barely missed both of them.

"He was not very clear about that," answered Verron. "And I have not had an opportunity to question him further."

Egon briefly inspected the ax before tossing it aside, as one might do with a chewed-off bone. "Why not?" he asked.

"General Finton arrived and took him from me. He's been holding him ever since and has accused him of deserting."

Egon shook his head in disbelief and turned to Finton. "Deserting? Lucas? Are you out of your mind?"

"I have my reasons to believe that he did, yes," answered Finton.

"You know the boy better than anyone else, Verron," said the king. "What do you believe happened?"

"Truthfully?" asked Verron. "I think the fight took too much out of him, and he lost self-control. At first, I had assumed it was because he was shaken, sire, but knowing him, it is more likely that it troubled him, that he didn't get to finish the fight. The hunters retreated, and I suspect that he wanted to go after them."

"That could be a plausible explanation," said Egon, "and would be more in line with his character."

The king was ready to head back down the hill, but Verron hastily stepped forward when he started to make his way. "Sire?" he said.

The king stopped and turned to face him. "Is there something else?"

Verron took a deep breath and glanced over to Finton. "Just that I am taking full responsibility for what occurred after General Finton took Lucas, sire. My men acted on my orders."

Egon had paused his descent down the hill and turned to hear what else Verron had to say.

The king eyed him quizzically. "Would you mind explaining?"

"The general convicted Lucas and was going to carry out an immediate execution by hanging the boy. I could not allow him to do that, sire." Verron paused as if to choose his next words carefully and watched the faces of the two men stare at him with anticipation. "I'm afraid I commanded my soldiers to pull their swords against Finton to stop him." Lucas waited anxiously for the king's reaction. He half-expected Egon to step forward to arrest the officer, but Egon did not move. Verron then added, "The intent was not to cause harm, but to hold off on what I perceived as a rash act . . . until your arrival and ultimate approval, sire."

"Is that all, Officer?" asked the king, after a moment of silence.

Verron nodded.

"Good," answered the king. "Then I dismiss you. Tell Lucas he's released from all charges and gather your men to return to Lord Aron's castle. We're finished here!"

Relief flooded through Lucas when he heard the words that would free him from the clutches of the man who hated him and the rope that lay waiting by the tree. He scrambled down the hill before the group of men could spot him and kneeled by the creek to quench his thirst. The king and Egon soon passed, with Finton right behind them.

"Itan," said Finton as the king crossed the stream. "Are you serious about releasing him?"

"I am," answered the king.

"I don't understand. The boy deserted."

The king lifted himself into the saddle and took the reins. "General," he said, "I cannot convict someone of desertion when his motivations for leaving are not telling of that—and when his commanding officer is willing to risk his own life to stand behind him, merely on principle. You should have been grateful for not stumbling onto a massacre here, General. I suggest you focus your attention back to the real reasons as to why we were here," said the king, before abruptly turning his horse and riding off, the fur cape over his shoulders rippling and his officers lining up neatly behind him.

Lucas rode at the back of the column with Zera by his side. They were on their way back to the king's camp, which was stationed outside the walls of Aron's castle and would possess the comforts of the adjacent castle, unlike the rustic camp they had just dismantled. After midnight, they rode past the stalls that functioned as temporary workshops for the artisans that traveled with the king's army. He could only see the chandler still working by the light of a small fire, dipping a wick in a heated substance.

Zera sat up and lifted her nose in the air. "I can smell the beeswax," she said softly. "I love that smell."

"Me too," said Lucas. "I prefer beeswax candles over tallow."

"Animal fat doesn't burn that long," said Zera, "and produces a smoky flame."

Lucas nodded and steered his horse when Officer Verron led the troop into the king's camp and between the neat rows of soldiers' tents. Most of the camp was quiet, and only the guards standing by firepits observed their arrival. They turned off to the right just before reaching the king's tent, and the matching red and black tents of the king's guard surrounding it, and rode along the dark stone wall encircling Lord Aron's castle to the horse corrals.

Lucas was surprised to see chosen waiting by the fence to take the horses this late at night but then felt their eyes on him and understood—they had heard what had happened.

Patrols continued for a few more days, but, with no more sightings or evidence that hunters were still crossing Lord Aron's land or committing any raids on it, the king soon stopped sending troops out. Egon announced that Lord Aron had invited the queen and princess for a stay at his castle, and for that reason, the army would remain camped for another week.

For the chosen ones, it meant they had more free time after completing their chores. Every afternoon, they gathered near a gameball field on the outskirts of the camp, sometimes climbing up on the empty wagons and barrels that were stored there. Some spent the time mending holes and tears in their clothing. Others just talked or kept themselves busy with little games.

Lucas, feeling restless, jumped off the wagon he had been sitting on with Zera. "We are all getting lazy," he said. "If we're not careful, we might lose focus and be of no use if there's another sighting of hunters."

"I don't know," said Zera. "I like being here. The rules of where we can and can't go are not defined like they are in the castle, and it has given me more freedom. I like watching the tradespeople at work. I have seen you talk to some of them."

"Only because they wanted to know what happened with the hunters," answered Lucas. "Some said they had a family member or friend in our troop that had come under attack." He looked at a chosen yawning and shook his head. "We can't just sit here every day," he remarked. He stared at the white-painted outlines that marked the perimeter of the gameball field in front of him and stepped away from the wagon.

"You have something in mind?" asked Zera.

"Maybe," answered Lucas and walked away. Several people he had talked to had asked him if he needed anything—he decided he would take one of them up on their offer. He made his way to the tent of a gentleman skilled in leatherwork, who was repairing the heel of a boot when Lucas approached.

"Did you change your mind about purchasing new boots?" asked the leather smith looking up from his work.

Lucas shook his head. "No, sir," he answered. "The boots I have are fine, but I was wondering if there was something else you could make?"

"Like what?"

"A ball."

"A ball?"

"Yes."

The smith put the boot he had been working on aside and stood up. "Have a seat," he said. "This may take a little time, but let me see what I can do."

Lucas sat himself down on a stool and watched the leather smith cut three pieces of leather—two round ones and one straight. He used an awl to puncture holes into the leather along the edges of all three pieces and then carefully stitched them all together with a bone needle. Observing the work of craftmanship brought Lucas back to a distant memory of his father transforming a crude piece of steel into a work of art.

Pleased with the newly acquired toy, Lucas walked up to the chosen ones with a melon-sized leather ball in his hand. "I'm not exactly sure what to do with this," he said, holding the ball up. "But I'm sure one of you does."

Several boys jumped up, big smiles on their faces. "Where did you get that?" asked Warrick, taking the ball and inspecting it. The wind lifted his waves of blond hair, and the way the sun lit up his usually pale complexion gave him a game-ready look.

"It's for us," answered Lucas. "I had it made."

"But are we allowed to play with it?"

"I have already asked Verron. He's allowing it."

"All right then, two teams!" shouted Warrick, marching to the middle of the field, the rest of the chosen jumping up and running after him.

"Here," said Davis, picking up two baskets and handing Lucas one of them. "We need to place those on either side of the field," he explained.

"What are they for?"

"They will be the team bases," answered Davis, brushing his long black hair away from his face. "Each team will try and get the ball to their sideline. I guess you have never played a village field game before?"

"No," answered Lucas. "The kids I grew up with didn't accept me, so I tried to stay away from them."

Davis nodded. "It's not a difficult game," he said. "There'll be two equal teams. The ball is placed on the ground in the middle, and both teams back away to their side of the field. When the start signal is given, they'll run towards the ball, and whoever gets it will then try and pass it around teammates to get it to their base. Do you want to have a go?"

"Sure," answered Lucas and walked to the far right of the gameball field. He placed his basket in line with Davis's on the opposite side and joined Zera and Warrick's team already lining up before it.

When Archer dropped a shirt on the ground as the start signal, Lucas followed his team by running towards the ball. They reached the middle line before Davis's team did, and Zera was the one who picked up the ball. She turned around and started running back, with the rest of the group following her. The ball was passed back and forth, with the other team in close pursuit. When Warrick had the ball, someone tackled him and he lost it. Now it was Davis's team who was running to their base and Lucas's team who ran after them.

The game was rough, but Lucas had fun, and after an hour of playing, he saw they were starting to gather an audience. When he noticed Carleton standing close to the field with a group of elites, he let his team run past him and stopped.

Zera paused next to him with her hands on her hips, trying to catch her breath. "What're they doing here?" she asked, gesturing to the elites.

"Just watching, by the looks of it," answered Lucas. His eyes fell on the dark-haired elite-born leading the group. "Maybe I should ask Carleton if the elites want to join?"

"I don't think that's a good idea," said Zera.

"Why not?"

"They will expect to win."

"I wasn't thinking chosen against elite," said Lucas. He walked towards the sideline and stopped before Carleton, who had watched his approach with interest.

"Do you want to play?" asked Lucas.

Carleton shrugged. "Sure," he said.

"There's one condition, though."

"What's that?"

"You split your group to join both chosen teams, and we are equals on the field." Lucas knew it was a tough request, but the chosen were having fun for the first time in ages, and he didn't want any kind of ranking order to interfere with that. Today wasn't about who won versus who lost.

Carleton hesitated for a moment before extending his hand. "Agreed," he said, and they shook on it.

CHAPTER 2

Itan could hear shouting and cheering in the distance. He was sitting in his tent behind a small wooden desk with a scroll spread out before him. Several more lay rolled up within arm's reach on the narrow travel bed directly behind him. With no natural light coming inside the tent, he held a four-prong candle holder above the scroll and tried to read the text. He cursed under his breath when the shouting outside got louder, and a drop of wax fell onto the parchment. He called for an officer to come inside his tent to tell him what was going on.

"It is the chosen and the elites, sire," the officer reported.

Itan looked up from the scrolls that he had been reading. "Are they fighting?" he asked.

"No, sire, they are playing ball in the gameball field Lord Aron has set up for his soldiers."

"A ball game? Together? Elite against chosen?"

"It appears that the teams are mixed, sire," answered the officer. "Do you wish for me to bring a stop to this?"

Itan sighed and picked up the feather pen to sign the scrolls. "No," he said. "Let them play. It could be good for morale." He dipped the pen into the inkpot and then held it over the rim to allow the excess ink to fall off. "Oh, and officer . . ." he said before he left the tent.

"Yes, sire?" asked the officer, turning back around.

"My wife and daughter will be arriving for a stay at Lord Aron's tomorrow," said Itan, lifting the pen from the inkpot.

"Do you wish your belongings to be moved to the castle once they are here?" asked the officer.

"No," answered Itan. "I will remain here at camp. As the commander of this army, I need to remain accessible to all my officers. The whole reason my soldiers are here, after all, is to protect you from these marauding hunter clans. You only need to ensure that my wife and daughter have clear passage on the road leading to the castle. I saw it was blocked by merchants' wagons today."

The officer nodded. "Is that it, sire?" he asked.

"Yes, that's all," answered Itan as he wrote the first letter of his name.

He assumed the game would be a one-off, but when he kept hearing noises from the field the next day, and was notified that boys and soldiers alike were now playing the ball game, Itan decided it was time to have a look himself. He walked outside and waited when he saw Egon coming from the road walking towards him. "I'm taking a walk out to the gameball field," he said when Egon came near. "Will you walk with me?"

"You've been informed then?" asked Egon stopping before him.

"About the entire army now playing?" asked Itan. "Yes, I have."

"No, that's not what I meant," answered Egon. "I came to tell you that the queen and princess have arrived."

"When?"

"About ten minutes ago."

Itan frowned and turned to see the castle gates closed. "Why didn't I hear the horn blown from the guards' tower to announce their arrival?"

"They didn't have to," answered Egon. "Lord Aron is watching the games at the field, and that's where the queen's carriage stopped."

"Oh, well, in that case," said Itan, making his exit. "We better hurry, so I can join my family and Lord Aron before they continue."

"I don't think there's a need to rush," said Egon, quickening his stride to keep up. "The carriage stopped after the princess jumped from it. Amalia is currently watching the games as well."

Itan gave Egon a sideways glance, then inhaled a deep breath. "Why am I not surprised my daughter would do such a thing?"

Itan saw Lord Aron standing next to Officer Verron, just behind a field line. His red hair and beard made him stand out in the crowd. He was also the loudest and most enthusiastic spectator. With cupped hands, he shouted words of encouragement at the players on the field, which appeared to consist of chosen, elites, and a handful of soldiers.

Itan saw the queen's carriage waiting on the road, and further down the painted line was his young daughter. With the hem of her green velvet dress dragging over the grass, her brown curly hair bounced as she ran up and down.

Itan decided to let his daughter run off some steam after her long carriage ride and joined Lord Aron and Verron just when Carleton got knocked to the ground, and he watched Lucas helping him up.

"Those two are getting along, then?" he asked Verron.

"Yes," answered Verron. "There is a mutual respect and under-standing between them."

"Where is Eli? I only see his friends Milton and Baldric on the field."

"I believe Finton restricted him from playing, which, given the his-tory, was a wise move."

"Agreed," said Itan. It was likely why he had not heard of any inci-dents occurring during the games, and he had to give Finton credit for that. As intense as the game appeared, he could see there was good sportsmanship, as well as a great deal of laughter and cheering from the people watching. Amalia was still jumping up and down, and it pleased him to see her so amused. He saw far less of her now that she was older and her mother had become more involved in her upbringing, and he missed her company and endless questions. He let out a deep sigh when he watched her run along the side of the field to keep up with the ball. "I wish she would start behaving like a princess," he mumbled.

"She is just like you when you were her age," said Lord Aron. "Your father could not pin you down either."

"Hmm, yes, but she is twelve now. Almost a lady."

"Who is she cheering for?" asked Lord Aron.

Itan watched her more closely and noticed her become louder whenever Lucas had the ball. He had passed the ball to a teammate just before getting tackled to the ground, and Amalia stopped jumping and let out a loud yelp of alarm. Her hands were placed over her mouth, and the king could not tell if it was playful or genuine concern. He saw Lucas lift his head and look at her for a moment too long before getting up and running back into the game.

"I guess that was obvious," remarked Lord Aron, to answer his own question. "She is acting more like a lady than you thought, Itan! She has her favorite picked out, and not a bad choice either. He is strong, well respected and . . . very good looking."

"But a chosen one," said Egon. "He should not be receiving her attention like that."

Itan shook his head and turned on his heel. He had seen more than he had cared for. "Egon," he said, "have my wife and daughter escorted to the castle immediately."

"Forgive me if my words offended you," said Lord Aron, who had decided to follow him. "I did not mean anything by them. She probably was just shocked by how rough the game gets, and it just happened to be Lucas who fell. I apologize."

"It is not so much her reaction that I am concerned about," responded Itan, "but more his! It appears I have missed something."

The candles inside had flickered in the breeze when Egon entered, but quickly settled to cast long shadows on the linen walls. Itan was not pleased to have to interrogate his closest confidante, but he had called Egon to his tent for just such purpose. "Tell me what you know about my daughter and Lucas," he demanded.

Egon looked confused. "What is it that you want me to tell you?"

"You were the only one who did not appear surprised to see Amalia cheering Lucas on in that . . . very personal way. Has he been trying to get her attention? And has she responded to that? I'm no fool, Egon. He is fifteen, and she's a pretty girl and a princess, at that." Unable to keep himself still any longer, Itan stood up from his desk and began to pace.

"No, sire," answered Egon. "If nothing else, he has made a strong effort to distance himself from her."

Itan stopped and stared at him. Where was the stoic guard that he knew Egon to be? "What do you mean, distance himself? Have they been close? When?"

Egon cleared his throat before he spoke. "They had a few encounters when Lucas worked in the storeroom, before his accident, but I can assure you they have not met since that time. I made sure of that."

"The storeroom. Of all places." Itan rubbed his face with both hands and let out a deep sigh. "And you never told me about this?"

"It did not come to my attention until the day I brought Lucas to the monastery, after his accident with the well. At that point, his survival was still in question, and I got the impression that these encounters had been unintentional on his part, as well as respectful. If anything, the princess was looking for a friend and solicited his company. I do not doubt that, when the time comes, Lucas will give her his loyalty, much as he has done for you."

"I hope you are right," said Itan, sighing. His daughter had often expressed being lonely and had seized any opportunity to play with children of staff members. He also understood why Egon had kept the information from him. The period of time Egon was referring to, immediately after the accident, had been a dark one for all involved, but for Lucas most of all—the boy's fall down the old well had not been an accident but rather a deliberate act, and by persons unknown to this day.

"You may go now," he told Egon.

Egon gave a quick bow. "Goodnight, sire," he said and left.

The tent flap dropped behind Egon as he passed through, and Itan sighed heavily. He was returning to his desk to look over his documents when he heard the rustling of the tent opening again. He looked over his shoulder to see Lord Aron stepping inside. The lord removed his brown fur mantle from his shoulders and tossed it aside on a chest by the entrance.

"You don't feel the need to knock?" he asked after Lord Aron had planted himself on the seat behind his desk.

"Well," said Aron, "Egon just exited a moment ago, and since you called me here—"

"It's all right," Itan grumbled, waving his hand dismissively. "I have a great deal on my mind, is all."

"Anything I can help with?" asked Aron.

"Perhaps," answered Itan. Ten years his senior, Aron had been a friend for many years, and Itan valued his opinion. "How do you think my men view me at the present moment?"

"They respect you, as has always been the case. Why would you ask such a thing?"

"You don't think they perceive me as weak? Lucas seems untouchable."

"Ah," said Aron. "Now I see where this is going. You are pondering today's ball game."

"Yes. That, and everything else. He's refused orders, turned his back on a superior, and then the desertion this week. What's next? Murder? Oh, wait . . . that was the first thing he managed to get away with." He couldn't help but suppress a chuckle, though really there was nothing very funny about it.

Aron sat down in one of the chairs and rubbed his red beard. "It sounds like he breaks every discipline and rank order you have in place. But . . . what if he were to be an elite? Would that justify his behavior?"

"It would help, but he isn't one."

"No, but you can change that."

"Change what?"

"Change it. Change his status. You are the king. I remember you telling Lord Killeand, last time we met up to renew the five-year alliance, that Finton branded him as a chosen when your officers were still debating other possibilities. And I have heard your men refer to Lucas as the King's Chosen. I don't think they would find it strange if you officially declared him as elite born."

"You think?"

Aron nodded. "He didn't come to you in the usual way. Your soldiers remember you hunting him down and the lives he has saved since joining you. Verron said it was Lucas who got them all playing that ball game. The boy's a born leader, and that's not what chosen ones are. Your soldiers treat him with respect, and I think you do well by protecting him from the likes of Finton. I've seen how he looks at that boy, and I don't think he'd hesitate to kill him if an opportunity arose that justified it for him."

"Perhaps," said Itan. "Finton is one I've started to worry about. He has changed." Itan got up from his seat and poured wine into two chalices and handed Aron one. They drank in silence for a minute, each with their thoughts, before Aron spoke again.

"I'm sure you didn't call me here solely to discuss Lucas," said Aron, finishing his drink and setting his empty chalice on the table.

"No," answered Itan. "I did not." He walked over to his desk again and picked up a scroll that he held up for Aron to see. "I received another message from Meloc today."

Aron leaned in, squinting at the scroll. "Your brother? Is he still reporting the same issues?"

"Yes. Meloc insists I come south to see for myself. He fears he may be losing control over the people. He feels they need to see their king in the flesh, to restore order."

"I thought you allowed him to lower the taxes, because of the drought this year?"

"I did. He says it has helped some, but now the greater difficulty, and most recent development, has become thieves . . . these bandits that rob people in the middle of the night. He cannot catch whoever is responsible. Calls them *ghost thieves*."

"Your brother has always been one for the mysterious and unexplained," laughed Aron. "Is he blaming this on yet another one of his legends?"

Itan looked at him sternly. "This is not a laughing matter. Whoever it is, it's causing the people to look at Meloc for answers, and he cannot give them any."

"What are you planning to do? Go down there? You are halfway already, but to move the entire army?"

Itan shook his head. "No. I have enough concerns over here without worrying about my brother's inability to manage his affairs, so I have asked him to come here to explain to me in person what is happening."

"You asked your brother to come here?"

"Yes, I am sending the bulk of my army back to my castle tomorrow with General Finton. Egon and the king's guard will stay here with me. With your permission, I would like my wife and daughter to remain here also."

"Of course," replied Lord Aron. "They will be my guests for as long as you like them to be."

"Thank you," said Itan. "It should be no more than two weeks, at the most—we will all go home once I have spoken with Meloc."

Itan stood watching from the walls of Lord Aron's castle when his army finally moved out the following afternoon. It had taken the entire morning to break up the camp.

"Where are they going, Father?" asked Amalia. She had been rolling her ball along the grooves in the stones of the battlement but now stood next to him and looked over the wall.

"They are going back home, sweetheart. We are staying, so that you may visit with your uncle, who is coming here in a few days."

Amalia looked up at him with rosy cheeks that matched the reddish pink color of her dress and smiled. She had not seen her uncle for a few years, and he knew it would please her greatly to see him soon.

Itan smiled back and then looked at her hand, which clutched the little leather ball she loved so much. He frowned, remembering that she had shown him the engraving of her name on it shortly after Lucas had returned from the monastery. "Who did you say carved your name on the ball for you again?" he asked. He watched her pull the toy behind her back and quickly turn around when she heard her lady-in-waiting call for her in the distance.

"I have to go, Father," she said hastily and ran off without giving him an answer, the sound of her boots clicking on the stone.

CHAPTER 3

The younger boys, who had been made to stay at the castle, were happy to have the older chosen ones back and wanted to know everything that had transpired during those long weeks. Lucas found it endearing. They begged Zera to tell the story over and over in the evenings, and the hunters became bigger and scarier each time she told it.

"Was their leader really as tall as the entrance gate? And with big, sharp teeth?" asked Ando. He was sitting on Zera's bed and looked over at Lucas, who was lying on his own bed with his arms folded behind his head.

Lucas propped himself up onto his elbow when he heard Ando's question and smiled. "He was big and tall, but he was not the monster Zera would have you believe he was. Mind you, I did not see his teeth. He had a full black beard and dark brown eyes."

"But was he scary?" asked Ando. "Were you scared?"

"Lucas isn't scared of anything," said Davis, "Right, Lucas?"

Lucas swung his legs over the edge of his bed and sat up. "He wasn't scary, and he was no monster," he answered. "He was a man. And everyone gets scared sometimes. Even me."

Once settled back into their normal routine, the chosen continued playing with the ball during their rest period in their training grounds. Since they had walls to use now, they played a different game. One team would hold the ball and stand behind a line drawn in the sand. They had to pass the ball quickly and move forward towards the back wall where they had marked two stones as a target to hit. If the other team intercepted the ball, it was their turn to stand behind the start line and try to get the ball to hit the stones.

After the first goal was scored, Lucas stood hunched with his hands on his knees, catching his breath and scratching an itch underneath the red headband he wore—his team's color. They were switching sides, and it was an opportune moment to take a break. He watched as the ten elite borns filed through the gate and stood up to greet them. They had come a few times now and were wearing white shirts, like the chosen, instead of the red elite shirt they would wear to distinguish themselves. Eli had been the only one who never played, but Lucas was surprised to see him following Carleton this time.

"Mind if we all join in again?" asked Carleton.

"Not at all," answered Lucas, stepping aside to let them through. He caught Eli's easygoing look when he walked past and was wondering what had changed. He was glad when he saw that Eli picked up a red headband to join his team, so they would not be each other's competition, but he had an uneasy feeling all the same.

He watched Eli giving Warrick a friendly tap on the shoulder as if they were comrades just before saying something to him. Warrick didn't reply and looked confused but then shrugged off whatever thought he might have had.

Something told Lucas he should stop the game. He watched the chosen line up, excited to begin. Eli looked unsure of what to do—he hesitated and only lined up once he saw everyone else do so.

"Are you coming, Lucas?" shouted Zera.

Lucas paused for a moment longer, staring up into the sky. He was looking for the magpie—but then shook his head to dismiss the thought. He was being silly, he told himself, and then ran to take his place on the defensive team.

The start signal was given, and the ball was handed over quickly across the line of boys going for the goal. It got handed to Davis first, who ran fast, and—before Lucas or any of the other boys could take him down—he passed the ball back to Carleton and they scored. After that, they played a few rounds back and forth until Lucas noticed that Eli was not going after the ball when it was their turn to defend. Instead, he seemed to enjoy knocking the younger chosen down, even if they did not have the ball. Lucas tried to avoid eye contact, but he was very aware that Eli was trying to get his attention by not playing fair.

"Let it go, Lucas," warned Zera, who was standing next to him on the start line. "He's trying to get under your skin."

Lucas nodded. He stood in the middle and was holding the ball. At the start signal, he charged forward but quickly passed the ball over before Carleton could take him down. They passed the ball up and down the line, and when they got close enough, one teammate threw it up against the stones and scored.

When they lined up to be the defensive team again, he felt someone's eyes on him and saw Eli grinning at him. Lucas quickly turned his head back to face forward, but not before realizing that Eli had put himself in front of Ando, who was half his size. Fearing Eli would hurt Ando, Lucas did not go after the ball when the game resumed but rushed to get to him instead. He had to weave in and out between all the running boys and watched in horror when he did not arrive in time—he was still running when he saw Ando roll over Eli's shoulder and land hard on the ground. Eli was already on the move, heading for his next victim. Lucas sprinted and bumped him from behind before he could take another boy down. Eli fell to the ground but quickly jumped up to face him.

"Enough's enough, Eli," said Lucas. "You play fair, or you're out!"

Everywhere around them, boys stopped in their tracks and watched them.

"You don't tell me what to do! I'm your superior, and you're to obey me," shouted Eli.

"Eli!" said Carleton, walking over. "He's right on this—you play fair, or you don't play at all. I've seen you take boys down as well, when there was no need for it."

Eli half turned to Carleton without taking his eyes off Lucas. His face was red, and his eyes were angry slits. "You can shut it, Carleton. I outrank you as well, but I'll deal with you later. First, I want to hear Lucas apologize!"

"For what?"

"Just do it, Lucas," said Carleton with a heavy sigh. "Apologize for causing him to fall, and we can get back to the game. Right, Eli?"

Eli nodded, but Lucas wasn't convinced. When he hesitated, Carleton walked over and put a hand on his shoulder to turn him sideways. "With the king not due back for another day," Carleton said softly, "Finton's the one in charge. Eli will do anything to get you into trouble. So apologize to him, and I promise I'll deal with him myself."

Lucas nodded. As much as he hated having to do it, Carleton was right. He turned back around to face Eli. "I'm sorry," he said. "I should not have bumped you or have spoken as I did."

"You are *still* not speaking as you should—how is it that you are to address me?"

Lucas took a deep breath. Every single boy had his eyes on him, and he could cut the tension in the air with a knife. He wished he'd followed his gut and stopped the games when they had returned to the castle. Instead, Eli had him right where he had always wanted him. "I'm sorry, sir," muttered Lucas.

"See," said Eli. "That wasn't so hard. Was it? Now, say it again . . . but on your knee this time."

A few gasps came from the chosen nearest to him. Lucas knew as well as they did that he could never bring himself to do that. "I apologized. That's what you asked for, and that's what I did."

"Kneel!" said Eli, more loudly this time.

Lucas just stared at him and did not move.

"Kneel!" shouted Eli again. Some of his friends had gathered behind him, and Lucas knew that made him feel even more powerful.

"Lucas," he heard Carleton warn him again, and he turned to face him. Beads of sweat rolled down over his red cheeks.

"Don't you see what he's doing?" Lucas asked. "Even if I did go on my knee, he will not stop. But, superior or not, when it comes down to it—he's a bully, and I will never go down for a bully."

Lucas was still facing Carleton when he heard Eli rush up behind him.

"I will not have you disrespect me," hissed Eli.

Lucas turned and grabbed his arm to avoid being hit, ducking when Eli came swinging at him with his other fist. Lucas knew he should be walking away, but the last time he did that, he'd been threatened with a flogging. Eli had him trapped. Walking away or striking a superior—either meant flogging, so he might as well deserve it. After deflecting Eli's second hit, he planted his fist in Eli's stomach. Eli doubled over and gasped for breath. His eyes turned wild, and he lunged again, this time hitting Lucas on the side of his head. Davis ran up to stop the fight, but Milton and Baldric blocked him.

"Stay out of this," shouted Baldric, placing his hand on Davis's chest. "This has nothing to do with you."

"You're wrong in that," said Davis. "What affects one chosen affects us all."

Shouts could be heard from the wall, and Lucas knew the training grounds would soon be overrun with soldiers. Davis had grabbed Baldric by his shirt to try and push him out of his way, but Baldric swung and hit him in the side of the face.

Davis shook his head as if trying to shake it off. He looked to Zera and Warrick, and the three of them jumped at Eli's friends. Other chosen and elites soon joined in the fight, while Carleton and Rhys struggled to keep as many boys out of it as possible.

"Stand down!" shouted Carleton as he grabbed boys by their arms in an effort to pull them away from the skirmish. "Stop fighting, all of you!"

Rhys tried to block any boy trying to reenter the fight by shaking his head and holding his hand out. "Don't," he warned.

Soldiers filed in, quickly surrounding the chosen and elite and breaking them up. Lucas had Eli in a headlock when Finton walked through the gates. He caught a glimpse of the general heading towards them but could not bring himself to stop.

"Grab them both," ordered Finton. "I want this madness stopped at once."

Lucas stopped fighting when he was pulled off Eli, but Eli still wanted to land the last punch after getting to his feet—until he noticed his father and dropped his arms at his sides. Verron came running in but was held back by guards at Finton's command.

"Can anyone explain what just happened here?" Finton shouted, loud enough for everyone to hear.

Most boys hung their heads and avoided eye contact with the general as he scanned the groups of boys. Finally, his eyes came to rest on Lucas and Eli.

"Eli, care to tell me why you were fighting like a commoner?"

Eli took a deep breath and cleared his throat to speak. "It's all Lucas's fault, sir. He was knocking down the younger boys in the game we were playing. I confronted him and told him to stop. He talked back, and punched me in the stomach."

Lucas lowered his head. There was nothing he could say or do. His fate was sealed. He knew what was coming.

"Who else was involved in this?" asked Finton, turning to the group of chosen boys closest to him.

"They all were," said Eli.

The entire group was surrounded by soldiers, even though there were boys there who had not joined in the brawl. Finton turned to Lucas and looked at him with a sinister glare. "I'll have you flogged in the bailey for this," he said. "As an example for others." He looked closely for a response from Lucas, but Lucas refused to give him one. When soldiers grabbed him by the arms, he willingly started walking with them.

"Wait!" Finton called out to his soldiers. When they stopped, he ran his fingers through his hair—he was staring at the ground and pacing. But then his face lit up. "I've a better idea," he said, smirking. "Someone else will receive his lashes and Lucas will watch instead—this will better demonstrate to him that his insolence has real-world consequences, especially upon those he holds dear."

Finton had finally figured out how to get to him. When he saw Finton march towards the group of chosen, Lucas pulled himself loose from the soldier's grip. It was of no use, though—he was blocked by other soldiers and restrained once again, this time with a firmer grip.

"General!" called Verron.

"Stay out of this, Officer. Do not stand in my way again. It's time we establish order and discipline these chosen." He took his time, ambling past each boy, and stopped when he reached Ando. Ando trembled when he looked up at the general, his thin arms pressed against his sides. He looked like he might cry.

"I think this one will do," said Finton and grabbed Ando by his collar.

"I didn't fight, sir," pleaded Ando, fear flashing across his face.

"You are bleeding from a cut above your eye—looks very much like you've been fighting to me."

"Sir," said Davis, stepping forward. "Ando is telling the truth. He got knocked down before any of the fighting started. By Eli! He did not fight—I promise you—but I did. Take me."

"Or me," said Warrick.

Several other boys stepped forward as well, but Finton shook his head. "If I punish this little one," he said, pulling Ando out of the group, "I know it will influence all of you."

Lucas looked frantically to his officer, struggling against the soldiers in a final attempt to free himself. He couldn't let Ando get punished for something he was responsible for—he would have to draw the general's anger back towards him. Using his mind, he located several horses held by handlers in the bailey, waiting to be seen by the farrier. With Finton dragging Ando past him towards the gates, Lucas focused on all six animals. Shouting could be heard in the bailey when the horses reared up and broke away from their handlers. They came cantering through the gate of the training grounds, causing soldiers to jump out of the way to avoid being trampled.

Lucas broke loose from the men holding him and was able to grab Ando from the general in the chaos. "Take him!" he cried, pushing Ando to Davis, who immediately pushed him further back behind the group, where the rest of the boys would protect him. The horses were bucking and kicking, making everyone scatter. Lucas ran up and jumped on one of them. Then, to his horror, he saw Tanner run towards the barrels in the back, where they kept their practice swords. He started pulling one out, but Lucas called to him to leave the blades.

"No fighting!" he shouted. "Nobody needs to get hurt."

The five riderless horses continued their erratic behavior, forcing the soldiers and elites out of the gates. Every time a soldier tried to grab a horse by its halter, it would rear up and kick its front legs. When the horses ran out of the training grounds, Zera, Davis, Warrick, and Tanner rushed up to the gates to close them. Lucas spurred his horse into a gallop, and when he made it through the gates, he heard them shut behind him. Before him, the five horses were prancing in front of a group of soldiers holding shields. The horses' handlers rushed forward to grab them by their halters and led them away.

Lucas raised his hands in the air to surrender. He was pulled from his horse by Finton and slammed up against the wall. One of the soldiers then yanked him around to face Finton, who was beet red in the face. Some soldiers tried to open the gates to the training grounds. When unsuccessful, they headed for the stairs to the top of the wall, but Finton called them back.

"We can deal with the rest of the chosen later," he said. "First, this one! Bring a wagon out!"

Lucas had a good sense of what was about to happen. He also knew no one could help him. Verron tried to protest on his behalf, but Finton was not having any of it, and Lucas hoped the officer would not further object and make matters worse.

"Face the wagon, boy," the general commanded, pushing him towards the ladder railing of a hay wagon.

Lucas did as told. He would take whatever pain he had to endure as long as the chosen were safe. Soldiers tied a rope to each of his wrists and secured him to the wagon with his arms spread out. He stood quietly, not even flinching when they ripped his shirt open to expose his bare skin. Though facing the wagon, Lucas could see with his mind that Finton looked surprisingly grave and somber. Eli, however, could not contain the smile on his face, and Lucas hated him for it. Hate was an emotion his teacher Father Ansan had warned against time and time again during Lucas's childhood years spent at the monastery, but Lucas felt himself slipping.

The gathered crowd fell silent when one of the officers stepped forward with a whip in hand to carry out the flogging, but Finton took it from him. He turned to Eli and handed him the whip. "It is you who he disrespects," he said, "so it should be you who is going to put an end to that."

Eli stared at the whip in his hands and looked to his father to see if he was serious. He made a motion to hand it back and opened his mouth to say something, but his father shook his head and made Eli step forward to stand behind Lucas.

"What are you waiting for?" asked his father. "He's all yours. It's time to demand the respect he has been withholding from you."

Eli glanced over at the elite born standing by Carleton, but their faces were stony towards him, their arms hanging limp at their sides. There was no doubt in Lucas's mind that Eli wanted to see him hurt but would rather have someone else do it for him, as he had relied on in the past. His friends, however, now also stood with Carleton. Lucas watched as they looked at Eli in shock, the hurt in their eyes palpable—as if it were them he was about to wound.

Eli looked down to the ground where the long whip was lying like a snake, ready to strike. He bent and took it in his hand, shaking as he lifted the handle of the whip over his head. The long, narrow end of it swung through the air, and when he lowered it, he let it strike Lucas's back.

It should have sliced his skin open, and he should have screamed out in pain, but to Lucas's surprise, it barely touched him before dropping to the ground.

Several muffled little laughs came from the soldiers standing around.

"What are you doing?" scolded Finton. "You've seen this done a thousand times, but you barely left a mark on him. Step back a little and do it again."

Eli took a step back and lifted the whip a second time. It came down, but again was ineffective, and Lucas didn't have to move a muscle. Perhaps, because Eli felt his father's wrath building up next to him, he raised the whip again, but Finton stepped forward and grabbed it from him.

"Do I have to do everything for you?" he snapped and, with the same motion, lifted the whip and made it come down on Lucas.

The intense pain made Lucas recoil and buckle at the knees. The crowd gasped as Finton raised the whip again and again. The next floggings seemed even worse, and Lucas reckoned that Finton was going well beyond administering punishment. He was venting. "There will be order! And discipline!" he shouted repeatedly.

"General!" called Verron. He had managed to brush Finton's soldiers off and stepped forward from the crowd. "That is enough, sir. I think we can wait until the king returns before we punish him any further."

Lucas breathed a sigh of relief when Finton paused to address Verron. "You saw what he did! He's out of control. All of the chosen ones are, and *you* most of all because you've done nothing about it. I am changing that *today*—I won't stop until the boy submits."

"Do we even know *why* he incited a riot?" Verron roared. "I am sure the king would like to know, but, at this rate, the boy will not be in any state to be questioned when he arrives."

With the words of his officer and the general fading into the background, Lucas had begun focusing on something else. He had his head turned towards the gates and was watching closely. He used his seeing mind to go beyond the castle walls. "Come on," he muttered when Finton was preparing to strike again. "Come on . . . they're right there." Then, just when Lucas thought he would have to endure another flogging, the horn finally sounded from the gates, and the creaking of the drawbridge being lowered was music to his ears.

"Take him away!" he heard Finton order. "All soldiers to resume posts!"

The ropes holding him to the wagon were slashed, and the men grabbed him by the arms. He could barely feel his legs because of the pain coursing through his back, and they had to drag him away. The soldiers were struggling to get him down the slippery steps to the dungeon, just as thundering hooves on the bridge indicated that the king, who was not due back for another day, had entered the castle grounds.

CHAPTER 4

Itan knew something was amiss when no chosen stood waiting in the bailey to take the horses after he rode over the bridge underneath the gatehouse. He saw a wagon pushed off to the side and two ropes dangling from it. The gates to the training grounds were closed, which was never the case at this time of day.

"Now this is curious," Egon said dryly, as he stopped his horse next to Itan's.

"What has happened here?" Itan called to Verron, who stood by the gate trying to get it to open—it appeared to have been closed so roughly that it was jammed. But something else was at play as well, beyond the condition of the gate. "Are the chosen ones in there?"

Before Verron could answer, Finton approached Itan. "We had an uprising," he said, "but everything is under control now."

"What do you mean, an *uprising*?" demanded Itan, jumping off his horse and marching towards the gates with Egon at his side.

"The chosen were fighting the elites," answered Finton. "We were able to separate them, but then they barricaded themselves inside their grounds."

"The king has arrived," Verron called out through the slit in the gates. "It is imperative that the gates be opened. Zera, Davis? Open the gates."

There was silence as they waited for a response, but then Itan could hear the barricade being removed. When the gates opened, the king's guard flooded in. They found the boys and Zera standing unarmed, their backs against the wall. Some of the chosen showed signs of having been involved in a fight. Zera's braid had come loose, and her hair was a tangled mess. Davis had a dark bruise on his cheek. Archer and Tanner's shirts hung in shreds. Warrick was wiping blood from a cut above his eye, and a handful of the others looked like they had been dragged behind a horse.

"Where is Lucas?" Egon called out, walking down the line of chosen.

"He was the one who agitated his peers and started the fight," said Finton before any of the boys could answer. "For his primary role in this confrontation, I had him taken away, lest he stir up the chosen all over again."

"How did he get separated from the rest if they locked themselves in?" inquired Egon.

Itan was wondering the same thing and looked at Finton for an explanation but then decided it mattered little. Itan's conversation with his brother about the uprising in the south was still troubling him, and coming home to a revolt in his own house was the last thing he had needed on his plate. What did it matter how Lucas got separated from the others if he was the one to blame? What mattered was that Itan had come home to this mess and was surrounded by incompetence. He turned on his heel and marched back through the gates.

"Where is he?" he bellowed for anyone in the bailey to hear. Despite Itan's desire to ignore the mountain of nonsense before him, he knew he had to determine what had transpired in his absence. He could feel his blood boiling, and it didn't help that the soldiers avoided his stare, pretending they didn't know who he was referring to. "Where is he?" he shouted again.

"The dungeon, sire," one of the guards finally answered.

Taking a deep breath and what amounted to only a few long strides, the king crossed the bailey. He would get to the bottom of this himself if he had to! Egon followed him, barely keeping up as he took the steps two by two to the dungeon.

"Why not keep the boy locked up for now and talk to him later?" tried Egon. "I can have him brought up when you have a clear understanding of today's events. You are very angry, sire. And understandably. Perhaps we should wait until—"

"I think we all know what happened here," Itan shouted without slowing down. "And it's going to stop."

He rushed down the last few steps and burst through the door at the bottom. Two guards sidestepped as he stormed past them. "Tell me where he is!" he shouted at them, taking in the long line of cell doors. He hated the smell and the dark, confined space of the dungeon deep underground—he had never enjoyed spending time there.

"He wasn't put in a cell, sire," answered one of the guards. "He's down at the far end."

The king hesitated. The far end of the dungeon was where the torture room was—the innermost room of the entire castle, its gloom and darkness unparalleled by any other space. He'd avoided it ever since he was made to come down to watch a torture when he was a ten-year-old boy. He could still hear his father's words as if they had only been spoken yesterday. "When a king orders a man's torture," his father had told him, "he has to be willing to watch it being carried out." He had slowed down and started to quiver when he heard a man's screaming come from the shimmering darkness at the end of the passageway. His father had grabbed him by the arm and had pushed him along in front of him to the far end of the dungeon. There he was forced to watch the torture of a man who had been accused of spying.

The man had succumbed to his injuries well before he could admit his guilt, but the sight and sound of the torture had stayed with Itan.

He now marched down that same dark hallway to the room at the end, which was lit only by the flickering light of torches on the wall. The light refracted weakly in the many devices of torture that hung along the wall. In the center of the room, hung Lucas, bound by his arms to the heavy chains suspended from the ceiling. He had his head down but raised it slightly before lowering it again. The king stopped still at the entrance, and Egon rushed past him.

"How bad do you think it looks?" asked Itan. Egon was examining Lucas's back.

"Not good," answered Egon. "But it looks like he only received three lashes."

"Then they were not finished," concluded Itan. "We clearly interrupted something we were not supposed to see."

"Maybe the flogging was not justified?" asked Egon. He stepped around Lucas, who had his head down, and bent at the knees to look the boy in the eye. "Lucas? Was it?"

"Leave us," said the king sternly before allowing Lucas to answer. "I want to talk to him alone."

"Sire," protested Egon. "I should hear what he has to say."

"And you will."

Itan waited until he could no longer hear Egon's footsteps, and the entrance door of the dungeon opened and closed after he left before turning back to the boy that hung in chains before him. He started pacing the floor, appreciating the total silence between them so that he could collect his thoughts.

"I arrived home to an uprising and was told that you were the one responsible," Itan finally started. "You know that the punishment for that is severe if that is indeed the case?" He stopped and waited for Lucas's reaction, but when he remained silent, he continued. "You have pushed boundaries and broken rules vital for the running of this army. On the other hand, you have also served me well and proven your loyalty."

He paused again and studied Lucas for a moment to make sure he was listening. His shirt was tattered, torn open from the back, and his head hung low, his eyes seeming to fix on one section of the stone floor. Itan looked down but did not see what Lucas was staring at. "I have people tell me that you do not belong here," he continued. "That you are not a true chosen . . . that I should never have taken you on. Others claim you're precisely what we need here—that you are something more than a chosen."

Again, he looked at Lucas. No longer was he staring at the boy he had first spotted performing in a circus act. He was older now, stronger, confident and fearless, and braver than anyone he knew—all the qualities that made for a great warrior. As king, he owned everything around him, including the people, but he never felt he owned Lucas. He would soon have to hear the allegations made against Lucas, and he would have to act accordingly. If Lucas had turned against him, he would have to put his affection for the boy aside and be the king his people expected him to be.

Lucas raised his head. There was no fear in his eyes, no sadness, no defeat. There was also no rage or hate. He simply looked self-assured in the knowledge that whatever was happening to him would happen for a reason. He had seen Lucas broken once, and no one thought he would recover, but he proved everyone wrong and came back even stronger than before. The king sighed. "I'm going to give you this one chance," he said, "to save yourself. I will give you a horse, a sword, and a letter of passage if you require one. After that, you may go wherever you want and find employment."

"You wish me to take leave of here?" asked Lucas in a subdued voice.

The king shook his head. "No," he answered firmly. "If truth be told, I don't, but if you are proven to be guilty of all the charges, I will no longer be able to justify having you in my army. And there could be other, very grim consequences for you. If you leave now, there will be no trial."

Lucas shook his head. "I'm thankful for the offer you give me, sire, but I'll have to decline."

"Are you telling me you were not responsible for today's uprising and therefore fear no punishment?"

"I'm responsible for trying to stop injustice," answered Lucas, "and for the fight that followed as a direct result. But I would do it again if I had to. If my actions are seen as an uprising against the king instead of standing up for what is right and fair, then yes, I will accept whatever punishment is assigned to me. I do not fear it."

Egon was waiting on the steps outside the dungeon and eyed Itan with concern when he emerged. He stood with his hands laced together, and did not make a move to leave, though Itan knew their presence in the Great Hall would be required immediately.

"He's fine," Itan told him. "No further harm came to him. He told me what I needed to know. So now I am ready to hear what really happened."

The Great Hall was buzzing with talk when they arrived, but a hush came over the space when Itan entered and made his way past his senior staff to the front. Egon followed in silence.

Itan took his place on the throne and began calling people forward one by one to listen to their reports of the events. Egon stood by and listened, his hands folded behind his back and his eyes fixed on the people who spoke before them. No doubt he, too, was very curious about what would be revealed. The first few witnesses all told Itan that Lucas had started the fight, but Lucas had admitted that already, and so that information was nothing new. Verron also confirmed this to be the case, but he had more to report.

"Six horses then came running in who had broken loose in the bailey," Verron was saying. "Lucas jumped on one of them."

Hearing about the horses spiked the king's interest, and he sat up straight to hear more. Verron had gone quiet, as if contemplating the event as well.

"Then what happened?" Itan asked.

Verron cleared his throat and cast a glance sideways, as if uncomfortable relaying the next bit of information. "The five other horses were wild and had every soldier scrambling for safety—the soldiers were fleeing the training grounds, for fear of getting kicked. The horses followed them, as did Lucas, on the sixth."

"Is that how he became separated from the chosen?" asked Itan.

"Yes, sire," answered Verron. "He rode through just as the chosen were pushing the gate closed. It seemed to be a deliberate act on his part."

"To separate himself?"

"Yes, sire."

"You are making assumptions, Verron," said Finton, who had just walked up to join them at the front of the room, despite Itan's request that witnesses approach him one at a time. "The boy most likely lost control of the horse when it wanted to follow the others out. I am guessing he would have much preferred to stay back with the chosen and continue to build their solidarity against the elite born."

"Lucas has never lost control of any horse before," replied Verron. "I doubt he did this time. His exit was almost certainly intentional."

"None of that matters," said Itan, though he believed the officer to be right. "At any point, were weapons used by any of the chosen?" he asked Verron.

"No, sire! One of the chosen went for the barrels at one point, but Lucas ordered him not to arm himself."

"When was this?"

"When he was on the horse and about to charge out."

"How did those horses get loose?" he called out to the horses' handlers and the farrier, who stood together in a group.

"We have no idea, sire," answered one of the handlers, stepping forward to speak. "Something spooked them. They reared and went straight for the training grounds. It happened quickly. We could do nothing to stop them."

"So, tell me," said Itan, turning back to Verron, "if those horses had not come in, would Lucas, in your opinion, have accepted his punishment for starting the fight, or was he ready to rebel regardless?"

Officer Verron cleared his throat before stepping forward. "No, sire," he replied. "He was detained after the fight and was cooperative. Until the general changed his mind."

"Changed his mind to what?" asked the king. "The type of punishment?"

"No, sire. He changed his mind as to who was to receive it." Verron glanced sideways at Finton before continuing. "Lucas only resisted when the general chose one of the younger boys to receive the flogging in his place. Some of the chosen offered to be taken instead, but the general had made his decision. Then the horses came in."

Itan saw that Finton wanted to say something, but he raised his hand to silence him. He only wanted facts at this point. He called Eli forward. "You don't have to tell me that Lucas defied you and initiated the fight," he said. "I've heard the story, and Lucas himself is not denying it either. What I don't know is *why* he did it, so go ahead and shine some light on that."

"Yes, sire," answered Eli. He glanced briefly at his father, as if seeking guidance as to what to say, but Finton avoided looking at his son.

As Eli relayed his version of the events, Itan noticed how Carleton dropped his head and was subtly shaking it—an indication that Eli wasn't giving him the truth.

"Allowing the boys to engage in these ball games was asking for trouble," Finton said quickly before the king could silence him for speaking out of turn. "It deteriorated the necessary and established boundaries between chosen and elite."

"The games did not make Lucas lose respect for your son," interjected Verron. "We all know that happened long ago. They may have hastened the opportunity for a fight, but the fight itself was inevitable. I have never witnessed Lucas disrespect other elite borns."

"That is because Carleton steps down every time. He doesn't put Lucas in his place and demand his respect."

"You don't have to demand respect when it's already given," said Verron, turning his head to face Finton. "Or brotherhood—Carleton has grown closer to Lucas in these short years than he ever has been with your son, whom he grew up with. I would go a step further to say that Eli has difficulty maintaining any significant bond with his peers."

A blush came to Eli's cheek. The king was surprised to hear Verron voice his opinion on the subject and let them bicker for a few minutes. Verron was usually quiet when it came to his nephew and Eli, but he had likely noticed that Carleton had stepped up in taking control of the elite borns. And Lucas had played a role in that.

"Sire, all of this could have been prevented," said Finton. "Allowing the chosen ones more freedom was a mistake. We need to reestablish discipline if we want to prevent anything like this from happening again. I think we can all agree that Lucas is trouble and will have to be removed."

Itan raised his hand when people erupted in agreement and disagreement. "Thank you, General," he said loudly. "Your statement is duly noted, and I will consider it. I agree that for this army to function efficiently, some sacrifices will have to be made. I cannot and will not tolerate anything like this again. You are all dismissed until I have thought this through and have settled upon the best way possible to move forward."

CHAPTER 5

Finton went to sleep that night quite satisfied with the knowledge that Lucas was finally going to be dealt with. Killeand had warned him once that Eli's everlasting feud with Lucas could hinder Eli in securing a high-ranking position in the future, and Finton knew as much to be true. No one wanted a general who constantly let his emotions get the better of himself, especially over a rival at a lower rank. Something Finton had not needed to be told, as that had been his fear for some time. Now that concern was finally being dealt with. He slept like a baby and only woke up when someone knocked on his door.

"What is it?" he shouted.

"The king is requesting to speak to you, sir!" the officer on the other side of the door answered.

"I'll be there shortly," replied Finton, leaping from his bed, eager to hear what the king had to say. He combed his fingers through his hair and dressed quickly before opening the door and following the officer who waited for him by the stairs. When they reached the lower floor, he saw the doors to the Hall open and people going inside. He had assumed he had been called to a private meeting with the king, but apparently not. He was just about to question the officer when he began to turn the corner—they were moving away from the Hall. Now, this was quite strange.

"Where did you say the king wanted to meet me?" he asked.

"Library, sir."

"Of course," muttered Finton. One was only ever called to the library when sensitive matters were to be discussed that the king did not want anyone else to hear.

The officer knocked on the library door and waited for a response from the other side before ushering Finton in.

The library walls were lined with shelves on which many books, scrolls, and maps were kept. A desk and several comfortable chairs stood in the middle of the room. The king was standing with his back to the door, looking at a map pinned to the wall. He was still wearing the same clothes he had worn the day before and held an old book in his hand, which he placed on a side table before taking a step forward. Finton noticed the puffiness under his eyes, indicating he had little or no sleep.

"Did you have a rough night, sire?" inquired Finton.

"You could say that. I had a few grave decisions to make."

"Anything I can help with?"

"No, this was for me to contemplate," said the king, settling himself into a leather chair and tipping his head back to rest it. The king shut his eyes. "But you are probably pleased to know that I agree that Lucas overstepped the line when he started the fight with Eli yesterday."

"I am," said Finton, tapping the side table in approval. The sound made the king startle, and he lifted his head and opened his eyes. "It is time that the boy is put in his place once and for all."

The king nodded. "And I will do that today."

Finton smiled inwardly. He could not wait to hear what the king had in mind. He waited for the king to elaborate further, but Itan seemed distracted or locked in deep thought. "So, aside from inciting a riot," started Finton, "striking a superior means punishment of ten lashes. He received three yesterday—"

"You forget the four that Eli gave him," interrupted the king.

Finton held his breath for a moment before speaking. "Well," he said, "you could barely call them lashes, but, if they are to be counted, I assume you want him to receive the outstanding lashes?"

"No," responded the king, straightening in his chair. "I think what you did to him yesterday was more than sufficient."

Finton felt a chill run up his spine. This was suddenly going in a different direction than he had expected it to. "What about punishing him for the riot he started?"

The king gave him a hard look. "I have determined there was no uprising," he answered. "From what I gather, he acted as he did to protect one of the younger ones. Which certainly adds to the list of queries I have about him." The king pointed to the chair opposite his. "Please sit," he said. "There is something I want to discuss."

Finton sat down in the red suede upholstered chair that he had always favored. He let himself sink into the soft cushions, but they offered no comfort. He watched the king pick up the book from the side table and let his hand slide over the soft leather cover. It was quite worn, showing it had been in someone's hands often.

"Do you recognize this book?" asked the king.

Finton shook his head. "Should I? It's true that I don't read much . . . but I don't think I have seen that one before. It looks well-loved."

The king nodded. "It was. My brother carried this book everywhere he went when he was young. Are you sure you have not seen it?"

Finton furrowed his brow, studying the book the king was twisting back and forth in his hand. Something about the ornate gold lettering . . . Yes—he did recognize it. "If I did," he lied, "then I don't recall it. May I ask what the book is about?"

"It is about the Great Battle," answered the king. "And it is about Toroun, and the prophecy that was written right after."

"Ah, yes," responded Finton. "Meloc's obsession with the prophecy. I thought you did not share his beliefs."

"I didn't," said the king opening the book, "but my grandfather did, and recent events have forced me to question my outlook. There is a passage here, on the last page, written in my grandfather's hand. In it, he talks about the chosen ones, about who and what they are, and why they are among us. One of the things he states is that they will become stronger and more skilled than elites, but only if they acquire the right leader."

Finton shrugged. "That will not happen. They see one another as equal. We all know that."

"Yes, but according to my grandfather, an exception exists. He says that chosen ones will follow *the one who is born from the stars*."

"What is that supposed to mean?"

"I wish I knew," said the king. "I consulted Verron on this. He had heard of it but didn't know what it meant, exactly."

Finton shook his head. "It sounds like nonsense to me. I don't see the chosen ones giving up the life you have provided for them to follow Lucas into uncertainty—if that is what you are implying. I agree he is different, and that his behavior confuses them."

"Because he is not a chosen?"

"No, yes . . . maybe," said Finton. "Where are you going with this?"

"Meloc believes it has happened before."

"What did?"

"Chosen ones behaving differently around someone," answered the king. "I had not made the connection, but when I saw Lucas yesterday—the way he handled himself and how he spoke? He reminded me of *Nolan*." The king paused, clearly waiting for his response, or to see if he recognized the name, but of course he did.

How could he not, despite the many years that had passed?

Nolan had been an imposter, much like Lucas. Finton recalled being a fifteen-year-old elite when Nolan had first shown up at the castle gates. Alone, on his horse, no older than thirteen, with a sword and a letter from his family stating the claim that he was of noble blood. He was accepted after being tested and became the most combat-skilled elite in the group, winning competition after competition and gaining the admiration of many. He never bragged, shrugging away all compliments that came his way. No one could resist his charm—his charismatic laugh and maddening humility.

He was effortlessly kind to everyone. Finton had lost friends to Nolan, one after another, much as Eli had, to Lucas.

Finton's animosity towards Nolan had grown stronger by the day. Especially when Meloc, not much older than them at the time, became convinced that Nolan was someone his grandfather had made notes about in the book that he was always reading. "Nolan is the one," Meloc once declared as he sat studying in the library with him one evening. "The one the prophecy spoke of. The one who will lead the chosen ones in a final battle of two kings!" He kept pointing out to Finton the chosen ones were behaving differently around Nolan. "No," Finton had insisted, "it's Nolan who takes interest in them and not the other way around. He panders to them!"

They were returning their horses to the stables after training a week later. They had just walked past Nolan and Egon, who were talking together. They were both smiling, something rarely seen with Egon, who was the strongest, most dedicated chosen they had. "Have you ever stood among them as if you were their friend," said Meloc, "and still commanded their respect, as Nolan has?"

He had not answered and had walked his horse into its stall, hoping Meloc would just stop talking about it for once but, of course, he didn't. "It's a quality my father will look for in a general," Meloc had continued in the stall next to him. "If I am right and Nolan is the one born from the stars—the position will be his for sure."

Finton could still feel the anger well up inside of him. It would be the last time he heard anyone speak of Nolan or the prophecy again—the fire had broken out in the stables shortly after, and Nolan was one of the three boys who perished that day.

Finton loosened the collar of his shirt to help him breathe. He felt the king's eyes on him. "I remember him," he answered softly. "It was a terrible thing that happened to him."

"Yes," said the king. "It certainly was."

"So, Lucas reminds you of Nolan?" he asked, trying to sound casual. "I do not recall Nolan having anything to do with the chosen ones. They certainly were not following him, nor do I think they are following Lucas now."

"Oh, they are," said the king. "Yesterday's events could not have come together as they did if they were not."

Finton shifted to the edge of his seat. "Then, what is it you're going to do? Change his status to an elite born, even though we have no proof of his bloodline?"

The king shook his head.

"Then what? You cannot keep him with the chosen if what you say is true, but there is always the option of sending him away. Didn't Lord Hammond make the offer to take him once?"

Again, the king shook his head and rose from his seat. "Lord Hammond has more than enough good fighters already. He does not need him. I gave Lucas the option to leave us voluntarily," he said, walking over to the shelf, "but he has declined. I cannot keep him here as an elite with all that has transpired, and Egon feels strongly that he needs to remain near the chosen if he stays." The king placed the book back on the shelf, running one finger down its gilded spine before abandoning it to resume the conversation. "Why did you have him chained up in the dungeon?" asked the king, his tone suddenly dark. "Why not have him locked up in one of the cells?"

"I don't know," answered Finton. "Because he was out of control?"

"Good enough reason," answered the king. "You know you did me a favor, and thereby Lucas?"

"I don't think I follow," said Finton, a second set of chills running up his spine.

"Seeing Lucas in actual chains made me realize we've had him chained from the moment he arrived here. I have only been able to see a glimpse of his qualities and strengths." The king paused to walk back to his chair. "I am going to change that," he continued once he sat down again. "Starting today, those chains are coming off."

"What do you mean?" asked Finton.

"While we have had this talk," answered the king, "all relevant staff has been informed that I intend to give Lucas the king's mark today."

Finton jumped out of his seat. His mouth dropped open, but he was unable to utter a word. Instead, he flopped back down in the chair and shook his head wildly. "You cannot do that," he was finally able to say. "That will put his rank above everyone's . . . generals, elite, officers, guards, soldiers . . . everyone."

"That's right," nodded the king. "He will only answer to me and, until he is of age, to Egon as well. I want to see what he will become when he is no longer subdued by his low rank. I am aware this may be hard for you to accept, but this is how it's going to be. My decision is final."

The betrayal was a slap in the face. All his years of service, the sacrifices he had made, and now the king was choosing a boy who'd been nothing but trouble? "I don't know if I can accept this," he said, his hands beginning to tremble. "It was an affront to you when your father gave the mark to a chosen, and now you are willing to do the same. What about those who have been loyal to you for years? How does Verron feel about this, and Egon, when he finds out?"

The king let out a deep sigh. "Verron already knows. He is making the announcement as we speak. And Egon agrees it is the only way to keep yesterday from repeating itself."

"Why was I not a part of this discussion?"

"Do you really want me to answer that?" asked the king sternly, gazing at a painted portrait of his grandfather. "If I had not come home a day early, would Lucas still be alive?"

"Of course he would be."

"Not according to Verron. Let's be truly honest with one another, even if it is just for a moment."

Finton placed both hands on his knees and nodded. The room seemed to spin, but he managed to stand. "Then you have made your decision," he said, once he had positioned himself near the door, "and I will have to make mine."

CHAPTER 6

Lucas could hear an iron bar lifting from its latch and a door being opened. How much time had passed? He had no idea. The muffled voices from the other side caused a chill to come over his body—it occurred to him that they could be coming to use those devices on him. He had felt the king's anger when he had entered the dungeon and seen the worried look on Egon's face. He had also noticed some bloodstains in the grooves of the stones beneath his feet. He wondered if the blood belonged to the taster that tried to poison Lord Hammond, and he moved his feet away from it. He then looked at all the strange devices that hung on the walls and tried to come up with a use for them other than inflicting pain.

Garrad and Verron approached him, and Lucas was surprised to catch the officer's reassuring look. He flexed the muscles in his shoulders that were getting stiff but stopped when the movement caused more pain.

Verron followed Garrad to the table with the spikes, and Lucas watched him place his bag on top of it. Lucas had yet to come up with a good use for that table, other than its intended purpose.

"You'll be all right," Verron said. He must have noticed the tremble in his body. "It's not like you've never had to deal with the ointment before."

Lucas wanted to say something but then saw the jar Garrad had taken out of the bag and immediately recognized the potent smell.

"Here," said Garrad. He passed Verron a brown glass bottle full to the brim. "Give him all of this to drink. We will wait a moment, then apply the ointment."

"What happened to the other chosen?" asked Lucas.

"Nothing so far," answered Verron, stepping closer and uncorking the bottle. "They are locked up in the dormitory. I have yet to hear the king's decision on what to do with them. I only received orders to bring Garrad to you." Verron put the bottle to his lips, and Lucas felt a bitter liquid slide down his throat. "I cannot promise you anything, but the fact that this order came after the king listened to everyone's version of events is a good sign."

"I don't think he will allow me to stay," said Lucas, after swallowing the last of the tonic. "He knows it might happen again." Verron stepped back, and he saw Garrad move in behind him with the jar in his hand. His eyesight started to become blurry, and Verron's voice was distant when he finally heard him answer.

"Then you will have to convince him that it won't."

"I can't," whispered Lucas. "Things have happened . . ." He struggled to keep his eyes open, but the elixir was too powerful to resist. He was only vaguely aware of the burning sensation of the cream as it was applied into the lacerations on his back and of the two men exiting the room after they had bandaged him up.

The rattling of chains startled Lucas awake. Two guards were standing by his side and supporting him while a third lowered the chain that was holding him up. Lucas raised his head when his arms came down and saw Egon observing him from the entrance of the torture chamber.

"Can you walk?" asked Egon.

Lucas rubbed his sore arms when the shackles were removed from his wrist. He still felt a bit groggy, and he could smell himself. How long had he been down here?

"I think so," he answered. He was shivering and felt a blanket placed over his shoulders when the guards let go of him. He was not sure what to do when Egon turned around and started to exit the room. Confused, he looked over his shoulder and saw the guards step away from him.

"Are you coming?" he heard Egon call out to him from the entrance of the dungeon.

"Yes, sir," answered Lucas. He took one last look at the guards, and then carefully stepped away from them.

Lucas noticed Egon's demeanor towards him was different. Warmer . . . or at least less distant. Lucas even caught a glimpse of an understanding nod when he held the door open for him. He showed concern when it took Lucas some effort to climb the steps up to the bailey but waited patiently. It was dark out, and the castle seemed to be asleep except for a light that still flickered through the window of the tailor's room when they walked past. They started to cross the empty bailey and the cool night air made him wrap the blanket more tightly around his body.

"Are you cold?" asked Egon.

"A little," answered Lucas. He had started to shiver more, but he couldn't tell if it was from the cold, the injuries he sustained, or the stress of not knowing what was to come next. It was clear to him that he was not being taken to the chosens' dormitory; they were heading straight for the king's guard barracks.

Egon opened the door and let him enter what looked like the king's guards' communal room. Lucas counted five tables where food could be consumed and saw a comfortable seating area in front of a large inviting fireplace on the far right of the room. Some of the guards were still awake and sitting at one of the tables, playing a dice game. They paused when he came in and stared at him with much interest. Lucas was glad when Egon gestured to the fireplace, where he could sit away from them and stare into the flames.

"Go and warm yourself up," he said.

Lucas sat down on one of the stools by the fire and waited for Egon to finally explain why they were here and what was to happen to him.

"You are probably wondering why I have brought you here," Egon said at last, picking up a stool to sit opposite him, "and why I didn't take you back to the chosens' dormitory."

"Because the king does not want me there?" responded Lucas, still staring into the fire. "It's all right. I saw this one coming."

"No, you didn't," said Egon, giving Lucas a sly look. It was an expression he had never seen on Egon's face—almost a smirk, but there was an earnestness there as well. "No one saw this one coming, including myself. The king has decided to give you *the mark*."

"The mark?" he asked, turning to look into the fire. "What you have? The king's mark. Why?"

"Will you accept it?"

Lucas dropped his head and stared at the floor for a moment. He didn't know how to respond. So many questions ran through his mind. "Can I—not accept it?" he asked, looking back up. "Not that I won't, but . . . is there a choice?"

"You don't feel you deserve it?"

"Yes," said Lucas. "I've just been punished for disobeying orders and accused of starting a riot, so none of this makes sense to me now."

"You must understand, Finton—and not the king—carried out

your punishment." Egon took a deep breath and leaned closer. "Look," he said, "do you think I felt I deserved it? All I did was go into a burning stable and pull people out. One of those just happened to be Meloc, the king's son. But it's not what you have done that matters. It's not the reason the king wants you to have it—it's what you will be able to do with it. Who you'll become when you're free to make your own decisions and only have to answer to the king, or to me."

"Will I still be able to train with the chosen?" asked Lucas. "To live among them?"

"That is for the king to decide," answered Egon, "but I have recommended that you do, at least until you are of age. The king did not seem opposed to that idea. It won't be the same, of course. You'll no longer fall under their rules. You will have to make it clear to them, so that they don't adopt any bad behavior."

Lucas nodded. Yes, there would be a change, but one that would benefit everyone. Finton's hostility towards him had increased. He had been caught by him twice now, and he could not risk a third time.

"It's a great honor," Lucas said, "one that I won't take lightly. It'd be foolish to even contemplate turning it down." He rubbed his eyes, trying to get his head on straight.

"Come," said Egon. "The ceremony will take place in a few hours and you look exhausted." He stood and picked up an oil lamp from one of the tables. "Follow me. I'll take you to your room."

Lucas yawned and gladly rose with the prospect of being able to lie down soon. He followed Egon down a hallway with doors on either side. When they turned around the corner, Egon stopped by the second one and opened it. It had a bed up against the wall and a nightstand. A wardrobe stood on the opposite side, and next to it, a table with an empty washbowl.

"It will be filled in the morning," said Egon when he noticed Lucas looking at it. "It is time you get some rest first." He placed the lamp down on the nightstand and gave him a friendly tap on the shoulder before heading out the door. Lucas stood in the middle of the room and watched the door close. He listened for it to be locked, but all he could hear were Egon's footsteps disappearing down the hallway.

Lucas opened his eyes to see a middle-aged woman pouring hot water into the washbowl from a pail. Her long dark hair, only somewhat streaked with gray, was tied with a pale blue ribbon. The water made a pleasant sound as it filled the bowl, and steam rose into the air. Where was he, and was he dreaming?

It was the pain in his back and the tight bandage around his torso that brought back the events of the day prior. Without looking at him, the woman left the room, and Lucas dozed off again. She came back eventually, and this time, the bowl of porridge placed on the nightstand woke him up. The woman smiled when he opened his eyes, and helped him sit up when he struggled to.

"Thank you," he said.

"My pleasure," she answered, placing the tray with the porridge on his lap. "Is there anything else you need before I go?"

Lucas shook his head. He didn't think so.

"Then I will inform them you are awake," she said.

After only a few spoonsful of the food, Lucas heard someone knock. The door began to open before he had a chance to answer. The tailor came in carrying a neatly folded stack of black and maroon clothes, which he put on the table next to the washbowl.

"These garments should fit you," said the tailor, stifling a yawn, "but if not, let me know. I still have some time to make alterations." With red, puffy eyes and tousled hair that stuck out in all directions, the tailor looked like he had not slept all night.

"Thank you," said Lucas. It always amazed him that the tailor always knew everyone's size just by looking at them.

The clothes the tailor left with him didn't resemble any uniform he recognized, but Lucas didn't have a chance to try them on because Garrad came in to check on his wounds as soon as the tailor left. He applied more cream and replaced the bandage with one that allowed for more movement. As Garrad left the room, two older men entered. Both had short-cropped gray hair, hunched backs, and blue eyes. Their skin was thinning, and they had exceptionally large noses. They were clearly brothers, possibly even twins, but Lucas did not know them.

"We are the artists," the slightly taller of the two explained. "And were informed this morning that our assistance is needed to give another the mark."

"You gave Egon the mark also?" asked Lucas.

"We did. It was some years ago. Our hands are not as steady as they used to be, so we want to make sure you know what to expect." He waited for Lucas to nod before continuing. "The mark will first be drawn on your shoulder by my brother here. Then I will cut into the lines before we can apply the pigment. There will be discomfort, but it is important that there is not the slightest movement on your part."

Lucas took a deep breath at the thought of these two men cutting into him. He wanted to tell them that he would try, but the door opened before he could say anything. The artists were ousted by the barber, a man of dark skin who said he had a job to do and needed space.

With a comb in one hand and scissors in the other, the barber went to work, and Lucas watched the locks of hair fall onto the ground. It reminded him of the day he became Father Ansan's student, except his head had been shaved entirely then.

When Lucas was finally alone, he washed himself with the now lukewarm water and got rid of the loose itchy hair the barber had left sticking to his neck. Then, he pulled on the new black trousers with a solid maroon stripe on the outside of each leg and buttoned up his black shirt.

"Look at you," remarked Egon, making his appearance at the door. "You clean up quite well." He walked over and ruffled Lucas's freshly cut hair. It was a gesture of kindness Lucas was not used to getting from the usually stern-looking king's guard. He had noticed Egon's change in demeanor the moment he saw him enter the torture room in the dungeon with the king the day before. As if Egon suddenly cared for him. What had changed that made him behave this way?

"Thank you," said Lucas. He finished buttoning his shirt and tugged on the maroon vest, which he noticed was made of soft suede. "I'm just not sure about these new clothes. Am I to wear this all the time?" He didn't want to sound ungrateful, but it felt like a little much.

"Remember, the clothes are not so much about you than they are the king and the reputation he must uphold. You represent the king at all times now, so you will only wear the best," said Egon. "But the tailor will make you another set that is a bit less formal." He then gestured to Lucas's back. "Did Garrad come to see you?"

"He did," answered Lucas. "Along with a lot of other people."

"Hmm, yes. The king is making sure that everyone understands the importance of the mark. He has also summoned as many people to the Hall as it can hold, to bear witness."

"Was it like this for you?"

Egon shook his head. "It was different for me. The king was on his sickbed, so there was no ceremony. It was done in his bedroom with only a few people watching. Without many witnesses, it took a while before everyone accepted that I carried the mark. King Itan doesn't want that for you. Here," he said, holding out a new belt with scabbard and sword that he had been holding when he entered the room. "Wear it all the time from now on, and whatever the king asks of you—don't disappoint him. He thinks highly of you, as do I."

Lucas took the sword with both hands and admired the weight of it. "I will not disappoint him," he said and strapped the belt around his waist. When he finished, Egon eyed him up from head to toe and nodded approvingly.

"Are you ready?"

"I think so," answered Lucas and followed Egon out the door.

He walked the long empty corridor with Egon by his side, their footsteps echoing as they neared the entrance of the Hall. Lucas glanced sideways at the imposing king's guard, whose eyes were trained forward. Egon's black hair glistened and looked freshly greased, with not a strand out of place. A red velvet ribbon tied his long hair together and rested between his shoulder blades.

Lucas was straightening his posture to match Egon's when the guards opened the doors, and they were allowed through. Hundreds of heads turned simultaneously when Lucas entered, and a large lump rose in his throat. He had underestimated the mark's significance. As he walked towards the front of the room, the crowd parting to create a path for him, he watched the king on his throne, sitting motionless and stone-faced. The queen was seated on one side of him and Princess Amalia on the other, equally still. Only Verron stood nearby. No sign of Finton, fortunately, who had likely not taken the news lightly. Lucas didn't know what he would do if he saw him. The pain on his back had subsided, but the memory of it had not.

Eli, on the other hand, was present. Lucas saw him standing among the elite borns on the left side of the aisle. He looked defeated, with his head hung low and shoulders slumped—not the overconfident boy Lucas was used to seeing.

The chosen ones stood on the right side. He had not seen them since he told them to close the gates behind him. He looked at the group, and his heart raced faster. The connection he felt with each one was stronger than ever before. It was as if he could feel them, hear them. He had no idea what the king had in store for him, but he knew he could not leave the chosen.

"Keep walking," he heard Egon whisper. Lucas had not realized he had slowed his pace. "You are doing this for them as well. You cannot refuse."

Lucas took a deep breath and gave Zera, Warrick, and Davis one last look as he walked past them. All three gave him an encouraging nod. When he reached the front, he stopped, and Egon walked up the platform to take his place next to the king. Lucas made a low bow and then watched Verron step forward to make the announcement.

"You have all been summoned," Verron's voice boomed through the Hall, "at the king's request, to bear witness to the mark, which will be given to Lucas here today. This decision was made in recognition of past service and continued loyalty to the realm." Verron paused, and Lucas saw he was now looking directly at him. "Lucas," he continued, "receiving the king's mark is an honor that will bind you to his service until death parts you. It will permit you to do what is necessary to protect and serve the king and the people. You will be free to act and make decisions in the king's name, and the king trusts that you will do so in a fair and just manner. Can you accept this honor?"

"Yes," replied Lucas, loudly enough for all to hear. "I accept it."

"Then we will commence," said Verron, nodding to a guard who stepped towards Lucas and placed a two-tier step in front of him. He knew from the instructions of the artist brothers what to do. He took off his vest and started to unbutton his shirt, conscious of the eyes staring at him when he removed it and thankful for the bandage concealing the worst of the lacerations. He caught the shocked look on

Amalia's face and felt the chosens' rage when their suspicions of what had happened to him were confirmed.

He kneeled on the lowest tier of the steps before him and placed his forearms on the top. It was silent in the Hall when he heard the doors open and the artists walked in. He listened to their footsteps coming slowly nearer and then stopping right next to him. One of the brothers was holding the inkwells—one black, one red, one white. The other brother had several sharp and pointy devices on a tray. They waited until the king gave them a nod to start and then positioned themselves on Lucas's left side. Lucas lowered his head and felt the tip of a pen move over his skin as one of the brothers began to sketch the mark onto his left shoulder. He took his time, stepping back when satisfied.

Lucas bit down on his lip when Verron gave them the approval to continue, and he felt the first small break in his skin. He held himself still while they slowly and methodically followed the outline of the drawing with their tools. Some felt to Lucas like straight cuts, while some were curved, and others were pinpricks. After each section of the mark was completed, there was a pause before Lucas could feel ink brushed into the openings of his skin. He knew that, slowly, the king's shield with the black and white horses' heads facing each other was taking form in his skin, and a new chapter of his life was about to begin.

A low whispering could be heard throughout the Hall when the two artists were finally finished and stepped aside to reveal the mark. Lucas continued to kneel as the king descended from his throne to inspect the work. Everyone in the Hall remained silent and held their breath while the king took his time examining every detail. When he was satisfied, Egon handed him his sword, and he raised it above Lucas's head.

"Lucas," said the king, "you have pledged loyalty by accepting the mark engraved into your skin. Now I will give you my loyalty by let-ting my sword seal the bond already created. A bond that only death can break." The king lowered the sword, and Lucas felt the cold steel soothe the burning sensation on his shoulder.

When the sword was lifted, the crowd erupted in a cheer, and Lucas noticed Amalia standing close by. Her elegant maroon dress made her look taller and the flower braid in her hair more mature. He assumed she must have left her seat at the same time Egon had approached with the sword. She leaned towards him when he was told to rise and whispered in his ear. "You looked like a prince when you walked down the aisle," she said. "I hope that getting the mark did not hurt too badly."

"No, my lady," he reassured her. He knew no one could hear them over the cheering, and the king was focused on the excited crowd. She smiled, stepping away when a guard came to hand Lucas his shirt. He watched her go while slipping it carefully over each arm, making sure to keep the fabric loose over his shoulders. When he heard his name called, he turned. The king was motioning for him to stand next to him, and, when he did, Lucas let his eyes roam over the group of people that were assembled and cheering for him.

He tried to smile and look as happy as the king was, but a blinding light suddenly blurred his vision, and a series of images assaulted his mind. First, the moment he'd stood on the hill with Sable, overlooking the castle, on the night he had first arrived with the circus. Next, the sight of Egon galloping towards him on his horse after he had stopped the runaway wagon. Then . . . a face he did not remember ever seeing, and a castle he did not recognize, at least twice the size of Itan's, with two high round towers on the rear corners. It stood at the opening of an inaccessible valley—the castle walls spanned the width of the valley and blocked the entrance to it. There was no moat around the large structure, and only one gatehouse stood at the center of it all. The images came and went so fast that they made his head spin. He started to buckle at the knees, and Egon rushed to his side to hold him up.

"Are you all right?" asked Egon.

"Yes," answered Lucas quickly. "Just lightheaded. Probably from having had my head down too long. I'm fine now." His mind was clearing, but the confusion of seeing those many scenes and faces left Lucas distracted and disoriented. The experience had reminded him of another ceremony he had been part of—when he had taken his place on the stone to become a master warrior. Images from the past had flashed before him then, but they had been initiated by the stone, whereas these seemed to come on their own.

"Unless something else triggered them," said Davis.

"Maybe," answered Lucas. He was lying on his bed in the chosens' dormitory. Davis was sitting on the bed next to his, and Zera sat at the foot end of his. "It's possible."

"Could it have been the sword?" asked Zera. "The words the king spoke seemed to indicate he was sealing a bond between the two of you?"

"That part is just symbolic," said Davis.

"You don't know that. The mark changed Egon. Everyone knows that."

"And I'm sure it will change Lucas, but only because his life as a whole here, at the castle, will be changing."

"Well," said Lucas, pushing himself up to a sitting position. "Speaking of changes . . . I am probably going to get in hot water for being here. I'm supposed to be using a room in the king's guard barracks from now on."

"I didn't think you could get into trouble anymore," said Warrick, who had just walked in with the rest of the chosen. He grinned. "Those days of being a human child are over."

"I still answer to Egon and the king," answered Lucas. "So, I'm not completely off the hook."

"Will you get to eat at the king's table, like Egon?" asked Ando, who had flopped himself enthusiastically in between Lucas and Zera on his bed.

"I'm supposed to tonight, but I think that is only because of the ceremony today."

"Will you tell us what you get to eat and what the king eats?"

"Snails and rats' tails," chimed Warrick.

Davis rolled his eyes. "The king eats what we eat, Ando."

"No, he doesn't," said Ando, giving Davis a stern look. "And neither do his officers. Some have a big round belly. We don't have that, see!"

All the boys started laughing when Ando stood and lifted his shirt to show his protruding ribs and then tried to do the same thing to other boys standing around. Some boys took off, and Ando chased them up and over beds as they tore away laughing. The rest of the boys cheered and chanted, egging Ando on. It was moments like these that Lucas cherished—when all of them were just boys being boys.

He was sitting on his bed with his back to the door, laughing at everyone's antics, when the door to the dormitory flung open and Verron stepped in. Lucas was the first to notice, followed by Zera, but none of the other chosen had, until Verron's booming voice echoed through the room.

"By God's bones," yelled Verron, "what is going on here?"

Every boy froze where he stood, their smiles disappearing when they saw the unimpressed look on Verron's face. Ando was standing on one of the beds and quickly stepped off when Verron strode into the middle of the dormitory.

"Can anyone tell me why you are not in your beds?" he shouted. "Anyone?"

All the boys stood silently, lowering their heads and pretending to study the floor. None of them answered, and Lucas did not know what to say, either. He watched Verron stare down each boy, making his way around the room until his eyes fell on Lucas.

"Lucas," he said firmly, "isn't there somewhere else you are supposed to be?"

"Yes, sir," answered Lucas and reluctantly stood up. He did not want to leave, and it was with a heavy heart that he forced himself to do so. There was complete silence when he stepped into the aisle and walked past Verron on his way out.

As soon as he was two steps down the stairs, he could hear Verron start to shout orders to get the dormitory tidied from top to bottom—nobody would be getting any dinner that night otherwise. A unanimous *yes, sir,* could be heard coming from the chosen, followed by the shuffling of feet and beds being pushed straight. Lucas was nearly at the bottom step when he heard Verron call his name.

"Yes, sir?" he answered, turning around.

"First of all," said Verron standing on the top landing, "you will need to learn to drop the *sir* when answering anyone with a lower rank than yourself. Second, I am not going to stop you from coming here or remind you where you ought to be."

"Yes, s—" Lucas began to say, stopping himself.

Verron smiled. "You're a fast learner," he said. "You'll be all right. The change may be difficult for you at first, but I'm sure you will excel in your new role."

"How am I supposed to address my superiors who are no longer my superiors?" asked Lucas.

"Any way you want," answered Verron. "By their rank title, their name, or both."

CHAPTER 7

Finton had left the library that morning and gone straight to his private quarters, where his anger had gotten the better of him. He had kicked over the chair and swiped his desk clean. A maid had come running when alerted by the noise, and he had demanded she leave at once if she knew what was good for her. He then opened the window to allow fresh air to come in. He had begun to pace the length of his room, and did so until Eli had knocked on his door to come in.

"Father?" Eli had started, his voice soft. "The king—"

"I know," answered Finton rubbing his hands through his hair. It was tough for Finton to look his son directly in the eye. "I have just been informed."

"What am I supposed to do now?" he asked desperately. "Lucas will make my life miserable, and there will be nothing I can do about it."

"You'll do what you always do," shouted Finton. "You will mess things up, over and over again, never learning from your mistakes. Like a stone! Did I not tell you to leave him alone? Did I not tell you that under no circumstance were you to join those ridiculous games?"

"You did, but—"

"But what?" Finton roared. "You felt left out because all the elites went? You felt sorry for yourself, and then what? You decided to have a little bit of fun and started taking out boys half your size?"

Eli shook his head. "That was Lucas."

"That was not Lucas," scolded Finton. "That was you! Do you think that I even for a moment believed that boy would intentionally hurt any of the chosen? He *defends* them, Eli! Don't you see? That is why we've been having all these issues! Because he is *not* a chosen!"

"He isn't?" asked Eli, a look of meek surprise covering his face. "I thought he was one, and is to be given the mark as an honor. Is that not the case?"

"No, it isn't. He was never a chosen, not from the moment he first set foot within these castle walls."

"Why did you not tell me?"

"Because none of us know what he is," he answered. A shocked look registered on Eli's face.

He took a deep breath and turned around to walk to the window. It always soothed him to watch the gentle swaying of the grass in the fields beyond the castle. Occasionally he had seen a fox frolic with its kits or a deer step out from the protection of the forest. But, today, there were no animals to see, and the grass stood still under the windless sky.

"What do you think he is?" he heard Eli ask after a moment of silence.

"An imposter and nothing more," Finton answered calmly. "But one who has infected the king and many others with a radical belief. One I do not share and never will."

When Eli remained quiet, Finton continued. "I need you to give me time to think. I cannot tell you right now what I am going to do, but I agree that having Lucas in a position of power will not benefit either of us. However, he's still young, and that will give us time to see how this is going to play out." He turned to face Eli. "I will not attend the ceremony for obvious reasons, but you will have to."

"I, I—" stammered Eli, but Finton stopped him.

"I know this will not be easy for you to swallow, but you will have to rise above your pride. It is my understanding that the king will not be having Lucas join the elite, so *they* should now be your only focus. Regain their respect."

Eli shook his head. "I am the laughingstock, Father. After yesterday . . . after that flogging I gave him . . . they will never take me seriously again."

It had pained Finton to hear his son speak those words, and now, at the king's dinner banquet that he was politely informed to attend, though everything inside of him rebelled at the thought, he couldn't help but recall his son's distress. He looked across the table to the one who was the cause of the predicament he was now in. The king had welcomed Lucas at the table as if he had always belonged there but, to Finton, he looked out of place. He had barely taken any food, and what items *were* on his plate seemed to be going to waste. Lucas had only briefly glanced at Finton when he had walked in with Egon but was now avoiding his stare and picking at the items on his plate. Sensing the king watching him as he stared at Lucas, Finton turned to him.

"The food is excellent, sire," commented Finton, loudly enough for all seated at the table to hear, "but it appears not everyone is enjoying it." Finton looked back at Lucas, and everyone at the table followed his gaze. He smiled inwardly when he saw Lucas shifting in his seat.

"Is there something wrong with the food?" asked the king, eyeing Lucas's plate. An array of different meats decorated with garnishes filled the table, along with various cheeses and pastries, creamy white ones and bright yellow hard ones well-aged, but all Lucas had eaten was a small piece of the fish. "Is it not to your liking?"

"No, sire," answered Lucas. "The food all looks wonderful."

"Then why not try some of the finer foods?" asked the king. "You don't have to be bashful. It's all here to be eaten."

Lucas looked at the food but shook his head, and Finton couldn't have been more pleased when he saw that. He leaned closer to the officer seated next to him. "The king will soon have to realize that elevating the boy's status has been a huge mistake," he said softly. "Perhaps he is good with the sword and can save lives, but he is just a soldier who does not appreciate the finer foods and cannot make proper dinner conversation."

"It is true that I have only heard him speak a few words since the meal began," replied the officer, "and only to answer questions directed at him."

"Then you agree that he will probably not be able to survive the social aspect demanded of a high-ranking officer," said Finton, loudly enough for others to hear.

"Well, no," stammered the officer when the eyes of the king fell upon him. "That's not what I said."

Finton reached forward to help himself to more of the duck meat on the platter in front of him. "You have given him the mark," he said to the king, "but he does not appreciate the privileges and basic etiquette that come along with it. I would suggest not wasting fine clothing or food on him in the future." He put a piece of meat in his mouth and gave Lucas a spiteful look. He looked around and saw the shocked faces of Verron and several other officers across the table from him.

"I don't see why you all look so surprised," he told them, raising his arms in mock surrender. "I am just stating the obvious. He may be a good soldier, but dressing him up and giving him a taste of our diet won't make him one of us."

Everyone had set their food down on their plates and stopped eating. The officers all waited for a response from the king, but he remained silent. Finton looked at Lucas and noticed the cold stare he gave him. Then the boy suddenly spoke. "The general is right," he said calmly. "Dressing me in fine clothes and putting delicacies on my plate I couldn't even have dreamt of in my wildest dreams . . . it does not make me one of you. Nor do I think that is the king's intention or the reason I accepted the mark." Having the attention of everyone at the table, Lucas took his eyes off Finton and continued. "I'm a soldier, and I need to remain one if I'm to continue to do my job. As much as I would want to indulge in the food before me, it's not the kind of food I grew up with or what shaped me into who I am today. I'm afraid it will not agree with my body."

There was a moment of silence before an older, more rounded senior officer erupted in laughter. Everyone looked puzzled at first, including Finton, but then he understood that Lucas had very tactfully implied he didn't want to gain weight. Finton looked at the king and saw the pleased smile he bestowed upon Lucas.

He had underestimated Lucas yet again. Who would have thought that the boy could be this clever when pushed in a corner?

He had told Eli they would have time before deciding what they must do, but now, surrounded by the wistful smiles of the men, he realized he was wrong in that as well.

At the second hour after midnight, Finton took the carefully composed note from his desk. Giving it one last glance, he tucked it into the small bag hanging from his belt before leaving his room. The halls were quiet, and he was confident that those he did not want to be seen by would be fast asleep. The guards on duty were his own, and he did not fear them reporting his nightly stroll. He took a moment to breathe in the cool night air and then stepped out into the bailey. He was pleased to see the gates already opened and the soldier he had chosen for the task waiting on his horse.

"You know where you're going?" Finton asked quietly, handing the soldier the note.

"Yes, sir. I was born not far from there, so the area is not unfamiliar to me."

"Good," said Finton, patting the rump of the soldier's horse. "Then you best be on your way. Don't stop for anyone, and if you fear you are compromised—destroy the message."

CHAPTER 8

The dinner finally ended, and Lucas made a beeline for the exit doors. He had been made to take a seat among the most prestigious men of the castle, men he had been taught to obey and fear for years. And now he was expected to share food with them? His stomach had become one big knot, and the smell of grease from the wild boar had made him feel nauseous. He knew he would have to eat something, and decided the fish might stand the best chance of keeping down. He added the cheese just in case his stomach would settle and for his plate not to look too sparse compared to others around him.

Finton had watched him through the entire meal, and Lucas had avoided his gaze by concentrating on carefully dissecting the bone from the fish. When Finton had drawn everyone's attention to him, he had looked down at the tiny little fish bones on his plate. They looked like small sticks—fragile, like kindle to start a fire with—and he remembered how Father Ansan had laid sticks out on the ground once, to show his path in life. He had placed a stone on one of the sticks and broken it. The stone had symbolized the obstacle in his life at that time. He was to find a way around if he wanted to continue the path he was on.

As he listened to Finton trying to humiliate him, Lucas had pushed a few bones in a line and placed a piece of cheese on top of one. The cheese was soft—the bone sharp and flexible. The stick could not have gone through the stone, but the bone could easily pierce the cheese if it had to.

Lucas raised his head and stared at Finton—it was this man who was the obstacle. If he was meant to have the mark—had earned his right to sit at the king's table and was expected to fight for him, and to protect the chosen—then he could no longer allow the sticks to be crushed at every opportunity.

Lucas opened his mouth and spoke the words that came to him, and, at long last, the general grew quiet. As the others continued their conversations at the table, Finton made his excuse to retire to his room for the night.

Lucas left the Hall on his own. Everyone dispersed into different directions, and no one minded him or told him what to do. He walked slowly and took his time to look around. It felt strange to walk on his own, without anyone watching his every move. The guards he passed stood to attention as soon as they recognized him and made no attempt to stop him, not even when he decided to walk into the little courtyard and sit himself down on the stone wall encircling the fountain.

He let his hand touch the water that dropped down from three different-sized round basins, spilling from one basin into the next. The bottom basin was the largest and sat on top of four large horse heads that would come up to his waist if he was to stand next to them. The second basin sat on top of a stone pillar in the center of the large basin. The third was the smallest and the source of the initial water flow. The sound of the water calmed him. Egon had told him that he was expected to sleep in the king's guard barracks from now on, but he wasn't ready to go there yet. He lay himself stomach-down on the fountain wall and trailed a hand back and forth through the water and closed his eyes. He listened to the noises of the castle dwindling as more and more people retired for the night.

The chosen ones would have finished their work by now and would be in their dormitory. He let his mind go there and saw most of them were already asleep. Davis was sitting on his bed and got up to walk to the door. He opened it and peeked around the corner. "I cannot come tonight," whispered Lucas. Davis closed the door again and blew the last candles out.

Lucas had no idea how long he had been at the fountain. He had nodded off. He sat up and walked back inside. He passed the guard station he had walked by earlier and told them goodnight. They did not respond, and he looked back over his shoulder. They were not the same guards that had been there earlier. The guards on the wall always changed out at seven o'clock in the evening. It had been after seven when he had left the Hall, but maybe, he thought, it was different for the castle guards.

When he walked out into the bailey, Lucas looked up at the clear starry sky. He wanted to try out his newfound freedom and headed for the stairs to the walls. He ran up the steps two at a time. He had done this many times in his mind, but it felt different to be able to walk the wall walk in actuality. The first guard he encountered was startled to see someone on the wall so late and called out to him to identify himself.

"It's me, Lucas," he answered. He stopped, not sure if they would know him.

"Go ahead," said the guard. "I know who you are—I was at the gatehouse when the lever for the portcullis broke. But you may want to use the code word when you pass other guards."

"What code word?" asked Lucas.

"They did not tell you?"

Lucas shook his head.

"Well," said the guard. "As you are the king's chosen—the code word for this week is *merlon*. Code words change weekly, or whenever the king sees fit, and either General Finton or Egon will let you know when it does."

"I see," said Lucas.

"You know, many of us are on your side. Finton had no right to . . . well, let's just say we are glad the king recognized the general's error."

Lucas used the code word when he passed other guards, but most already recognized him before he had to. He walked the entire wall system, including along the back of the main castle building, until he came back to his starting point, where he noticed there had been a guard change on the wall. Before descending the stairs, he paused for a moment, wondering if it would be worth inquiring about the irregular shift, but then shrugged his shoulders and continued to the king's guard barracks. Perhaps today's events had required they change the schedule.

Egon was waiting next to the door to Lucas's room, looking somewhat displeased and still in his formal dinner attire, which included a long black jacket. "Where have you been?" he asked.

"I dozed by the fountain," answered Lucas, taking the doorknob. "And then I walked the walls." He half-turned around in the hope Egon was not mad and hoped he had not overstepped.

"Alone?"

"Yes."

Egon furrowed his brow. "There's a code word for walking the walls at night. Who gave it to you?"

Lucas held his breath for a moment. He didn't want to get the guard in trouble, but he couldn't lie. Egon always knew when someone lied. "One of the guards on the wall told me," he answered. "Did I do something wrong?"

Egon shook his head. "It's fine," he said, and smiled. "I, too, explored the entire castle the day I received the mark. Just stick to daytime exploring next time around, will you?"

"Yes, sir," he said. "But can you tell me . . . at what time does the evening guard change take place?"

Egon had stopped in front of the door to his own room. "Seven," he answered and looked back at him over his shoulder. "You know this."

"What about the guards inside the castle?"

"Seven as well."

"Every night? Even tonight?"

"Yes."

Lucas let go of the doorknob. "Perhaps then, I should inform you that they changed well after seven."

Egon stepped away from his door. He looked alarmed. "Are you sure about this?"

"Yes," answered Lucas. "I saw different guards at some stations when I passed a second time."

"But not everywhere?"

Lucas shook his head. After noticing the second guard change by the stairs, and thinking it might be useful to know how guard-change irregularities were handled—or in the event that something was truly misaligned—he had decided to see where else a guard change had taken place and had used his mind to go around the walls again. "I counted seven."

Egon took a deep breath. "Come with me," he said. "Our night just got longer."

Lucas followed Egon as they made their way through the empty hallways to the king's private room, where Egon knocked on the door.

"Sire," said Egon, his head close to the door. "Sire, it's me—Egon." When no response came from the other side, he knocked again. "Sire, I need to speak with you. It may be urgent."

This time Lucas could hear some shuffling and the king's voice telling Egon to come in. "You may enter," the king said.

Egon turned to Lucas and gave him a grim look that belied his reluctance to disturb the king at such an hour, and with nefarious news. "Wait here for now," he said, and went inside.

A short time later, Lucas found himself in the library, where the king was fumbling through rolls of maps on a shelf. He was in his night tunic with a black cloak over it.

"These should do," said the king, removing the ribbon that held a set of scrolls together. He brought them over to a desk and spread them out for Lucas to look at. The scrolls appeared to be very old, with the parchment torn in places and the colors fading. The king had to hold the ends down with his hands to stop them from rolling up again. One of the documents was a map showing the top view of the walls surrounding the castle, and the second map showed the layout of the internal hallways. "Can you point out exactly where you saw the guard changes?" asked the king.

Lucas nodded and leaned over the maps. He first located the Hall and then traced his movements of that night with his finger on the map, stopping at every location where a guard change had taken place and placing a chess piece on it. "That's it," he said when he finished and stood upright.

"Seven," counted the king. "Are you certain a guard change took place in each of those locations?"

"Yes," answered Lucas. "The new guards were wearing tall black boots with buckles on the side. The boots from the earlier guards were plain, with no buckles."

"Only two inside and the rest around the gate area," commented Egon. "I passed the guards inside earlier. They are Finton's men."

"Yes," muttered the king. "He's up to something. He has never replaced the guards during a night shift before."

Lucas had no idea what they were referring to and remained quiet.

"Do you want me to question his guards?" asked Egon.

The king shook his head. "No, I would like to avoid Finton knowing we are onto him, and I don't want anyone else involved in this. Put a watch on him and be ready to act if necessary."

CHAPTER 9

ll week long, Itan had to pretend that all was good, but in truth, he wanted to confront Finton every time he laid eyes on him.

"He will never tell you what it was about," said Garrad, after the king shared with him that he'd learned Finton had sent a messenger out in the middle of the night after Egon put a watch on him. The physician often stopped by to check on him, but with no ailments to report, they simply talked as friends about anything that came to mind. "On the other hand . . . have you considered that you may be jumping to conclusions here? That there is an innocent explanation?"

Itan was writing a message to his brother at his desk in his bedroom and lifted his head to look at Garrad, who had made himself comfortable in his armchair and was cleaning his spectacles with the fabric of his surcoat. "An innocent explanation for replacing guards mid-shift only in areas where Finton could be seen?"

Garrad shrugged his shoulders. "I'm just trying to give him the benefit of the doubt."

"Since when?" asked the king. "You have not trusted Finton for some time now."

"Exactly. Let's wait and see what he is really up to. Keep a watchful eye out—the messenger might come back with a response, and when he does, Egon can extract the information from him. That is, if Finton has not revealed everything to you by then himself."

"I fear I have bad news," said Egon, as he barged into the room without knocking. "We may have no way of knowing what message Finton sent out unless we question the general directly."

"Why is that?" asked Itan.

"We just had a messenger enter the castle for Finton," answered Egon, "but it's not the same one he sent out. This one's not even one of ours."

"Are you sure?" asked the king.

"Positive," answered Egon.

"Where is the messenger now?"

"Still in the bailey, waiting for Finton."

The king jumped up from his desk and darted to the window just in time to see Finton handed a message that he read straight away.

Not long after, a guard knocked on the door.

"Yes," answered Itan and turned to face the opening door.

"General Finton is requesting private council, sire," said the guard. Itan inhaled a deep breath and looked at Egon and Garrad before replying to the guard. "Give us a minute," he said. "They are just leaving."

The guard nodded and closed the door.

Garrad sat upright and put his spectacles in the top pocket of his surcoat. "Well," he said, pushing himself out of the chair. "I would love to hear what he has to say, but I know when my presence is not wanted."

"Do you wish me to question the messenger?" asked Egon softly. "Find out where he came from?"

"Not yet," answered Itan. "Let's wait and see what Finton has to say first."

Finton walked in after Garrad and Egon left the room. He was still holding the note in his hand and held it up for the king to see. "I have just received a message," he said. "From my uncle."

"Not bad news, I hope," said the king, barely looking up from his writing in the hope—albeit skeptical—that his casual demeanor would inspire Finton to talk openly.

"He is not well, apparently," said Finton. "He is asking for my help to run his estate while he recovers."

Itan looked up. "I am sorry to hear of your uncle's compromised health, but what is your purpose in telling me this? Surely your uncle knows of your position here and that you do not have time to play farmer."

A brief silence passed, during which Finton rubbed at the back of his neck. Finally, he answered. "I am resigning," he said, and before Itan could respond, he continued. "You asked me to accept that Lucas was given the mark, but I cannot. It will be in everyone's best interest if I leave."

"And when exactly did you decide this? Before or after you received the message from your uncle?"

"It has played on my mind for a few days," answered Finton. "But yes, hearing of my uncle's bad health has hastened my decision, to be sure."

Itan walked out into the bailey to the group of men waiting on horseback. It was raining and showed no signs of stopping, but Finton was preparing for immediate departure and was taking fifteen of his soldiers with him. They were clothed with no identifiable colors upon them, and the king's crest had been removed from the horse's tack. Itan had not tried to stop Finton, although it troubled him that something was not adding up. Two separate messengers, and all in one week, when he couldn't recall Finton ever sending or receiving messages before.

Or perhaps he had sent messengers in the past, and no one had ever known. If it had not been for Lucas, this time would have been no different.

Garrad had said his goodbye and was stepping off to the side when Itan approached Finton.

"I'm sorry it had to come to this," said Finton, turning to face him. "I wish it had gone differently." There was no sadness or regret written on his face, so his words held little meaning.

"Yes," answered Itan. It was a cold goodbye, but he really didn't know what to say. Instead, he looked at Eli, who sat sullenly on a horse behind his father, the rain plastering his bangs to his forehead. "You don't have to take him," Itan said. "Whatever differences you and I have, they should not dictate your son's future."

Finton looked over his shoulder and shook his head. "They already have. You've made your choice, and I've made mine."

When the gates opened and Finton rode out, Egon came to stand next to him.

"Did you inform Lucas?" asked Itan. "Does he know to stay out of sight, follow to see where they are going, and then come straight back to report to me directly?"

Egon nodded. "I told him all of that, and he is preparing."

Itan nodded, satisfied. "Send him out in half an hour. That should be plenty of time."

"Are you really sending him on his own?" asked Garrad, looking puzzled. In his distracted state, Itan had barely noticed him standing a few feet to his right.

"Yes," he answered. "Finton will expect to be followed, and he'll expect it to be Egon who follows him, with one or two of the guard.

He will not expect a lone man, and least of all Lucas, though the goal, of course, is that Lucas not be seen at all."

"*Boy*," Garrad corrected gently, pulling his cloak more snuggly around his thin frame. Large puddles were beginning to form all around them. "It is a big risk you are taking. If Finton gets his hands on him, he'll kill him."

Itan waited for the gates to close entirely before turning around. "It's a risk and a sacrifice I am willing to take on," he answered before walking away.

CHAPTER 10

Lucas had his horse saddled with supplies and was ready to mount up. He was pleased to be useful. All week he had been with the chosen ones, but, as his back was still healing, all he had been able to do was observe and give instructions to the younger ones.

A half hour had passed since Finton had ridden off with his men, and Lucas was tacking up his horse inside the stables. He was ready for his task, but he could see the concern on the faces of the chosen who had gathered around him. "I'll be all right," he said as he fastened the throatlatch on his horse's bridle. "You don't have to worry." He spoke with perhaps a tiny bit more confidence than he felt.

"You know I will," said Zera, who stood closest. "I don't understand why the king is sending you out alone."

"Me neither," said Warrick, leaning against a post with his arms folded across his chest. "And to go after Finton, of all people."

"You're making it sound as if I'm to fight him," said Lucas. "All I have been instructed to do is to follow at a safe distance and find out if he's truly going to his uncle's place."

"Why does the king need to know?" asked Ando. The younger chosen had climbed on hay bales and dangled his feet down. "I'm glad

General Fusstown is gone. I hate him, and I don't care where he is going."

"Ando, get down from there," said Davis after looking up. "You know there's no climbing allowed. You could fall and break a bone."

Ando pulled a face but scrambled down when Davis gave him a stern stare.

"We all hate him for what he was about to do to you, Ando," said Lucas. He double-checked the girth of his saddle and took the reins of his horse.

"But why you?" asked Ando, stepping next to him. "I don't want you to go."

Lucas looked down at Ando, who was small for his age, and placed his hand on his head. "The king thinks I'm the best for this mission," he answered. "So I've little choice but to go."

"He'll be all right," said Davis, holding Ando back. "Lucas has the seeing mind, remember. Finton won't even know he is there." He locked eyes with Lucas. "Right?"

"Right," answered Lucas leading his horse out. He hated leaving his friends, but it was time to go, ready or not.

"Be careful," said Egon, standing ready at the gates next to Lucas on his horse. "Finton is experienced and will have his wits about him. He will no doubt send scouts behind him on occasion, to monitor if he is being trailed."

"No one will see me," answered Lucas. "I won't get too close."

"If you do," said Egon, his eyes earnest, "don't let him catch you. He'll not let you live."

Lucas looked down at Egon and nodded. He waited until all gates were open before spurring his horse to ride out. He didn't stop until he rode over the last hill and then briefly turned around to look at the castle in the distance, as he always did—the view evoking that moment when he had stood on top of the circus wagon to get a glimpse of the castle for the first time. It never failed to remind him of the road he had traveled to get to where he was now.

He scanned the forest ahead of him, letting his mind wander to the group he was following. There was no sight of them, and he figured their head start had put them far ahead of him. Egon had let him study the maps and had pointed out the area where Finton's uncle's estate was so he could go in that direction before catching up with them—if that was, in fact, where Finton was going.

Heeding Egon's warning of discovery, Lucas decided not to travel the road but to go alongside it, through the forest, remaining a safe distance from where he could be seen and heard. It was a decision he started to regret at nightfall when he failed to get a sighting of the group. When it became too dark for his horse to navigate the uneven terrain safely, Lucas dismounted. He took his horse's reins from its neck and continued on foot. He hoped that Finton had stopped for the night and that a campfire would help guide him to them. If that was not the case, he didn't know what he would do.

Lucas made his way to the road to check for fresh tracks. He got down on one knee and felt the ground with his hand. The soil had been disturbed by horses, their tracks fresh enough that they could not have passed all that long ago. Grateful for the recent rain and relieved that he had not failed his mission in the first few hours, Lucas followed the road along the edge. He had not made it far before he heard muted voices. He crouched behind the thick trunk of a tree and listened to determine what direction the sounds were coming from. Once he had a good idea, he crawled closer, until he saw the dark silhouette of two men sitting with their backs against a large boulder.

It was just the two of them. No one else was in sight. Egon was right—Finton expected to be followed and had ordered two men to stay behind to watch the road. Lucas carefully picked his way around them to see how far ahead the rest of the group was and found their camp no more than a mile up the road. Eli was sitting on a log close to the fire, as was his father. Lucas located the positions of the other thirteen soldiers and got as close as he could to their camp. He was hoping to find out which way they were going.

Eli did not look pleased. He had his head down and was drawing in the sand at his feet with a small stick.

"You need to cheer up," Finton said. "You know full well that I couldn't have left you there. Lucas would have made your life miserable."

"It's not that," answered Eli, gouging the dirt more aggressively with the stick. "He made my life miserable from the moment he showed up."

"Then what? Having to leave your friends behind?"

Eli did not answer and kept his eyes to the ground.

"I have told you, time after time, that you don't need friends. Friends will make you weak. Your compassion for them will make you flimsy . . . cause you to lose focus. Friends will stab you in the back when you least expect it. Family will not."

"That's not how I see it," said Eli, dropping the stick and glaring at his father. "Carleton and Rhys's friendship has made them stronger, and they lead the elites now. Lucas has always kept Zera, Warrick, and Davis close, and see where that has got him? I lost my friends some time ago. But that's not what's eating at me." Eli picked the stick back up and threw it in the fire. "It's that you didn't consult me . . . didn't ask *me* what it was I wanted. I'm like a pawn you simply push across the board with your fat little finger. I am seventeen and should have been able to make my own decision."

"Enough!" Finton interrupted, giving Eli a stern look. "You should be thankful that I've secured a guaranteed high position for you. You have a few days to get over your sulking. After that, I need you to be the son they expect me to show up with."

Lucas had never seen Eli stand up for himself, or show anything but fear of his father. This was different. Had Eli begun to see his father for the person he truly was? When no more words were spoken, Lucas backed away. He made no fire that night and only ate a few bites of the dried meat he had brought with him.

He was up before sunrise and moved closer to Finton's camp. He watched them wait for the two soldiers to report they had not seen any signs of anyone following before moving out. The group followed the road for a few more miles until they came to a junction and then veered right towards the west.

Lucas used his gift of seeing and stayed a safe distance behind. He stopped from time to time to let his horse drink by a stream or rest. A few times, he had experienced an uneasy feeling of being followed himself, and it had made him move on faster. It was a feeling he had in the past, but there was no one there when he used his vision. He attributed it to his own paranoia and tried to push the feeling aside, but he found himself looking for the magpie more often.

By the end of the second day, when Lucas was beginning to feel strained by using his power of sight, a fortified farmhouse came into view. A large stone wall surrounded it, with one entrance that was closed off by two black iron gates. Lucas halted his horse and used his mind once again to watch one of Finton's soldiers dismount and bang on the gates. It was soon opened by a man who did not appear to be a soldier. He wore a plain tunic over work trousers and permitted the group to ride in without questioning who they were or what they wanted.

Finton was the first to dismount inside the small courtyard after the gate closed behind them, and he gave his men instructions on where to put the horses. He then marched up to the house with Eli in tow and opened the door as if he lived there.

Finton clearly knew his way around. No one had come out to greet him, which indicated to Lucas that he might have spoken the truth about his uncle being sick, but Lucas could not leave before he was certain of this. He secured his horse and climbed up a large elm, nestling himself in the fork of the tree. From that vantage point, he could see over the walls and watch the entire estate. He sat perfectly still, waiting for Finton to make another move, which he didn't think was going to be any time soon. Lucas allowed himself to relax and was just beginning to doze off when the familiar sound of a gate closing alarmed him so much that he nearly fell out of the tree.

He only just barely caught sight of a single rider leaving the grounds. It was the same individual he'd watched riding into King Itan's grounds the morning Finton had announced his departure— notable because of the dimple that pressed into each cheek. Lucas contemplated following him, but it was Finton he had been ordered to follow.

Not much else happened in the two days that followed. Eli had come out a few times and thrown a stick for a large brown dog on the meadow in front of the house. It was strange for Lucas to see him affectionately stroking the dog each time it retrieved the stick. When the dog grew tired, Eli sat down in the grass, and the dog flopped down next to him. Lucas watched as he continued to pet the dog on its head and neck. He had never before seen Eli so happy and carefree.

Finton's soldiers mostly hung around in the courtyard and tended to the horses. Only once did he see Finton himself come out of the house to take a stroll into the garden, accompanying a man much older than himself. Finton had to support him while they walked over to a bench, where they sat and talked for a good hour.

Lucas was finding the entire spy mission to be fruitless, not to mention a little bit boring. The elm tree had long since become uncomfortable. He was just considering returning home when a horse inside the barn let out a loud neigh, which was answered by another horse, not in the vicinity. He sat up straight and watched the road—the messenger who had been sent out previously was now coming into view.

Not long after his return, Finton's men were mounting up in a hurry. Lucas climbed down out of the tree as fast as he could and rushed over to his horse. Finton and Eli had already exited the house and were mounting up as the gates opened. Everyone was off in a rush and heading directly south, further away from Itan's castle—the same direction the messenger had taken. He wished he'd asked Egon for a map to look at, but there'd been little time to get ready, and he hadn't thought of it. Now he wondered where they could be going—if the messenger had been able to return in two days, it couldn't be too far.

Lucas followed closely, but had to increase his distance when rocks and cliffs forced him onto the road. When the forest disappeared altogether, and only a rocky landscape remained, Lucas knew he had gone further south than he had ever been. He increased his horse's speed when Finton and his men rode beyond the reach of his seeing mind, and he lost the group as they disappeared over the crest of a hill. When they came back into view, he saw them descending towards lush green pastures.

A small, fortified castle stood in the distance. Lucas could see no moat around it, but the walls were vertical with embrasures all around. He could no longer follow Finton, or he'd be seen from the castle, so he rode his horse between the rocks as far as he could and, leaving his horse grazing on a patch of grass, climbed the rest on foot. From his viewpoint, he watched Finton slow down to a walk and stop within a hundred yards of the castle's gate.

Lucas narrowed his eyes and focused on the tower banners blowing in the wind. They were colors he had seen before and belonged to none other than Lord Killeand. Lucas sighed, recalling the conversation between Eli and his father. The high position Finton had told him he had secured? It made complete sense now to Lucas when he also recalled the conversation between Killeand and Finton in the king's stables. They had spoken about Itan still having too much power, and Finton had indicated that he was behind the attack on the treasury to do something about that. It was clear to Lucas then, and it was even more apparent now—they were in a conspiracy together, and it was time to return and tell the king what he knew.

Lucas had just started backing down from the rock he had been lying on when something caught his eye. More riders were approaching the castle from the other side, a group of maybe thirty. They could be soldiers, but they were not Killeand's. They wore no distinctive uniform or colors. Moving back into position, he watched them enter through the gates without delay. His curiosity renewed, Lucas stayed and watched a third group arrive a few hours later—it was the smallest, with only five riders, but the same thing happened. The gates opened automatically and without question, as if the riders were expected. He could go back to the king and report what he had seen, but he didn't feel it was enough—he needed to know who they were.

There was nothing but the flat open ground in every direction. Even in the dark, he would not be able to approach any of the walls without being seen. A town, visible in the distance to the southeast, could provide him cover, but its distance to the castle was too great for his seeing mind.

Lucas watched the comings and goings into the next day and hoped either Finton or the unknown soldiers would come back out, but neither happened. When the day came to an end, he felt he could no longer wait and would have to return to the king with the information he had. He retrieved his horse and traveled east towards a road he could see in the far distance. A caravan of five wagons was making its way slowly towards the town. They were high wagons, pulled by two horses each. Lucas's eyes lit up, and his heart jumped when he recognized what they were. Circus wagons! The sight brought back memories of his life as a performer. Something Eli had mocked him for on more than one occasion, as had Finton.

He remembered Killeand approaching him before the start of the tournament at Itan's castle some years ago and asking him why the people called him "the king's chosen."

"They call him that," Finton had interrupted, "because the king put him on the list rather than a village official. He was a circus performer, acting out the great Toroun, and impressed the king enough that he wanted him."

Lucas had expected Killeand to lose interest in him after that and walk away, but Finton's words had the opposite effect. The lord's eyes had lit up upon hearing he had worked in a circus.

"Really?" said Lord Killeand. "I do love the circus. I never miss a performance when they come into town."

Lucas had never performed for him, but it gave him an idea. If this circus was going to perform in town, there was a chance Killeand would show up, and as those other riders were guests, there was a chance he would bring them along. It might provide Lucas a good look at them. Making up his mind that it was his best option, he waited until nightfall before taking the road south. He spotted the circus camped just outside the town, and he could not help but be drawn towards it. He stepped his horse off the road and went a little closer before coming to a halt.

In the glow of their campfire, he could see a young girl watering the horses and a man fixing some broken back steps on one of the wagons. A large cauldron hung off a hook above the fire, from which the aroma of fish stew made his stomach growl. Flashes of memory washed over Lucas, of tending to the horses or sitting by the fire and eating the food that was cooked over it. Of seeing Rosa and Lisette's bright-colored wagon with flowers—the sight of which would put a smile on his face even in dark, miserable weather. These wagons were plainer and were not as cheery as the ones he remembered, but yet, now that he looked closer at them, they seemed familiar. He didn't recognize any of the people, but then again, it had been more than three years since he had last seen them.

He noticed himself gripping the reins of his horse a little too tightly and was about to turn around when he heard a voice behind him.

"Can we help you, sir?"

Lucas peered over his shoulder and saw two people coming towards him in the darkness. Could it be? One was as big as a giant, with broad shoulders and a thick head of hair, and the other was a dwarf, compact and muscular. His heart leaped as he instantly recognized the two men who had stopped a few yards away. Alive, both of them! With the way they had been separated . . . Lucas had always wondered about their safety, and how things had resolved on their end.

They had come from the town, and Lucas knew they would be naturally wary of any visitors. He scrambled to think how he should make his identity known to them.

"We have a flyer to give to your lord if indeed you are here to inquire about the performance?" continued Everett.

Lucas slowly turned his horse around and faced them, but they still did not recognize him. It was very dark, and he was dressed in nice clothes—they could see he had a sword and clearly thought he was a soldier.

Lucas smiled. "I do not serve a lord," he replied. "I serve King Itan."

"My apologies, sir. I assumed you had come from the castle yonder," said Everett, pointing in the general direction from where Lucas had come. "Or is that where the king currently is stationed?"

"No, he is not," answered Lucas. He had sensed an edge in Everett's tone but decided to hold off on revealing who he was just a little longer.

"I am curious to know if you remember a boy, one who impressed the king. It was some time ago. He did a sword-fighting act with you."

Everett froze and cleared his throat while Bernt shuffled uncomfortably behind him. Lucas wanted nothing more than to leap off his horse and embrace the man once very dear to him, but he resisted the temptation and waited patiently for Everett to pull himself together. No . . . if he was honest with himself, it was him that needed the moment to process his own emotions. Tears were forming at the corners of his eyes, and he swallowed hard to keep them at bay.

"Yes, sir," Everett finally said. "I certainly do, but unfortunately, after his performance for the king, we lost him. We hoped he would find his way back to us but then received the unfortunate news that he had died." There was a deep sadness in his voice. "I am surprised the king is still looking for him . . . that he does not know about this," he added.

"The king is not looking for him. And that boy never died," answered Lucas.

Everett's eyes lit up, and he shook his head in a confused kind of way. "How do you know this, sir? We were told he did."

"Well, I am afraid you were misinformed," sighed Lucas, slipping from his horse. "But you can stop calling me *sir*. I don't remember you ever addressing anyone like that. Didn't you always tell me it would put you beneath someone, and you were much bigger than any man, despite your stature?" He smiled and watched the faces of his long-lost friends lift with wonder. Everett let out of cry of joy when Bernt rushed past him and embraced Lucas. Lucas saw the man he had seen fixing the step coming towards them.

"Ned!" Everett shouted. "Ned! It's Lucas!"

When Everett and Bernt let go of him, Lucas walked towards Ned and stood in front of him. Now of the same height, he looked Ned in the eye and held his hand out.

"Is it really you?" stammered Ned, who was frozen to the spot.

"Yes," answered Lucas softly. "It's me."

Ned's eyes filled up with tears as he took Lucas's hand and embraced him. He held on to him for a long time until Nadia walked up behind him and spoke. "What's going on here?" she asked, her arms folded over her chest.

Ned held Lucas by the shoulder as he turned towards her. "He is alive, Nadia," he whispered. "He is alive."

When Nadia's mouth dropped open, and she started to cry, Ned let go, and Lucas ran towards her. When she fell into his arms, his own eyes released the tears he had been holding back. It was she who had last held him when he was still a child. She held onto him and would not let go until Ned eased her away. Lucas then hugged Rosa and Lisette, who had come out of their wagons, bewildered at first, then shrieking with delight.

"You will have to tell us everything," said Rosa, "but maybe you want to meet someone else first?" She pointed behind Lucas, and he turned around to see the young girl watching from a small distance.

"Do you recognize her?" asked Nadia. "She has grown, just like you have."

"Ana?" he asked, a lump forming in his throat. Although no longer the small girl he remembered, Ana still had golden curls like her mother.

"Yes," said Nadia, and told the girl to come closer.

Ana stepped in front of her mother and smiled shyly when she looked up at him.

"You don't remember me, do you?" asked Lucas, smiling. "I used to look after you and play with you. The last thing I remember we did together was at the camp outside the king's castle. I was walking you by the hand, past all the different artists who were showing off their skills. We stopped at a music group and listened until you got tired and fell asleep on my lap."

"I don't recall that," said Ana. "But I do remember being looked after by a boy when I was little. I just don't remember what you looked like."

"That's all right," said Lucas. "You were only four or five at the time."

"Well," said Everett in the silence that followed. "All pleasantries aside, you nearly gave me a heart attack back there—we thought a soldier was watching our camp. So, the king did find you then? We heard from Stan's brother that you were sentenced to death after a murder had taken place at the inn?"

"Yes, well," said Lucas, taking his eyes off Ana and facing Everett again. "Clearly, Stan's brother never went to the courthouse to hear the sentencing."

"So, you were arrested then?"

"I was—charged and convicted. I was sent to work in the mines and was headed there when an officer from the king's army passed the prison transport I was on. He recognized me and took me with him instead."

"Why don't you go and sit by the fire?" said Ned when everyone started asking more questions. "I'll take care of your horse, and when we eat, you can tell us everything."

Lucas gladly accepted the offer of a warm meal and followed the group over to the campfire. He warmed his hands on the wooden bowl Rosa gave him and inhaled the aroma of the stew. He remembered the food to be always seasoned with herbs grown in baskets hanging off Rosa and Lisette's wagon or collected from the side of the road. It made for a nice change from the bland food he had been served at the castle as a chosen and from the dried meat and fruit he'd eaten in the past week.

"Still as good as always," remarked Lucas, cherishing every bite of his food.

"Thank you, Lucas," answered Rosa, and Lisette nodded in agreement. The twins embarked on some friendly banter over who had cooked that night. He was offered seconds, at which point Ned came back and joined them.

Of all the people in the group, except for Ana, Lucas felt Ned had changed the most. He looked thinner, with protruding cheekbones, and his weary eyes told of the hard circus life he was living. Once Ned sat down, he started telling them his story, beginning at the moment when he remembered arriving at the inn, to the moment he was given the king's mark.

"So, you think the king does not believe you are a chosen anymore?" asked Everett.

"I don't think so. Maybe because I was the only one breaking every rule they had. I may have gotten some of that from you though!"

Everyone laughed, and Nadia reached out and patted his hand.

"Do *you* think you are a chosen one?" asked Ned.

"Part of me does," answered Lucas, "and part doesn't, but I am happy not to fall under the strict ranking rule anymore."

"I'm glad the king recognized how special you are," smiled Nadia. "You've grown into quite a handsome young man."

"You say that about everyone who wears nice clothes," joked Ned.

Lucas blushed and then looked around the group that had felt like family once. "Are Stan and Rowan not here?" he asked. "I see only five wagons, and they are all different colors from what I remember."

Everyone went quiet and stared at Ned.

"Rowan has passed on," said Ned with a deep sigh.

Though he had never harbored warm feelings towards Rowan, hearing that he was dead was not something he'd expected, and the news chilled him. "How?"

"On his way back from the inn. After dropping you off," said Ned reluctantly. "He was found underneath the wagon, which had rolled off the road. The people who found him said it looked staged . . . made to look like an accident. Both horses were found loose with no injuries and the harness intact, as if someone had set them free. We thought he might've run into king's soldiers who tried to get information from him, and we feared for our safety. That's when we painted our wagons a different color and headed further south than we had planned."

Lucas shook his head. "The king would never have ordered to have him killed."

"How do you know?" asked Everett. "This was when he was still desperate to find you. And this General Finton you spoke of—he sounds capable of something like this."

Lucas didn't think Finton was ever involved in trying to find him, and the only person he knew to question people by any means necessary was Egon. He didn't think he had anything to do with Rowan's death, either, but he couldn't be entirely sure. "What about Stan?" he asked, steering away from the topic.

"Stan took it hard," answered Ned. "He blamed himself for not going with him. He lost interest in the circus. His drinking had us moving on from whatever town we happened to have arrived at before we even had a chance to perform. Then he got the news about you from his brother. Things got worse. He decided to leave us. Last we heard, he was living with his brother at the inn."

A silence came over the group.

Bernt cleared his throat. "You have not told us yet what you're doing all the way down here. And all by your lonesome," he said.

"I was sent to get some information," answered Lucas reluctantly. He wasn't sure how much—if anything—he should tell them, but he told them about Finton leaving the king's army and that the king had him follow Finton to see where he was going. "I watched some people enter Killeand's castle," he told them. "It looked like their arrival was expected—planned—and, though I can't put my finger on it yet, I feel something's going on that the king should know about."

"Like a conspiracy?" asked Everett.

Lucas nodded. "It looks that way to me. I watched the castle to see if any of them would reappear, so I could find out who they are, but not one of them has. I had decided to give up and was just about to take off when I noticed your wagons on the road."

Lucas then told them the plan that had formed in his mind, about hoping to see at least some of the men, and perhaps Killeand and Finton, at the performance in town.

"You're right—he loves the circus," said Ned. "That is why we come here at least once a year. I have no doubt he'll attend tomorrow."

"Then I will be there as well," said Lucas, "and hopefully, I can get the information needed to relay back to the king."

"But what if Killeand does bring this Finton with him?" asked Rosa. "Would he not recognize you? Your clothes will make you stand out."

"I'll have to keep my distance," answered Lucas. "And stay far enough away from them."

"That," said Everett, biting his lip, "might pose a problem."

"Why's that?" asked Lucas.

"We're to perform inside the market hall," answered Everett. "And when Killeand attended in the past, he didn't use the same doors used by the townspeople."

"How did he get in?" asked Lucas. With the lack of sleep he'd suffered of late, he wouldn't have enough strength to use his seeing mind, so he had to get close.

"He used the narrow walled-off merchant's road and entered at the back of the market," answered Everett. "Unless you have a way to blend in with the crowd, Rosa is right, you might be recognized."

"We can disguise him," said Lisette enthusiastically. "Change his appearance."

"Yes," added Nadia. "I am sure I can find some old clothes of Ned's you can wear."

Lucas shook his head. "I appreciate all of you wanting to help," he said. "But I can't accept. If I get caught, you could . . . well, these are not nice men. I worry that any bit of assistance you might give me could implicate you somehow."

"Lucas," said Nadia softly. "Then that gives us even more reason to help you. We've all lived with a lot of guilt over the decisions we made. When we heard you were dead, we could not help but feel responsible." She paused and looked at Ned, who lowered his head.

"Let us do this," she continued. "Give us the chance to make it right."

Lucas took a deep breath. Maybe he should just return to the king, tell him where Finton went, and leave it at that? Except that he was curious who those men were himself. He looked around the group and, after seeing encouraging nods all around confirming Nadia's words, he relented. "All right," he said. "Changing my appearance might work."

They stayed up till midnight talking around the campfire, and when everyone was finally making their way to bed, Lucas found Everett sitting on the roof of his wagon.

"I used to sit like that, up there with you, to look at the stars," he said, looking up. "Mind if I join you?"

"Be my guest," answered Everett and waved him up.

A gentle breeze blew in Lucas's face while he looked at the dark shadow of the castle in the far distance.

"Are you sure you need to do this?" asked Everett.

"No," answered Lucas. "I don't. But something tells me I should."

"Still acting on that intuition of yours, then." Everett leaned back on his elbows and stared at the sky. "I should never have believed when they said you were dead. I should have looked for you. I'm so sorry."

Lucas watched a bat swoop up and down around them catching bugs. Everett was not who he remembered him to be. He had been quiet after the initial reunion and seemed troubled. "You couldn't have known," said Lucas.

Everett sighed and looked at him. "But I could have told that officer the truth when he came for you that morning. I could have resisted when the others made the decision to send you away."

"I don't think you were supposed to do any of that," replied Lucas, gazing up at the millions of stars in the night sky. "I think whatever happened was meant to happen in the way that it did. I've cheated death several times—when I shouldn't have."

"Someone is watching over you, I think," said Everett, following his gaze just when a trail of light shot across the sky. "You can make a wish."

Lucas nodded. "I just did."

"What did you wish?"

"I can't tell you that, or it won't happen," smiled Lucas, nudging him. The unexpected push made Everett nearly fall off the roof, but Lucas caught him just in time.

"You've gotten too big," responded Everett when he recovered.

"Or you are just too little," said Lucas. He looked at Everett's face and saw his smile appear. His old friend was back.

Everett sighed and looked at the stars again. "You may know my wish," he said. "I doubt it will come true anyway."

"You don't know," said Lucas. "It might."

Everett shook his head. "No," he said. "I don't think we'll ever be able to earn enough money to be able to retire from this life for good."

"Is that what you want?"

"It'd be nice not having to worry anymore," answered Everett. "After we lost you, we struggled with our performances. You drew in the crowds for so long—they were expecting to see you. They'd walk away disappointed when they discovered you weren't there."

"How bad did it get?" asked Lucas. He remembered refusing to perform for a few days after discovering Stan had lied to him about introducing him to King Itan, and everyone had gone hungry.

"Pretty bad," answered Everett. "But it could have been worse if Rosa and Lisette had not been resourceful enough to forage for food. After Stan left, we changed things up. I was doing more performances intended to make the people laugh. Like a jester. Hated every minute of it at first—resented being laughed at for being small. When Ana was old enough, I did an act with her. It became popular with the crowds, and things started to look better. Then Ana followed in her father's footsteps . . . started throwing knives. Only ten, and the best female knife thrower I've ever seen."

"That explains her build," said Lucas, recalling the muscles in her arms and shoulders when he had observed her earlier. "I thought she might have taken after her father."

"She's very good at it," said Everett. "Ana's our star performer now, just like you were."

"Then maybe you should come north again. There seem to be fewer towns here in the south. The king's likely to have forgotten about you by now—I could ask him to pardon you, though I imagine he already has by now."

"Rosa and Lisette would like that," said Everett. "We had to move away from the area Meloc controls. Too much civil unrest there."

Lucas knew Meloc was the king's brother, and that the king had met with him recently, but they had never gone down there. "What do you think's changed?"

"A drought, two years back," explained Everett. "Crops withered away, people starved. The taxes were lowered to help the people, and things got better again. Then, the robberies started. Lots of them. All in the middle of the night—sometimes entire livelihoods taken. No one knows who's doing it, and no one's immune to it—there seems to

110

be no distinction between rich and poor. Some farms are burned down after a robbery, for no reason."

"Is Meloc doing anything about this?"

"I think he's tried. Some believe they can't be caught. They call them *ghost thieves*."

"Ghost thieves?" asked Lucas.

Everett nodded. "Yes, because no one has seen them or lived to tell their tale. The only thing people have reported is hearing multiple horses galloping off, but only ever getting a glimpse of one—a black horse with a white mane."

"The king met with his brother a few weeks ago," said Lucas. "That must explain why."

"Yes, probably. It has caused disarray, and the people blame Lord Meloc. Anyway," said Everett, taking a deep breath, "we didn't want to run into the ghost thieves, so we came west and have been here ever since. Killeand has his land and his people under control, which makes it safer. More people are starting to move this way."

Lucas sat quietly, thinking this through. Was that why Finton had come here? To help with the influx of the population and keep the ghost thieves from coming onto Lord Killeand's lands? Finton might have contacted him with that very proposal, after he decided he no longer wanted to serve the king, but Lucas could not shake the feeling that there was more to it than that.

When Everett fell asleep, Lucas climbed down from the wagon. He would check on his horse, then put his own head to rest. He was passing one of the wagons on his way when he noticed the large white goat tied on a rope on the other side. Walking closer, he noticed the black spot just above its nose. "Hello, Tiny!" he said, stopping to stroke the animal behind his ear.

"He likes that," someone spoke. He looked up to see Ana leaning out of the window of the wagon.

"I'm sorry," said Lucas. "I didn't mean to wake you."

"You didn't," said Ana. "I wasn't asleep yet." She pulled herself away from the window to join him outside. She stood next to him stroking Tiny on the nose.

He looked at her. Like her mother, she still had the same curly white-blond hair, but longer and kept back in a ponytail. She had her mother's smile as well, but other than that, she was very much her father's child.

"I do remember you living with us," said Ana softly. "My last memory of you was the same as yours. I didn't understand why you'd left. Nobody would tell me. My mother just cried when I asked about you, and my father would get angry and walk away. So I stopped asking."

"Do you know what happened now?" asked Lucas.

"Yes," answered Ana. "Everett told me. He explained that my father wasn't angry, but felt guilty for sending you away."

"He didn't have to feel that way," said Lucas. "I never blamed anyone for what happened."

At dawn, Lucas collected a pail of mud and carried it over to his horse. His horse had already been untacked and given a plain halter, but he still stood out as too valuable to be owned by a circus group. Ana came to help, and the two of them worked silently, rubbing the mud into the horse's coat and onto his feet to change his appearance. When they finished, they both stepped back to admire their work. Ana smiled and showed him her dirty hands. He showed her his and then smudged some mud on her nose. She giggled and started to chase him, her dirty hands reaching for him.

"Still a bit of the old Lucas in there, I see!" shouted Rosa, and Ana and Lucas gave up their frolicking to go see what the women were up to. Rosa was standing behind Lisette, who was bent over a big open trunk and now looked over her shoulder at Lucas.

"A lot of trust and responsibility the king has put on those young shoulders," Lisette said as she continued to rummage in the trunk that was full of jars and kitchen equipment. "I am glad to see you can still find some joy, Lucas."

"What exactly are you looking for in there?" asked Rosa.

"Something—ah, got it!" she said, straightening up with a cork-sealed bottle in her hand. "I knew I would find a use for it someday."

Lucas could see the small bottle had something black inside of it but had no idea what it could be. Before he could ask, Lisette was pulling a chair over. She held the bottle up to him and smiled.

"What's that?" he asked, wondering if, in fact, he wanted to know.

"Pickled leeches!"

"Pickled what?" asked Lucas.

"Pickled leeches! To dye your hair. You mentioned you had met Lord Killeand. He may recognize you if he sees you, so we need to dye your hair black."

Rosa shook her head and smiled. "You always amaze me with your finds. This is precisely what we need."

Lucas couldn't wipe what he knew was a grimace of disgust from his face. "Where did you get it?"

Lisette pulled a chair up for him to sit on and removed the cork. The smell of fermented leeches made them all nearly gag. Ana covered her nose and turned away. "I bought it from a lady in a village once," she answered, wrapping his shoulders with an old rag. "Don't worry. It won't smell once you rinse your hair. A good rinse later on, after the performance, and your hair will be back to its natural color."

Lucas sat down and let Lisette rub the concoction in, and Ana ran off to help her mother. Lisette wore an old apron to protect her clothing and used a soft brush—like a paintbrush—in order to avoid getting it on her hands. The smell was terrible at first, but after drying in the sun, it disappeared, and his hair was a solid black. Nadia gave him some of Ned's old clothes to wear, a black, hooded shirt with brown trousers that she altered to fit him, along with some old boots.

"No one will recognize you now," commented Ned when he passed him that afternoon. "Unless they know your face."

"I will keep my head down," said Lucas, noticing Ned's concerned look, despite his encouraging comment. Ned had been the only one who was reluctant to help and had watched from a distance. If it had not been for Nadia, Lucas doubted he would have agreed to be of service.

"I just want you to be careful," Ned told him.

"I will be," said Lucas and continued to his horse. He picked up a pail of water and held it up for his horse to drink from, all the while watching everyone getting ready to head into town. He remembered those busy moments. The rushing around, the panic to grab the last few things. The nerves and the thrill, even though they had performed a thousand times. They never knew exactly how the crowd would react, or how willing they would be to give their money away.

Lucas pulled the pail back for a moment when his horse bit the edge of it instead of drinking the water. He noticed Nadia heading his way. She stopped next to him and waited until he finally got the horse to put its nose in the pail and drink.

"You seem content," Nadia finally said, "but are you being treated right?"

Lucas glanced over to her and saw she looked concerned.

"Yes," he answered. "Being a soldier has its moments, but we don't want for anything. Why?"

"I saw you as you were changing your shirt this morning," admitted Nadia, "and I couldn't help but notice the lines on your back. They look recent. Whatever happened to you must have been difficult to endure."

Lucas's horse splashed the water over the rim, getting him wet. He pulled the bucket away before answering.

"That was all Finton's doing," he said. "Not the king's. And Finton will not be able to touch me ever again." He smiled, and he watched as Nadia forced a little smile back.

Lucas joined the townspeople and shuffled his way through one of the double-door entrances into the market hall. The size of a gameball playing field, the rectangular building had been cleared of its stalls and, apart from a small stage at the end, it was empty. Lucas could hear Everett's voice and people laughing as he slipped off to the side. He found a space at the back of the crowd and looked towards the stage. He caught a glimpse of Everett in his checkered black and white jester outfit. He appeared to be entertaining the first row of people while Nadia was urging the entering crowd to form a semi-circle around the stage.

"Plenty of space left at the front!" she said, waving people forward in her short ruffled purple skirt and a cropped shirt with puffed sleeves. "The show will begin in two minutes!"

Ana stood on stage. She was wearing a purple, cropped jacket over a white shirt and maroon pants and juggled knives in the air to warm up. She smiled at the crowd each time she took a break.

Lucas looked behind him and was pleased to see the doors remained open with only the odd person still entering.

Everett jumped on the stage and stamped his feet in a rhythm on the floorboards. He then waved his arms in the air to encourage the crowd to join in. As the sound of stamping feet echoed off the white-washed stone walls, Lucas noticed a door near the back of the stage open. He lowered his head when Killeand stepped through with a few of his officers and let his eyes go over the crowd before him.

Everett peered over his shoulder. "Lord Killeand!" he shouted, smiling while encouraging the crowd to keep the rhythm going.

When Killeand stepped forward, Everett silenced the crowd with a single motion of his arms. "Let's welcome your lord," called Everett and held his hand out to Killeand.

Killeand raised his hands in the air, beaming as the crowd cheered.

"And now," shouted Everett when Killeand stepped off the stage and found a place in the front row, "let the show begin!" He moved to the side to allow Ana to take center stage and for Ned to push the rotating board forward.

While Ana threw her knives at different targets on the board with precision, Lucas kept a close eye on Killeand and his officers. He was disappointed that none of Killeand's guests had joined him. He was now no closer to finding out who they were, but decided to make the most of the afternoon by watching his old friends perform. Everett made sure he involved Killeand in his acts, and he was a willing participant who basked in the crowd's attention. The lord was as boisterous and outgoing as Lucas remembered him to be during the tournament at Itan's castle.

Lucas pulled the hood over his head to disguise his face, left before the show finished, and returned unnoticed to the circus camp.

They all sat down by the fire when the others got back, and Lucas enjoyed more of Rosa's cooking. He knew that, very soon, he would have to say goodbye. Everyone around him was quiet, and Lucas thought they were enjoying their food. Then he noticed the glances Nadia was throwing at Everett.

"Is anything wrong?" asked Lucas, looking around the group. "Did anything happen in town after I left?"

Everett hesitated but then put his bowl down on the ground in front of him. "I have found a way . . . a way for us to get you the information you need."

Lucas stopped eating and stared at him. From the expressions on the faces of the others, he didn't think he was going to like what he was going to hear next.

"The group's been invited to the castle," continued Everett. "I offered Killeand a private performance, and he accepted. We will be able to go and see who all those people are and tell you if you are willing to hold off from returning to the king a little longer?"

"What?" responded Lucas. This was madness. "No. You can't go in there."

"Why not? It will be easy for us. Killeand let us know the timing was perfect since he has guests over—he'll be focused on their enjoyment. We'll do a show, see who's there, get some names, and get out. And we could use the coin—we charge a fair amount for the private performances."

"It's not worth even a hundred pieces of silver." Lucas shook his head. "I don't want you to risk it. I have no idea who the other people are, and Killeand's not to be trusted. Neither is Finton. He's unpredictable and cruel."

"Yes," said Ned. "We know. Nadia told us what Finton did to you."

Lucas saw all the sympathetic faces staring at him and sighed. "I can't have you going in there asking questions. He lied to the king about where he was going, and I'm sure he feels paranoid about being followed. I don't doubt that he is a man on edge right now. Even just one wrong look will rouse his suspicion."

"Then to back out and cancel now would rouse even more," Nadia said. "We might even be followed."

Lucas blinked at her, impressed by her astuteness. He tried to

117

think. Since Everett had offered and Killeand accepted, it would be unwise to cancel. Especially with Killeand's obsession with the circus.

"When are we supposed to give this performance?" asked Ana. She was sitting next to her mother and had been listening quietly.

"Tomorrow night," answered Everett. "At eight o'clock."

"It will be dark then," muttered Ana and turned to her father. "Lucas could lay flat on the roof of the supply wagon, and we can smuggle him inside the gates. He can then sneak inside the castle and see those men for himself."

"Ana," said Ned offering her a bemused smile. "There are guards on the walls, and even in the dark, they will spot him right away."

"We will hide him inside the wagon then," said Ana, not giving up on her idea.

"Ana, stop," said Ned. "The idea to smuggle Lucas inside is preposterous."

"Well, I don't know about that," interjected Everett. "Is it?"

Lucas looked up when he felt Everett's eyes on him.

"Is it, Lucas?" asked Everett. "Do you think you could get the information you need if you had a way to get inside the castle?"

Though Lucas was reluctant to agree, given the danger it would put his friends in, a plan was already slowly forming in his mind.

CHAPTER 11

"**D**id you manage to get the straps in place?" asked Lucas.

Ned was crawling out from underneath the supply wagon. "Yes, all finished," he said, wiping the grit from his hands on his trousers. "There are two straps to put your feet through, and two for your hands, and I added one across for your waist—you'll be able to pull yourself flat against the bottom of the wagon. With the two storage boxes on the side, and if we drop the back hatch, someone would have to get on their knees and look underneath to see you. Are you sure you can do this?" asked Ned, suddenly looking serious.

"Yes," answered Lucas. "I'm sure." Although reluctantly at first, Lucas had hammered out a plan that had the best chance of success. It wasn't going to be without risks, and several times that day, he had thought about calling it off. His need to get the king some answers and an opportunity too great to pass on ultimately made him decide to go through with it.

They waited until close to nightfall before heading towards the castle. Their party was divided into two wagons. Lucas crawled underneath the supply wagon and secured himself with the leather straps. He knew it would be hard to hold on, with all the bouncing up and down on the sandy road. Ned had suggested he wait until they were closer to the castle before climbing under, but Lucas didn't want to chance it. He felt that the wagons would be under watch the minute they set off.

The road to the castle felt longer than he had anticipated, and he was glad when he sensed the wheels slowing down and finally stopping. He pressed himself up as snugly as he could against the bottom of the wagon. He listened as the gates opened, and the wagon rolled forward again. The second wagon came close behind, but no one approached the wagons for inspection. A couple guards did walk by, but at a casual pace, and Lucas was able to make out the buckle on the black boots of two of them. They had to be Finton's men, he concluded, since he had seen them wear buckled boots at Itan's, but why were they working the gates? Was Finton not a guest?

"Right over there, all the way over to your left, if you would, sir!" he heard someone call out, and Lucas guessed it was a guard instructing Ned on where to stop the wagon. The second wagon stopped right next to them, offering what Lucas knew was still only a thin veil of protection—his every move would have to be guarded.

Everyone got out and helped unload. Lucas listened to the familiar sound of the circus unpacking. Except this time, there was no offbeat banter or giggling. Even the typical crunch and stomp of Bernt's footsteps felt muted.

As he clung to the straps, Lucas could see the boots of several soldiers who came to assist them. The soldiers were laughing and chatting merrily when directed on what to carry out of the wagon by Ned. At Itan's castle, it would have been the same, thought Lucas. Any entertainment was a welcome break from routine. Everett did his best in making jokes and keeping the soldiers distracted while they were close to the wagon, but Lucas had no intention of coming out of hiding yet. Only when the bailey was clear, did he get himself loose from the straps and let himself drop to the ground.

The bailey was small, no bigger than the chosens' training grounds. The stables and the soldiers' living quarters were spread along one side, and the main castle building stood opposite. Lucas could only see one main entrance into the castle, where wide steps led up to a set of double doors. He would have to find another way inside.

He stayed on the ground underneath the wagon when some guards passed and then rolled out from underneath. When he glanced up at the wall, he could see that there were four groups of two guards apiece, all facing outward, and none watching the inner part of the castle. The walls themselves were not smooth. They were built up with rough stones, the mortar between them not leveled. There were plenty of handholds for him to use to climb. It was how he had managed to climb the monastery's walls as a little boy.

Swiftly, Lucas pulled himself up on the roof of a low shelter and waited to make sure none of the guards were changing positions before he started climbing the wall that connected with the main building. When he reached the parapet and wall walk, he noticed a door to his left, but using his mind, he could see guards on the other side of it. He crossed over to the battlement and climbed between the merlons to reach the outer part of the castle wall. Again, he was able to use the holes where the mortar was missing or uneven to climb along the outside until he came to a window. Precariously balanced on its ledge, Lucas grabbed his dagger with one hand and slid it in between the two adjacent windows until he found the latch that held them together. He then pushed the knife upward and felt the latch swing back.

He was about to push the windows open that appeared to give him access into a hallway, when he heard a door open and saw a man coming out of a room. He shot out of view, nearly losing his grip, his heart beating in his throat when he saw how high up he was. His fingers were going numb from the tight grip, and he could feel his feet starting to slip from their holds. He closed his eyes so he didn't have to look down, and used his mind to concentrate on what was happening inside instead. The man walked past the window, adjusting his big fur cloak around his shoulders. He made his way down the tower staircase, and Lucas breathed a sigh of relief in knowing he would soon be able to move . . . but then he heard another door open. This time there were voices, and before he could see who they belonged to, he recognized them straight away.

"Father," said Eli. "I am *telling* you, that is Lucas's old circus group down there. I recognize the dwarf."

Finton stopped and shook his head. "Every circus has a dwarf these days," he said and continued walking.

Eli caught up with him. "The giant, the knife thrower, the twins—I'm sure it's them!"

Eli's father stopped again and turned to his son. "Even if you are right," he said, "and it is the circus group associated with Lucas? What of it? They haven't seen him or heard from him for years. The king had people keep an eye on that as well. They let him go and never showed any interest in getting him back."

"Yes, but Lucas has the mark now," continued Eli. "He is free to go as he pleases, and certainly they mattered to him. What if he decides to look for *them,* and they then tell him we are here?"

Finton put a reassuring hand on Eli's shoulder. "Why would they? They have no idea who we are." He paused for a moment. "Let's go. Killeand doesn't like to be left waiting." He started walking again, and Eli followed.

Lucas waited until they were gone before pushing the window open and slipping inside. He crossed the hallway and went straight for the door where he'd seen the man with the fur cloak exit. He slipped inside the room behind it, quickly and quietly closing the door behind him. A burning fire in the hearth lit the room. He looked around, trying to discern anything about the occupant's belongings that would give him a clue of who he might be. The man hadn't worn any identifying colors, but the gray fur cloak indicated someone of wealth and status.

Lucas spotted a saddlebag on the back of a chair, and he opened it. Inside, he found a comb made from horn, a bone knife that folded closed, and some parchment. He pulled out the parchment, but it was blank. He then reached deeper inside the bag and let his fingers wrap around something that felt like a small handle. He pulled it out and saw that it was a wax seal stamp. He placed it on the ground to get another that appeared to have slipped behind the lining. He carefully worked it out of the hole it had fallen through and studied it. It was different than the first one. It looked much older, and the wooden handle was cracked. The stamp itself was chipped in the center. The symbol looked familiar, but Lucas could not remember where he had seen it. Since it didn't appear to have been used for quite some time, he put it back where he found it.

The first seal piqued his interest more. The symbol depicted a shield divided into two parts—with two swords crossed on an inner shield and four stars along the outside in a cardinal direction. He was sure he'd never seen it before. It appeared to have been used recently, with some wax still attached to the side. Lucas looked over to a desk and spotted a block of brown wax. He picked it up, along with some parchment from the saddlebag, and kneeled by the fire. He held the wax close to the heat until it started to melt and let a glob of wax fall on the parchment that he had laid on the floor. He then carefully pushed the seal into the wax until the symbol pressed into it. He let it all cool down before putting the seal back in the bag and the block of wax back on the desk, precisely the way he had found it. He then folded the parchment with the seal inside and stuck it in his pocket before making his way out of the room.

Lucas walked the empty hallway in the opposite direction of the tower and went down a narrow staircase, that was likely used by servants, that came out onto a gallery overlooking the banquet hall. He crouched down behind a balustrade when he could hear laughter down below. Tables were set up in a semi-circle, where people were eating and drinking while the performance was taking place in the center. Lucas could see Everett doing his jester act, with Killeand at the center of it all. Soldiers and castle staff stood behind the people sitting at the tables. Eli was sitting next to his father at the head table, his expression distant. Occasionally, he forced a smile, but he was not paying attention to the show.

Both Eli and his father were wearing well-fitted clothing in Lord Killeand's colors—light blue and gray. Lucas felt certain the king would feel betrayed once he heard this.

Eli wore an officer's uniform, a shirt with two rows of buttons, and a vest in Killeand's colors. His father had regained his position as a general. On the opposite side of Finton sat the man with the fur cloak. From his clothes, Lucas could not tell if he was a lord, a high-ranking officer, or even a king. The cloak was striking, but the rest of his clothes were plain, although tailored. He was leaning towards Finton, and the two exchanged a few quiet words every now and then. It was hard to say if they knew each other or were just getting acquainted, but whoever he was, Finton seemed to respect him and kept nodding in agreement with whatever he heard.

Killeand's seat was in between the man with the fur cloak and someone who looked to be the leader of a large group of rowdy soldiers who were sitting at other tables. Lucas could tell this by the way he was keeping an eye on their behavior. It was clear they were mercenaries and, therefore, the most dangerous type to have around.

The first time Lucas had heard about mercenary soldiers was after the treasury attack on the road, when he'd asked Zera what would happen to the men they'd taken prisoner.

"It all depends on who they are," Zera had responded. "If they are common thieves, then they'll be tried and most likely sent to the mines. If they are suspected to be mercenary soldiers, then they'll be handed over to the king's guard for questioning."

"To be questioned about what?"

"Who paid them to attack," clarified Zera. "Mercenary soldiers are soldiers who'll work for anyone, long as the price is right. They don't fight for a cause—they fight for money."

Lucas wondered why Killeand would need to hire soldiers, as he seemed to have plenty in employment. He watched Everett do his juggling act with Killeand adding more objects for him to juggle with. Engrossed, Lucas nearly forgot the time until he saw Ned standing ready on the side with his rotating disk. Before Lucas had joined the circus, that had always been the last act, and he suspected his time was running out.

He made sure it was all clear around him and then slipped back up the stairs, the way he'd come.

CHAPTER 12

Everett had stretched his act as long as he had been able to and was ready to end it. Having to be cheerful in front of the general, who made his blood boil when he thought of the harm he'd done to Lucas, had not been easy. On top of that, the group of soldiers had gotten drunk to the point of obnoxiousness. He no longer felt like putting a smile on for this lord who thought too highly of himself.

"Well done, my lord," said Everett when Killeand attempted to juggle. "It is time for our last act of this evening, and I will kindly ask you to take a seat, as this act will involve risks to your safety." He gave a slight bow and sighed with relief when he was able to step to the side.

Everett looked at the soldiers, who were no longer interested in the entertainment happening in front of them. Instead, they had set their attention on the four women, Ana included. When Nadia stepped towards the rotating disk and strapped onto it, the soldiers started to whistle, and everyone was distracted long enough for Everett to walk over to Bernt and whisper to him. "Start loading up," he told him quietly. "And take the women out. I have a feeling we need to make a quick exit."

Everett turned back around and saw Ned approach the rotating disk where Nadia had secured herself, to give it a spin.

A soldier whistled and called out to Nadia. "You look like an easy woman. Why don't you show us everything you have?"

Ned ignored the soldier's comments to his wife and threw the first knife. It was at that moment Everett noticed someone was about to leave—the soldier at the head table who had looked uninterested in the performance for most of its duration was standing up to head out after Bernt. Everett didn't know if Lucas had made it back yet, but they could not afford to have anyone get near the wagons. He had to stop this soldier from leaving. Everett took a deep breath and then quickly stepped back between the tables.

"And now, gentlemen," he announced, "for the finale of tonight's performance, we invite someone from the audience to take the place of this lovely lady."

Ned had his knife ready to throw and stopped to look at him curiously.

"Let's see . . . you, sir!" announced Everett, pointing to the soldier who was about to leave. "Yes, you sir," said Everett, when the soldier stopped and pointed questioningly at himself. The other soldiers started laughing and chanting, urging him to volunteer. "You look like a brave young man."

"What're you doing?" asked Ned when Everett stood next to him. "I can't throw knives at a soldier. What if he moves?"

"Let's hope he doesn't," said Everett. "We don't have a choice. He was going to follow Bernt out to the wagons." He stepped away from Ned and promptly stopped the disk, getting Nadia loose quickly to minimize the chance of the soldier changing his mind.

The soldier walked reluctantly into the center of the room and was now looking at Ned, who was still holding a knife. "I don't think so," he said, shaking his head.

127

"Oh, come on, Harbert," said Killeand, suddenly rising from his seat. "Show my friend here how brave you are and that you're the right man for the job you'll be paid for. You don't want to give the impression that you'll run at the first sign of trouble, now do you?"

Killeand's words instantly changed the banquet hall's atmosphere from a joyous one to one of tension, and Everett's heart sank when he realized he was the cause of it. Perhaps it would have been better to have let him go, but it was too late for that now.

Harbert looked from Killeand to the man with the fur cloak, and Everett saw Harbert's demeanor had changed. It was as if he was offended, but his hands were tied, and he had no option but to comply. The soldiers had all grown quiet. Even Finton and his son looked alarmed. Everett knew he had to find a quick way out of this—but then watched as Nadia did it for him. She had stepped towards Harbert and spoke softly to him. Everett could not hear what she said, but Harbert's body language relaxed, and he even smiled at her as he listened. He then followed her to the disk and let her strap him onto it.

"You're not trying to kill me, are you?" Harbert asked Ned, flashing a nervous smile.

"I'll try not to," answered Ned, taking his position. "We'll try without a spin first."

Everett held his breath, sighing with relief when the knife lodged itself in between Harbert's legs. Ned threw two more, and when he was comfortable enough that Harbert wasn't going to flinch, he asked if he wanted to spin.

By now, Harbert seemed to have gotten over his nerves and cheerfully answered, "Sure. Why not?"

Much to Everett's relief, that caused his men to become loud again and cheer. The tension dissipated, and several more men requested to get pinned to the board. When he felt he had given Lucas more than enough time, he told the crowd the show had come to an end and turned to Lord Killeand and bowed. "Thank you, my lord," he said, "for the opportunity to entertain you tonight."

"The pleasure was all mine," said Lord Killeand.

After the last piece of equipment was loaded in the wagon, Everett dropped to one knee, pretending to examine the worn wheel by the light of the torches that lit the bailey. Lucas was there but was giving him an alarmed look, shaking his head wildly. It was then that Everett heard Killeand's voice. He quickly got up and turned to see him walk down the stairs from the castle. Finton was at his side, and they were coming towards the wagons.

"Well, we best be on our way now," he said, meeting them halfway. "We are traveling south tomorrow and have an early start."

"You are leaving so soon," said Killeand. "Why not stay and hold another performance in town? You have my permission to stay as long as you like, and can keep your wagons here overnight if it suits you."

"That is very kind of you, my lord, but us circus folk are of a restless mind," said Everett, feeling Ned's eyes on his back, urging him to get on with it. Ned had taken his seat at the front and had grabbed the reins. "We never stay anywhere for too long."

"Let me ask," said Killeand before Everett was able to turn around and walk away. "Since you travel a great deal . . . have you, by any chance, ever performed for King Itan? It would have been some years back."

Everett's heart stopped, and a lump entered his throat, but he hoped they did not notice when he shook his head. "No, we never have," he answered as casually as possible. Had Finton recognized them and said something? Perhaps the timing of their arrival had made him suspicious. He might suspect they were sent to spy on him for the king, and he was going to have to be very careful with his words. "It is my understanding that the king does not care for entertainment that much."

"That may be true," said Killeand, "but he did invite entertainment groups some years ago . . . for the princess's birthday."

"Really?" asked Everett.

Killeand nodded and continued. "Yes, he did, and he enjoyed watching a young boy doing a sword-fighting act."

Everett knew both Finton and Killeand would be watching him closely for his reaction, and he was glad for having been in the business of role-play all his life.

"Well," he responded, keeping his voice flat. "If he caught the king's attention, he must have been something."

"He still is," said Killeand. "He joined the king's army, and I got to watch him a few years later. His name is Lucas. Maybe you knew him back then?"

"Doesn't ring a bell. I don't think I've ever had the pleasure of seeing anyone doing a sword-fighting act. Mostly knife throwing, fire breathing, juggling . . . that sort of thing. Do you know the name of the circus he was with?"

Killeand looked at Finton, but Finton shook his head. "I guess we don't," answered Killeand, "but he worked with a dwarf."

"Ah, now I understand why you are asking me. You think I should know because I am a dwarf," said Everett, forcing a chuckle. "Well, there are lots of us, and we are not all one big happy family. Most of us don't like each other. The competition, you see."

Killeand smiled, and Everett was relieved when he didn't follow up with any more questions. He didn't think he could take much more.

Killeand observed the wagons standing ready to ride out the gate. "Your people seem eager to get going. Here." He handed Everett a small pouch of coin. "You have earned it."

"Well, thank you, my lord," said Everett. He took the pouch and let it weigh in his hand. It was more coin than he had expected. "The pleasure was all ours, but it is greatly appreciated." He turned around quickly, before Killeand would notice the little droplets of sweat forming at his temples. He grabbed the side of the wagon and climbed onto the seat next to Ned.

"Are we good?" asked Ned when the gates opened, and Bernt was rolling the first wagon through.

"Finton knows who we are," Everett answered. "We have to move out quickly."

CHAPTER 13

Lucas had thought Everett was going to give him away when he got down on his knee to see if he was underneath. He knew Killeand and Finton were coming. He'd already had a close call after he had dropped himself too loudly on the shelter's roof, and one of the guards on the wall had peered into the bailey. As luck had it, Bernt was coming out of the castle with the women and had distracted the guard long enough for Lucas to slide underneath the wagon.

His arms had grown sore from holding himself against the bottom of the wagon while Killeand questioned Everett, and he was glad when the wheels were set in motion. As the wagon passed through the gate, Lucas could hear a horse whinny in the stables, and he felt compelled to let his mind wander towards it. In the dark stable, a horse was moving restlessly in its stall, catching the moonlight coming through a window on its white mane.

As soon as they arrived back at the camp, Lucas let go of the straps and dropped to the ground. His entire body was sore, his skin caked with dust and dirt. Ned jumped off the wagon and looked underneath to see if he was all right. "I'm sorry for the rough ride there," he said. "Everett thinks Finton knows who we are, and that's why we rode out at such a speed."

Lucas rolled from underneath and dusted himself off. "I think so too. Which means I need to get going straight away."

"Can you not stay the night?" asked Nadia, coming to stand next to Ned.

"No, love," Ned answered for him. "He'll put us all at risk if he does."

Lucas gave her a sympathetic look but then followed Ned, who ordered everyone into action. Bernt took the horses off the wagons with Ana's help. Rosa and Lisette stoked up the fire and prepared the camp for the night. Nadia fetched Lucas's clothes for him to change back into as Ned set about removing the straps from underneath the wagon, and Lucas went to get his horse ready. It was still crusted with dirt, which he had to remove before he could saddle up for the long ride—at least where the saddle could cause sores on the horse's back. Everett came to help him.

"Did you get the information you needed?" asked Everett, as they brushed.

"Yes," replied Lucas, "but I'm sure the king will want to know why Killeand has hired mercenary soldiers when the alliance they have in place guarantees one another military support."

"There's a possibility it wasn't Killeand who hired them," said Everett. "Killeand told the mercenaries' leader, who he called Harbert, that he was to show the other guest at the table what he was getting for his money. So it sounded like the man in the gray cloak was the one paying the mercenaries."

"Did you happen to get his name?" asked Lucas.

"No," answered Everett. "Killeand only referred to him as 'my friend.'"

"Seems I will be providing the king with more questions than answers," said Lucas with a sigh.

He led his horse away from the wagons and the light of the

campfire. His friends stood waiting for him. He embraced each of them and thanked them for their help. It was hard to say goodbye so soon, especially when he stood in front of Nadia. "I'm sorry I have to leave," he said, a lump forming in his throat when he saw the tears in her eyes.

"It's all right," she said, smiling. "It was a gift to learn you are alive, and I am grateful for that." She then hugged him tight before letting go.

"Rosa," he said, mounting his horse, "do you remember us passing through a forest once and you telling me that the biggest blueberries grew there at the end of summer?"

"I do," replied Rosa.

"Can you show Ana when they grow?" he asked. He swung his leg over the saddle.

"Should we harvest them?" asked Rosa.

Lucas gripped the reins and looked around the group of confused circus members before smiling at Rosa. "I am sure she would like that," he answered and rode off into the night.

At dawn, Lucas stopped by a creek to let his horse drink and decided to wash the leech dye out of his hair. He kneeled and leaned over to put his head in the water. If it had not been for Father Ansan insisting those many years ago that he get over his fear of water, he would have been stuck with black hair for quite some time. He rubbed his hands over his scalp until the water no longer turned black around him. Lucas was tired, not having slept all night, and splashed more cool water over his face before looking over to the other side of the stream. With his mind busy with other things, he'd failed to check his surroundings and only now saw the magpie in the tree across the creek. Behind the bird, two riders—dressed in black—emerged from the mist hanging between the trees.

They rode towards him.

Lucas felt for his sword and realized he had made another huge mistake by leaving it on his saddle. If he got up fast, he could run to his horse and get it before they made it across the creek, but then he froze. Not only did he see the danger in front of him, he felt it behind as well. He spun around on his heel, but he was too late. Lucas was struck down by the dark rider with the eye patch and scar—the leader, from the inn!

"Secure him, Byram!" the man with the scar called out.

The rider named Byram jumped off his horse and rolled Lucas over onto his back. Lucas remembered this blond-haired, blue-eyed man as well. He'd given him the chills then, and he was still the one Lucas felt he should fear most. Byram grabbed his arms and tried to tie his hands together with a rope. Even though he was still dazed from the blow to his head, Lucas did his best to fight him off. He clenched his hands into fists and jerked his arms back while thrashing his body around, making it hard for Byram to keep his grip on him.

"Hold the boy!"

"I'm trying, Garam," answered Byram, "but I may need some help here!"

The other man, Garam, leapt off his horse and helped pin Lucas to the ground. With no way out, Lucas tried to connect with their horses but failed. Their minds appeared to be blocked, and he could not reach them, which was strange but he had no time to worry about it.

Lucas continued to struggle and kick, but these men were strong and seemed to anticipate his every move. With his hands now almost tied and two more riders ready to cross the creek, Lucas connected with his horse, who stood some distance away. His horse snorted, threw his head up in the air, then turned and came charging. The animal kicked at Lucas's attackers with his back legs, and the men had no choice but to let go and dive to the side. Lucas jumped to his feet and grabbed the pommel of his saddle with both his hands. He lifted himself over the back of his horse, swung his leg over, and let his horse take off. He pulled at the rope around his wrists with his teeth until it was loose enough that he could undo the knot and grabbed the reins when he was free.

All four riders pursued him on their horses, splitting up across the rocky forest terrain in an attempt to cut him off.

Before long, a rider appeared on Lucas's right, pulling up alongside him. The man grabbed Lucas's arm and tried to yank him off his horse. Lucas reached into his saddlebag with his left hand and drew out a knife, which he thrust into the rider's neck. He watched the man first try to cup the blood that gushed from the wound, then slump to the side and fall off his horse. Before Lucas had time to correct himself in the saddle, Byram appeared on his other side and jumped behind him in the saddle. Stunned by this move, Lucas realized these were not regular soldiers. They were highly skilled and were going to great lengths to get him. They didn't falter when one of their comrades fell—they stayed focused on catching him, and by any means possible.

Lucas fought hard to try and get Byram off his horse. Byram had his arm around his neck and was squeezing hard. As he struggled to breathe, Lucas directed his horse with his mind through the trees towards some low-hanging branches and pretended to lose consciousness. When Byram released his grip on him, Lucas managed to duck, and just in time. The branch hit Byram across his forehead, and Lucas felt Byram's body go limp before he fell from the back of his horse and hit the ground.

Lucas's horse dodged branches and jumped over logs and rocks as Lucas tried to lose the remaining two riders. One of them Lucas now knew was called Garam. Every time he thought he might have lost them, he caught sight of one of them in his peripheral vision. His horse's neck was outstretched, and the animal's breathing became increasingly labored as they raced through the forest. With his horse having ridden all night already, he was losing ground, and Garam suddenly cut him off and made his horse come to an abrupt stop. Lucas looked over his shoulder and saw the other rider not too far behind.

"Give it up, boy," said Garam. A sinister smile was playing on his face. He had lost the eye patch in the scramble by the creek, revealing a milky white eye. "You can no longer outrun us, and there's no need to get yourself hurt again."

Lucas shortened up the reins and weighed his options. Garam was right—his horse was too exhausted to go any further, and escape seemed impossible. He had no idea what they wanted from him, but there was darkness surrounding these men, a darkness that raised every hair on the back of his neck. He was going to fight them no matter what happened. He took his sword from the strap on his saddle, and turned his horse around to face the rider coming up behind him. With less than thirty yards between them, he gave his horse free rein and charged. With his sword in hand, he was ready to strike the rider down, but the rider turned his horse inward. Lucas's horse veered sharply to the right to avoid a collision, causing him to lose his balance and fall.

He scrambled to his feet, bracing himself for an outcome not in his favor, when he suddenly heard someone whistle behind the dark riders. Both dark riders looked over their shoulders to see who it was, and Lucas took advantage of the distraction by running forward and jumping up to thrust his sword into Garam's stomach. For a moment, Lucas stared up into the cold eyes of a man he knew was responsible for the death of his father, then stepped out of the way to let him fall off his horse. He turned to see a man he didn't know charge the last dark rider and watched him take the rider out with the throw of a dagger into his chest. Lucas then watched the stranger jump off his horse and check to ensure the dark rider was dead.

"That was a close call," the man said and held his hand out as he walked towards Lucas. "It is good to see you again, Lucas."

Surprised the man knew his name, Lucas eyed him up. His light brown skin and soft brown eyes were familiar, but Lucas could not place where he had seen him. "We have met before?" he asked.

"We have," the man answered. "At an inn a few years back. My name is Dastan."

Hearing the name and looking at him closer, Lucas now remembered him to be the traveler who had spoken up for him at the courthouse. His leather trousers, white-laced shirt, and suede vest were of good quality but coated with dust. Dastan's unkempt shoulder-length hair and stubbly beard gave the impression that he had been on the road for some time.

Lucas gestured towards the dead riders. "You were at the inn before they came there."

Dastan nodded. "Yes," he said. "I was going to try and get you away from there, but then they showed up sooner than I had anticipated. Your name threw them off—it made them hesitate to take you right away, and I thought we had a chance. Unfortunately, I was wrong, and I'm sorry for that." Dastan put his dagger back in its sheath and went to retrieve his horse.

Lucas followed him. "Who are they, and who are you?" he asked, confused. He was confident it was no coincidence that Dastan had shown up here. "And why were they trying to kill me?"

"They *were* the dark order," answered Dastan. "And they were not trying to kill you. They had orders to take you alive. I am the one tasked with preventing that from happening. It appears they are all dead now, so that was the easy part. The hard part of my job is yet to come."

"And what is that?"

"Answering all the questions you have about yourself," said Dastan, mounting his horse.

Lucas looked at him. "What is that supposed to mean?"

"You already know that you are not what people think you are," said Dastan. "But if you are not a chosen, and not an elite, and not ordinary, either—what are you, then?"

"And *you* know?" asked Lucas. "You can tell me?"

"I can," answered Dastan, "but I doubt you will believe me if I do."

"None of this makes sense to me," Lucas said, shrugging, "so why don't you try me?"

Dastan shook his head, tightening the reins. "For you to believe who you are is for you to see it," he said. "If you are willing to come with me, I can help with that."

Lucas shook his head. "I appreciate your help here today," he said. "But you are a stranger, and I have to get back to the king, where my duty lies. I have already been absent too long."

"Very well," said Dastan, turning his horse around. "I had hoped you were ready to hear the truth, but if you are not, it will have to wait."

Without another word, Lucas watched him ride off and disappear over the crest of the hill, leaving him standing alone. He looked at the ground and the two dead soldiers of the dark order and let out a deep sigh. He then mounted his horse and hoped it would be all right if he did not return to the king just yet.

Lucas followed at a distance as they made their way through the foothills and onto higher grounds. They rode through a forest and occasionally got a glimpse down the deep ravines when there was a break in the tree line. Dastan had slowed down once for him to catch up, but, still skeptical of whether he was making the right decision, Lucas had stopped and waited until he got going again. He kept looking for a magpie but did not see one and, after several hours, he felt more at ease. When they reached a narrow ridge, Lucas finally started riding closer. "You finding me was not a coincidence," he said.

Dastan looked back at him, a brief knowing look flashing in his eyes.

"And you knew I was on my own." Again, Dastan did not answer, but Lucas knew he was right. "Up until three weeks ago, I was a chosen one, and it would have been impossible for me to ride out alone—you must have been told that my rank at Itan's had changed. By someone who knows me. Someone at the castle." He was guessing at the last part, but he felt there was no other possible explanation. He waited for Dastan to respond this time, but when he didn't say anything, Lucas stopped his horse. "I am not going any further until you tell me."

Dastan sighed, halting and turning his horse to face him. "Egon," he said.

"Egon?" asked Lucas. "Egon knows what I am?"

"He does now."

"How?"

"Because I told him," answered Dastan. "I contacted him when you were all camped at Lord Aron's."

The surprises kept coming, and it was hard to sort through which ones he should believe and which ones should give him pause. "How is it that you are acquainted with Egon?"

"I wasn't, up until recently. I knew *of* him, but we had never met."

Lucas shook his head. He doubted that Egon would be approachable by a stranger and certainly would not readily provide information about anyone in the castle.

"You don't believe me, do you?" remarked Dastan and set his horse into motion again. "Egon knew my brother, growing up. I mentioned his name before Egon pulled his sword to strike me down. It was enough to save my life, but it still took some heavy explanation as to who I was before he agreed to hear me out."

Dastan continued down the trail, and Lucas followed in silence again. He thought about how Egon's attitude towards him had softened after coming back from Lord Aron's. He had thought that was because of Finton and what he had done to him, but Egon would not have hesitated to use flogging himself if he had thought him to be guilty of revolting against the king. Egon had shown concern—too much concern—but for what?

"Why did they try to take me and not kill me?" Lucas asked. When Dastan did not answer, he pulled his horse up alongside him. "The dark order?" he asked. "You said they had orders to take me but could not kill me? Why?"

"Killing you would have consequences neither they nor the person they worked for were willing to take," answered Dastan without looking at him.

The path became narrower, and when it went downward at a steeper incline, Lucas had to drop back again so they could traverse it single file. He leaned back, letting his horse do the work of finding his footing.

"You are creating more questions than answers for me," Lucas called out.

Dastan turned around in his saddle. "Have you heard of Toroun?" he asked.

"Yes," answered Lucas. "Who hasn't?"

"Then, you may also know that the people responsible for his death died soon after him?"

"I do."

"And do you remember why?"

"Because of a curse that the gods allegedly released after his execution."

Dastan nodded. "The same will happen if you get killed. That's why the dark order needed to capture you alive."

They had reached level ground, and Lucas started riding next to Dastan again. "I am not Toroun and, in any case, Toroun is a legend," he said, shaking his head. "His story is exaggerated, and the curse most likely made up."

"Is that what you think?" asked Dastan, giving him a sideways glance. "Or that is what you have been told?"

Lucas shrugged. He remembered asking Father Ansan once if the story about Toroun was real after reading it in a book but had never received a clear answer. He had then acted out the story so many times with the circus that he had come to view it as fiction and never questioned it again.

"It's all right for you to believe it didn't truly happen," continued Dastan. "That's one of the reasons you were brought across the river border and allowed to grow up with King Itan. Only here, on Itan's land do the people believe the prophecy to be the writings of a storyteller, and they are not looking for a boy with extraordinary powers." He paused and looked at him in earnest. The wind had picked up, and it blew through his brown hair. "The story, however, is real, and the curse, not a mere fable."

Lucas took a deep breath. He didn't understand what this had to do with him. "If that's so, and I am to believe everything about Toroun was real, what does this have to do with me? I am not Toroun."

"No," agreed Dastan. "You are not." He stopped his horse where there was a gap in the trees and looked towards a mountain on the other side. "You will soon become more powerful than he ever was."

Lucas stopped next to him and followed his gaze to a village in the distance and the red-roofed, whitewashed stone building that lay beyond it. They had approached it from the south side, but he recognized the building. "It's the monastery," he said. Seeing his former home basked in sunlight on the rocky plateau above the village brought back memories. Good ones, from when he was a child, but the most recent ones he quickly pushed to the back of his mind. They were from a painful part of his life he had been trying to forget. "You mentioned I needed to see, to believe who I am?" he said after a moment of reflection.

"I did," answered Dastan.

"Then you know what lies behind those walls?"

"I do."

"How?" asked Lucas. "No outsiders are allowed near it."

"That wasn't always so," answered Dastan. "The stone has been part of our people's heritage for a long time. You also saw my brother at the monastery once."

"Your brother?"

"Yes, after Einar died. You were young and probably don't remember."

Lucas lowered his head and went deep into his thoughts. He did recall a stranger in the courtyard one time. The stranger had watched him practice and had tested his skills by sneaking up behind him to try and take the sword. It was after he had talked to Father Ansan that the decision was made that Lucas was to become Father Ansan's student.

"You should have told me you wanted to take me to the stone," he called after Dastan, who had already started descending the ridge towards the village. "I could have saved us a lot of time."

"Why is that?" called Dastan over his shoulder.

Lucas turned his horse onto the path to follow him. "Because I was there not more than a year ago. The stone didn't tell me then who I was when it very easily could have."

"You weren't ready then."

"And you think I am ready now?"

"No, but there is only one way to find out."

They rode around the village, passing his old house on the road leading up to the monastery. Dastan gave him a look of understanding when they passed the abandoned structure in silence. The window shutters were hanging off their hinges, and parts of the house were overgrown with moss and vines. The door to the forge hung off its hinges. Lucas could almost see his father standing there, scanning the road to see if he was on his way home from wherever it was that he had been that day, sweat dripping from his face from the heat of the forge.

The memory made his eyes water, and he looked away.

Dastan dismounted when they reached the monastery and knocked on the big wooden door. Lucas waited and got down only after Dastan had spoken to a monk through the little hatch, and the door opened. Two monks came out to take their horses, and Lucas followed Dastan over the threshold into the dim entrance hall.

"It seems like yesterday when I sat on the floor over there by that door while my father went in to talk to Father Ansan," said Lucas. "That was the day they accepted me to come and train with them, but I thought I was in big trouble for climbing their walls."

"You are right to think you should have gotten into trouble for that," said Dastan, smiling. "Those walls are high. You could have easily killed yourself."

A monk entered, and in the dim light, it was hard to be sure if it was who he thought it was. "Father John?" he asked, thinking he did indeed recognize the monk who used to look after him when he was a boy, and again during his recovery the year before.

"Master Lucas," said Father John, coming up to him to embrace him. "Is it you? You have grown yet again. Father Ansan will be delighted to see you looking so healthy. Come, let us not delay!"

They followed Father John down the hallways, and Lucas looked around, recognizing places as he went by. The room where he had spent many hours learning to read and write with Father Ansan, the chapel where the monks would go for morning prayer, his bedroom with the tiny window that would let the moonlight in, the stone tiles of the hallways where he would step on every other one for fun, and finally the dusty courtyard where he had been taught the ways of the warrior monks. He stopped near Dastan while Father John approached Father Ansan, who stood with his back towards them as he instructed a large group of monks with shaved heads and all wearing gold-colored robes. Only Father Ansan wore the gold-trimmed red satin robe of a master warrior. Father John whispered a few words in his ear, and Lucas saw Father Ansan spin on his heel, a smile appearing on his face when their eyes met.

Father Ansan turned the lesson's instruction over to one of the monks in the foremost row, and then walked over to stand before him. Lucas pressed his hands together in front of him and bowed to greet his old teacher. Father Ansan did the same and then held him by the shoulders to have a good look at him.

"You look strong, my son," said Father Ansan. "I am pleased we get to meet under better circumstances this time."

"Thank you, Father," said Lucas. "I continued to heal after leaving here, and I practice what you taught me."

"Perhaps you can give a demonstration of your skills?" asked Dastan. "I would love to see what you are capable of . . . now that I am not trying to save your life." He briefly looked Father Ansan in the eye. He gave a nod in return and called out over his shoulder before Lucas could give a reply.

Lucas watched a young monk, not much older than himself, leave the group and come over quickly.

"Yes, Father?" asked the young monk.

"You remember Master Lucas," said Father Ansan. "He has honored us with another visit. Have him show everyone what it takes to defeat a master while I go and have a talk with Dastan."

"Can it wait?" asked Lucas. "I'm not in top form right now after nearly getting killed this morning and then having to spend hours in the saddle. Not to mention my empty stomach."

"Then the timing to show them what it takes to defeat a master is perfect," said Father Ansan. He let go of Lucas and gave him a friendly slap on the shoulder. The young monk gave a bow. "Please, come with me," he said.

Lucas followed, looking back once to see Father Ansan and Dastan walking away together. It was clear to him that they knew each other, as it had been clear Father Ansan had also known the stranger that came to observe him all those years ago, and who he now understood to be Dastan's brother.

Lucas recognized most of the monks from the brief time he had trained with them when his legs were still healing. None were masters yet and were eager to see what he could do. They formed a large circle around him and handed him a wax wood stick. He admired it, twisting it around in his hands. It had been a long time since he held one. Father Ansan and Dastan walked over to a bench nearby and sat down. Their lips parted as they engaged in conversation, but their eyes remained on Lucas as he readied himself for the first attack. The young monk was the first to charge him, and his attack was swift. Lucas kneeled on one knee and held the stick above his head with both hands to reflect the blow. He then dropped onto his bottom, swung his leg around, and deflected an attack from behind. The entire fight lasted only a few minutes, with him rolling, jumping, and swinging the stick in all directions until every monk had attacked him once.

Lucas paced the circle while catching his breath to prepare for a second round when Nasai came over to him.

"Will you fight us blindfolded next time?" asked the young monk. "Father Ansan says that when a person loses one of his senses, it can heighten others, so when an opponent has lost his sight . . ."

"And the hearing increases, it can make an opponent unpredictable and dangerous," interrupted Lucas, smiling. "I remember him telling me that."

"Then, will you?"

"I can," answered Lucas, "but if you have heard about me, then you know that a blindfold does not prevent me from seeing."

"A seeing mind is not the same as using your eyes," said the young monk. "Do you know if your hearing increases when you are blindfolded?"

"I'm not sure," answered Lucas. His hearing was heightened already as one of his abilities, but he had never tried the two together. "Let's find out." He allowed the young monk to come up behind him and tie a scarf over his eyes. When he was blindfolded, Lucas stood still and unlocked his seeing mind to look around the group of warrior monks. They were all quiet and were watching him without moving a single muscle. He knew their attack would start with the slightest, most subtle movement, one that would be barely perceptible, so he concentrated on listening for just that—a foot moving over the sand, a deep breath that might be inhaled, or a piece of clothing that rubbed over the skin. He tried to tune out the sounds coming to him from outside the circle, which appeared to be getting stronger with every passing second, until he heard Father Ansan's voice and the words he spoke.

"I must say I was rather surprised to see Lucas with you here today," said Father Ansan. "I did not think he would be able to leave the castle alone as a chosen. It's what we all agreed would keep him safe."

"I know," answered Dastan, "but he is no longer a chosen, he . . ."

Dastan had paused, and Lucas could see him pay closer attention to the warrior monks. Then he heard it—the bottom of a stick shifting the sand beneath it as a monk behind him switched hands. Lucas turned and deflected the first attack, then heard Dastan's voice again while he continued to defend against other monks now engaging him.

"Did he just see that attack coming or hear it?" asked Dastan. "Does he have the power to increase his hearing? Do you think he can hear us right now?"

Father Ansan chuckled. "With Lucas, there is no telling what he can do," he answered, "but what were you saying about him not being a chosen?"

"Itan changed his rank by giving him the king's mark," answered Dastan.

"Why?" asked Father Ansan. "I know you have someone at the castle in a position of importance who could have put a stop to it."

"Yes, we do," answered Dastan. "That would be Egon. He's a king's guard."

Lucas dropped his knee onto the ground and held his stick overhead to block an attack. He then swung the stick to the side—blocking another. Hearing Egon's name spoken spiked his interest again, and he focused to listen to the two men on the bench.

"I have met Egon," said Father Ansan. "He was the one who brought Lucas here last year after his fall, but he never told me we were on the same side."

"That's because he didn't know at the time," said Dastan. "I only informed him of Lucas a few weeks ago when it became clear that he might need an ally within Itan's walls."

"But he wasn't able to stop Lucas from being given the king's mark?"

"No," answered Dastan. "Itan made his decision quickly and without consultation. I was only informed a few days ago, after Egon became concerned that Lucas had not returned from a mission. I have yet to find out where he has been, but I found him fighting off the dark order, well outside the area where Egon thought he had gone and might be. I took the opportunity to get close to him and convinced him to follow me here."

"Do you think he is ready?"

Lucas twisted the stick in his hands. The two monks circling him were waiting for the right moment to attack. Father Ansan's words echoed in his mind. Ready for what? he wondered.

"I'm not sure," answered Dastan. "But I was told by Egon that the chosen ones have started to follow Lucas. If he doesn't find out who he is, he will not be able to take full control over them. I feel he is also resisting the powers within him or not utilizing them to their potential. I don't think the dark order would have been able to get their hands on him otherwise."

"I think deep down—he knows who he is," said Father Ansan. "Lucas has shown his capability to your people in the past, but he has forgotten. All it will take is for him to remember."

"He was an infant then."

"In our eyes, he was," replied Ansan.

"I told Lucas that the stone could show him who he is," said Dastan with some uncertainty in his voice.

Father Ansan nodded. "It can, and it will . . . if it is time."

Lucas rotated his body over the ground, extended his leg to hook his foot behind the heel of the last monk, and took him down.

"And?" asked the young monk when Lucas stood up and removed the blindfold from his eyes.

"Hearing heightened," answered Lucas, smiling, and handed him the scarf. He saw Father Ansan and Dastan get up from the bench and walk over to him.

"You are a master warrior to be admired," said Father Ansan. "You have improved your skills since I last saw you."

"Thank you, Father," answered Lucas, walking alongside him. Dastan followed close behind.

"I still remember you standing on the wall behind me when you were a young boy," said Father Ansan after a moment of silence.

"I do too," answered Lucas. "I was persistent in wanting to join, but you told me I was too young."

Father Ansan nodded. "Have you ever wondered what changed my mind that day?" he asked.

"I hadn't," answered Lucas. "Although I get the impression now that I should have."

"You would have been too young to understand, and then when Einar died—"

"My father," said Lucas. He looked over his shoulder to Dastan behind him and back to Father Ansan to see their reaction. They had both held their breath long enough for Lucas to confirm what he had started to suspect the moment Dastan had first told him he wasn't who he believed he was. "Einar wasn't my father, was he?"

Father Ansan slowly shook his head. "No, he wasn't."

Lucas stopped walking. "I don't know if I'm ready to hear much more," he said. "I'm going to lay down for a while, and then I have to go. The king will be wondering what is keeping me."

"Lucas," said Dastan firmly when he started to walk away. "You need to know. You need to know the truth about who you are and who you will become. Let the stone show you."

"No," said Lucas sharply. "No one bothered to tell me before, so why would I want to know now?" He picked up a stone and threw it at the small bell tower on top of the roof. He didn't care that the sound caused him to get angry looks from monks walking the cloister. "I don't even know who *you* are and why I even followed you." He saw that Dastan wanted to step towards him, but Father Ansan put his hand on his arm to stop him.

"You followed Dastan because your whole life you have reacted on impulse," said Father Ansan in a calm voice. "You knew it was the right thing to do. It makes you who you are."

"But why now?" asked Lucas. He threw his hands up. "Why not last year when I was here?"

"You know that was not the right time," answered Father Ansan.

Lucas sighed, rubbing his hands through his hair. He felt like a young child being lectured, and the lack of sleep wasn't helping his tolerance levels. But he knew what Father Ansan was referring to. He had gone to the stone for answers without the guidance of the other warrior monks. He had touched the stone, but its hold on him had been too strong for his weakened body. It had caused him to black out and collapse onto the ground. He had been lucky not to have fallen into the water and drowned.

"Maybe you should rest," said Father Ansan. "You look tired, and I don't want you to make a decision you may regret later."

"Yes, I am exhausted," he said. "I will rest. But it may not change how I feel about this."

Lucas fell asleep straight away and did not wake until he heard the bell for evening prayers. Candles were burning in niches on the wall in the otherwise dark guest room. He rolled onto his back and stared at the ceiling. The familiar smell of smoke from incense burning made him feel like he was home again. Father Ansan had been right. He did frequently act on impulse. It was something that had gotten him out of trouble but also in trouble many times. When he had dreamt of his own death, warriors had stood by the stone. He had always thought those were just dreams, but now he felt he could not be so sure anymore. He sat up and saw the deep red silk robe with golden trim neatly folded on the bedside table. On top of it, a sash with a black tip. He gently picked it up and felt the smooth material.

When he entered the courtyard, heads turned in his direction, the monks gathered there acknowledging his arrival. The stone stood glistening in the moonlight from its position on the island in the center of the pond. Candles were burning in a circle around it, and all the warrior monks were present and waiting.

Dastan walked up to him and put a hand on his shoulder. "I'm glad you are going through with it," he said. "Father Ansan never doubted you would."

"He knows me too well," answered Lucas.

Dastan gave him a little smile. "They tell me I can't stay once the ceremony starts, but I hope the stone will show you the path you need to follow going forward." He then gave Lucas an encouraging tap on the shoulder and left.

Lucas walked to Father Ansan. He saw the plank across the water to the island. Unlike when, as an eleven-year-old boy, he had been worried that the stone would not accept him, this time, he only worried that he was not ready for what the stone could show him. He took the bowl of brown rice handed to him by Father John and forced himself to eat, despite his lack of appetite. There was no telling how long the stone would keep hold of him and his body needed energy.

"Thank you," he told Father John, handing him the empty bowl and moving to stand silently next to the plank, which in his memory had seemed much bigger. A few short steps took him across to the island. He could hear the monks removing the plank when he climbed on top of the flat part of the stone. There he sat cross-legged, watching the monks seated at the water's edge in meditation. He looked down at all the ancient carvings around him on the stone. He now understood they were family crests of the warriors long gone. He counted thirteen. The same number of warriors he always saw in his dreams. He took his time tracing every single one of them with his fingers, then closed his eyes. He could feel the stone's energy flow up inside, giving him a warm, tingling feeling. Within moments, he was surrounded by darkness.

He felt submerged in blackness and eternal silence for what seemed like forever, until he started hearing people in the far distance, their voices coming closer and closer. He heard them talking, whispering— even arguing. He heard laughing, crying, screaming . . . and then the cries of a baby who was making it known he had entered the world. And finally, voices, but drifting away. When the darkness began to lift, Lucas found himself in a sparsely lit bedroom. A single candle stood on a table, and he watched a man enter. He looked worried and was closing the door behind him quickly.

"We have to go," he heard the man say. "They can be here within the hour. It's no longer safe to stay."

A middle-aged woman who had been sitting on a chair in a corner with her hands folded on her lap stood up to address the man. "Your wife is too weak," she said, "and the fever still not broken. She won't make it."

The man looked desperately towards the bed, in which a woman lay gravely ill. Her face was pale, and her skin clammy. He lowered his head and let out a deep sigh. He then walked over to the crib next to his wife's bed and tenderly picked up the baby, holding him tight against his chest. When noises could be heard coming from outside, he held the baby out in front of him and kissed his little forehead. Finally, he turned to face the woman standing in the room and held the baby out to her. "I need you to take him to the elders," he said urgently. "He is the gift our people have been waiting for, and he cannot fall into the hands of those who want to stop him."

"What about you?" asked the woman, taking the baby from him. Her voice and hands trembled.

"I have to stay here with my wife," the man answered. "Take my son before it is too late," he pleaded. "If I am right—if we are all right and he is our future—then the gods will protect you on your journey."

The woman left the room with the baby held tightly in her arms, and the man went to sit by his wife's side.

People of all ages had gathered outside the house, all carrying heavy bags strapped over their shoulders. They all stood waiting for the woman with the baby and, once she joined them, they began walking together as a group. They walked silently into the hills, none of them exchanging any words. When they reached a high vantage point, they turned around and listened to the screaming down below in the village. Several houses were already engulfed in flames, and the fire was slowly spreading. Some children in the group started to cry and their mothers tried to keep them quiet by covering their eyes and ears.

The woman looked down at the baby in her arms and saw him looking at the fires, the reflection of the flames visible in his eyes. He then turned his little head and looked up towards the sky. The woman followed his gaze and saw a thick mist coming down over them. With the mist providing the cover to escape, the people continued their journey farther into the hills until they reached the mountains, where warriors on horseback stood waiting for them. The woman handed the baby over to one of them.

As the people began to follow the warrior group deeper into the mountains, their image began to fade.

The next thing Lucas saw was a group of men standing on a high mountain plateau. The ground was covered in ice, and the wind was blowing snow into the men's faces. They all wore heavy brown furs to keep the cold out and stood together as a man dressed in black fur approached them. Lucas recognized the face of the man he knew as his father. Einar stopped a few yards from the group and waited for one of the men to come forward and hand him a bundle wrapped in wolves' fur. He carefully took it and pulled away the flap covering the baby's face to see that he was fast asleep.

"His name is Baelan," said the man who had handed the baby over. "He is Dax's son and a direct descendant of Toroun. He is the one sent by the gods and destined to unite our people and protect the true realm. Those who fear the prophecy will try to stop it, and Baelan is to be guided and protected until he is ready to fulfill his destiny."

"I will keep him safe," answered Einar and covered the baby up again. He then secured him under his fur coat before walking back the way he had come.

Alone, Einar walked down the mountain through thick forest until he came to a fast-flowing river and stopped. He put the baby down on the ground while he uncovered a raft from the brush and pulled it closer to the river's edge. He threw a hook with a rope attached to the other side, and the hook lodged itself into a tree.

When he was satisfied that it would hold, he lifted the baby from the ground and laid him down on the raft. He looked behind him as if he had heard something and pushed the raft into the river, stepping on it and grabbing the rope to pull them across. When they reached the halfway point, Einar again looked anxiously behind him. Five riders dressed in all black had appeared at the river's edge. The raft struggled against the river's current, and he had to pull hard to keep it under control. He glanced down at the baby by his feet. The small bundle of fur was getting splashed and had started to slide closer to the edge. Einar held on to the rope with one hand and kneeled to grab the baby, but by doing so, the raft tipped, and both fell into the water.

Lucas felt he couldn't breathe. Einar grabbed the bundle, which had miraculously stayed afloat, and held it up to keep the infant out of the water. They made their way to the other side. Once across, Einar and the baby's journey continued until Lucas saw him knock on the monastery's door. Answers were beginning to form. Then, when Lucas finally understood, he found himself on the hill overlooking the stone.

A soft wind was blowing, moving the tall grass around him and ruffling his hair. He turned to face the thirteen warriors standing in front of the stone, staring at him. He watched as twelve of them pulled their swords and inserted them into the ground before them. They then slowly kneeled, and with both hands on the sword's pommel, they bowed their heads in silence and respect. Toroun had remained standing and waited until Lucas started walking down the hill towards him. It was then that he raised his sword and dropped down to one knee. Unlike the others, he did not insert his sword into the ground. Instead, he laid the sword on both his hands, and held it out in front of him.

Lucas stopped before him. He had been offered the sword once before—when he had died after the chosen test. He had not been able to take it then, but he felt he was ready to accept it now. He touched the cold steel and then gripped the hilt with both hands.

Lucas opened his eyes with the late afternoon sun warming his face. He knew a few hours had passed and that he was alone in the courtyard. Lying still and watching the clouds move overhead, he listened to the sounds around him. He felt very calm and focused, and his mind was clear. Everything made sense.

He climbed down from the stone and made his way over the plank, which had been put back, and to the training courtyard, where he found Dastan observing the warrior monk's practice. Father Ansan was giving some final instructions before finishing up.

Lucas went to stand next to Dastan. "You are one of my family's people," he said. "The man who raised me was not."

"No," said Dastan. "And he was not supposed to raise you either. He was from the hunting tribe and had been asked to bring you across the river and give you to the warrior monks. My brother had a vision that you were supposed to be among them, even though our people had lost contact with the protectors of the stone after the Great Battle. There was no way of knowing if they were aware of your birth, but Einar agreed to take you anyway. When he arrived here, it became clear that they did not know about your existence. They refused to take you and told Einar there was no proof you were the one sent by the gods."

"Why did no one believe him?" Lucas asked Father Ansan, who had joined them.

"News of your birth had not reached us," answered Father Ansan. "And we wrongly thought the stone had not revealed it either."

"But it had?"

Father Ansan nodded. "We now think it did, to a master warrior named Oswall. He was my teacher and the strongest master warrior I have ever had the pleasure to know. He started to travel as he got older and would visit from time to time. The last time that happened was a few months before your birth, and he has not been seen since."

"Then what happened?"

"Einar was unsure of what to do next, after being turned away," continued Dastan. "He sat down some distance from the door and laid you down by his feet. While he sat, slumped forward with his elbows on his knees and his head buried in his hands, he didn't notice you were reaching up to the dagger that hung from his waist. When he looked down, he saw that you had both your hands wrapped around the blade. When he pried your little fingers off it, your eyes met his and you smiled. He was surprised you had not cut yourself. You then looked straight at the door of the monastery. It was clear the monastery was where you were supposed to be. Einar was a man of his word and committed to seeing his mission through.

"Familiar with forging swords, Einar returned to the monastery gates and asked to speak to the warrior monks again. He made a deal with the monks that he would set himself up in the village as a blacksmith and would make their swords. In return, they would assess you when you were older to see if you were, indeed, the one. Einar kept our people informed. The elders thought you to be safe until they learned that the black order had killed him to find you. By that point, the warrior monks had taken you in."

"So, whose orders were the dark order following?" asked Lucas.

"King Boran's father's," said Dastan. "He created the order after you were born."

"Why?"

"To stop the prophecy," answered Father Ansan.

Lucas looked at both of them and wondered. "Can that happen? Is that even possible?"

"It is believed so, and that's why your people want to keep you safe."

CHAPTER 14

When the castle appeared in the distance, Lucas increased his horse's speed. The guards recognized him when he came over the last hill and sounded a horn. The bridges were lowered, and the portcullises pulled up, and he was able to ride in fast. As he crossed the last drawbridge, he saw Egon break into a run towards him.

"Tanner!" yelled Egon. "Get ready to take a horse in!"

Lucas quickly dismounted and handed his horse's reins to Tanner, giving him a quick nod. Tanner looked relieved and happy, while Egon's face showed mixed emotions.

"The king expected your return two weeks ago," he said. "I hope you have a good explanation for your delay."

"I do," answered Lucas. "I bring news of Finton, but something else as well."

Lucas looked up towards the Great Hall, where he saw the king standing by an open window.

"Itan will be pleased to see you," said Egon, looking over his shoulder to follow Lucas's gaze, "and I will be happy to see him stop pacing in front of those windows."

"I didn't realize there was a timeline I needed to be back by," said Lucas.

"No one expected you back for the first four days," replied Egon, "but after a week, the king grew impatient and started to doubt his decision to send you out on your own. In the beginning, I joined him on his walks along the wall, sharing in his desire to see you come riding through the gates with news and to reassure him that your return could occur any day. When that did not happen, the king became more and more short-tempered. Even Amalia, who initially accompanied us, has avoided her father for several days now."

"He will want to hear the news I have for him," said Lucas as they watched the king close the window. "It is not just about Finton, and it was the reason for my delay."

"Do I need to assemble senior officers for this?" asked Egon, turning back to him.

"Yes," answered Lucas. "I think they should be present."

Egon nodded, eyeing him up from top to bottom and noticing the dust and sweat. "Then you'd better clean yourself up first," he said. "You look a mess."

Lucas stood before the washbowl in the entrance of the chosens' dormitory, hastily splashing water over his face and through his hair. He was reaching for the cloth hanging from a hook on the wall when he heard someone coming down the wooden stairs.

"You're back?" called Zera, jumping the last few steps. She had a grin from ear to ear, and Lucas thought she might have embraced him if it wasn't for her brother and Warrick coming up behind him and stopping just inside the entrance.

"I am," answered Lucas, drying his face with the fabric and then rubbing it over his hair. "And it feels good to see everyone again. Once I've spoken with the king—"

"We've all been worried," said Zera. "You were gone so long that we feared Finton got to you."

"He never saw me," replied Lucas. "I took so long because his uncle's house wasn't his final destination."

"Where else did he go?" asked Davis.

"I'll have to tell you later," answered Lucas. "I'm to report to the king right now, so it will have to wait." He hung the cloth back on the hook and noticed a black stain that was likely from leech dye left in his hair.

He wasted little time in heading down to the Great Hall, where he found the king, Egon, Verron, and two other senior officers seated at a table. He noticed their intense stare when he entered, and he thought for sure he was going to get scolded for not returning sooner. He approached the table and stopped on the opposite end from where the king sat and waited for the king to address him. Verron and Egon sat on either side of the king. Their stares seemed to last forever, and Lucas found himself shifting his weight from one foot to another.

"So," said the king finally, "where did Finton go? Did he go to his uncle's house as he said?"

"He did, sire," answered Lucas. He saw the surprise on the king's face. "Or at least I assumed it was his uncle's house. Looked more like a fortified farmhouse, out west, two days' ride from here."

The king nodded. "Yes, that would be his uncle's house, but why did you not return after confirming his arrival there?"

"I decided to linger, to see if anything else of interest might occur. Soon after Finton arrived, a messenger was sent out. It felt strange to me, so I waited two days for his return. When he did, Finton, Eli, and their men all left again to head south for another full day of riding."

Both Verron and Egon turned to look at the king, but Lucas noted that he did not seem surprised.

"You followed them?" asked Itan.

"I did."

"I hope you kept your distance. You know where they went?"

"I recognized the colors on the banners raised above the castle's towers."

"And you saw them go in?"

"I did."

"Lord Killeand?" asked Egon, who had put two and two together.

"Finton and Killeand always got on quite well together," said one of the officers. "I'm not surprised he went to go and visit him."

"He's not visiting," said Lucas. "He wears Lord Killeand's uniform of a general now, and Eli, that of an officer."

The king furrowed his brow and eyed him sternly. Lucas understood what it must look like—Itan suspected that he had not kept his distance in order to know these things. "And you know this, how?" he asked, as if on cue. "Killeand's residence is well-protected by open fields. You cannot approach without being seen. So, I must assume you saw them coming out in their new uniforms?"

"No, sire. I never saw them leave the castle, so I went in."

Five pairs of eyes bored into his. Verron then looked towards the king.

"You were under no orders to approach or engage with anyone," said the king angrily. Only now did Lucas notice how dark the circles were under his eyes. Though only a couple weeks had passed, his face had a gaunt look to it, and it occurred to Lucas how much was at stake here. There was still so much Lucas himself did not understand.

"I talked to no one, and no one saw me," said Lucas. "Two more groups of riders arrived soon after Finton did. No banners, no colors, but all were received formally, as if their arrival had been planned. I got a bad feeling about it. When an opportunity showed up that could get me into the castle unseen, I took it." Egon shifted back in his seat, avoiding eye contact with him. Now that he knew who Lucas was, he would not feel the need to question him about his actions as he would have before.

Lucas explained how he'd run into his old circus group, and how they had helped him. The king was not amused but held his tongue and let him finish.

"That's when I saw Finton and Eli in new uniforms, and most of the soldiers there appeared to be mercenaries, except for one."

Lucas reached in his pocket and pulled out the piece of folded paper with the seal on it.

"He arrived separately from the mercenary soldiers and carried this," he said, unfolding the piece of parchment and handing it to Egon, who sat closest to him. Egon looked at it and passed it to the king.

"How were you able to get this?" asked the king, staring at the wax seal.

"I saw the man who did not look like a mercenary coming out of the room he was staying in. He looked like a man of importance, and I was curious about him. I went in his room to see if I could learn who he was and found the seal and parchment in a bag. There was a block of wax on the desk, so I made the seal."

The king took one look at the parchment and then slammed it on the table in front of him. "King Boran's crest," he said, anger flashing across his face.

They were all dead silent until Verron cleared his throat. "Their families go a long way back. Killeand's grandfather and King Rodin were cousins. They may have stayed in contact. It could mean nothing," he said, but quickly stopped when the king threw him the evil eye.

"It suggests betrayal, Verron," said the king. "Even if nothing comes of it, the fact that Killeand and now Finton might be in contact with him . . ."

"How do we know for sure? Who was it that Lucas saw?" Verron asked.

They all turned to Lucas again, and the king asked if he had managed to get a name.

"No, sire," answered Lucas. "I can only tell you what he looked like. Tall, muscular build, short stubble beard, and he was wearing a gray fur coat." He saw them all shake their heads and try to recall anyone by that description. When none of them could, the king looked up at Lucas again. "Is there anything else you feel the need to report?" he asked.

"Only one thing," answered Lucas. "Everett seemed to think that the unknown man was the one paying for the mercenary soldiers."

"What made him come to that conclusion?" asked Egon. "Did he hear Killeand say that?"

"It doesn't matter who is paying for them," interrupted the king. "The fact that they were with Killeand, and he appears to be conspiring with Boran, tells me enough of his treachery." He turned to Lucas. "Is that all?"

Lucas nodded.

"Very well," said the king. "You can go now, and rest."

Lucas made a bow and caught Egon's eye, and Egon then pushed his seat back. "I'll walk you out," he said.

When they were outside the Great Hall, and the door closed, Egon stopped and waited for Lucas to face him. "You wanted to talk to me?" he asked.

"Yes," answered Lucas. "I believe I can tell you that, on my way back from Killeand's, the dark order attacked me." He watched Egon's reaction and saw him wrinkle his brow. "There were four men, on horseback. I was able to take them out, with help from Dastan." He waited a moment, but Egon remained silent. "He convinced me to follow him back to the monastery. I understand that I am Baelan, here to protect the true king and to unite the people. I was told that you know this as well?"

"Yes," answered Egon. "If I had only known this when you first came here, I could have prevented many of the events that transpired." He narrowed his eyes. "You will have to start trusting me now."

Lucas raised his head slightly. "The mercenary soldiers, at Killeand's . . ."

"What about them?"

"I think they're responsible for all the trouble Lord Meloc has," said Lucas.

"How do you know of Meloc's issues?"

"Everett, my circus friend. He told me about the robberies. He said that people had reported seeing a ghost horse. A black horse with a white mane. They are rare, but there was one in the stables at Killeand's. I don't think it was a coincidence."

Egon took a step back, placing both his hands on his head. He let out a big sigh. "The king is never going to believe this," he said, clearly frustrated. "He's convinced his brother is inventing all this. I'm not sure he will change his opinion based on any hunch you might have. Not without him knowing who you are, and I doubt he will believe that either."

"That's why I didn't say anything," said Lucas, watching Egon pace up and down.

Egon released another sigh. "Let's leave it for now," he said. "At least for the time being. As they are mercenary soldiers, there's no telling who put them up to it and for how long that individual can sustain the cost of hiring them—if that is in fact what we are dealing with."

Lucas did his best to adjust to his new status. He ate at the king's table, but only when he was specifically told to attend. Otherwise, he took his meals with his friends. His bed at the king's barracks was more often than not unslept in, and even though he was no longer required to do chores, he did them anyway.

Lucas reached for the rye bread and broke a chunk off before passing the rest of the loaf to Zera. Davis and Warrick were eating their food across from him. He then dipped the bread into his bowl of stew and took a bite.

"I noticed the king stop you outside the stables this afternoon," said Davis. He had rested his spoon and lifted his head to look at him. "He didn't look pleased."

"He wasn't," answered Lucas before taking another bite from the now broth-soaked bread.

"What did he say to you?"

Lucas swallowed before answering. "He scolded me for working in the stables and told me I was not living up to my new title."

Davis nodded. "He's right."

"I know," said Lucas, "but it's hard. I don't feel I fit in among the senior staff."

"Who cares?" said Warrick, barely looking up from his food. "You carry the mark now and should be eating meat from the bone instead of . . ." He paused and lifted a gray, slippery half-solid substance from his bowl with his spoon and crinkled his nose. "What is in this broth anyway?"

"It's a mushroom, Warrick," responded Zera moving her braid back over her shoulder. "They must have had too many delivered for the king's table for them to end up in our food. They don't keep very well. I remember sorting through them a few times when I was working in the kitchen . . . before the king accepted me as a chosen."

All three of them watched Warrick bring the piece of mushroom into his mouth and chew it slowly. "Doesn't taste much of anything," he said after he had swallowed it. "Perhaps we don't miss that much."

Davis shook his head and turned back to Lucas. "You need to try and adjust to your new status," he said. "You may be carrying the mark, and are above some of the rules you once had to abide by, but angering the king is not a good thing. For you, or for us."

"I'm not intentionally trying to push boundaries," Lucas replied a little too stiffly. Davis had been the only one Lucas noticed reacting on occasion to his elevated status. It made sense—regardless of their closeness, the mark had set him apart.

"Did you get in serious trouble?" asked Zera with marked concern but also, Lucas thought, to diffuse any tension.

"No," answered Lucas. "Egon stepped in and told the king that I needed time to adjust. He suggested I join the elite in combat training from now on in the afternoons and train horses in the early mornings. It would still give me a chance to be near all of you, but at the same time, I would be doing something more fitting to my new role here at the castle."

"How did the king respond?" asked Zera.

"He didn't object," answered Lucas and picked up his spoon.

Training horses had been a job Lucas gladly accepted. He loved riding at dawn, especially on those mornings when the fog would rise, and it felt like he was riding through the clouds.

Lucas heard from Egon that Amalia had spotted him from her window as he rode through the fog, and that she was begging her father to allow her to do the same. The king had been reluctant but, in the end, had relented, and Lucas was told she would join him on the next foggy day. A week later, when that day finally did arrive, he stood with her horse ready, out in the bailey, waiting for her to dart down the steps of the castle, as she was often seen to do whenever anything excited her.

"I've been waking up early for days," she said, appearing in trousers and with a grin on her face. "And it is finally here."

Lucas helped her mount up and then got on his horse. The king ordered four of Egon's guards to accompany them, but as soon as they were outside the gates, Amalia ordered them to stop and wait.

"I'm sorry, my lady, but we have strict orders regarding your protection," one of the guards told her. "We must follow, but we will keep our distance."

"I'm perfectly safe with Lucas," Amalia objected, but the guard shook his head.

"Your father wants them to come with us, my lady," said Lucas. "He will not be pleased."

"I don't care," she responded with a determined face. "I've waited long enough for the fog to come, and I don't want them to chase it off."

"It rises from the ground," smiled Lucas. "They will not chase it off."

Amalia gave him a stubborn look and then kicked her horse to take off. Within seconds, she disappeared in the thick fog, and Lucas sent his horse after her in a hurry.

"You are quite the rider," Lucas told her, when he was able to catch up.

"Thank you," she said, smiling graciously. "Father insisted that I was taught, when I was very little. Same with reading. I remember him telling me once that I would need to be independent if I ever became queen, and mother had objected by saying it was not ladylike."

"And now here you are, riding, just as well as any boy your age," he said, grinning. "I wonder what else you can do!" He spurred his horse on, looking over his shoulder to see her already moving swiftly behind him.

The horses raced next to each other, and Amalia was wearing a serene smile on her face. The first time Lucas had been able to ride like this, in the coolness of the morning, with no one around telling him what to do, he had felt an immense sense of freedom. He realized it must be the same for her. Being a princess, she was rarely left alone, and seldom left the castle. Seeing her so happy now, riding in the thick fog with no one being able to see her, he wanted to make the moment even more special for her. He called out to her and waited until she looked at him. "Do you want to feel free, my lady?" he asked. "Like a bird, flying in the sky?"

Amalia looked at him, puzzled, but nodded her head eagerly.

"Then let go of the reins," he continued, "and lift your arms in the air—like this." He showed her what to do and watched how she first hesitated but then followed him in his actions. "Now close your eyes," he continued. "Feel the rhythm, and trust your horse."

Amalia did what he asked her to do, and the two of them rode until they reached the hills and the fog disappeared. They briefly let their horses catch their breath before turning around and riding back.

"Thank you," said Amalia as they neared the castle. "That was amazing."

"My pleasure," he replied.

The king's guard fell in behind them as they approached the castle. When they crossed the last bridge and rode into the bailey, Lucas saw that something was wrong. The king was in deep conversation with his senior staff, his face vexed. Amalia got off her horse and ran up to her father, but it was as if he didn't even see her. Egon broke away from the group and approached Lucas as he was leading the horses back to the stables. "Hold up," he called, increasing his stride.

"Something wrong?" asked Lucas when Egon caught up with him.

"You need to get ready to ride out this morning," he said. "The robberies on Meloc's land continue, and we just received news that a hamlet was burned down two days ago. The king wants to get down there as soon as possible with a large delegation. Officer Verron will be staying here and is taking charge of the castle. This means you will be in charge of any chosen we bring along. Speak with Verron, select those chosen you are bringing, and get them ready," Egon said. "We'll ride out in two hours."

The castle erupted in activity as everyone assigned to ride out rushed about in preparation. Lucas chose five of the oldest, strongest, and most experienced chosen. He watched Carleton and three elite borns take their place near the front in the column behind the king's guard. He stood waiting to be told where he should go, unsure how his new status affected placement. He saw Egon turn around and look at him questioningly.

"I think you can choose your place, Lucas," said Davis behind him. "Just tell us where you want us to go."

"We will all ride in the back then," he responded.

"You'll get used to making these kinds of decisions," said Davis, leading his horse to the back. "You'll have to."

"I suppose so," answered Lucas and followed him.

CHAPTER 15

It took several days to reach the far south. They had to cross a river and some of Killeand's land to do so. The king kept sending scouts up ahead, to ensure their safety. Now they were only a few hours out from reaching Meloc's castle, and Lucas could tell the king had relaxed. Rolling hills of lush green grass stretched out for miles in front of them, and stands of trees dotted the hilltops. The line of soldiers moved like a slithering snake as they slowly made their way through the landscape. Lucas was still on higher ground and could see that the king was now at the front, leading the entourage, with Egon next to him and Verron right behind. Lucas understood why the king's guard had changed formation a few miles back—the king wanted to be seen as leading when they approached their destination.

A decision that left him more vulnerable, which Lucas did not think was wise.

No one spoke. The only sounds were that of the gentle clanging of swords and the occasional snorting of a horse. The sun was shining in the cloudless sky, and the grass moved gently in the breeze. Lucas peered over his shoulder. Davis and Warrick were casually looking forward, their bodies at ease, swaying to their horses' walk. Tanner and Archer behind them were no different.

Only Zera, who was next to him, followed his every move, but relaxed again when he turned back around in the saddle and tried to settle as well. They were going down a hill and would have a flat road in front of them for a while. The men in front were already there. Those in the back still had an elevated view of what lay before them.

Lucas was letting himself rock to the motion of his horse when, all of a sudden, his senses sharpened, and a burst of energy took hold of him. His horse felt it and jerked up, tensing its neck muscles in the process.

"What is it?" asked Zera, following his gaze to the forest on the far right.

"I don't know yet," answered Lucas. "We have to get closer."

"Do we need to alert the king?"

"No time," said Lucas, suddenly aware of the danger. "Follow me," he shouted to the chosen as he broke away from the column of soldiers in a fast gallop towards the forest.

"Stay with me," called Lucas to Zera and Davis. "Get bows ready!" His shouting alarmed the rest of the soldiers, and they came to an abrupt halt just as Zera and Davis released their first arrows in the direction of the trees.

"Protect the king!" shouted Egon, and the king's guard formed a tight circle around him just as an arrow whooshed through the air from the forest, striking one of them in the arm. A second arrow lodged itself in a shield. Lucas now turned his horse and headed straight for the forest with the chosen in a line and several of the king's guards at their rear.

"Pull your swords," Lucas ordered softly, as they entered the forest. Using his mind, Lucas was able to see that Egon had split his men and sent them around to circle the forest while Lucas and the five chosen worked their way through it. Zera and Davis's arrows had hit their mark on two archers who had been lying in wait, and they saw four more fleeing on foot.

"Warrick, Davis, to the left," shouted Lucas. "The rest with me." He led the way in the pursuit of the fleeing men, jumping over logs to cut them off. He'd already seen the horses the men had waiting for them at the back of the forest with his mind, and if the men were able to get to them, there was a chance they could get away.

The chosen were able to take out three of them and were in pursuit of the fourth, who had nearly made it to the horses. Lucas saw this man look over his shoulder to see how far behind they were. By doing so, he failed to notice the king's guard who stood waiting at the edge of the forest to take him out. He was struck by two swords as soon as he left the tree line.

Egon looked at the number of horses and then at Lucas. "Did you get them all?" he asked.

"Yes," answered Lucas. He looked at the dead man on the ground, whose lifeless eyes were facing the sky. "He was the only one who made it past the tree line."

Egon nodded and followed his gaze. "He is wearing plain clothing," he remarked. "Nothing to identify him by."

"The others were the same," said Lucas. "No colors."

Egon turned to the king's guard. "Check the horses," he ordered. "Find me anything that can tell me who they are or where they came from."

Lucas watched the king's guard walk over to the horses and empty the saddlebags. They scattered the contents out over the ground before unrolling the blankets.

"There is nothing here, sir," reported one of the king's guards.

Just then, the king rode up and stopped his horse next to Egon.

"Mercenaries," said Egon. He looked to Lucas to see if he recognized them, but he shook his head no. "Could have been hired by anyone."

The king cleared his throat. "I don't think another attack is likely, but we can't take any chances. Lucas, take the chosen up ahead to scout and stay up there until we reach Meloc's castle."

The sun was setting when they rode in through the outer gates. The soldiers veered off to the left to set up camp in the outer bailey, and the king rode on to the inner bailey. Lucas waited by the second gate to let the king pass, and watched as a man who looked to be a younger version of the king came out of the castle to greet them. The king was taller, and his brother's brown hair reached his shoulders, but they had the same pointy chin with a stubbly beard. When the king had dismounted and embraced his brother, the chosen ones turned their horses around. They left the castle to do a last sweep of the area, before returning and settling down for the night. Lucas rode with them, though he found it difficult to suppress the yawns. It had been a long day, and he rode with blood still on his hands.

CHAPTER 16

The sun had barely shown itself, and the dew still hung in the air. Itan had woken well before dawn and was now walking the inner walls with his brother. There were six years between them, and they were nothing alike. As the eldest, Itan was made to follow his father's footsteps, whereas Meloc had been raised in a carefree way—of the two of them, he was the dreamer.

Growing up, Itan had sometimes envied his younger brother, especially in those moments when he would see him sitting with a book on his lap, or going out with hunting parties and returning to boast about the trophies they'd brought back, or even just playing with the kittens in the stables, while he was made to go to yet another combat practice or to attend one of his father's weekly council meetings, which could go on for hours.

They stopped on the bridge connecting the inner and outer wall and leaned over it to observe Itan's soldiers camped below. A group of elite borns and chosen stood together in a circle around one boy. He was blindfolded, and the others took it, in turn, to come up to him from different angles. They tried to tap him with sticks on parts of his upper body and he would try to block them. Their relaxed laughter and the fact that no one was trying very hard made it obvious they were playing a game rather than engaging in any kind of training.

"Is that him?" asked Meloc, gesturing to the boy in the middle who blocked most, but not all the attempts. "If it is, then I must say I am greatly disappointed."

Itan shook his head. "No, that is Verron's nephew, Carleton." He watched as Carleton missed a block and got tapped on the shoulder with a stick. The boys laughed, and Carleton took his blindfold off. He smiled as he tried to hand it off to another boy, who refused. With the blindfold raised in his hand, he walked around the circle to find someone else to have a go, but found no one. Some of the boys looked behind them over their shoulders, at someone who Itan guessed was out of his view.

"The center stage is waiting here for you," called Carleton, holding up the blindfold. "If I'm willing to stand here and be laughed at in the name of entertainment, perhaps you can as well."

Itan leaned over the wall to see who Carleton was calling out to, and it did not surprise him when he saw Lucas walking up. "That's him," he said, when the circle of boys opened to let Lucas walk through. "That is Lucas."

"I still cannot believe you gave a chosen the king's mark," said Meloc. "I remember how you thought father had lost his mind when he gave it to Egon."

"He *had* lost his mind," Itan reminded his brother. "He was unwell and wasn't thinking straight. He'd made several poor choices already, prior to that."

"You mean like when he signed a contract with the Hammonds? To let them run the mines up north?"

Itan nodded. "That was one of them. We all knew it would make them richer than it should."

"Yet *you* claim to have been thinking straight," said Meloc. "From what Egon told me, the boy was about to be severely disciplined when you decided to give him the mark. That is not the Itan I know. You've gone soft, bestowing mercy on a guilty boy like that."

"I had a choice to make, between someone who had saved my life and the lives of many others, and someone who had served me for many years, controlled a vast number of my soldiers, and carried a superior title. In the end, it was a case of whose loyalty I would lose, and I had every indication that I had already lost Finton's some time ago."

They watched Carleton put the blindfold on Lucas, and Carleton asked to be handed a second one, which he also put on him.

"Why the second blindfold?" asked Meloc.

"You will see," answered Itan.

A crowd of soldiers started to gather around when they noticed Lucas was about to play the game. Three boys came forward and started to circle him until one stepped in and started the attack. Lucas blocked and swung around to block the next and the next. They started coming faster now, and two more boys joined in, but none were able to get close enough.

"I'm impressed by what I see. He could be the one, you know," said Meloc. "The child written about in the prophecies. 'When the bright star shines in the night sky, the one who will pledge loyalty to the true realm and unite the people will be born.'"

"There are many bright stars," answered the king. He kept looking down to watch Lucas, but his body had tensed up. "You know I don't believe in prophecies. Lucas was raised by warrior monks in the early part of his life, and this is how they train to become a master."

"Some prophecies have proven themselves to be true," continued Meloc. "And there is only one bright star appearing every hundred years. That was fifteen years ago."

Itan gave a deep sigh and backed away from the wall. "Just because he's of the right age doesn't make it true," he said, continuing the walk. "Prophecies are the words of one person who believes he can foresee the future. Many interpretations can be read from them, and we only read the one we are willing to believe."

CHAPTER 17

Lucas followed Carleton into a small circular room on the second floor of the back tower. With the only natural light coming from two narrow windows, the lit candles, resting in sconces along the walls, were necessary. They'd been called to attend a meeting, with staff from both the king and Meloc in attendance. Lucas took his place at the long rectangular table, as did Carleton, and when the last officers entered, the doors closed.

One of Meloc's generals unfolded a large map and spread it out.

"I've been trying to keep track of where and when this plundering occurs," began Meloc. He pointed to dots on the map, each marked with a number. "The numbers indicate the order of events. There are two areas the robberies happen most frequently. Over here, on the north side, and then way back here, in the south. The first time I received a report, it came from the north side. The second took place way down south, and so it jumps back and forth. Some nights we have two occurrences only hours apart."

Lucas noticed Egon narrow his eyes and shift his position across the table.

"What is the distance between the two areas?" asked Egon.

"Anywhere between ten and a hundred and fifty miles," answered Meloc.

"What is the distance when you have two on the same night?"

"The same night?"

"Yes. I mean to ask, is it possible for one group to be responsible for these attacks, or are we dealing with two groups, possibly even more?" asked Egon.

Meloc stared down at the map and placed a finger on two of the dots. "Well," he said, "the first time we had two attacks, they were about ten to fifteen miles apart."

"Which is doable for one group," interjected Lucas.

Meloc looked at him and agreed. "Yes, absolutely. That pattern continued for a few nights, but recently, incidences have been farther apart. One night it was nearly thirty miles between them. Which, at a fast pace, is doable in a few hours during the day, but not at night. I believe we are still dealing with one group—my general here believes we are dealing with two."

"Because of the distance between them?" asked Egon.

"It doesn't matter whether it is one organized group or multiple little bands," said Itan. "What matters is how are we going to predict where they will strike next. We can dispatch enough patrol troops to both areas and catch them in the act if we know where they are going to be. Have you tried to figure that out?"

Meloc nodded. "Yes, I have sent patrols out, but the robberies appear to be random. It could be a farmhouse one day and a merchant the next."

"Nothing happens at random," urged the king. "There is always a reason, so there has to be a pattern of some sort."

Lucas saw some officers nod in response, and others were shaking their heads at the daunting task of determining where to send troops. Then, several heads bowed over the map, and fingers were drawing lines between the dots. Lucas stood at the back and had watched and listened in silence. The officers had all crowded the table, and he had not been able to get a good look at the map, but that didn't matter. "They take goods, right?" he said, loudly enough that he knew he would be heard. Meloc's general peered over his shoulder to see who had spoken and looked annoyed. Unfazed, and understanding what his youth must look like, in terms of his experience, Lucas continued. "How much is stolen in one night?"

The general began to object, but then Lucas heard Meloc speak up. "Do we know the specifics on this, general?"

The general took a deep breath. "Mostly food, some livestock, some valuables," he answered reluctantly.

"How much?" asked Lucas.

Again, the general gave him a look of irreverence and didn't seem to want to answer. Lucas caught the king's eye briefly before he turned to the general.

"Your insolence towards Lucas is unacceptable," said the king. "I believe you should answer him. I think he may be on to something that you have overlooked."

"Please answer the boy's questions, general," said Meloc. "He is the one my brother gave the mark to, and I am curious to see if that was the right decision."

Lucas noticed brief glances between the king and Meloc and saw the general straighten up and turn to him, a look of surprise on his face. "I apologize," said the general. "I had not realized who you were." When Lucas nodded agreeably, he continued. "You were asking how much is stolen during one heist?"

Lucas nodded. "How heavily they load their horses will determine the speed of their travel afterward," explained Lucas. "Or are they taking substantial enough of a load that they require a wagon?"

There was a silence in the room before Meloc answered. "Yes, in some cases, there was enough taken that it would have required a wagon."

"Then we don't need to know where they are going to strike next," continued Lucas. "We need to discover where they are hiding the loot."

"And how we would go about doing that?" asked the general. He stepped aside to let Lucas through to look at the map.

"Wagons require roads," said Lucas, pointing to several roads on the map. "If we can determine which roads are most likely used to move a wagon unseen at night or with the least amount of attention, then we can stake those out. I only see several roads on this map that seem suitable, and only three of those come together. I am fairly certain they will lead us to their storage place."

"I am impressed with your theory," said Meloc. "I am *not* impressed that we failed to come up with that ourselves," he said, looking to his generals and officers.

"That is because you were focused on catching the thieves," said the king. "Not on recovering the stolen goods. I believe Lucas has a point. Finding out where the goods are taken might be easier than predicting where the next attack will take place."

"I agree," answered Meloc. "But why narrow it down to just these three roads? I can see several that could be used as well, and some of them link up."

"The people want these thieves caught," said Lucas. "I understand they have been reporting any suspicious behavior, but that none of the reports were related to the storage of goods?"

"That's right," answered Meloc. "So, why do you think that is?"

"I don't think the goods stay here. They are taken out of your territory. These three roads link up into one single road that leads out west," explained Lucas, pointing to a location on the map. "This is where I think they're taking it. We find the goods, and we find the people responsible." Lucas looked towards the king, who gave him an approving nod.

"That's on Killeand's land," remarked one of the officers. "Why not ask him if he's had any reports?"

"Getting a message to him would take too long," said Meloc. "My brother is here now and ready to deal with this. We have enough men to stake out all of these roads and find out where they are hiding the goods."

Lucas shook his head.

"Is that not exactly what you said to do?"

"I think Lucas is going to tell you that too many soldiers on the roads will draw unwanted attention," said Egon. "Word that the king has arrived has no doubt spread as well, and anyone thieving will be on the lookout for patrols. I propose to only send Lucas with the chosen ones, as well as Carleton and Rhys. They can handle the stakeout and report back any suspicious activity. Once we know where they are, who they are, and how many we are dealing with, we can send in more troops to go after them." Egon turned to Lucas. "Is that what you might have suggested?"

"Yes," he said, nodding. "We can send them out in civilian clothing and split them up into groups. It sounds like a solid plan to me."

Lucas and Egon's proposal was accepted, and the scouting group rode out that same afternoon. They traveled in an easterly direction first, in case anyone was watching the castle, and then split up. Lucas took his group north to stake out two of the three roads they had decided on, and Carleton took Rhys to the southern road. Upon reaching the first road, Lucas left Davis, Tanner, and Archer at several different strategic locations—and where there were decent hiding spots—before doing the same with the second road, where he left Zera and Warrick. They would remain at their posts for the next two nights to watch any activity on the roads and would then all come to the appointed meeting point—a junction where the three roads came together, and where Lucas and Carleton were going to do their stakeout together.

Lucas whistled when he reached the crossing. Carleton was already there and whistled a reply. They hid their horses and then settled behind a fallen log. From there, they had a full view of the junction.

That first night, Carleton and Lucas took turns watching the road, but they saw no one. During the morning, they saw a few wagons pass, but none of them looked suspicious enough to follow.

"I want you to know I never shared Eli's beliefs about you," Carleton said later that afternoon, when they were watching the road together. He had cut an apple with his knife, and his dark eyes locked onto Lucas as he held a slice out to him. "You should know . . . I never agreed with the way Finton treated you. I tried to talk to Eli—"

"I know," Lucas said, taking the apple from him. "You stood by my side when it mattered most. I have not forgotten that."

He was about to say more but stopped. A slight sound that didn't sound like the movement of an animal had caught his attention, and he motioned to Carleton to hold still. He then put a finger to his lips and pointed to the road. They could hear the creaking of a wagon struggling under the strain of its cargo and ducked, leaving only enough of their faces exposed to watch it pass. Two people were sitting on the front bench and both had swords by their sides. The cargo itself was covered with a canvas tarp secured with rope.

"What do you think?" said Carleton. "They don't look like farmers or merchants to me, and their wagon seems overloaded."

"Yes," responded Lucas. "I don't think they are going far with it."

"Do you want to follow that one?" whispered Carleton. They had talked about what to do if a wagon passed and had decided that one of them would follow it while the other would wait for the others to get to their appointed spot.

"I think so," answered Lucas, keeping himself low to the ground as he backed away from their hiding spot. He retrieved his horse and, once he had quietly mounted, pursued the wagon from a safe distance.

Two hours passed, at which point he moved off the road when he noticed the wagon had stopped and pulled over to the side. Both men remained on the wagon and appeared to be waiting. Then, when darkness fell, Lucas heard a second wagon approach. It slowed down, and Lucas could hear one of the drivers talking to the horses. "Whoa, whoa," he said to stop them. The wagon came to a halt next to the first one.

"Good evening," greeted one of the men from the first wagon. "You finally made it, then? We started to think you weren't coming."

"It wasn't an easy task. We had to take more caution with the arrival of the king in the area. I do not doubt that he is here at the request of Lord Meloc, and if his soldiers had stopped us—well, we would have had no reasonable explanation as to how we acquired some of the items in our wagon."

"Here," said a man from the first wagon. Lucas saw him passing a jug over to the second wagon. "Looks like you fellows could use this."

The men continued to talk. They shared food and drink with each other.

As quietly as he could, Lucas retreated through the brush. Retrieving his horse from where he had secured it to a tree, he made his way back up the road. He wasn't surprised when, at length, he saw a single rider coming down the road. Carleton! He'd had a feeling Carleton would follow him, and he stepped onto the road to stop him before the men on the wagons could spot him.

"They've stopped," explained Lucas when they were both safely off the road. "Just a little ways up."

"Why?"

"I don't know, but the wagon I followed is there too, and they are taking a break—it's clear that they are working together. Did the second one come from the southern road as well?"

"No, from one of the northern roads," answered Carleton.

"Two separate instances of plundering then. I think we got them."

"I think so, too," said Carleton, smiling. "Now we have to wait and see where they will lead us." He crept closer to the road and looked over his shoulder at Lucas.

"They are moving on," said Lucas, mounting his horse. He waited for Carleton before getting back on the road.

When darkness was surrounding them, they stepped off the main road again onto a small side path. Leaving their horses behind, they continued on foot until they saw the light of torches and heard voices ahead. A big barn came into view, and the men were in the process of pushing one of the loaded wagons inside. The second remained outside. With the large barn door wide open, Lucas caught a glimpse of the crates of goods lining the walls in towering stacks.

When the wagon was in and the barn doors closed and locked up, the two cart horses were tied to the back of the second wagon, and all four men got onto it to continue down the side road. Less than half a mile down, they came to a farmhouse with another large barn nearby. They were met by some men coming out of the house who helped them push the second wagon into that barn. When they finished, all of them went inside and, after a while, Lucas could hear laughter and talk.

"You were right," commented Carleton. "They *are* storing their loot."

"I wonder if they keep it here for very long though," said Lucas.

"What makes you say that?"

"They've been plundering for months, right?" started Lucas. "There doesn't seem to be enough in the barns to suggest that."

"You think they have other storage places?"

"Possibly, or it gets moved on from here and sold or distributed," answered Lucas. "Maybe that's why they didn't offload the wagons tonight. We can find out in the morning."

"The others will be at the meeting place at dawn," said Carleton. "If we both stay to see what happens with the loot, they won't know where to find us. So why don't you go and get them, and I will stay here to keep an eye on things?"

"Are you sure?"

"Don't look so worried," said Carleton, flashing a smile. "You don't think I can handle this?"

Lucas did not like the idea at all, but he didn't want to offend Carleton by giving him the impression he wasn't capable. "I'll be back as soon as I can," he responded and, when Carleton nodded, he began to back away, watching for any twigs that might snap under his feet.

Lucas made it back to the junction before dawn and, one by one, the other boys and Zera arrived soon after, all except for Warrick. Most of them reported seeing the two wagons pass, but some reported seeing riders on horseback accompanying them.

"How many riders?" asked Lucas. He suddenly had a bad feeling about having left Carleton alone.

"I saw three," said Davis.

"Six on the southern road," answered Rhys.

Lucas paced the ground and rubbed his hand through his hair. If those riders were not with the wagons, then where had they gone?

When Warrick finally made it, he was able to confirm that he had seen riders abandon the wagon to take a different road towards the west. Fearing they were in over their heads, Lucas sent Warrick for backup while he took the rest of the boys and Zera back to the farm where he had left Carleton.

It was mid-afternoon when they arrived at the spot Lucas had left Carleton, but he wasn't there. The house looked abandoned, and the door to the barn unlocked. The wagon was gone, along with everything else that had been inside.

"Where do you think Carleton went?" asked Rhys.

"I suspect they were moving out, and he decided to follow," answered Lucas, stepping out onto the road towards the barn. The others followed while they checked the house. He sent Archer and Tanner to check the first barn, and they soon returned to say that it was also empty.

With his back to Rhys, Lucas knelt to the ground and studied the tracks on the road, then closed his eyes to focus on surveying the surrounding area. A caravan of six heavily loaded wagons was not far out and moving west. They were on open ground, but he did not see Carleton following them. He stood up quickly, turning to face the others. "The wagons left not too long ago," he said, rushing to his horse. "But they're not our concern. We have to get to Carleton."

"Maybe he's following the wagons?" called Rhys after him.

"He's not," answered Lucas, mounting up. "There's another farm a mile down the road."

"How . . .?" started Rhys, but Lucas saw Davis put a hand on his arm to stop him from asking further questions.

"He knows," said Davis, rushing past him to get to his horse. "And we have to hurry."

They rode half a mile before Lucas pulled them off the road. They continued another few hundred yards through the brush before dismounting and moving forward on foot. Soon a clearing came into view, with a house in the middle and several horses tied up to a fence nearby. Lucas could see another big barn on the far left, some ways off, and facing the front of the house. He also saw what he had not wanted the others to know yet, but a chilling howl of pain made them all aware. They immediately set off towards the front of the house and watched from the cover of the brush surrounding it. From this vantage point, they saw a group of armed men. In their center, they had Carleton. He was down on his knees with his hands tied behind his back. His face was bloody, and he was being hit repeatedly with the hilt of a sword held by one of the men who stood near him.

"Carleton!" whispered Rhys. "We have to do something. They are killing him."

They watched as the mercenary circled Carleton and asked him another question. When Carleton didn't answer, he was struck again. He doubled over with the force of the blow. Pain was written all over his face when he straightened himself up and spit blood out of his mouth.

Lucas looked at Rhys. The elite born was tight-lipped and tense, ready to charge forward. The chosen, on the other hand, were looking around for options.

"We are outnumbered two to one," said Zera. "Even with the element of surprise, it will be too risky."

Davis was staring at the ground. "I hate to agree, but yes. We'll have to wait for Warrick to come with reinforcements."

Rhys shook his head. "Who knows how long that will take."

"Maybe we should ride up? We are king's soldiers, after all," said Rhys. "Once they realize that, they might just release him."

"Carleton's already told them that, I'm sure," answered Zera. "It is not stopping them. The king's name means nothing to mercenaries. And our youth and plain clothing won't lend us any additional authority. Anyone can claim to be a king's soldier, at that."

Lucas looked closer at the group of men and realized something. There was someone in the group he recognized. "I think I might be able to buy us some time," he said.

"How?" asked Rhys.

"By offering a trade. Carleton for me."

Zera's mouth dropped open, and she shook her head wildly. The others all looked at him as if he had lost his mind.

"Look," said Lucas, before anyone could say anything. "We need to get Carleton out of there, and we don't have much time. Zera, did you not tell me once that mercenaries are money-driven? That they'll work for anyone as long as the price is right?"

Zera nodded. "You are not thinking of offering yourself up as ransom, are you?"

Now it was Rhys who shook his head. "If you go put that idea in their heads," he said, "you'll have just given them two to bargain with."

"It will not come to any deal," continued Lucas. "All we need is to convince them of a ransom trade and have them send Carleton back to the king with their offer. Once he is clear, we can do the rest."

"I don't like it," said Rhys. They all watched Carleton receive another blow. "But I'll go with it since I do agree we cannot wait."

"Then wish me luck," said Lucas.

CHAPTER 18

"Are you alone?" Carleton heard the leader of the group ask for the twentieth time. "How much does the king know?"

"If what he's saying is true and he's even *of* the king's men," another member of the group grumbled. "Looks like any dirty kid to me."

The leader turned to the man who had spoken. "One more word out of you, and you'll be trading places with this dirty kid," he spat.

Carleton remained silent and looked down at his opened and bloodied shirt. Four buttons were missing. They must have been torn off when he was pulled from his horse and dragged to the house. How was he going to explain this to the king? He had foolishly assumed that the road was clear after he watched the wagons move out and head west that morning.

"Answer me!" shouted the leader and swung his arm back.

The blow of the hilt of the sword that struck Carleton's head was more painful than the previous ones and he didn't know how much more he could take.

"Last chance," said the leader. "How many of you are there?"

"I told you already—I'm alone," gasped Carleton, swallowing the blood seeping down his throat. More blood streamed down his face from a cut on the side of his head. It pooled in his left ear and made everything sound far away. "We always work alone. To cover more ground." His face was swollen, and one eye had nearly shut, and his body ached from being dragged, but he still tried to stay strong.

He was preparing himself for another hit when he heard a familiar voice.

"No, we don't," he heard the voice say. "There are always two of us."

Carleton lifted his head with great difficulty and saw the men draw their swords and turn their heads towards the road. He saw Lucas advancing warily, his sword out in front of him. Their eyes met, but then Lucas turned his attention to the men, and he wondered if Lucas had lost his mind. Where were the chosen and Rhys? Did they have a plan? Carleton carefully scanned the edge of the forest but saw nothing.

"I am offering a trade," he heard Lucas say. "Me for him."

The man in front of Carleton—who he could only assume was their leader—laughed. "You might be the biggest fool I've yet to meet," he said. "What's to stop me from having the both of you killed?"

"You don't want to kill me," he heard Lucas say. His voice was steady and confident, and Carleton could detect no fear in it.

"And why not?"

"Because I'm worth more alive to the right people," answered Lucas and then pointed towards one of the men within the group. "You can ask him! He knows."

Carleton turned his head, as did everyone else, to look at the man Lucas was gesturing to. It took him only a moment to recognize that he used to be a delivery man for the castle. Why had he not made the connection until now? He had seen him drive in supply wagons and unload goods into the storage room near the kitchen for years. He looked different with his mustache and stubbly beard. He wondered how Lucas knew him, as the man had stopped delivering not long after Lucas arrived.

"Is that true?" asked the leader. "You know him?"

"I do," answered the delivery man. "And yes, he is right—there are people who would want him alive."

The leader eyed Lucas from head to toe before walking to the delivery man to have a quiet word. "All right," he said after a brief moment. "I've heard your name mentioned before, but why should we make a trade when we can take you and kill him?"

Carleton looked at Lucas and felt the presence of the leader close to him. There was no doubt in his mind that he would make good on his word and put a knife to his throat in an instant. He could see that Lucas was aware of this as well, but he did not let that show.

"I will not go with you willingly if you don't let him go," said Lucas. "I will fight you to the death, and that would not be in your best interest. Besides, my friend here will save you the trouble of sending one of your own to the king to report the hostage situation. You can leave one or two men here to wait for the coin that the king will surely pay for me."

The leader rubbed his chin and walked a few steps away, visibly contemplating his options. Carleton had no idea why Lucas would indicate that people would pay money for him and offer a trade. The only person who might do that would be the king, but if all they had to do was give these men the impression that they could make a great deal of money, then he was going to play his part. He dropped his head down and pretended to be in worse shape than he was, and Lucas picked up on it.

"We can be well on our way before my friend here will get far," said Lucas, his voice bitter. "You've beaten him to a pulp."

Carleton felt the leader's eyes on him. "Seems like we might have," he responded. "All right then—hand over your sword, and we have a deal."

"Not until he is mounted up and is on his way," said Lucas sternly. "*Then* we will have a deal."

Carleton heard someone get the order to fetch his horse, and a moment later, he was lifted onto it. He leaned forward on his horse's neck, struggling to stay on, and watched Lucas throw his sword on the ground to give himself up. Lucas made a slight movement with his head that told him to get out of there while two men were tying his hands in front of him. Reluctantly, Carleton grabbed the reins and kicked his horse into a gallop to get out of the way. He had not made it far up the road when he met Rhys.

"I will help you get back to Meloc's castle," he said, but Carleton shook his head.

"No," said Carleton. "Lucas needs you more than I do. I can make it alone."

CHAPTER 19

L ucas let the men tie his hands but kept an eye on his sword, which was lying a few feet from him. He saw the leader look at him and then at the forest around the farm. He raised his eyebrows, and then cursed under his breath. "It's a trap," he roared. We're surrounded."

He started shouting orders to his men, but it was too late. Lucas kicked the two men who were holding him out of the way and dove towards his sword. He landed with his hands on the hilt, but before he could lift it, he was kicked hard in the ribs and flew off to the side. He rolled onto his back and saw the leader towering above him, his sword raised and his face distorted with anger.

Lucas knew this man no longer worried about the consequences of killing him. But just when he was about to let his sword strike Lucas in the chest, an arrow hit him through his neck, stopping him in his tracks.

Lucas rolled out of the way, grabbing his sword just as the leader sank to his knees. The others now came charging out of the tree line, and Lucas saw Rhys coming towards him from the road. He raised his hands, and Rhys swung his sword to cut the rope in passing. Lucas then jumped up to join the fighting. Most of the boys were still on horseback, but Zera and Davis had leapt off their horses and were chasing three men who were fleeing into the farmhouse.

Lucas located his target and ran towards it. "He's mine," he shouted to Tanner, who was in a fight with the delivery man. Tanner stepped away and found another fight nearby to engage himself in.

Lucas watched the eyes of the former delivery man grow large with fear when he saw him approach. He looked around to see if anyone could help him, but when he saw no one, he started backing away towards the barn. Lucas was in no rush, though he could feel his blood boiling—this was the man responsible for giving information to the dark order and for tainting the water barrel that had made them all sick. He had seen it when the stone revealed the answers to his questions. No one ever suspected it could have been as simple as that, an outsider dropping poison in the barrel. To this day, it had remained a question that had hung like a black cloud over the army.

Just as the man was about to round the corner of the barn, Lucas heard the thundering sound of horses' hooves coming from the road. It was Warrick, with the king's guard! The moment they pulled their horses to a halt, they joined the fighting. Lucas didn't doubt the mercenaries would soon be dead or on their knees, begging for mercy, with the king's guard here. He concentrated again on his target in front of him.

The delivery man had clearly noticed Lucas's distraction and was coming at him, sword raised. Lucas blocked, and a bitter fight ensued. Only when the delivery man paused to look at the cut he'd received on his arm, did Lucas take a deep breath and kick the sword out of the man's hand. It dropped to the ground, and he pinned the man against the wall, his sword aimed at his chest.

"Why did you do it?" asked Lucas. "The king employed you, paid you, fed you . . . and you placed mistrust among his troops. And what did I ever do to you? I offloaded your wagons while you went to the kitchen to chat up the scullery maid and consume a meal."

The delivery man looked at him, puzzled. "How did you know?" he asked.

Lucas didn't answer. At that time, he had made it his business to know since Amalia would often come to see him.

"I never meant for you to get hurt," continued the delivery man. "They threatened to kill my family if I did not provide them with information. I thought the underground river would be the easiest way to get you out of the castle alive. How was I to know the river had changed its course?"

The man's eyes pleaded for mercy, and Lucas backed off. Perhaps he was telling the truth. When he saw Zera come around the corner, Lucas took a step back and turned to walk away. He saw Zera trying to shout a warning, but he had already seen how the delivery man had waited for his opportunity to pick up his sword. Lucas ducked, missing the man's sword from striking him in the back. He spun around on his heel and, with both hands on the hilt, sliced clean through the delivery man's neck. He then stood unmoved as the man's body slumped to the ground. He watched the head roll down a bit of slope and come to a stop at the side of the barn—the man's lifeless eyes staring upward to the darkening clouds above.

Zera walked up to him and stopped by his side. "I didn't know you had the strength and speed to separate a man's head from his body," she said softly as she stared down at the still face of the delivery man.

"I didn't either," replied Lucas. His body was trembling from the force that had rushed through him, and he felt nauseous by the sight of the carnage he caused.

"How are we to explain this to those who don't know who you are?" asked Zera. "It's near impossible to decapitate a moving target with such precision."

"I don't know," answered Lucas trying to collect himself. It had been a long time since he'd felt so intensely affected by the energy that had surged through his body. He used to vomit when that happened, and he had needed to learn to control his reaction. "Perhaps we should keep this between us?"

"Yes," answered Zera. "For that, we'll have to hide the body." She placed a hand on his shoulder and turned him to face her. "Why don't you go before Egon sends someone to come looking for you? I'll get Davis and Warrick to help me take care of this."

Lucas nodded. He hated leaving Zera to deal with the gruesome task, but she was right. There was a reason why executions by beheading were done by tying someone down and placing their head on a block—it stopped the person from moving and increased the chances for a clean cut. Even then, it sometimes took more than one blow, Lucas knew.

Lucas walked back to the farmhouse, where Egon was taking account of the number of dead mercenaries, and Carleton was sitting on the steps of the house.

"How're you doing?" asked Lucas, taking a seat next to him.

"I've been better," answered Carleton. "But I could have been a great deal worse if it had not been for you."

"You brought reinforcements," said Lucas, gesturing to the king's guard.

"Met them on the road," said Carleton. "And apparently, Warrick met Egon before he got to the castle."

"It all worked out then," said Lucas and put a gentle hand on Carleton's shoulder before standing up.

Carleton tilted his head slightly to one side to be able to look up at him with his good eye. "You told those mercenaries that you were worth more alive to the right people," said Carleton. "And that Itan's former delivery man knew. What did you mean by that?"

"Nothing," lied Lucas. "I simply tried to keep us from getting killed."

"I don't believe you," said Carleton, turning away from him to look at the king's guard. They were busy loading bodies onto a wagon. "Will you ever tell me what your conversation with these men was about?" he asked.

"One day," said Lucas and walked away to help with the cleanup.

Upon their return, Carleton had done most of the talking, much to Lucas's relief. He explained how Lucas had convinced the mercenary soldiers that he was valuable to the king because he carried the mark and that they would be paid for his safe return if he went free. Meloc had listened but had never taken his eyes off Lucas and was watching him with what felt, to Lucas, like too much interest.

Egon had picked up on it as well and met with Lucas in the stables.

"He is a believer of the prophecy," explained Egon. "He doesn't believe in coincidences and probably feels there is more to the story than what Carleton told." He paused for a moment. "As do I. But I am sure you have your reasons for not telling me how you knew where to find these mercenaries."

"Do you think he knows?" asked Lucas. "About me?'"

"No," answered Egon. "I think he is more fascinated by the fact that his brother gave the mark to someone so young. That said, Meloc has always been looking for the one, so I think it's best if you stay out of his sight and don't draw attention to yourself."

"You don't think the king needs to know who I am?" asked Lucas.

"I do," answered Egon, "but now is not the time. I don't feel Itan is ready to accept that the fate of his kingdom may lay solely in your hands, and I haven't figured out what my role in that will be."

"What do you mean?" asked Lucas. He was looking at a horse that had its ears back. It was trying to bite the horse in the next stall over, to keep it from reaching over to get his hay. When it succeeded, nipping the other in the neck, both horses shrieked and reared.

"As a former chosen," answered Egon after the horses went back to eating hay as if no argument had taken place, "I'm bound to protect you, but my moral duty lies with the king. What if the two are not aligned?"

Lucas wanted to reply, but he wasn't sure how. The thought that Itan might not be the true king had not occurred to him. "I should wait to tell the king then?" he asked.

"I believe that would be for the best," answered Egon. "At least until he needs to know, or it becomes obvious to everyone that you were born with a unique purpose."

Over the next few days, Egon made sure to send Lucas on every patrol that left the castle and found tasks for him to do when he returned, but this only seemed to fuel Meloc's suspicions more. On the final evening, before they were due to leave for the return trip home to Itan's castle, Meloc decided to hold a banquet to celebrate their success in putting a stop to the plundering. He invited everyone involved.

"He has invited us as well?" asked Warrick when Lucas told the chosen about the banquet. They were all sitting together at the soldiers' camp in the outer bailey, sharing two whetstones, in order to sharpen their swords.

"That's what I was told," answered Lucas. "You'll be sharing a table with the elite borns."

"Where will you sit?" asked Zera, holding her sword up to inspect the blade. "Will you be allowed to sit with us?" She lowered her sword and passed the whetstone to Tanner.

"I doubt that very much," answered Davis before Lucas could. He was sliding the whetstone he was using in even strokes along the edge of the blade.

"Me too," interjected Warrick. "It'll be the king's table for him!"

"I can ask," said Lucas. "With his brother there and all the high-ranking officers, it will be a full table already."

"That's out of the question," replied the king in a sharp tone when Lucas asked if he could sit with the chosen and elites. He had stopped the king, who was already decked out in his best formal attire, in the hallway on his way to the banquet hall. "You are to sit at my table," he continued, "where you belong. It will be frowned upon if I allow you to sit with the chosen when I wasn't in favor of allowing them to come in the first place."

"Then may I be excused from the banquet?" asked Lucas.

The king stared him down. "Why would you even suggest something so outrageously outside of what is reasonable?" he asked. "Because I'm not giving in to your demands? Do you wish to embarrass me?"

"No, sire," answered Lucas. "It's just that I don't feel I'll have anything to add to the adult conversation, and, if you recall, Meloc's officers did not appreciate it when I spoke at the meeting. I think they will be more than pleased if I do not sit with them."

The king sighed and stepped closer. "Look," he said. "You are the reason we put a stop to this thieving, and I don't care how incompetent that made my brother's officers feel. If they are to be reminded of that by laying eyes on you while we celebrate tonight, then so be it." He paused and placed a hand on Lucas's shoulder. "Don't let your age stand in your way of claiming ownership of your accomplishments," he continued. "You deserve to sit at my table, and I want you there."

"Yes, sire," replied Lucas and watched the king give him a nod before walking on. Lucas stayed behind for a few minutes, before following with a heavy sigh.

Lucas found himself seated in between two of Meloc's officers, with Meloc close by and the king on the far side of the table. Plates piled high with fresh fruit and meats were brought in by the dozen, and Lucas watched how the chosen ones—at a separate table from him—eagerly tucked in. He wished the king had allowed his request to sit with them, so he could enjoy eating the food and engage in conversation instead of having to listen to local gossip he knew nothing about.

Egon gestured for him to eat from across the table, and he reluctantly took a piece of meat. He was not hungry, but Egon's gesture warned him that he should not draw attention to himself. He forced himself to eat while the king and Meloc and the handful of generals seated near them were engaged in a bitter discussion about the low rent charged to tenant farmers and whether higher rent would encourage the growth of more crops. Finally, the topic seemed to bore Meloc as well, and he changed the subject. Lucas had been observing the space and only partially listening to the conversation, so he was caught off guard when he heard his name. The conversation had returned to gossip, and he had not noticed when it had looped back around to the current issues the king faced regarding his people's safety.

"I'm sorry, my lord—you asked me something?" he said, turning towards Meloc, who was waiting for him to answer.

"I was asking your opinion about the possibility that we may not have caught all those responsible for the plundering."

Lucas shrugged. "I don't think anyone can know that for sure," he answered. "We will have to wait and see if the raids continue."

"Yes," said Lord Meloc. "You are probably right on that." He kept his eyes on him, and Lucas felt the question had only been a way to get his attention and to get everyone else at the table to put their focus on him as well. "Tell me," he started. "I was told that you spent time with an order of warrior monks and that it was they who taught you to fight. Is that correct?"

"Yes," answered Lucas casually. "That's right." He tried to show more interest in his food and started eating. Not that he thought it would do much good—Meloc had everyone's attention now and continued.

"Fascinating," he said. "It is my understanding that you cannot even become a warrior monk unless you are specially selected and have been an ordained monk first. This means you must have lived within the walls of the monastery and given your vows before they would even consider you. My brother here has not questioned your story, but I have an issue with it." Meloc looked at Itan before returning his gaze to Lucas. "Can you enlighten me as to how monks who have little or no contact with the outside world became interested enough in a young boy to want to teach him their ways? You must have been rather special to them."

Lucas took a deep breath. He felt an interrogation had begun for which he would need to be careful with his answers. Meloc was clever and would try and ask the right questions to fuel his suspicion that he may have found the one. Lucas saw Egon shift in his seat and clear his throat to say something.

"Are you questioning Lucas in order to determine if he has been telling the truth, Lord Meloc?" asked Egon. "Because, if you are, I can tell you that his story was verified."

Meloc shook his head. "No. I am merely asking *how* it could be true. What possible motivation could they have in wanting to teach a child? That's the part I take interest in, and I am hoping Lucas can enlighten us."

"Answer my brother, Lucas," said the king when he remained silent. The king was looking at him with a renewed interest. Having been in his brother's companionship these last few days had no doubt affected him. Everyone else at the table had stopped eating and waited for his answer.

Lucas put his food down and sat back a little. "They didn't want to," he answered. "They did not want to take me in, and they did not want to teach me. Not initially, at least."

"And what is that supposed to mean?" asked Meloc. "If they didn't want to teach you, what changed their minds?"

"Me nearly falling off the wall."

Some people at the table chuckled, but then quickly became silent again, eager to hear the rest of the story.

"My father was a blacksmith, and he supplied their swords," continued Lucas. "As soon as I was old enough, he gave me the task of delivering them to the monastery. I became curious to see what was behind those walls, and one day I just climbed them. I saw the warrior monks practice, and from that day forward, I kept going back to watch from a place on top of the wall. I then started to copy their moves."

"And they let you?"

"Well, they did not kill me. They did try to stop me, but I kept finding different ways to climb up the wall. So then they just ignored me . . . until I took the sword my father had made for me up the wall. I nearly lost my balance. Maybe it was my persistence that persuaded them. Or their relationship with my father. I don't know. I never asked." He paused in his story and looked around the table. Everyone was facing him, and no one was eating. The goose lay untouched on its platter in the center of the table. "Then my father was murdered," he continued, "and I ran to the only place I knew I would be safe. I had no other family, and the monks allowed me to stay."

"But then you left and joined the circus?" laughed Lord Meloc. The two officers next to Lucas laughed as well, but Lucas was careful to show no emotion.

"I wanted to learn to fight so that I could become a king's soldier. I never wanted to become a monk, nor did they encourage me to. When the circus was passing by, they told me I would be able to meet the king if I were to join them, so I went with them. The rest, I'm sure you've been told."

"Are you satisfied now, brother?" asked the king. When Meloc gave him a nod, the king continued. "Then maybe you can leave the boy be and let him eat."

People started to talk among themselves again, and the noise in the hall returned. The king engaged in a conversation with a general and officers at the table, and their attention was no longer on Lucas.

Lucas picked up some food again when he noticed Lord Meloc had finally taken his eyes off him to talk with the general next to him. He wanted to leave the table, but he needed the king's permission to do so.

He was rolling a grape around his plate when another basket of bread was placed on the table near him. He looked up to watch the servant walk around the table to pass behind him. He briefly caught the servant's eye, and Lucas's senses sharpened.

Something wasn't right. He could feel it.

He waited until he knew for sure and felt the presence of the servant right behind him. He then jumped up, turned around, and grabbed the servant by the collar of his shirt. He pushed him back roughly, pinning him against a pillar in the process. He had moved so fast that his stool fell over and hit the floor with a bang, causing everyone in the Hall to freeze and stare at him. The chosen all jumped up to come to his aid but stopped when the king rose from his seat and raised his hand.

"Lucas!" shouted the king. "What is the meaning of this? What made you lash out at this servant?"

"He is no servant, sire," answered Lucas. "He's a soldier, holding a knife." He applied his entire weight against the man, twisting his arm so he would drop the knife he was holding. When it clattered to the floor, Lucas kicked it away, and Egon picked it up.

The king stared with bulging eyes at the bone-hefted knife Egon held up, then shouted, "Take that man out of here. Find out what his intentions were and who he is working for."

"Hold up, brother," said Meloc. "No harm was intended. That soldier is one of mine, and he acted on my orders."

"What?" asked the king. "Are you telling me you deliberately set this man upon Lucas with a knife?"

"I did," answered Meloc with a satisfied look on his face. "I wanted to know if your boy is attuned to threats and what his response might be." He picked up a grape and popped it into his mouth. "Now we both know."

Lucas was breathing hard and staring the man in the eye. The poor soldier was lucky to be alive, and from the way he stared at him, he knew it too.

"That was a reckless thing to do," said the king, staring furiously at his brother. "Either could have been hurt."

Meloc shrugged and kept eating the grapes from his plate.

Without releasing his grip on the soldier, Lucas peered over his shoulder and looked towards the king. "Can I release him now, sire?"

"Meloc?" asked the king. "He's your man."

"You may release him," answered Meloc.

The soldier let out a sigh of relief when Lucas released him and hastily left when Meloc dismissed him. Lucas straightened his clothes and looked across the tables to see Zera, Warrick, and Davis still standing. He took a deep breath and felt Egon's hand on his shoulder.

"I think you can go now," he said.

"Thank you," answered Lucas. He gave a quick bow to the king and Lord Meloc, who smiled stiffly at him.

Lucas was happy to leave Meloc's castle the following day. He traveled ahead of the king in order to scout the land on the long journey back. The king's brother had not come out to see him nor any of the other chosen off, and Lucas was guessing it had something to do with the night prior and Itan's display of annoyance. "I'm pretty certain we could go the rest of our lives without laying eyes on Meloc again and that would be just fine," Davis had said, trying for some levity as the chosen rode out. They stopped every couple of miles to wait for the king and soldiers to catch up before riding off again. When they came to the big open countryside where the previous attack had taken place, they stayed closer to one another, and Lucas saw Carleton break from the column to ride over to him. He slowed his horse and waited, as he knew Carleton was still hurting, and riding hard made it more painful.

Carleton pulled his horse next to Lucas's, and they rode silently, watching the boys ahead of them and the column of soldiers on the road in the distance. Carleton shifted his weight in the saddle and rested his hand on his knee. "I never thanked you properly," he said after a while. "For what you did for me. For risking your own life."

"You don't have to," answered Lucas. "I saw an opportunity, and I took it. I am sure you would have done the same."

Carleton nodded and continued to ride next to Lucas through the tall grass. Little grasshoppers jumped out of the way with every step their horses made, and bees were flying from flower to flower.

CHAPTER 20

Killeand stood at a window in the gallery above the banquet hall. He watched Harbert gallop through the gates on his black horse, its white mane flowing. He was followed by fewer riders than Killeand had known him to show up with in the past, which was concerning. As was the way he slid off his horse before coming to a complete stop.

"What's the hurry?" shouted Killeand when he could hear Harbert's hastened footsteps downstairs. He turned around and walked down the grand stairs into the Hall.

"My lord," said Harbert, arriving at the bottom of the stairwell before Killeand had even made it down. He put his hand through his tousled hair and tried to catch his breath before continuing. "We have been compromised. We've lost all the wagons from this last run, and to the king's guard, no less."

"How?" Killeand roared, putting both hands on the side of his head. "How were you compromised?"

"I have no idea," answered Harbert, beads of sweat prickling his brow. "We'd made solid plans to move the last of it out as soon as King Itan made it to Meloc's castle, but they came straight for us the next day. Meloc must have received a tip for that to have been possible."

Killeand turned in a circle and inhaled deep breaths before lowering his hands and facing Harbert. "Were any of your men captured alive?" he asked. "Is there any chance this could come back to me?"

"I don't know," answered Harbert, then changed his mind and shook his head. "I don't think so. I had the best men on the job—men who are fully aware that one doesn't survive an interrogation from the king's guard. They would likely have fought to the death."

"How many patrol troops did the king send out?" asked Finton, who had walked into the Hall and heard the last of the conversation. He frantically tugged at the collar of his shirt and avoided looking at Harbert.

"Only a group of young boys left, but they headed east."

"How many boys?"

"Not many. About eight."

Killeand cursed under his breath. "I knew it," he said. He could feel himself trembling. "From the moment I laid eyes on him. You should never have left Itan's side, Finton. Now we have no control over him, and he is releasing the boy as his secret weapon."

"There is no reason for Itan to suspect you had anything to do with it," said Finton, wringing his hands. "And neither should Meloc. The plan may still work. We have to move it forward."

Killeand thought for a moment and then directed himself to the mercenary Harbert. "How long before you can mobilize the rest of your men?"

Harbert shrugged his shoulders. "A couple weeks, maybe less?"

"Get it done," said Killeand. "And I will do the same." He waited for Harbert to agree and leave before turning to Finton. He looked around the Hall and to the gallery above to make sure no one else was there but still spoke in a hushed tone. "I think you and Eli should move on to the other part of our plan while I take care of this."

"I believe I should stay and see this through first," said Finton. "I can be of help. I know how Itan thinks."

"No," said Lord Killeand firmly. "You may know how Itan thinks, but we have that boy to deal with now, and you *don't* know how he thinks, or we would not be in this mess."

"He may not have had anything to do with it," said Finton. "It's like Harbert said—they could have been betrayed from inside."

Killeand looked even more irritated. He shook his head. "Don't be a fool, Finton. Eight boys ride out, one of them being Lucas, and the whole operation falls apart," he said. "No, he had something to do with it for sure, and I need you gone. When this is all over, I need Lucas with me, not against me. He probably hates you more than words can describe for what you did to him, and I can't say I blame him. If Lucas knows you stand with me, he will never want to listen to anything I have to say to him. It will jeopardize everything that I and others believe in."

"I thought you told me that the prophecy you so wholeheartedly believe in is going to come true soon," said Finton. "If that's the case, and it cannot be changed, what difference does it make what side Lucas is going to be on?"

Killeand narrowed his eyes and stared at Finton. "I never told you that it could not be changed," he said. "And Lucas is the key to that."

CHAPTER 21

Lucas walked alongside the temporary corral that was built in the field outside the castle. A hundred horses were divided into smaller groups and separated by fences built within the corral. He saw the king on the opposite side, talking to the breeder, who had herded in the horses the night before. Egon was with the king, as was Amalia. She never missed an opportunity to get out of the castle these days. Lucas walked over to them and leaned over the fence to look at the horses. Amalia joined him, getting her dress stuck on a nail sticking out of a fence post and smiling as she pulled it loose.

"Your mother will not be pleased to see that you now have a hole in that nice dress," Lucas whispered to her. He was teasing her since he knew how much she hated wearing it.

Amalia looked over her shoulder to see if her father was paying attention, but he was still in conversation with the horse breeder. "Then she should not insist I wear dresses," she replied. "They are a nuisance with riding, with climbing . . . with everything."

"You are a princess," said Lucas, helping her up the rest of the way. "You will be a queen one day. What do you think the people will say about a queen who does not dress like a lady?"

Lucas could see that Amalia wanted to respond, but her father had finished talking with the breeder and was coming over to them. He looked at her, saw the hole in her dress, and shook his head disapprovingly, but said nothing.

Then he turned to Lucas. "Walk with me," he said.

Lucas jumped down from the fence and hurried to catch up with the king, who had already walked away.

"Amalia will be thirteen soon," said the king. "And I want to give her a horse for her birthday. You have an eye for horses, and a way of understanding them, so I would like you to choose the best one for her."

Lucas looked at the herd of horses when they stopped. "These are all courser horses, sire," he said. "They are warhorses and not suitable for pleasure riding."

"You have been riding with her," said the king. "Do you not think she can handle one?"

"Oh, she could certainly handle one," replied Lucas quickly. "But—"

"Well, then I trust you see to it," interrupted the king. He left Lucas standing and started making his way back to Amalia, then paused and turned back around. "Oh, and Lucas?"

"Yes, sire?"

"When you have chosen the right one, I want you to start teaching her."

"Teach her what, sire?"

"Skills that will protect her. Keep her safe no matter where she is or what happens," answered the king, a smile playing on his face as he turned to walk away.

Lucas spent the rest of the afternoon walking among the horses, trying to find the best one for her. Horses were taken out as they were chosen by other officers and soldiers, but he finally settled on a small, fast gray mare.

The king brought Amalia to the stables the following day to see her new horse. Lucas had spent an hour brushing and cleaning the mare's coat to make her look presentable and just finished when he heard Amalia's excited voice outside the stable doors.

"I still cannot believe I am finally getting my very own horse," said Amalia. "Is she as big as your gray horse?"

"You will see," answered the king as they entered.

Lucas noticed that Amalia was wearing riding clothes that would allow her to ride like the boys. Her face lit up when she spotted the mare and, still holding the halter, he watched as she ran up to the horse and placed her hands on its neck, her eyes shining and wet with emotion.

"Careful now, Amalia," the king called after her. "You don't want to spook your new horse."

"She won't spook, father," Amalia answered, looking back over her shoulder. "She is perfect."

King Itan stopped behind her. "She still needs schooling but as long as you like her."

Amalia let go of her horse and turned around to hug her father. "I love her," she said. "Can I take her for a ride?"

"I will leave you to discuss that with Lucas," answered the king. "He will be overseeing your training."

"Training?" asked Amalia, taking a step back and looking up at her father. "What kind of training?"

"Lucas?" asked the king. "Do you mind explaining this to her?"

"Yes, sire," answered Lucas.

"Good," answered the king and turned around to walk away.

Amalia watched her father leave, and when he was out of sight, she turned back to Lucas. "What training?" she asked. "Horse schooling? I get to learn how to teach a horse?"

Lucas shook his head. "No," he answered. "I will finish working

213

your horse for you. Your father was referring to combat instruction. If you like, you can start this afternoon."

"*Combat?*" asked Amalia, her eyes wide. "This afternoon? That's when the elite born train."

Lucas nodded. "And the chosen from now on," he answered. "It will be new for some of them as well, so you are not the only one learning from the beginning."

"Really?" asked Amalia. "My father is allowing me to train with the chosen and elite?"

"Yes," answered Lucas. "Unless you don't want to, then I am sure I can—"

"No, no," interrupted Amalia. "Don't tell my father I don't want to." She put her cheek against her horse's neck and smiled when she closed her eyes.

"I'm glad you like your horse," said Lucas. "She'll be good for you."

"She will be the best," replied Amalia.

Lucas couldn't help but like the princess. He always had. From the time of their first encounter, she had treated him as if he were her equal.

Amalia playfully tickled the mare under the chin and then turned to Lucas, a soft smile on her face. He returned her smile but then picked up a brush he had left on the floor and put it back in the tack box on the other side of the aisle. The responsibility he felt for her well-being, which the king had put onto his shoulders, wasn't lost on him.

For Lucas, the training came with an additional dose of pressure, for the king watched his daughter and the chosen's progress every afternoon from the wall above the training grounds.

One afternoon, a week after training began, the king and Garrad chose to observe the training from the sidelines rather than from the wall. Watching Amalia with Lucas, Garrad said to the king in a whisper loud enough to overhear, "Not so long ago, you were bothered by the fact that she paid him too much attention. Now, you're handing her to him!"

Amalia blushed at Garrad's words. Lucas was relieved that no one else seemed to have heard Garrad's comments, which he took to be an out-in-the-open warning.

"True," Lucas heard the king say. "But that was when he was a chosen. Lord Aron suggested I change his status so it would no longer trouble me." The king smiled at Garrad's shocked expression and slapped his friend on the shoulder. "Don't worry. That was not the reason I gave him the mark. I take the mark very seriously indeed. As for Amalia, I need her to learn how to handle a horse in combat in the event that it ever comes to that."

"Can Egon not accomplish that?" asked Garrad.

"He can," answered Itan, "but he has more than enough responsibility already. Lucas is the only other person I can trust to get it done and the only one she's willing to listen to." At this point, the king made eye contact with Lucas. "Besides, he has Carleton and Rhys to help him teach her, and with all the chosen and elite there, they will never be left alone. That, of course, would be highly improper."

They fell quiet as Lucas gave instructions and then watched as Amalia made a charge at a dummy, but she was swinging her sword too high and missed the target. Lucas followed up by shouting at her to do it again, his voice as stern as he could make it without embarrassing her.

"He's not letting her off easy," commented Garrad, giving Lucas a nod.

"She doesn't need easy," replied the king, looking to Amalia now.

"I told him to treat her like the rest of them. Her life may depend on it one day."

It was sweet relief to Lucas when the two men finally wandered away.

"I think that is enough for today," said Lucas when Amalia came back from a second charge attempt. "We will have to work more on your positioning."

"Why? What did I do wrong this time?" asked Amalia. "I struck every target."

"These dummies are rigid," answered Lucas. "In real life, you will have a moving target, so you have to know exactly how high your aim should be in every situation." He stroked her horse's neck and then called out to the chosen. "For those of you older than fourteen, stay on your horse and line up before the west wall. Anyone younger . . . you may dismount, but I need you to place the dummies in two long rows going west to east, twelve feet apart."

Lucas jumped on his horse and joined the older riders at the far end of the outer bailey, where they set off two at a time to make a charge at the dummies, hitting each one as they went past and charging on to the next. Carleton and Lucas were the last to go, and they held their horses in until the field was clear. Then with a nod to each other, they let their horses go straight in a canter to make the first charge. They hit one dummy after another, never slowing down, never missing their mark. They reached the other side, crossed over, and did the same thing on the way back.

When they finished, Lucas dismounted and followed the rest of the boys back to the stables. As he passed underneath the inner gate, he heard calls for officer assistance coming from the front entrance. He continued to the stables but saw Egon coming down the stairway used to climb the wall. A guard was advancing towards him at a brisk pace. "What exactly is going on here?" Egon asked. "We aren't expecting visitors."

"A messenger is demanding to be let in at once, sir," answered the guard. "Says he is from Lord Meloc's castle, but he carries no identifiable colors on him."

"Single rider?" asked Egon.

"Yes, sir!"

"Then open the gates but be on guard."

Lucas was still busy with his horse in the stables when the request came for him and Carleton to come to the Hall at once. They arrived just as they heard the messenger say he was a civilian, a farrier, who just happened to be at Meloc's castle when it happened. The king was sitting on his throne, and the man claiming to be a farrier stood before him with his back to the gathered audience.

"How did he get in?" the king asked.

Lucas went to stand next to Verron. "What happened?" he asked.

"Lord Meloc's castle has fallen," whispered Verron. "Lord Killeand took it."

"What? How is that possible?" Carleton asked, his mouth dropping open in disbelief.

Verron pointed towards the messenger, who was still trying to explain what happened.

Lucas leaned closer to Carleton. "He doesn't look like a farrier," he said softly. "The farrier we have here at the castle wears a long tunic, like most civilians."

"You're right," replied Carleton. "This man is wearing brown cropped trousers with a belt, a tucked-in shirt, and boots for riding."

"There is something oddly familiar about him," said Lucas.

Carleton turned to him. "You have seen him before?" he asked.

Lucas nodded. "I might have."

"It appears he was let in, sire," continued the farrier. "Lord Meloc passed me in the bailey, and I overheard him tell his general that Killeand had come to discuss some plundering he was experiencing on his lands. When Killeand rode in, his men pulled their swords and

217

demanded surrender. Lord Meloc was taken hostage, and his men laid down arms soon after that. It all happened quickly. I escaped before the gates closed and came here to tell you, sire."

Lucas moved away from Carleton and walked over to the side where he could have a better look at the man.

"I appreciate you traveling all the way here to tell me," said the king. "But I am puzzled by the fact that a civilian would make an effort to do so."

"He is no civilian, sire," said Lucas, stepping forward after he'd had a look at the man's face. He recognized him as one of the mercenary soldiers. "I have seen him before. At Lord Killeand's." He saw the fury in the man's eyes as he spoke, but the mercenary managed to contain it and looked at the king.

"I have no idea what this boy is talking about, sire," said the man. "I'm a farrier working for Lord Meloc."

The king turned to Lucas. "Are you completely certain as to where you've seen this man?" he asked.

"Positive," answered Lucas.

"He is lying," called the mercenary. "I—"

"Silence," interrupted the king. He motioned for guards to come forward as he rose from his seat. He then descended the throne's steps and stopped before the mercenary, now pushed down onto his knees. "Tell me what that traitor is up to," he shouted. "Tell me what Killeand has done to my brother."

"I don't know, sire," answered the mercenary. He lowered his his eyes to avoid the king's stare. "I am telling the truth. The boy is mistaken. I never laid eyes on Lord Killeand . . . until a few days ago."

"Egon!" roared the king. Lucas saw Egon step forward. "Take this man to the dungeon and kindly encourage him to talk."

"Certainly," said Egon and motioned to the guards.

Lucas watched the mercenary resist when the guards grabbed him by the arms and dragged him out of the Hall. He then saw the king face him.

"Go with them, Lucas," said the king. "See how it is done."

Lucas wanted to object, but he knew he couldn't and turned to follow Egon.

"What are you doing here?" asked Egon when Lucas caught up with him at the end of the hallway. The king's guard was just ahead, prodding their subject of interrogation forward.

"The king wants me to watch and learn how you interrogate people," answered Lucas, walking by his side as they headed down the steps. "I didn't think I could refuse, but, in all honesty, I admit I have no desire to watch what you do."

"He may talk before it comes to that," said Egon. "Most do."

They continued crossing the bailey in silence and walked down the steps that led to the dungeon, the sound of their footsteps echoing off the hard surfaces all around them. Lucas took a deep breath when they reached the torture chamber, and he watched the mercenary chained up on the same chains he was suspended from not so long ago. Even though months had passed, his night spent here was still fresh in his mind.

The mercenary soldier's eyes were wide, and Lucas sensed his fear. He had given up the façade that he was an innocent farrier.

Egon was unfazed. He calmly stood in front of him and waited for the guards to step out of the way.

"Let's start with an easy question," said Egon after the guards had left, and only the king's guard remained. "What is your name?" When he did not get an answer, he nodded to a king's guard, who then punched the soldier in his stomach. The chains prevented him from doubling over from pain, and Egon followed it up with a second punch before stepping back again. "Your name," he repeated.

"Eric," the soldier gasped.

"And who do you work for, Eric?"

"I work for Lord Meloc."

"You were seen at Killeand's," said Egon, pacing in front of him. "What were you doing there?"

"I've never been to Lord Killeand's castle," said Eric, looking at Lucas. "He must've mistaken me for someone else."

Lucas saw Egon pause and turn to look at him. Lucas shook his head.

"I don't think he did," continued Egon. "So, tell me what Killeand is up to!" When Eric gave no response, Egon walked over to a wall and took what looked like a long pair of scissors. "I guess if you are not willing to talk anyway, you won't be needing your tongue."

"Egon," said Lucas, who knew the device was used to cut out someone's tongue. "I will not stay for this."

Egon nodded to him, and Lucas prepared to leave.

"Wait," said Eric. "Where is he going?"

Egon shrugged his shoulders. "He has been where you are right now. It brings back too many painful memories, I suppose."

"You torture your own?"

"If the king does not get the response he wants, then, yes, we do."

"I don't believe that."

"Suit yourself," answered Egon and pulled open the foot-long blades.

"I can show you," said Lucas, unbuttoning his shirt. "They didn't rip my tongue out as Egon will yours, but I was left hanging from those same chains for hours, and I have these scars to remember it by." He took his shirt off and turned around to show the scars on his back. "All I had done was start a fight."

He heard Eric take a deep breath, and Lucas turned back around to face him, rebuttoning his shirt as he did so.

"All right," said Eric. "I thought I was the one working for a madman, but it looks like it could be loads worse."

"So, you are working for Killeand?" asked Egon.

"No," answered Eric. "I work for a man named Harbert, and he will work for anyone."

"You are admitting to being a mercenary then?"

"Yes," sighed Eric. "We were asked to go and help take Meloc's castle, which we did, but I don't know for what purpose. I was sent here shortly after the takeover to inform the king his brother is now a hostage." Eric paused and looked up at Egon. "Killeand wants the king to come and negotiate a price for his brother's release. If he doesn't, Lord Meloc will die."

"When?" asked Egon.

"Four days from now."

A brisk wind was rustling the leaves, and Lucas shrugged off a chill. The group of elite and chosen stood in a line at the forest's edge. The shadows of the trees hid them as they observed the castle before them.

"Killeand's flag is flying on the towers, and his soldiers are patrolling the walls," said Carleton. His horse was chewing on his bit while Lucas's let out a soft snort.

Lucas remained silent and let his mind wander inside the castle. He didn't see many soldiers, and there was no sign of Killeand.

"Why do I get the feeling you are about to tell me something in regard to something I don't see?" said Carleton, taking a sideways glance at him.

"Right now, I see what you see," said Lucas. "But tell me . . . how many soldiers do you count?"

Carleton took another good look, shrugging. "There seem to be guards at every post—why do you ask?"

"As elite borns, they teach you battle strategies," said Lucas, without taking his eyes off the castle. "If you had just taken over a castle and you expected a counterattack, how many soldiers would you be posting on the walls?"

"Well," said Carleton, "I would cover every post for sure, and probably more on the side I would expect the attack to come from."

"And what would you have the rest of the soldiers do?"

"I would have them prepare for battle." Carleton paused, seeming to realize where Lucas was going. It was quiet at the castle—too quiet. "Killeand should expect King Itan to be coming," said Carleton, "but is making no preparations for it."

"I don't think Killeand is there," said Lucas.

"You mean he took the castle and just left? Why would he do that? And why leave a handful of soldiers behind to keep hold of it?"

"Yes," said Lucas. "He doesn't want the castle. He never did. Taking it was a way of getting the king here. He knows the king would try and get it back, and that's exactly what he wants."

"Where are you suggesting he is then?"

"Over there," pointed Lucas. "In the valley beyond those hills."

"And when the king attacks the castle . . ."

"Killeand will attack him from behind."

Carleton jerked at the reins and started turning his horse. "We have to warn the king," he said.

"We need to be sure first," responded Lucas. "And we need to secure Lord Meloc—if he's still alive—before the attack begins. At nightfall, I'm taking the chosen. We'll breach the wall and go in."

"Then what?"

"If we're right, and Lord Killeand is not there, I'll signal from the back tower. Then you and the elite born can go and warn the king."

They continued watching the castle the rest of the day, but when no other soldiers came and none left, Lucas made his way down to the castle on foot, at nightfall, with twelve of the most experienced chosen ones. When they reached the outer wall, the chosen divided into two groups and stood with their backs pressed against the rough stone, silently waiting for Lucas's directions. They had observed the pattern of the patrols all day and knew there would be a moment in the section on the wall above them where the soldiers tasked with guarding the wall passed and would have their backs turned. All eyes were on Lucas, who was using his seeing mind to wait for the final guard change of the night. Warrick and Tanner were standing ready, holding a rope with a three-pronged hook attached, and were waiting for him to give the all-clear. "Now," he told them when the last guard passed by, and all was clear above.

Both boys took a step away from the wall and threw the hook with the rope attached high up into the air in one swift move. The sharp prongs found grip on the embrasures above, and, after tugging at it to make sure it was secure, Lucas and Davis started to climb first.

When they reached the wall walk, Lucas looked down to see that a few fires were burning below. Some soldiers stood gathered around the fires, but their number was nowhere near enough to defend an entire castle against even a fraction of the king's army.

Lucas then rushed up to the closest soldier who stood with his back turned, looking down into the bailey. He put one hand over the man's mouth to stifle any noise, and as he pulled him away from the parapet, he stabbed him in the back with his dagger. Davis had rushed past him and taken out the next soldier in a similar manner while the rest of the chosen were making their way over the wall. When the entire group made it onto the wall walk, they hid behind the first turret and waited for Lucas to give them the go-ahead to continue. When he did, the chosen rushed past him two at a time and took out the next set of unsuspecting soldiers. They continued moving from turret to turret until no soldier remained alive on the walls. They made their way back towards the castle tower, hiding the soldiers' bodies inside the turrets along the way, hoping that this would delay the discovery of the chosen's presence within the castle walls.

When they reached the castle tower, and Davis was about to open its door, Lucas put his hand on his arm to stop him. "Shh," he said, putting a finger to his lips. He was using his mind and saw someone coming down. They stopped to listen and heard footsteps on the stairs inside. The sound grew louder as the steps came nearer, and the boys and Zera split up on either side of the door. Lucas could feel the energy of anticipation in all the chosen, but Tanner appeared the calmest. That's what he liked about him. Ready for any task, no fuss, and a let's-get-this-done mentality. Tanner put his ear to the door, and, when all was quiet, he opened it, and they slipped inside. Lucas led the way upward, with Tanner right behind him, while Zera and the rest of the chosen waited on the stairs.

As they reached the top of the tower, they could hear two guards quietly talking. Both guards stood by the wall, overlooking the countryside.

Lucas and Tanner, each of them with a dagger in hand, came up behind the soldiers, reaching their arms around their necks to cut their throats.

Then, with a torch taken from the stairway, Lucas signaled to Carleton and the elites still waiting in the forest that there was no sign of Killeand inside the castle.

"What if Carleton doesn't get to the king in time to warn him?" asked Tanner softly. "Not only will the king's army face an attack at the rear, but we're going to be on our own in here."

"We're going to be on our own either way," answered Lucas as he headed back down. "The king sent us to assess the situation, but never told us to enter Meloc's castle. That was never part of his plans."

When they rejoined the four chosen who stood waiting, Lucas gave them the thumbs up that all had gone well, and they continued down until they reached the lower floors. Voices were coming from the Great Hall, which was in the central part of the castle, and they saw a few officers sitting around a table by the fireplace. Waiting for the right moment, they crossed a hallway and went down the stairs that spiraled deeper down into the castle. Lucas was now grateful for the boredom he had felt at the banquet—he had taken that opportunity to let his mind go down every stair and hallway of the castle until he had memorized its entire layout.

Lucas stopped when they came to the dungeon's entrance door and knocked softly. He could hear the shuffling feet of a soldier coming to the door to answer it.

"Be prepared, all of you!" whispered Lucas to the chosen behind him. He heard the latch slide back, and he held his breath in anticipation. He sensed the others getting ready behind him, and when the door only partially opened, Lucas pushed it back roughly, knocking the soldier against the wall of the narrow passageway of the dungeon. The soldier let out a muffled scream of anguish when the heavy wooden door crushed his face, and Lucas heard a crunch that he imagined was the man's nose. Lucas put his full weight against the door to keep the soldier behind at, allowing the chosen to brush past him to take out the four other soldiers stationed inside the dungeon. When they'd been taken care of, Davis came back and killed the soldier behind the door.

Lucas let go and watched the soldier's body slump to the floor. "Zera!" he called. "Stand guard on the stairwell and warn me if you hear anyone coming." When she nodded and stepped out of the dungeon, Lucas grabbed the keys that were hanging off an iron hook on the wall. He looked through the little window in one of the cell doors while putting a key in the lock. Meloc's soldiers had already jumped to their feet and were eagerly waiting to be let out.

"Where's Lord Meloc?" asked Lucas as he opened the door.

"Over there, I believe," one of the soldiers said, pointing to another cell where Itan's brother could already be heard calling out to be released, and Lucas tossed the keys to Tanner.

As soon as Tanner unlocked the door and opened it, Meloc stumbled out. Archer rushed to his side to help support him, but Meloc recovered quickly. He looked fatigued but otherwise unharmed, and perked up as soon as he recognized Lucas and some of the chosen.

"Thank you for coming to my aid," Meloc said. "That was most uncomfortable, and I'm quite glad it is over." He stretched his back and adjusted his clothes. The cell he had stumbled from was pitch black inside and, by the stains on his trousers, Lucas could tell that Meloc had not been able to see where on the floor he had sat himself down these past days. "Now, where is my brother?" continued Meloc, blissfully unaware he needed to be quiet. "Take me to him."

"Shh, my lord," said Lucas hastily. "We need to—"

"Boy!" shouted Lord Meloc, interrupting him. "Don't you tell me what to do in my castle."

Lucas took a step closer. "My lord," he said in a calm voice, though he felt a bit like locking him back up, "you are not free yet. Us chosen are the only ones who have made it inside the castle thus far. Upstairs are Killeand's soldiers. They don't know we are here. We managed to eliminate the soldiers on the wall, but there are too many left in other parts of the castle for us. We have to wait."

"Then . . . where is my brother?" asked Meloc.

"Still an hour's ride from here," answered Lucas. "Until he gets here, we can't do anything rash. The chosen and I will go back upstairs and try to stay out of sight until morning. Down here would be the safest place for you and your men to wait."

"Do you really think I'm willing to stay down here while these imposters make themselves comfortable in my house?" asked Meloc.

"No, my lord," answered Lucas, "but right now, your soldiers are unarmed, and we have no way of getting weapons down here without risking everyone's lives."

Meloc looked around his group of soldiers. Only five of them held swords—and those were swords retrieved from Killeand's dead soldiers, who lay at their feet.

"I promise you," continued Lucas, "that when it's time for you to reclaim your castle, Tanner and Zera will come to alert you." When Meloc nodded, Lucas motioned to the chosen to move back up the stairs, but before he made it to the door, he heard Meloc call his name. He turned around on the threshold and looked at the lord.

"My brother has put a great deal of trust in you," said Meloc. "Don't disappoint him by failing to get me out of here."

Lucas nodded. "I understand," he answered and waited until one of Meloc's soldiers closed the door and locked it from the inside. Then he rushed up the stairs after his friends.

CHAPTER 22

Itan stood hunched over the table in his tent with Verron, several of his military officers, and Egon. He was dressed in battle attire with chain-mail armor underneath his tunic and sabbatons covering his boots. A map lay spread out before him. They had been staring at it for the better half of the past hour, but they had not been able to agree on a strategy moving forward.

"Attacking the castle would put Lord Meloc's life in danger," said Verron.

"As would a siege," said Egon.

Itan sighed and stepped away from the table. "We don't even know if my brother is still alive," he said. He walked over to a side table and picked up the jug to pour himself a cup of water, and his hand trembled as he did so. He was placing the jug back on the table and bringing the cup to his lips as steadily as he could when he heard a commotion outside, and he set the cup down so abruptly that half the water sloshed out. Horses were approaching, and someone was shouting out the passcode, followed by a number—specific to the one trying to enter—in order to be allowed into the camp. Itan had chosen "Caius," the name of the family dog that had been his and Meloc's companion when they were young. It seemed a fitting code for the occasion since the dog had also been a rat catcher, and that's what he felt Killeand was—a pesky little rodent that needed to be exterminated.

"Twelve," said Verron, lifting his head from the map, "that's Carleton."

Itan put his cup down and looked towards the opening of the tent when a horse with labored breathing came to a stop just outside. He could hear boots thump the ground, indicating the rider had jumped from the saddle in haste.

"Permission to enter, sire," called Carleton.

"Granted," replied Itan. The guards drew the tent flap back and Carleton stepped inside briskly. He looked exhausted and was drenched in sweat.

"What happened?" asked Itan. "Are you alone?"

"The elite are with me," answered Carleton, still trying to catch his breath. He took big strides to the table where Verron and Egon still stood near the map. "Don't attack the castle," he said. "It's a trap."

Itan nodded and joined them. "We suspected as much," he said, "but please explain."

"Killeand is not there," said Carleton. "Some of his men are, but not all of them. The majority are missing."

"How have you confirmed this?"

"We observed the castle as instructed and concluded that it did not look like the castle was well-defended. Lucas and the chosen breached the wall a few hours ago and signaled to confirm Killeand is not inside."

"What about my brother?"

"I do not know, sire." Carleton's face clouded, and Itan could see that the boy regretted not being able to relay brighter and more hopeful news. "We left as soon as we received the signal."

"Where are Lucas and the chosen now?" asked Egon.

"They were going to attempt to locate Lord Meloc," answered Carleton, "but even if Meloc is not held at the castle, Lucas told me he would not risk sneaking back out and would hide with the chosen for the time being. If they're caught, it will alert Killeand that we are onto them. He's staying put, until we get there."

Itan sighed and bent back over the map. "So Killeand left enough soldiers behind at the castle to make it appear he is holding it, but he's abandoned it?"

"Where do you suppose he went?" asked Verron, turning to Carleton.

Carleton pointed to an area on the map before anyone else could answer. "Lucas thinks he's here, hidden in this valley beyond these hills. He believes that if we attack the castle, Killeand will attack us from behind."

"Lucas has no battle-strategy experience," commented Verron.

"He may not, but we discussed it, and I believe he may be right," said Carleton.

"I think he may be too," said Itan softly. "Killeand is not after my brother or his castle, even though it would increase his wealth and prestige. He's after me, and likely at the order of King Boran."

"How did you come to that conclusion?" asked Egon.

"The guest Lucas saw at Killeand's castle . . . the one who had Boran's seal," answered Itan. "He was probably there to hand over the orders. It's the only explanation I have for him to have been there, and it makes sense." He stood upright and turned to his officers. "Get the army up and ready. We'll move out within the hour."

"What is the plan, exactly?" asked Egon, after the officers left the tent.

"Killeand wants me to attack the castle," Itan declared, rolling up his map with fury, "so that is what I am going to do!"

Itan had his army mobilized and marching for the duration of the night. They'd arrived just before dawn, and he was now moving them forward in long lines towards Meloc's castle. The wind was blowing, making the banners ripple. The first two rows were foot soldiers, followed by soldiers carrying long ladders that would be used to breach the walls. Then there were the archers. Itan followed immediately behind, with Verron and the cavalry. They all came to a halt a few hundred yards out and watched the castle in front of them. It was eerily quiet, but soon Itan could see movement on top of the walls.

"Are you ready for this?" he asked.

"As ready as I will ever be," answered Verron with confidence.

Itan turned in the saddle to look behind him. He could see nothing and hoped he had made the right decision. He gave a signal to the horn blower on his left, who put the horn to his mouth and blew the sound to start the attack.

The first row of soldiers immediately moved forward, with shields raised to protect themselves from arrows raining down on them. Archers had appeared on the walls.

"What if we have it wrong?" said Verron when they saw more soldiers on the walls than Carleton had estimated were at the castle.

"It's too late now for an alternate plan," answered Itan, signaling his archers to move forward. Before long, he watched the first of his soldiers reach the bottom of the walls and saw the ladders going up against it. Then the sound of a horn made him look over his shoulder—a dust cloud was rising from the hills behind him. Verron caught his eye and nodded with satisfaction when the first of Killeand's soldiers came into view as they made their way over the hills.

Itan turned his horse around to face the oncoming army, and the four rows of cavalry who had stayed back with him followed suit. He ran his horse along the lines and glanced over to the castle, where his soldiers continued to try and breach the walls. Ladders kept being pushed out by those defending, and soldiers were falling before reaching the top. He reached the end of the line and was preparing to face his own upcoming battle when he noticed a change on the castle walls. His soldiers were rushing up the ladders, and there seemed to be no resistance from Killeand's soldiers.

"It looks like our soldiers made it, sire," said Verron, following his gaze. "The fighting appears to be taking place on the walls now."

Itan narrowed his eyes. He could see the sun reflecting off the steel from swords on the walls, but the first of his soldiers had yet to make it over the embrasures. "Lucas," he muttered softly, raising his sword to urge the cavalry forward towards Killeand.

CHAPTER 23

After leaving Meloc, the chosen had made their way back along the outer walls and into the loft above the stables, where they spent the rest of the night waiting. Lucas used his mind now and then to make sure the dead soldiers lay undiscovered inside the turrets while the chosen kept a close eye on any movement inside the bailey by peering through cracks between the planks of the walls. With the first rays of light coming through openings in the roof, Lucas feared it was only a matter of time before a guard change occured and the bodies would be discovered. The thought of this weighed heavily on his mind. He sighed deeply and looked at Zera sitting next to him. She was braiding strands of straw and had been doing so for some time.

"What are you making?" he asked softly.

"Nothing in particular," answered Zera. "I'm trying to keep myself awake."

"You could make a crown out of it," said Lucas. "Tie all the braids together?"

"I could," answered Zera, holding the two ends together to make a circle. "If I have enough time to finish it." She reached for more straw by her feet but pulled back when a black and white bird startled her as it flew by. "Lucas?" she asked, raising her head to the rafters where the bird had landed and was peering down at them. "The magpie?"

"I saw it," answered Lucas and began to concentrate. He let his mind wander over the castle walls and down across the damp morning grass towards the west. "The king is close," he whispered with an overwhelming sense of relief. Around him, the chosen rose to their feet. "It's time to get ready."

Before the soldiers inside the castle could detect the king's army outside the gates, Lucas had Davis get his group ready to enter the bailey. Tanner and Zera had left earlier to prepare Meloc and his men for an exit from the dungeon. Never had he felt so much pressure—one poorly orchestrated move, and the strategy, and thereby the chosen— could be compromised.

When Lucas made his way onto the inner wall, he stopped. "Down," he whispered to the chosen behind him as he crouched behind the low wall of the parapet himself. Using his mind, he had seen one of Killeand's officers walk outside and stop on the castle's steps.

The officer looked at the smoldering fires in the pits and the soldiers who were starting to wake up around them. His gaze then wandered upward to the walls, and he frowned as he casually scanned along them. He appeared to mutter something under his breath before turning on his heel and disappearing back inside.

"What's happening?" asked Warrick, who was right behind him.

"An officer just discovered there are no guards on the wall," answered Lucas.

"Why is he not raising the alarm?" asked Warrick.

Before Lucas could answer, he saw the tower door thrown open, and the officer stepping out onto the wall walk. The officer looked annoyed and was undoubtedly expecting to shout at sleeping guards, but instead, he saw no one. Hastily, he walked to the first turret, where one of the guards sat with his back against the wall with his eyes closed.

The officer bent down and shook the guard by the shoulder as if to wake him, but instead of waking up, the lifeless guard fell to the side. The officer ran to the next turret, where he found another guard down. He looked confused until a movement outside the castle walls caught his attention.

When Lucas saw the king's soldiers reach the base of the exterior walls with his mind, the fight inside the castle had already begun. The first soldiers Lucas encountered on the inner walls after the officer raised the alarm were not expecting an attack from behind and were quickly overwhelmed. He had charged at them with sword raised overhead and struck them just below their helmets. The chosen followed right behind him as he continued moving forward towards the outer walls, all the while dodging incoming arrows from King Itan's army.

Once Killeand's soldiers turned around to fight the chosen, the arrows stopped coming, which gave the king's men a chance to climb over the walls. With every soldier engaged in a fight, Lucas retreated and looked down into the bailey, scanning it until he spotted Davis.

"Open the gate!" he shouted when he caught his attention. Davis gave him the thumbs up and ran to the gate with Archer joining him. As they were opening it, Meloc and his men came up from the dungeon and entered the fight in the bailey.

When the gate opened, the king's soldiers flooded in and were able to overrun the castle, and Lucas finished up on the wall. He looked around to account for all the chosen. He saw Zera and Warrick fighting soldiers off in the bailey, but Tanner was nowhere to be found. A wave of panic rushed over him as he headed down to the bailey to look for him. He had to push past soldiers who were coming up and found himself startled as a cheer rang out from one of the towers as Meloc's men took Killeand's flag down to raise their own. Lucas looked to see if Tanner was with them, but he wasn't. Finally, reaching the bailey, Lucas rushed over to Zera and grabbed her by the shoulder.

"Where's Tanner?" he asked.

"I don't know where he is now," said Zera, "but he was right behind me on the stairs after we got Lord Meloc out."

Lucas looked to Warrick, who had just finished a fight and was coming towards him. "Have you seen Tanner?" he asked.

"No," answered Warrick. "I haven't."

"Cover me," Lucas said to both. He had to use all of his concentration to locate Tanner among the chaos of fighting men. With so many moving bodies in the way, it posed a challenge in viewing the quieter areas. Lucas homed in on a wagon pushed up against the wall of the stables. He saw a human form not large enough to be that of a grown man lying curled inward like a sickle. Could that be Tanner? Lucas ran and dropped on his knees next to the wagon wheel. Tanner had his arms pressed against his stomach, and he was struggling to breathe.

"I'm sorry," said Tanner, looking up at him. "I was the last one to leave the castle. I thought no one was left inside."

"Don't talk," said Lucas, who looked down at him and saw the blood soaking through his shirt. "We've got you. You'll be fine."

Zera and Warrick appeared by his side, and together they lifted Tanner to take him inside the castle, where other wounded soldiers were being taken. Once inside, they laid him down on a table and applied more pressure on the wound in his stomach to stop the bleeding. Just then, shouts were coming from outside that the king was under attack from the rest of Killeand's army. Lucas looked over his shoulder towards the door before turning back to his friend.

Tanner attempted a weak smile. "You go," he said. "I might be done for today, but you are not."

Lucas shook his head. He didn't want to leave him.

"Lucas," said Zera softly. "You know you have to go. The king is relying on you. I'll stay with Tanner."

Lucas looked from Zera to Tanner, and he placed his hand on Tanner's shoulder. "I'll be right back," he said reluctantly, feeling his chest swell. He walked out of the castle and down the steps into the bailey. Riderless horses had started to make their way through the gate into the safety of the castle when Lucas stepped out, and he grabbed one of them. With the interior walls of the castle now largely under control, he jumped on the horse and headed straight for the battle outside. Davis and other chosen ones who happened to be down in the bailey followed his lead and rode out after him.

The battlefield spread out over a wide area in an open dusty field. There were no trees to obscure his view, and Lucas headed directly to where the heaviest fighting was occurring. As he got closer, he could see the king surrounded by members of the king's guard, with each one outnumbered in their fight. Among the soldiers fighting around them, Lucas saw mercenaries on horseback. He recognized their leader, Harbert, letting out screams of victory each time his sword found a target.

He couldn't see Egon and wondered where he was. Moments later, a horn sounded in the distance, and he saw Egon approaching from the south with a large group of soldiers. Then a second horn sounded from the north, and he watched Carleton come over the hill with another group of soldiers, including the elite borns.

Lucas was trying to fight his way closer to the king when he noticed that the king's guard, who had previously been able to surround the king, was slowly being drawn away from him. He too found himself pushed back as more and more of Killeand's soldiers blocked his way and engaged him in battle. The soldiers fought with raging anger, and their skilled swordsmanship slowed Lucas down. He slashed his sword down and around, making every stroke count. Looking to where the king was fighting for his life, he saw that Harbert was making his way towards him from the other side, and Lucas knew he had to hurry. He looked for a way to get to the king quickly, but he had a large group of battling soldiers in front of him, and there was no chance he would be able to push through them in time.

In a split second, Lucas turned his horse away from the fighting, stepping a few yards away, at which point he turned back around and rode forward at full speed. Some soldiers saw him coming and dashed out of the way, but most soldiers were too involved in combat and had to duck at the last second when Lucas's horse jumped over them.

Harbert had broken through the circle and was headed straight for the king with his sword raised. Lucas landed his horse in front of him. Their weapons clashed in midair.

Lucas leaped off his horse and took Harbert down with him to the ground. In his peripheral vision, he could see that the king's guard, aware their king was in danger, were working their way back to him. Two of the king's guard pushed themselves past him and Harbert. They had both jumped to their feet and were now engaged in a bitter fight. Harbert was a solid and skilled fighter, creative and surprising in his movements and quick jabs, but Lucas was faster, and his sword soon ended the fight, finding its way through the man's rib cage. Harbert fell to the ground in a heap.

"Who are you?" Harbert gasped when Lucas stood over him and kicked his sword away.

"My name is Lucas," he answered.

A slow smile crept over the grimace of pain on Harbert's face. "I have heard your name," he said. "Some refer to you as Baelan."

"It's not a name I use," responded Lucas.

"It doesn't matter," said Harbert. "I still know who you are." He paused to try and take another breath, and Lucas kneeled to the ground when he saw Harbert was saying more, but his voice had become much softer.

"They made me believe I was fighting for the true king, but seeing you here . . . I suppose I was fighting on the wrong side?"

"Killeand told you he is the true king?" asked Lucas.

Harbert shook his head weakly. "No," he said. "Killeand is just a puppet on strings. There are others who believe they have the right to rule."

"King Boran?"

Harbert coughed up blood and then said something Lucas could not hear, so Lucas got down lower. "They are coming," he heard him say. "And Boran . . . wants to meet you."

Lucas remained silent. He watched Harbert's breathing grow shallower until he took his last breath. He then stood up, grabbed the hilt of his sword with both hands, and pulled it from Harbert's rib cage. Looking around him, he saw that small groups of Killeand's soldiers were still attempting to put up resistance, but most of them had laid down their swords and surrendered. The chosen had all gathered close to him, and Archer handed him the reins of a horse.

Lucas had put his foot in the stirrup and heaved himself into the saddle when Warrick pulled his own horse up alongside him.

"Did you know that man?" asked Warrick.

"He was the mercenaries' leader," answered Lucas. "I saw him at Killeand's." He then gestured to Archer, who was walking away to mount his horse. He seemed relaxed, and Lucas wondered if he knew that his best friend lay wounded inside Meloc's castle. "Does he know about Tanner?" he asked softly.

Warrick followed his gaze and shook his head. "I don't think so," he answered. "He was fighting on the wall when we found Tanner and brought him inside."

"Let's go back and see how Tanner is faring," said Lucas. "I believe we've finished here anyway." He saw the king ride over to Egon and a group of soldiers who had captured Killeand. They had him down on his knees and held a sword to his throat. Riders were coming from the castle gate, and he saw Meloc dismount close to King Itan. The two brothers smiled as they embraced and slapped each other on the back. Lucas kicked his horse into motion and rode over. He stopped and looked at Killeand. The lord had held his head down when the king and Meloc appeared before him but now raised it to look at him.

They stared long and hard at each other before Lucas turned his horse towards the castle and rode off at full speed.

Lucas abandoned his horse as soon as he rode in. He ran up the steps into the castle, followed by Davis and the rest of the chosen. Zera was still by Tanner's side and had not left him. He caught Zera slowly shaking her head when she stepped aside to let him through, and Lucas felt a lump in his throat when he saw Tanner's pale face. He had hoped it had not been that bad, but, if he was honest with himself, he had known already what the outcome would be. He took Tanner's hand in his and leaned in to get closer to him.

Tanner opened his eyes. "Did we win?" he murmured.

"We did," answered Lucas, tears welling up in his eyes. Archer dropped on his knees beside him and stared at their wounded friend. His eyes were watery. The two of them were best friends.

"I would have liked to have seen Lord Killeand's face when he realized he was defeated," said Tanner, managing a smile.

"You will be able to watch his face when he stands trial," said Lucas.

Tanner closed his eyes for a moment, and when he opened them again, he gripped Lucas's hand more tightly. "I won't be," he said. "You know that."

Lucas wanted to respond, but Tanner stopped him by shaking his head. "What is it like?" he asked. "To die? What did you see when you died after the chosen test?"

"You are not going to die," said Archer.

"Archer," said Tanner, who now had tears in his eyes as well. "You know I am. I am sorry I will no longer be there for you. You were always a great friend to me, and I will miss you too, but I need you to be strong. The others need you." He turned back to address Lucas. "For the first time in my life, I'm truly scared, and I need you to tell me what it's like," insisted Tanner. "I want to know what's going to happen."

Lucas swallowed hard and wiped a tear away from his cheek. He looked up at all the chosen, who were standing in a circle around them. Carleton and the elite were there, too. Their faces said everything. Zera stepped forward and stroked Tanner's face, bending to kiss him upon the cheek before returning to her place. They were all trying to be brave for Tanner, and he needed to do the same. For Tanner, and for all of them. He gathered up all his strength and mustered up a smile before looking down at Tanner again.

"It's beautiful," he said. "When I died, I found myself in a field with high green grass. The softest grass you can imagine. The wind was blowing gently through my hair. The sun was shining, and it was quiet, but I wasn't alone. There were people there waiting for me, and they'll be there for you too."

"Are you sure?" asked Tanner. "I don't want to be alone."

Lucas nodded. "You won't be," he answered. "They'll welcome you. It's a place where we will all meet one day again and where we belong. In my case, they told me it wasn't my time yet, and I needed to go back. But I didn't want to. I wanted to stay. It was a good place to be. There was no pain, no suffering . . . only peace." Lucas took a deep breath before he continued. "You'll like it there, and you can wait for the rest of us to come and join you."

Lucas watched as a calmness came over Tanner. He closed his eyes, and Lucas thought he was gone, but then he opened his eyes again.

Tanner whispered softly so only he could hear. "How come you didn't tell me about that enormous black stone in the field?"

Lucas held on to Tanner's hand until he had taken his last breath, and his grip loosened. He slowly let go of him and took a step back so that the others could say their goodbyes. He watched the chosen ones, one by one, kneel by Tanner's side and bow their heads in respect.

Lucas stood fighting back the tears when he heard Archer whisper to his friend—"I will miss you." When Davis folded Tanner's hands on his chest, Lucas could take no more. He backed up and then walked straight past the king and Egon, who stood on the threshold, and stepped out into the bright sunlight.

By nightfall, the dead bodies had been laid on pyres outside the castle walls and set alight. The sound of crackling wood reached Lucas's ears as he stood by the pyre they had built for Tanner. With Davis standing next to him, torch in hand, he watched Archer and three other chosen climb down from the pyre after laying Tanner on it. He could see the despair in Archer's eyes as he walked past him to join the others.

Then Zera stepped forward. A crown of braided straw in her hand. She climbed the pyre as a gentle breeze picked up, ruffling Tanner's hair. Zera brushed a lock of blond hair from his face and placed the crown on his head. She leaned over and pressed her lips on his forehead before slowly backing away.

Lucas glanced over his shoulder to look at the line of chosen behind him when Zera had rejoined them and saw her wipe a tear from the corner of her eye.

"Tanner's death has been a blow to us all," whispered Davis. "But Zera came to me earlier, so . . . angry. I have never seen her like that. She doesn't understand why he had to leave us so soon."

"Neither do I," said Lucas, facing forward again. He struggled to keep his own tears away. "Maybe one day we will all understand."

"Let's hope so," said Davis, falling quiet for a moment. "Are you ready?"

"Yes," answered Lucas. He had a heavy feeling in his chest. What he was about to do was difficult for him, but he had no choice.

Davis gave him an encouraging nod and stepped forward to take his position at one corner of the pyre. Lucas followed his lead and walked over to the other side. He then waited for the chosen to kneel and lower their heads before placing his torch at the base of the woodpile.

CHAPTER 24

Itan stood on the wall, looking out over the sea of flames lighting up the night sky. He had watched the chosen from a distance as they had all gotten down on one knee. Lucas and Davis had lit the fire, placing a torch beneath the wood.

Tanner had been one of many losses that day, but Itan knew it had only just begun. Killeand had admitted to them, when a hot poker was held before his eyes, that he had worked with King Boran. "Finton is with Boran as well," he had told them, when they had demanded that answer. "The time to decide the one true king has drawn near, and I do not believe that king will be you."

Itan had turned away when he saw the hatred in Killeand's eyes. "Do what you must," he told Egon. "Find out why those I thought to be my friends have turned on me."

Meloc came to stand next to him, the fur collar of his black cloak standing up to protect his neck from the cold breeze. He sighed when he saw the fires. Without taking his eyes off the ground below, Itan spoke softly. "You've been right, brother," he said.

"About what?"

"About everything," said Itan. "The prophecy that you always have so loyally and wholeheartedly believed in. Toroun. The chosen ones, and the new king's protector . . . it is all true. I was a fool for not believing it when others did."

Meloc glanced at him. "What changed your mind?"

"He said he didn't know who he was until recently."

"Who?"

"Lucas."

"So, I was right, and he is the one?"

"He is," sighed Itan. "He was born in the night of the brightest star and given the name Baelan. After Boran's father killed his parents, Lucas was brought across the river. The man who raised him and who was supposed to tell him his destiny never got the chance. Lucas did not find out about his heritage until one of his people tracked him down."

"How do you know all this?"

"I spoke with him this afternoon, and he told me. I also read the book, the one you always spoke of, some time ago, and had started to come to my own conclusions. I felt a strong connection with him, from the moment our eyes first met, when he showed up with the circus group. Like I knew him and needed him close."

"It's clear that there were forces at work, beyond anything in this world, that have put him on your path," said Meloc. "The fact that you read my beloved book alone, a book that you once despised, gives me enough reason to believe this."

"I never hated you reading it," replied Itan. "I just couldn't comprehend why you lived by every word of it and what made you believe in the prophecy."

"Do you think it would have made a difference if you had believed in the prophecy sooner?"

"Perhaps," answered Itan. "I did not understand why I was drawn to Lucas for the longest time and resisted it often. At times, I distanced myself. It was not until I noticed Egon protecting him and the chosen behaving as if he was their leader that I felt maybe there was more to it, and I let things take their course."

He pulled the cloak tighter over his shoulders when a cold breeze made him shiver before continuing. "Today, the men were speaking with immense passion about how he saved my life. No one had seen the threat I was facing from the mercenary soldier coming for me, including the king's guard or myself. But Lucas had driven his horse into a group of fighting soldiers as if nothing was going to stop him. He was right there, at the right time, and I am convinced I would not be standing here if he had not." Itan paused and watched one of the pyres collapse, sending sparks high up into the air when the wood hit the ground. It continued to burn after the wood settled, and Itan continued. "One of the king's guards heard the mercenary ask Lucas who he was, and Lucas gave him his name. The mercenary knew who Lucas was. And I think Killeand knew as well. You saw how he only showed respect to Lucas when we had him down on his knees after the fight."

"Then why so glum, brother?" asked Meloc. "If he is the one—and it appears that he is—you have his unwavering loyalty. He has saved your life several times, which means you are the true king and have nothing to fear."

Itan shook his head. "It's not that simple, Meloc. You know more than anyone how Toroun served King Rodin until the end. It was not until the battle had started, and the gods spoke to him, that his loyalty changed."

"You feel Lucas could be a danger to you, then? That he will turn against you if you were ever to face Boran in battle?"

"According to Killeand, a battle is imminent. We extracted enough information from him to know that Boran is planning to come and fight me."

"Did Killeand reveal how he plans on doing this?" asked Meloc.

"There's no way he can bring a whole army across the river in time without us knowing about it and putting a stop to it."

Itan's eyes went to one of the burning pyres, and he sighed. "If he did, he has taken that information with him. Killeand suffered a wound during the battle that proved to be fatal. He collapsed and died before Egon could discover anything more."

"Then what is your plan moving forward? If Lucas is Toroun's descendant, and you are unsure of which side he stands on, all you can do is have him locked up until you defeat Boran—if he does indeed end up finding his way here."

The king turned to look at his brother. "Don't you think that, with all the forces that have been at work here, destiny cannot be circumvented?" He turned back to look at the fires one more time. "What you describe did cross my mind, but I have to accept what is to come. If I am not the true king and Lucas is the one who has a hand in changing that, or rather a force above him and far more powerful than him, then so be it. The only thing I can do is prepare for what is to come."

Itan heard someone cough behind them, and they both turned to see who it was.

"I'm sorry to interrupt, sire," said Egon, "but you wanted to know when they were ready?"

"I did. Thank you, Egon," said the king as he stepped away from the wall and began descending the stairs.

"What is happening?" asked Meloc, following him down.

"I am sending Lucas across the river," he answered in one breath.

Meloc's face dropped. "Are you insane? Why?"

"I need to find out what Boran's plans are, and Lucas told me that the mercenary who attacked me today told him Boran wants to meet him. So, who better to send than him?"

"You are sending the chosen ones as well?" asked Meloc.

"Yes. Hopefully, they can get word back to me," answered the king as they walked towards Lucas. They reached the inner bailey, where all the chosen were mounted up and Lucas stood by his horse. His hair was wet, and he had changed into clean clothes.

"We are ready, sire," Lucas told him.

"Then, I wish you all the best and will await news from you." Itan regretted the words as soon as he'd spoken them—there was an air of desperation to his tone.

"I will send word if and when I am able," answered Lucas, who had already started to mount his horse. The gates opened, and the boy was preoccupied, the king could see. He was already on his next mission.

CHAPTER 25

When the king had pulled Lucas aside after Tanner's death, he had expected it was to scold him for not acknowledging him as he had rushed out of the room where Tanner lay dying. He had reluctantly followed Itan to a quiet corner of the bailey, but the king's demeanor was far from angry when he faced him. Instead, he had stared at him in silence, then asked a question Lucas had not been ready for.

"I don't think I should ignore the rumors any longer," said the king, "or the prophecy that my brother believes to be true. Is there anything you need to tell me?"

Lucas had let Itan's words sink in. He had felt the evolving powers inside of him grow stronger every day, and he knew there would come a time when he would no longer be able to hide his gifts from the king. Harbert had told him King Boran wanted to see him and that he would be coming for Itan. A massive attack in the near future was imminent. "Yes, I believe it is time that I did, sire," he answered, and when the king nodded to indicate that he was listening, Lucas told him everything.

When Lucas finished, the king placed a heavy hand on his shoulder. "Thank you," he said. "For confiding in me. I don't know exactly what I am to do with this information yet, but I will think on it and let you know."

Lucas had found relief in having disclosed his identity to the king. He could finally be who he was supposed to be. Lucas mounted his horse and looked to Egon, who gave him an approving nod, and to Carleton, who now knew his identity as well.

Carleton stepped closer and stroked the neck of his horse as he looked up at him. "Be safe," he said. "The gods may have empowered you, but I have seen you bleed, and you are heading into unknown territory."

"I will," said Lucas before spurring his horse on to ride out of the gates with the chosen right behind him.

They slowed their horses as they passed the fires, out of respect for the dead, and Lucas looked to where they had left Tanner.

"He will still be with us," he heard Davis say next to him.

"Yes, he will," said Lucas and slowly moved them all past. Tanner's death hurt, but he was determined to find meaning in his loss.

Over the next few days, Lucas led them over hills and through forests until they finally reached the river border. They rode up to the water's edge and watched it splash against the rocks. An occasional log or island of debris floated by, and little whirlpools could be seen forming in the water, which was so muddy it looked like ale. The noise from the rushing water was deafening, and there was no easy way for them to cross. They were all tired and decided to make camp before looking for a crossing in the morning. Zera and Warrick went hunting and returned with a small doe, which they roasted above a fire that night.

Lucas laid his head down and observed the swaying tops of the trees and the glistening stars in the sky. With the wind gently rustling through the trees, he soon fell asleep.

He woke to the sound of a whisper sometime later, his eyes popping open in alarm. It was still dark, and all the chosen around him were sleeping. The fire had gone out, and only the embers were still glowing red. The wind had picked up a little, and he listened for the whisper to come again. His hand was resting on his sword, but he felt no presence of danger.

Then he heard it. The whisper that was carried down by the wind, calling his name. He sat up and looked towards the river, where the sound seemed to be coming from. He no longer could hear the thundering roaring of the water crashing on the rocks, only the whisper calling for him. When he got up and took his horse by the reins, the chosen slowly rose as well. Zera and Davis came to stand next to him when he reached the water's edge and stared at the river, which was now as smooth as a lake. The stars twinkled placidly over its surface.

"What happened to the raging river?" asked Zera. "How long will it stay like this?"

"Long enough for us to cross," answered Lucas. He mounted his horse, as did the chosen who had gathered behind him. He had no idea how the river's current had come to slow down but knew somehow that it would stay that way until they were over it. He wondered if, in his subconscious mind, he had been responsible. Like when he was an infant, and the fog had come down to protect his people while they escaped into the mountains. Could it be another gift he possessed but was unaware of? If it were, he would have to find a way to reconnect with it and learn to better control it.

A long-forgotten memory flashed through his mind as his horse stepped into the water. He had heard his name called before, in the night after the fight with the hunters, and he had followed it then, but the river had not been as calm.

The whisper in the wind became louder as he made his way across but stopped once they reached the other side.

They all looked back and watched the water starting to build up again, forming crests and little eddies—it was returning to its natural form. They followed the river's edge for a long time before moving inland. Nobody asked him where they were going, and he would not have been able to answer them if they had. All he knew was that he felt the need to find his people, and he let his intuition guide him. After they turned to go inland, Lucas felt a sense of familiarity around him, like he had been there before. They had been riding through an extensive pine forest, but now the trees had changed, and a denser wood enveloped them.

Lucas rode until they came to a clearing and stopped in the middle of it. The sun was warming his skin, a welcome feeling after the cold dark forest. A magpie flew overhead and landed in a tree close by—Lucas saw it but paid it no attention. His horse snorted gently as the chosen waited.

All was quiet when the first hunter appeared from behind the trees in front of them—a broad-shouldered man whose dark curly hair and full beard made it difficult to detect any facial expressions he might have. Lucas recognized him as the leader who had called off the attack on him when the hunters had caught him and Zera off guard. Armed with a battle ax and shield, he made his way into the clearing and stopped right on the edge of it. More hunters emerged—to his left and right and from behind—until they formed a tight circle around the group of chosen, all along the edge of the clearing. There was no way for them to escape, had they wanted to.

"They look fierce," said Zera softly behind him.

"Their numbers are at least ten times that of us," said Davis. "Fighting them will be impossible."

"Let's hope it doesn't come to that," replied Lucas.

The hunters banged their weapons on their shields, and some of the boys reached for their swords. Lucas held his arm out, gesturing for them not to do so. He had his hand resting on his sword, and without taking his eyes off the leader, he slowly pulled it out. He held his sword above his head and, after a short pause, threw it on the ground before him.

"What are you doing?" whispered Zera. "Have you forgotten that they tried to kill us last time?"

"And they could have," answered Lucas, "but they didn't."

The banging stopped, and all the hunters looked to their leader as he stepped forward and stopped a few yards away from Lucas. "We have met," he shouted, so all could hear.

"We have," responded Lucas.

"You killed eight of my men," said the leader, raising his hand to calm the angry roar of the other hunters.

Lucas sat motionless in his saddle. "I remember," he said. "I also remember I did not initiate that fight, and I do not wish to start one now."

The leader nodded in acknowledgment. "Indeed, you did not, and we would not have attacked you had we known you were there, among that group."

"You know who I am?" asked Lucas.

The leader nodded. "Your birth name is Baelan, and my people have been waiting for your return," he answered, dropping to one knee and bowing his head. "We are here to serve you, as our ancestors did before us."

The men behind him followed his example, and soon, one by one, the other hunters laid down their weapons as well and had dropped to their knees.

"Then we should sit down and talk," said Lucas.

The leader rose to his feet when Lucas jumped off his horse and walked over to him, holding out his hand.

"We shall," he answered. "The name is Orson."

Lucas signaled for the chosen to dismount, and they followed Orson into the forest with the rest of the hunters.

Davis walked next to Lucas and was keeping an eye on the men around him. "I don't like this," he whispered. "You killed some of his men. What will stop them from taking revenge and killing us all?"

"I hear what you are saying," answered Lucas, "but I don't feel we are in danger."

"I'm sorry, but that doesn't quite put me at ease," said Davis.

"Orson called off the attack that day in the forest," replied Lucas. "He could easily have killed me then, but he didn't, and I'm curious to find out how he knew who I was."

They walked a good distance through dense forest before Orson made the loud grunting sound of a buck claiming its territory and waited for a response up ahead. They continued when the call was answered, and Lucas started noticing huts made of upright wooden pillars hidden among the trees. The ground had been trampled, he assumed by the many women and children he saw observing them as they walked through.

Orson stopped when they came to an enormous cliff overhang, where houses were built into the rock. Smoke was rising from different locations throughout this entire hidden village, and women were busying themselves with chores. Children started running up to them when they were clear of the trees, touching the boys and the horses as if they had never seen outsiders before.

"Off you go," said Orson, trying to chase them off. "I apologize for their behavior. We don't get visitors often."

"No need to apologize," said Lucas. "They don't bother me."

The smell of cooked food became stronger as they got closer to the cliff overhang, and it made his stomach rumble. When they reached the cliff, Lucas saw that the only way to get to the houses in the rocks was by climbing ladders.

"Come and take the horses," called Orson to several hunters who stood watching. When they came forward, he pointed to a ladder. "After you," he said.

Lucas looked up the cliff wall before climbing. Curious eyes watched him when he reached the elevated rock dwelling and he stepped away from the ladder to allow Zera and the rest of the boys to come up. He could observe some of the houses below, but the trees obscured most of them. The overhang he stood under was bigger than he had expected. They could easily get every person down below up, if needed, and defend themselves.

Orson led them to two fires. Some hunters were already seated around one of them, and Lucas was asked to take a place near the fire with them. Orson pointed to the other fire for the chosen, but one suspicious look from Davis made Lucas split the group up, with Zera and Davis joining him.

As soon as they all sat down around the fires, three women came and handed out bowls of stewed deer meat in a broth from the pots hanging over the fires and fresh bread from the stone ovens. Lucas thanked the lady who handed him a bowl and waited until everyone else was served before he began eating. He noticed the women remained standing behind them, and a large group of children had gathered close by to watch with wide eyes. Orson looked up from his bowl and followed Lucas's gaze.

"They have heard the stories of our ancestors," explained Orson, as Lucas dipped a piece of bread into his stew. "And of the baby born to the mountain people, who we were asked to bring to safety across the river. They have just learned that you were that baby and are naturally curious."

"I know that the man I thought was my father and who sacrificed his life for me was one of yours," said Lucas before taking another bite. The stew was prepared with spices, and was more flavorful than any food he had ever eaten at the castle. Only the meals he had consumed in his time with the circus cooked by Rosa and Lisette could compare with the stew he was eating now. Some of the chosen boys around him accepted second servings, and he was pleased to see them all growing less tense.

"Einar was my older brother."

Lucas looked up and saw Davis stare at Orson as well. "I'm sorry he died because of me," said Lucas. "He was the only father I ever knew, and I loved him."

Orson nodded. "It is not you who is to blame. He knew how important you were in restoring peace for the people and did not hesitate when he was asked to take you away. His decision to raise you was no surprise to me. Nor was his death, when I learned of it. I am sure he would be proud if he could see you now."

Lucas collected his thoughts. "I have many unanswered questions," he said. "I only recently found out who I am, and you said you knew who I was when you saw me that day in the woods."

"I did," replied Orson. "You look like your father—your true father."

"You knew him?" asked Lucas, surprised.

"I only had the pleasure of meeting him once myself, but my brother and your father were friends. Our people have always known of your continued existence, and I have been kept informed by one of your people."

"Dastan?"

"Yes," acknowledged Orson. "Considering you now know who you are, I take it the two of you have met?"

"We have."

"Your friend here does not trust our intentions," said Orson, changing the subject.

Lucas looked at Davis, who was not eating and was watching everyone's moves. "We were trained to hunt you down and protect the border from you," Lucas said. "Sitting down and sharing a meal with you can't change years of being told we had to fear you."

"We are not the enemy," said Orson while looking sternly at Davis. "We only come across the river when our food supply is low. After King Rodin was defeated, my people have been hunted down and killed . . . ever since we helped Toroun hide his family. These woods have been the only safe place for us for some time now. Boran's soldiers believe it is haunted and will not venture far. Just as your people had to flee to the mountains in the east, mine fled to the woods."

"Why did you not try and discuss this with King Itan?"

Orson shook his head. "My ancestors spoke with his grandfather, but he had no interest in allowing us to come across to live and hunt on his lands. He corrupted the minds of those near him by making us out to be evil killers, who would not only hunt animals, but murder innocent civilians, whenever we pleased. King Itan grew up believing this, and so I do not blame your friends for maintaining those long-established beliefs."

Lucas put his empty bowl on the ground in front of him. One of the women, dressed in a brown, ankle-long tunic and fur vest, came to fill his bowl up, but he declined. She gave a graceful bow and moved to a hunter holding up his bowl.

"We are led to believe that King Boran might be planning on coming across the river to attack King Itan," said Lucas.

"Not the river," answered an elderly man who sat next to Orson. It was clear he was past the age for hunting, but he appeared important to Orson, as did two other men who sat near him. With snow-white hair and aging skin, Lucas took them to be the elders of the village. "There is no chance of him getting an army across without building a bridge. We have it well-patrolled, and there is no indication he is doing such a thing. He has been rounding up young men from villages near the castle in recent years to work in the mines again," continued the village elder, "except, this time, we think he is using them to build a new mountain pass."

"But you don't know this for certain?" asked Lucas.

"No," answered Orson. "We can't get close enough. Boran's castle blocks the way to the valley and the mountains that lay behind it. It's heavily guarded."

"I've been told Boran wants to meet me," said Lucas. "I'm planning on fulfilling his wishes there. I may be able to get close enough to the valley beyond his castle to see what is going on."

One of the older men startled at Lucas's words. He shook his head in disbelief, and another muttered under his breath.

"You will not make it out alive," argued the third elder, who had remained stoic. "You have been hunted like the rest of us. Your people brought you to safety for a reason, and you cannot let Einar's death be for nothing."

The other elders nodded in agreement, and Orson looked to Lucas for a response.

"Boran cannot kill me without my death bringing grim consequences to him. He will die with me if he does kill me, and he probably knows this."

"I do not think it is wise to rely upon the curse keeping you safe," said an elder who had been very quiet up until then. "We do not know with certainty if it applies to Toroun's descendants. The death of Boran's father after he saw to it that your parents were killed could merely have been a coincidence."

Before Lucas could reply, Davis spoke for him. "I'm sure it does apply to him," he said, waiting until he had everyone's attention before continuing. "Lucas has already died. It happened after he was put through the chosen test at King Itan's castle. The elite born responsible for his injury received a small scratch on his neck from Lucas's sword, but, when Lucas's heart stopped, it started to open and seep blood. The king's physician was able to get Lucas's heart started again, and the cut on the elite born's neck closed. I was there and saw it happen."

Lucas looked at Davis.

Even Zera stared at her brother. "You never told me this," she said.

Davis shrugged his shoulders. "It was never talked about, and for the longest time, I didn't want to believe it myself."

"Even so," said the elder, "if Boran doesn't kill you, he may put you in chains and have you locked up, to ensure that no misfortune befalls you. You may remain his prisoner, indefinitely."

"I may have to take that risk," answered Lucas.

"We may be able to help you get close enough to his castle," said Orson. "But it is something I will need to discuss with the others first. There is risk involved for our people. Maybe this will be a good time for you to take some rest." Without waiting for a response, he called one of the women over and introduced her. "This here is Aysla," he said. "She is my wife and will show you where you can stay while you are here. I will come and find you when we have an answer for you. If there is anything you need, ask her, and she will see to it."

"I will, and thank you," said Lucas. He thought it was in their best interest not to upset the hunters. The chosen stood up quietly and followed Aysla through the maze of houses built from stone and mud to a smaller structure at the far back, built against the cliff face. When they entered, Lucas saw it was the size of a small shepherd's hut. The chosen crowded into the space, where a few wooden benches were tightly fitted along the walls around an open space in the middle where a fire was already lit and producing heat. Other women came in to lay fur and woolen blankets down on the floor and benches and then left after Aysla approved their work.

"You can rest here," said Aysla. "If there is anything you need, just call for me."

"Thank you," answered Lucas and watched her leave.

"Now what?" asked Warrick.

"Now we take turns to rest," said Lucas.

"Do you trust them?" asked Davis, who still seemed tense.

"I'm not sure," answered Lucas honestly. He wanted to, but like the chosen, he had also grown up hearing stories about hunters. "I think we can," he said, "as long as they don't think we are a threat to them or bring danger to their people. They will protect their own first."

Lucas took his place on a bench by the door with Archer and took the first watch. The rest of the boys and Zera spread out over the benches and laid down. A hide that hung in the door opening prevented anyone else from seeing in, but it also prevented them from seeing out. Archer sat opposite him and pulled the hide aside a little to peer out.

"Are you all right?" asked Lucas softly. "We haven't really talked about this, but I know you miss Tanner."

Archer dropped the hide and looked down to the ground. "I do," he answered. "We came to Itan's within weeks of each other and became fast friends . . . but death can be around the corner for any of us. We all know this. Tanner did too."

"It doesn't make it any easier."

"No," said Archer, "it doesn't, but I like to think his death had meaning." He lifted his head and looked at Lucas. "Would you have told the king who you are, and would he have allowed us to come here if it had not been for Tanner leaving us?"

"I don't know," answered Lucas truthfully. He had not thought about it this way for the chosen, but everything that had happened to him seemed to have a meaning. "Probably not. But we also do not yet know what we will gain from coming here. My hope is that there will be purpose in our journey, and that no more of us will be lost."

They sat in silence after that, Lucas's thoughts churning, while the chosen behind them slept. A few hours later, they laid down their heads, and Davis and Warrick took over the watch.

Early the following morning, Orson came to them and asked Lucas to step out to talk to him. Lucas slipped his boots on, assuring Davis and Zera it would be just fine that he go alone. He stepped outside and saw Orson waiting for him on the other side of the narrow path separating the houses and headed in his direction, but had to come to an abrupt stop before crossing a footpath to prevent a collision—a group of children playing a game of chase was running past at breakneck speed.

"Hey," shouted Orson at the children. "No running up here. You know better."

Lucas saw the children slow to a quick walk and heard their echo of laughter die off underneath the cliff's overhang. He watched the children disappear between the houses and continued to join Orson. "You wanted to speak to me?"

"Yes," replied Orson. His expression was now serious. "A decision has been made. The elders feel that it's not our place to show you the way to Boran's castle without the approval of your people. Boran is dangerous and calculating. He will have crafted a plan for your arrival. You must see your people first before you go to Boran. They have been waiting for your return, and you owe it to them." Orson waited until Lucas nodded in agreement before he continued. "I have sent a messenger to your people to arrange a meeting. It will be a few days before we receive word. You can stay here and remain as our guests until then. You are free to go anywhere in the village if you like, but I advise you not to venture into the woods without being accompanied by one of us. There are many traps set up to prevent the village from being discovered—it will not be safe if you do not know where they are."

"I'll inform the chosen," responded Lucas.

"Then I officially welcome you to our village," said Orson, placing a hand briefly on Lucas's shoulder before walking off.

During the next few days, the chosen settled into village life by helping with general chores and building a new hut on the lower grounds for a young family. They looked after their horses and played with the children. Zera could often be found sitting on the ground, a circle of children around her. Lucas smiled inwardly whenever he walked past. Her voice grew animated as she told story after story, and Lucas even heard her laugh. He hoped it was a sign that she had found a way to heal and move past the loss of Tanner.

Davis and Warrick had not been pleased when Lucas told them they could not leave the village on their own, but they were soon invited to accompany a hunting party and cheered up after that. They returned from the hunt invigorated and in good spirits, excitedly informing Lucas of all the clever traps the hunters had set out for miles all around the village—anything from fall pits to spiked beams which would swing down when set off, to nets and poisoned darts, all very well hidden. The only way to know where they were was from memory or the subtle marks left on trees.

Orson had two young sons, Bo and Ari, who followed Lucas around everywhere unless their mother called them away to give him a break from them. Bo was the oldest by one year and slightly taller than his six-year-old brother, and both looked like their father, with their round faces and black curly hair. Lucas enjoyed their company. Entertaining the young boys reminded him of playing with Ana when he lived with the circus and Princess Amalia when she visited when he worked in the storage room at the castle—he had missed the presence of young children. The boys showed Lucas their fighting skills, and, in return, he taught them new skills.

"If our uncle raised you . . ." asked Ari one evening, as he stood facing Lucas with a stick as a pretend sword in hand ". . . does that make you our cousin?"

"To be our cousin, he has to be blood-related," said Bo, who was watching nearby.

"That's right," replied Lucas, "but your uncle was like a father to me, so I suppose I am your cousin in that regard." Ari came towards him, and Lucas pretended to be hurt when he let him stab him with the stick. He let go of his sword and held his stomach as he fell to the ground and lay still.

"It looks like you killed him," Lucas heard Zera say.

"He's all right," said Bo. "My brother didn't kill him. Lucas is only joking. Watch." Bo dropped by Lucas's side and started poking him.

"Well, he looks dead to me," said Zera when Lucas remained still and didn't move.

"No, he's not!" shouted Ari and ran over to join his brother. Now both boys were trying to get a reaction out of him.

Lucas waited a few seconds before letting out a roar and reaching up to grab both boys. They screamed at first but then laughed when he started to tickle them.

Zera stood over them and shook her head, smiling. "I don't think I've ever seen you horseplay quite like this," she said.

"These are my cousins," said Lucas. He lifted the boys up by their waist, one at a time, and put them back on their feet before standing up himself and brushing off the dirt from his clothes.

Bo and Ari nodded to Zera.

"Well," said Zera with a grin. "You may want to bring your cousins with you to the lower grounds then. They are holding a wrestling match between the older hunter boys, and some of the chosen have decided to join in."

"Oh really?" asked Lucas. "Which?"

"Warrick, Peyton, Silas, and Archer, I believe," said Zera as she put her foot on the ladder to climb down from the cliff. "It will be interesting to see."

Lucas agreed and followed Zera to a clearing in the forest where a crowd stood gathered. He saw the chosen standing among them, and Lucas went to stand next to Davis. In front of him were two hunter boys wrestling each other on the ground. One of the boys had the upper hand and was lying on top of the other, who was trying to wriggle out from underneath to no avail. People suddenly cheered, and the boy who had been on top stood up. He put his hands up in triumph and then helped the other boy to his feet.

"What made him win the game so fast?" asked Lucas softly.

"He was able to pin his opponent down on both shoulders for a few seconds," answered Davis.

"Is that the only rule?"

"No," answered Davis. "When you tackle your opponent to the ground, you have to do so within the perimeter of the circle, and you are not allowed to grab hold of any clothing."

Lucas heard Warrick called to the center. He was to face a muscular hunter boy much wider than him but shorter. Both boys waited until someone shouted "Begin!" and then the match was on. They grabbed each other by their upper arms, and struggled for some time until Warrick managed to get his opponent to the ground, but the hunter boy used his weight to roll over and was soon on top of Warrick.

"Come on, Warrick," shouted the chosen. "You can do this!" But Warrick couldn't, and the hunter boy won.

The wrestling games continued, with other boys facing each other until only one was left, much like the tournament Lucas had taken part in once. The hunter boys were more skilled in wrestling than the chosen, but they all put up a good fight.

There was much cheering and laughter that evening, and the chosen felt happy and relaxed when they settled into their sleeping quarters that night.

They all laid down, except for Davis. "I will take the first shift," he said and sat himself down by the door.

"I think we are fine without a watch, Davis," said Lucas. "Why don't you try and get a full night's rest?" Lucas had made his bed on the floor and was ready to close his eyes.

Davis shook his head and peered through the doorway. "I know we have been welcomed in their village, and they are treating us well," he replied, "but we are still outsiders to them."

Lucas rolled over onto his side. "Very well," he said. "Wake me when you want to go to sleep, and I'll take over." He yawned, feeling sleep take over almost as soon as he closed his eyes.

CHAPTER 26

Byram sat hidden in a corner of a town inn, by the shadowy flickering light of a large cobblestone fireplace that protruded from the back wall.

The waitress came over and placed a mug of ale in front of him. "Anything else I can get you, sir?" she asked.

"No," answered Byram.

"Something to eat, perhaps?"

"I said no," snarled Byram and waved her away with his hand. He wanted to be left alone.

The waitress left, looking over her shoulder as she went. He could tell he had unnerved her, but he didn't care. He wasn't there for polite talk nor to practice cordial manners.

He traced his finger over the lines carved in the table, each of which he imagined could tell its own story. Deep stab marks in the table spoke to moments when someone had stood up to prove a point, to threaten someone, or to claim what was owed. Long straight lines showed where someone had been lazy and cut their bread directly on the table instead of using the provided wooden board.

There were decorative swirls as well, evidence of a bored patron who sat at this table for some considerable time—he considered contributing to those, as he'd been sitting at this table for the last five nights in a row and was becoming restless. Watching men laugh, argue, sing—getting drunker and drunker as the evening progressed, and the occasional fight that resulted—all while he waited, sober and still.

He was waiting for a man he had seen for the first time at an inn not very different from this one many years ago. If he had known who he was, then his companions might all still be alive. The boy would have been theirs to take, and he would not have to sit here night after night, with his desire for revenge festering and growing.

After they had failed to secure the boy by the creek, his life had changed—he was all that remained of the black order. After Boran heard how close they had come to catching the boy, he had been fueled with anger and frustration.

"By God's bones," King Boran shouted, jumping to his feet from the marble throne he had been sitting on. "There were *four* of you and only *one* of him."

"The boy used his gift of controlling horses, sire," said Byram. "His horse charged at us, bucking, and kicking. There was nothing we could do."

"There was so much you could have done," roared Boran. "You knew he had the gift. I did not tell you to drug your horse to block their senses for nothing. You failed me."

"With all due respect, sire," said Byram, "Garam was the one in charge, and I followed his orders. If you allow me to recruit new men into the dark order, I promise I will deliver the boy to you."

"No!" shouted Boran. "I no longer see a need for the dark order. You are finished."

Byram had turned to Grant, who had been standing near the king, but saw him shake his head slowly, indicating that it would be unwise to further challenge the king's decision.

He had been stripped of his title after that day and all the privileges that he had become accustomed to. No longer feared or respected, he had been sent away with a group of disgruntled soldiers and officers to patrol the forest's edge. They were to find a way into the woods and track down the hunters' hideout. After lying in wait and patrolling for weeks without any sign of hunters, his troop had grown hungry and fatigued, and even more discontent.

Fearing mutiny, another failure, and more humiliation, he had told his officers to build a camp and wait for him while he would go and do what he did best. It had not taken him long to find someone who gave up the information he needed, after some coercion. He had found the shepherd boy sleeping underneath a tree in a field a few miles from the forest and just off the road leading into town. His sheep were grazing on the lush green grass, and a young black and white dog sat watching nearby.

Byram dismounted and took a piece of dry meat from his saddle-bag. "Come here," he said softly as he kneeled to hold the food out for the dog. "Here, puppy. Come and get it." He glanced at the shepherd boy, but he remained asleep when the dog started wagging its tail and started coming over. The dog sniffed the meat, but just before sinking its teeth into it, Byram reached forward. The animal yelped when he grabbed it by the scruff of the neck and lifted it off the ground.

The boy woke and jumped to his feet. "Sir! What are you doing to my dog, sir?" he called out.

"Shh," said Byram, holding the dog out in front of him. "No need to get upset." He put his arm around the dog and pressed it against his chest. He hated dogs, and every fiber in his being wanted to end its life right there and then, but that would not serve his purpose.

"I want to ask you a simple question," continued Byram and gestured to the sheep grazing in the field. "Do you always let your herd graze in the vicinity of the forest?"

"I do," answered the boy. His eyes moved away from the sword around Byram's waist and returned to the mutt Byram held pressed against his chest.

"And do you watch the people traveling this road, or are you in the habit of sleeping when you should be attending your sheep?"

"No, sir," said the boy. "I only took a short nap today. I'm always alert to who enters and leaves the town. My mother and father, they—"

"Perfect," said Byram. He stared hard at the boy. "Then you can probably tell me if you have seen hunters leave the forest?" He held the puppy more tightly, causing it to whine as the boy was shaking his head. He repeated the question, and released his grip when the boy nodded. "When?" he asked. "When do they leave the forest?"

"The only time a hunter leaves the forest is to meet with a man at the inn."

"What does this man look like?" asked Byram.

"Tall and muscular," said the boy. "Brown hair at shoulder length. Leather trousers and a suede vest."

Byram recalled the man immediately, and his heart skipped a beat with excitement. No longer bound to carry out the king's order to capture the boy that had cost him his dignity unharmed, he vowed to take his revenge.

"Another drink, sir?" asked the waitress, pulling him out of his head.

Byram looked up and shook his head. "Not right now," he answered, returning to his thoughts after he watched her go to another table. He wanted to kill the man responsible for standing in his way, and, when that was done, he would kill the boy who King Boran believed to be the key to securing the throne forever.

He'd been recruited into the order a short time after the rumor that the boy was still alive was fueled by stories of a circus boy with exceptional sword skills. Einar had already been killed at that time, but when Garam had filled him in after the fact, the story had made sense to Byram. Einar's last words—that the baby he was supposed to protect had drowned in the river—had felt plausible. Garam himself had seen the pair go under and they had failed to find evidence of a child at his house when they had finally tracked him down. The noise they had heard by the door, which had resulted in Einar's death, proved nothing more than a bird.

The bird had been responsible for the scar across Garam's face. It had flown up from the ground and attacked him after he'd gone outside to investigate.

After Byram became the sixth and final member of the black order, they set out to see if any of the rumors could be accurate but found no sword-fighting boy performing with any of the circus groups they observed. They were on their way back to report the gossip to be false when a chance encounter with a lone circus wagon changed everything. It had been a frigid night, and, not expecting anyone to be on the road that late, Garam had decided it would be safe to build a small fire. All six of them were sitting around it, trying to warm their cold feet and hands, when they heard the creaking sound of wagon wheels stop on the road. Not saying a word, Garam had gone to investigate. He returned a short time later with a scrawny-looking lad who immediately froze when he caught sight of the rest of them.

"I thought you said you were merchants?" the lad had said to Garam, unable to hide the tremble in his voice.

"We are!" said Garam, slapping him encouragingly on the shoulder as he walked over to the fire. "Come and sit. Warm yourself."

"You look more like soldiers," said the lad, still standing hesitantly some distance away.

"We are brothers," explained Garam. "We dress this way because it scares off the thieves and keeps our goods safe."

Byram noticed the lad looking around for a wagon, which they did not have, and he saw Garam realizing the same thing. "Our merchandise does not require a wagon for transporting," he quickly said. "Just strong saddlebags and daggers for protection, if you know what I mean."

The lad thought for a moment and then appeared to understand what Garam meant.

"Well," he said. "You don't have to worry about me. There are many of you and only one of me, and I'm no thief. I'm not even armed. I work for a circus."

"Really?" asked Garam, meeting his companions' gazes with a sinister smile on his face. "How interesting. Then I am sure you can brighten our evening with your tales as you warm yourself by our fire and drink some of our ale."

Byram had scooted over to make space and held out a cup.

Whether it was Garam's smooth-talking or the ale that took hold of him, the lad soon made himself comfortable and relaxed as the evening went on. Byram didn't like him. He found him to be arrogant and self-assured. The lad laughed at his own jokes, and they had to laugh with him to keep him at ease, which irritated him.

"So, tell me . . ." Garam had said, still snickering after the last story. Byram was astounded that the boy couldn't see through it. "You seemed startled when you thought we were soldiers. Any particular reason for that?"

The lad had stopped laughing, suddenly becoming more serious, and took another sip of his drink before answering. "Not really. Not anymore, at least. I got rid of the thing they are looking for."

Garam sat up. "So, you are a thief? You stole from soldiers?"

The lad quickly tried to take his words back. "No, no, it wasn't something that was theirs. It was something that we had, but they wanted."

"Hmm," said Garam. "What kind of *thing* could a circus have that would be of any interest to soldiers?"

The lad looked around, and when he saw everyone's eyes on him, Byram saw that his desire to captivate his audience took over, and he soon told his entire story. No one interrupted him, and they refilled his cup to keep him talking.

"Now, you told us that this boy knows what is happening all around him, without even looking?" asked Garam, after the lad finally finished his obviously exaggerated version of the story.

"Yes, pretty unbelievable, right? I tried to sneak up on him so many times, but he always turned around at the right time."

"But you also said you knocked him out and caused him to miss a meeting with the king?"

"Maybe that time was different because he was kneeling and pre-occupied with the goat. I had no intention to do what I did—it all happened so quick." The ale had made the lad tired, and he started to yawn. "Anyway, I don't have to worry about him anymore. My uncle will make his life miserable. He has a lifetime of hard work and a bed in a smelly barn at the inn to look forward to."

The lad took another sip and silently watched the fire, not paying any attention to Garam standing up and walking behind him.

"You're right," said Garam. "You don't have to worry about him anymore. He'll be our problem now."

Puzzled by the remark, the boy had sat up and started to turn to look at Garam, but the last thing he would have seen would have been Garam's hands grabbing his head and twisting it to break his neck.

It had come as no surprise to Byram that Garam had felt the need to kill him. He personally would have done the same—he had grown tired of the boy's presence as well. Except the manner of how and when would have been different. He preferred a clean cut to the throat and only after his victim was made aware of what was about to happen.

They used the wagon to make his death look like an accident—so perhaps no blade to the neck had been wise given the circumstances—and set off in the direction he had come from in search of an inn and a boy matching the description. The lad had never mentioned the inn by name, and they didn't know how long he had traveled prior to their encounter with him.

"We should have asked the name of the inn," Garam had repeatedly grumbled, until Byram was about ready to twist *his* neck.

They had stopped at several inns along the way, some of which had stable boys working for them, which slowed their search. They would stay at the inn, befriend the boy if he appeared to be of the right age, and then go on to see how eager and capable he was to fight. When they finally came across a boy named Lucas, someone else had as well. They were never able to get close enough because Lucas himself was guarded—this other person seemed to be protecting him. Then two of their members thought they had a chance when they saw him go into the woodshed alone. They must have seen him kneel to collect wood and recalled the part of the story where the only time the circus kid had been able to sneak up on the boy was when he had knelt and was preoccupied. Without time to get the rest of them, they had decided to take him on their own. They paid for it with their lives, and the group was suddenly down by two men.

Fearing exposure, Garam decided it was best for the rest of them to distance themselves from their fallen comrades and the inn. They had left in the midst of the chaos and watched Lucas driven off in the prison wagon.

Dressed in civilian clothes and hidden among the curious at the courthouse, Byram had witnessed how the other guest from the inn had stepped forward in the boy's defense. He made himself known as Dastan, and his words saved Lucas from the gallows and had him sent to the mines instead. They could have attacked the prison transport when some of the guards went to a tavern to drink one night, but they discovered King Itan's patrol troop resting not too far away and decided to let them pass first. They had no way of knowing that an officer in that troop would recognize Lucas amidst the other prisoners and rob them of their best opportunity of securing him.

No other chance would present itself for nearly two years, with Lucas safely tucked away behind the walls of Itan's castle. The few times he did leave those walls, he was surrounded by soldiers and chosen ones.

Becoming desperate, Garam decided that the only way they would succeed in their mission was to get Lucas out of the castle when he and everyone else would least expect it—an idea that seemed virtually impossible until they befriended the castle's supply delivery man at the local tavern by paying his drinking debt for him. He told them everything they needed to know, and after Garam put more coins on the table, he even agreed to put the poison in the water barrel that the chosen drank from. The plan was flawless, and he still could not believe how it all went so wrong.

Byram looked up when a group of men started to sing at a table nearby. When they quieted down again, he let his thoughts go back to the moment Garam told King Boran they had failed a second time. He'd watched the rage well up in Boran's face and had instinctively put his hand on his sword to protect himself from an outburst, which he was convinced would have happened if it was not for Boran's priest, who suddenly stepped forward.

"The boy survived the fall, you say?" the priest asked calmly. "And they took him to a monastery?"

"That's correct," answered Garam.

The priest turned around to face Boran and smiled. "Then that is a good thing," he said.

Boran shook his head, still enraged. "How is that a good thing?" he roared, waving his hand angrily towards all of them. "Those fools had him! They let him slip out of their hands and nearly killed him. If the curse is real, and Lucas had perished that day, then I could have been dead."

The priest nodded calmly. "But that did not happen, did it?"

"No, it did not."

"Then it is a good thing. If the boy had died, the gods would have had to punish you for it, but he did not."

"Meaning?"

"That the gods favor you, sire," said the priest. "They do not want you to die, so they arranged for the boy to be taken to a place where they will heal him and make him strong again."

"Only to be returned to Itan, no doubt," said Boran bitterly.

"This boy, Lucas, does not decide who is to become the true king," said the priest. "Toroun was loyal to your grandfather until the end. I have been trying to tell you for years now that it does not matter where the boy is and who raises him."

"Yes, but I need him in my sight. When the time for the final battle is upon us, I can make sure I have him locked up and nowhere near me if I sense the gods do not favor me as the true king."

Heeding the priest's advice, King Boran told Garam to stand down for the time being. It would be years before they were ordered to try again, and it was a decision that had proved to be deadly wrong. The boy had grown, and had developed a strong connection with people close to him. Having already developed the gift of knowing, which had caught them off guard at the inn, it was now believed he also had Toroun's gift with horses. The priest had given Garam an elixir to give to their horses when they were going to make a move on the boy. It would block the horses' minds, and Lucas would not be able to connect with them.

They approached him by the creek, but they had underestimated the boy's abilities. He saw his first comrade fall when they set in pursuit, and had then jumped into the saddle behind the boy, but was knocked unconscious by a low-hanging branch. When he finally came around and set in his pursuit, he had caught a glimpse of Garam and his last comrade as they were being killed, but he was too far out to do anything about it. The boy then disappeared with the man he recognized from the inn.

A cool night breeze came into the inn Byram currently occupied as the door swung open. Byram tilted his head slightly to see who would enter, but when no one did, and the door remained halfway open, his senses alerted him his wait might finally be over. He sat back and watched the waitress turn towards the door, and while she continued to serve some patrons their drinks, he noticed the slightest sideways movement of her head, as if she was telling someone not to come in. From where Byram was sitting, he could not see the person by the entrance door and knew it could easily be someone of interest only to the waitress, but then he saw the innkeeper make an excuse to the person he had been talking to and walk over to her. He whispered something in her ear and then made his way to a room behind the bar.

The waitress finished putting the drinks down, laughed at one of the patron's jokes, and discreetly walked over to the entrance. She exchanged a few words with whoever was there and then closed the door without letting the person enter. Byram caught her looking in the direction of the room behind the bar when she came back in. She then glanced in his direction, and, by her agitated body language, he knew his night had just become more interesting.

He had watched the waitress closely these past few nights. She was pretty, and pleasant, but older than waitresses he encountered at other inns he frequented. He could tell that working long hours with men who were trying to get her attention for reasons other than ordering a drink was wearing on her. She did not encourage their attention and served their drinks with a strained smile on her face. Why was she not with her husband, cooking his dinner and tending to his children? Perhaps she had no family.

Out of curiosity, he had followed her one night after she finished work to a small house at the edge of town. He watched her go in, and a few minutes later, another woman came out.

"I'll see you tomorrow," said the woman, waving goodbye to the waitress closing the door behind her. After the woman disappeared from sight, he peered into the window to see the waitress kiss a child on the forehead. The child was sleeping in a cot.

He waited a moment and then waved the waitress over to his table.

"Another one, sir, this late at night?" she asked when he ordered another drink.

"Why not," he said with a smile. "I have nothing better to do."

She forced a smile back and went to get him another drink. When the innkeeper came back, they spoke a few words, but Byram managed to avoid their gaze as they looked in his direction.

He ordered one more time after that, sipping slowly to pass the time, which allowed him to observe drinks being taken to the back room throughout the night by the waitress. He left with the last intoxicated patrons and first walked towards the back of the inn, but whoever had been let into the room near the back exit was long gone. He then made his way to the waitress's house, where he knew the other woman would still be watching her child. He knocked on the door, and after it opened, he forced his way in and did what he did best to leave no witnesses. He then waited for the waitress to return to her home, and before she could scream, he had her pinned to the wall with his hand over her mouth and a bloody knife pointed at her stomach.

"Do not scream," he said while she looked wild-eyed from her friend on the floor to where the child lay in the cot. "Your child is still alive, for now," he told her. "But you are going to tell me what I want to know if you don't want that to change."

He waited until she nodded, then slowly took his hand from her mouth but kept her pinned to the wall. "I know who it was, by the door tonight, and who was there to meet him in the back room. All I want to know is what was said and where I can find him tonight."

"I don't know, sir," the waitress pleaded. "He comes sometimes, and I bring the drinks. They don't talk to me."

Byram shook his head. "Come now. I know you are lying. You know him, and you know him well."

"I know nothing. Please, sir," she pleaded, but he dragged her towards the child's cot and pointed the knife at the little sleeping girl. Tears were streaming from her eyes as she begged him not to harm her child, but he never had any empathy, and it had no effect on him. She took another look at the child and then told him that the man at the door was someone named Dastan, and he came from the mountains.

"I already told you I knew that," Byram hissed impatiently, pointing the knife back at her. He had to restrain himself from using it already. He never left any witnesses alive, but she had not told him yet what he needed to know. "Tell me something I don't know, or you can watch your child die first."

"I don't know where he is now," she cried. "He goes back to the mountains to report to his people every time he meets one of the hunters in the back room. He doesn't hang around."

"What were they talking about?"

"About someone named Baelan. He came to the hunters—he is at their camp."

Byram stared at the waitress's face and knew she had spoken the truth. This information suddenly reset his priorities. He had a fast horse and over a hundred soldiers at his disposal. If only he could find the hunters' hideout while they were still waiting for their messenger to return, then he could take them all by surprise.

He glanced over at the sleeping child and smiled. "I think there is something else you can tell me."

CHAPTER 27

Lucas rolled onto his back and listened to the sound of the village as it was winding down and settling in for the night. Soon all he could hear was the crackling of burning wood in the fire. When the village had gone completely quiet, he turned to face his sleeping friends. They were lying spread out over the benches and breathing peacefully.

Davis was the only one who was awake. He was sitting by the door to keep watch and leaned down to grab another log. "Can't sleep?" asked Davis when he put the log in the fire.

"No," answered Lucas, pushing himself upright. "I feel the air shifting."

"Perhaps a storm is coming," said Davis. He pulled the hide aside and stepped outside. He was only gone for a few seconds before walking back in. "No, I don't feel . . ." He stopped and stared at Lucas wide-eyed before rushing over.

"Not a storm," said Lucas as his breathing became rapid, and he felt he was going to pass out. Davis caught him by the shoulders just in time and laid his head down.

"What's happening?" asked Davis as Lucas closed his eyes. "Lucas, talk to me."

Davis's voice became distant as Lucas let his mind drift beyond the hunters' village and into the pitch-black forest. As he advanced, leaves separated before his eyes until he saw a horse trying to find a path through. The horse's nose brushed against the damp leaves as he moved forward. His rider held him in just enough, so he placed his hooves gently on the moss below to prevent making too much noise. A second horse was close behind, with a third and fourth appearing to his side and more following, their riders all anxious like the first but determined to press forward as they followed the soldiers on foot in front of them—

Lucas sat up abruptly and saw all the chosen awake and watching him.

"They are coming," he told them.

"Who?" asked Davis.

"Boran's soldiers."

"But Orson said they did not dare to enter the forest. Out of fear of it being haunted."

Lucas pushed himself up and made his way to the door. "He did say that, but someone else is leading them in. Someone driven by his own motivations, who won't let anyone stand in his way."

"Do you know this person?"

"I have met him," answered Lucas, standing up. He looked at the group of chosen. "We need to get ready," he said and quickly left the sleeping quarters.

A sleepy Orson appeared outside when Lucas called him from outside his door.

"Why have you woken me?" asked Orson. He brushed his hand through his hair as he yawned. "It can't be more than a few minutes after midnight."

"You must get your men ready," said Lucas without wasting any time. "Boran's soldiers have entered the forest."

Suddenly alert, Orson stared at him wild-eyed. "How?" he started to say but then shook his head. "Forget it. It doesn't matter how you know. How far are they?"

"If they continue moving at the pace they have been, and encounter no obstacles along the way, then they will reach the village just after dawn."

Orson stepped inside his house and grabbed his weapons. "Still time, then," he said and put his hands to his mouth to blow a low whistle. The sound alerted four hunters who came out of their houses and gathered around him. Orson filled them in, and each of them disappeared in a different direction.

Lucas observed not a shred of panic as the village systematically awoke and began to prepare for an attack. Everyone knew what to do as if they had practiced for this day all their lives. There was no shouting, no crying from sleepy children lifted from their beds. Women, children, and the elderly who lived on the lower grounds made their way up with supplies, helped by those on the top. Barricades were put up all along the edge of the cave and traps set. Groups of men gathered with weapons in an open area by the forest's edge and waited patiently for Orson's instructions.

Lucas kneeled on the ground in front of the chosen and stared at the woods before him. When he rose, he approached Orson and the elders. "The soldiers on horseback have slowed down," he told them, "but the soldiers on foot have spread out and are pressing forward."

"They have reached the denser part of the forest already then," Orson frowned.

"The traps will slow them down," said one of the elders. "That will buy us more time."

Orson shook his head. "It may not. If they have spread out, any trap going off will only take out one or two at a time, and will only make them move forward more cautiously. It's not enough to deter an army on a mission."

"How many soldiers are coming?" asked the elder.

"Perhaps a hundred," answered Lucas.

"That is more than we can prepare for," said Orson. "They will overrun the village."

"Then we need to do our name justice," replied the elder. "Turn this around and let the hunted become the hunter again."

Orson's face brightened up when he heard the elder's words. He thought for a moment, and then Lucas saw him walk up to each group of hunters. After receiving their instructions, they headed off into the forest.

The last to go was Orson's group. Lucas and the chosen joined them.

They walked in silence through the dark forest. Orson stopped from time to time to get more information from Lucas, which he then passed on to the other groups by making different animal sounds. With the last message passed, they halted in a large fern field that grew between two ridges in the forest. Orson had everyone spread out and crouch down on the damp ground that soaked their clothes.

"This reminds me of the place where the hunters ambushed us," whispered Zera. "It was daylight then, but we had not been able to see them. Now, with the forest still in darkness, it is difficult even to see our own."

"Yes," said Lucas softly. "The only advantage we have here is that we know the soldiers are coming, and the soldiers have no idea we are here."

"And so, the prey becomes the predator," added Davis. For once, as if all his pent-up somberness of the last few days had bubbled over, he smirked. "Just like the elder suggested."

Lucas, with his sword in his hand, used his mind to see the first men advance over the ridge and stop when they noticed the field of fern in front of them. Having encountered traps already, no doubt they were suspicious—Lucas could only imagine that this was why they did not continue.

Orson was crouched close to Lucas, and after having waited several minutes with no further movement from the soldiers, he nudged him. "Listen," he whispered.

Before Lucas could ask him what he should listen for, he heard it. It was what the soldiers had been waiting for. Far in the distance, the faint sound of barking could be heard. Orson's eyes grew wild, and he looked panicked. Lucas knew all too well that if dogs were released into the ferns, their cover would certainly be blown, and a surprise attack would be out of the question, resulting in more casualties on their side.

"We have to move to higher ground," said Orson. He cupped his hands and mimicked the call of an owl, which, as Lucas had learned from the village children, was the signal to retreat. He was about to make the call once more, but stopped when Lucas shook his head.

"Dawn is almost upon us," said Lucas. "With the forest becoming lighter, the soldiers will see us. Leave this to me and the chosen."

Orson made the sound of a mockingbird, which was the signal for negating any previous command—Zera had shared that learned fact only a day ago. Their time spent among the village children was proving more useful by the moment.

Lucas tapped Davis on his shoulder and gestured to have all the chosen move forward slowly.

Davis nodded and tapped Warrick on the shoulder to pass the message on, but Warrick narrowed his eyes and shook his head.

"Go forward," mouthed Lucas when Warrick looked at him, but he didn't move, so Lucas crawled closer to him.

"I hear dogs," said Warrick when Lucas was next to him.

"I know," said Lucas, "but I need you to trust me." The chosen were strongly connected to him, but the hunters were not, and he feared that he would not be able to stop the dogs from attacking Orson and the others. The chosen would have to get in front, so that the dogs would reach them first. "Crawl forward until you feel you need to stop," Lucas told them, "and I'll direct you the rest of the way. I'm not going to let anything happen to you."

Warrick nodded reluctantly and then passed on the signal to the chosen next to him. The dogs had stopped barking, but they were coming. With the chosen now ahead of the hunters, they would be the first to be detected and attacked by the dogs and soldiers that followed. Except Lucas had no intention of allowing that to happen.

He closed his eyes and concentrated on the space all around him until dense fog began rising from the ground in front, which became thicker as it continued upward. The dogs' heavy panting could be heard as they ran over the ridge and passed the soldiers in the front lines. Lucas refocused his attention and connected with the dogs as he had with horses. The dogs' panting suddenly stopped, and all was eerily silent. With the fog still there, only Lucas could see each of the chosen with a dog laying on its belly next to them and facing the direction of the soldiers. The dogs were large, their jaw structures impressive, which gave Lucas hope that his plan might work. Each chosen kept one hand on a dog's head and waited until he gave the signal.

Lucas felt his heart pound in his chest. The tension of those around him increased, and he prepared himself for a fight that was inevitable. With chosen and dogs in place, the fog lowered itself, flattening out until it covered the entire field just above the ferns.

CHAPTER 28

Byram caught up with the foot soldiers standing on a ridge in front of a field of fern. "What are they waiting for?" he asked an officer. "Get them to move forward."

"They believe something is wrong with the fern, sir."

"Did the dogs go past them?"

"Yes, they did."

"And?"

The officer shrugged his shoulders. "They went quiet, sir."

"Then they need to move," shouted Byram. "With the dogs now well ahead, they'll soon reach the hunter's hideout. If the men are not right behind them, it will ruin the surprise element of our attack." He rode his horse into several soldiers, driving them from the ridge. He then watched as the rest of the frightened soldiers began to move down and, with stilted movements, enter the field of ferns. As soon as they were a few yards in, the fog rose behind them and blocked his view. It was quiet for just a moment, and then the sound of dogs growling and muffled howls coming from men in agony could be heard coming from the fog. The horses spooked and reared up, nearly throwing officers off. They looked frantically at each other to find an explanation for what was happening in front of them, and Byram had no answer for them. Before long, soldiers were running back out of the fog, some collapsing before they even reached the ridge.

"Get back in there!" Byram shouted to a soldier who was scrambling up the ridge to escape. The soldier raised himself, wild-eyed and panicked, when he reached the top. Blood was splattered all over his face, likely from a fallen comrade, and he shook his head wildly. "The dogs turned on us!"

"What's your point?" shouted Byram. "They're just dogs. Take them out."

"We did, sir," replied the soldier, now visibly trembling with fear. "But something else is in the fog that we can't see. The attacks are coming from everywhere. They're coming from the ground . . . from the trees. Men are being slaughtered in there."

The soldier then ran past, and Byram could hear him scream when he was taken out by a hunter's trap. The traps were all around them, invisible and very effective. Now he too feared that something evil and invincible was indeed in the fog.

"We need to get around this fern field," called Byram to two cavalry officers. "Take your men to the left and right, and let's deal with this once and for all."

"Yes, sir," replied both officers and directed his order.

Byram watched one group ride off, but as the first men disappeared into the fog that was now rising from the fern field, he could hear the arrows coming from the trees and the screams that followed.

The rest of the cavalry soon turned around and gathered back on the ridge. The forest became ghostly quiet, with no movement to be seen or sound to be heard until a black and white bird flew out of the fog and landed on a branch in the tree next to him. The officers looked to him for advice, turning their faces towards him, their eyes pleading for some sort of solution. He knew that none of them were eager to continue, but he had to his advantage that they feared him as much as they feared what was lurking beneath the fog.

It had not been easy to reestablish that kind of respect, but he had done so, and had done so deliberately. It was all in the details. After watching the flames take hold of the waitress's cottage, he had returned to camp with his face and clothes still splattered with the women's blood and the thirst for more in his eyes. He had told his men he knew how to get to the hunter's village, and they were to ride out within the hour. Two officers had dared to speak against him.

"We would have to send scouts out first," one of them had said. "Let's not be fools by going in totally blind. We have no detailed maps of that area . . . wouldn't know where to begin."

"Yes," another had agreed, nodding in support of the first officer's recommendation. "I refuse to risk the lives of my men by rushing into the unknown."

Byram had stared at them for a moment, and when it looked like he was going to walk past them in anger, he pulled two knives at the last moment and slit both their throats. After that, he regained the fear the men had always had for the black order. The fear that he was more than human, that he could kill men just by looking at them.

With all the horses lined up on the ridge and the fog thinning and rising, Byram decided to push forward. With swords raised, the last of his men charged forward and slashed down at the ferns, the horses trampling over dead soldier bodies as they went.

They made their way across, finding nothing lurking in the fern. They stopped, and Byram looked back at the field of ferns, which was no longer covered in fog. When his horse sidestepped, trying to avoid a body strewn across the ground in a heap, he caught movement in his peripheral vision. He looked to his men to raise the alarm, but it was already too late. A sea of arrows rained down on them from the trees and took the last officers and soldiers down all around him. Before an arrow found him and took him to the ground, he looked up and saw Lucas watching him from a distance. The boy had become powerful, he thought to himself as he felt himself fall. More powerful than anyone had foreseen.

CHAPTER 29

Lucas watched as Zera and Warrick dug some dried meat out of their saddlebags. The other chosen were all sitting or lying down on the rocks around him to rest before they had to move on again. Davis was sitting next to him. They were at a high point at the edge of the forest, in a small clearing between rocks. In this place, they were supposed to meet Dastan, who would take them across the land, towards the mountains where his people lived.

The hunters had celebrated their victory by roasting several pigs. When the messenger had returned that same night, the chosen had said their goodbyes to the village people the following morning. They had then followed Orson and several hunters to where they now waited. They were left on their own, as the hunters were not comfortable being this far out, and they settled down to wait.

Several hours had gone by since then, and Lucas had started to carve a drawing into a leather water sack. It wasn't the worst way to kill time, and given all of the commotion they'd had to endure, he was enjoying the relative quiet and solitude.

"When we were lying in wait in the ferns," said Davis sitting next to him. "I could hear your voice in my head. First, you were telling me to move forward, then to stop and concentrate on a dog." He waited for Lucas to respond, but Lucas just listened. "I then called the dog over with my mind and waited for it to come closer. I don't think it ever saw me until it jumped out of the fog, and I commanded it to obey me. I knew that I wasn't quite doing this myself—that I was controlling the dog through you. How is this possible?" he asked. "How could I hear you?"

"I don't know," answered Lucas. "I can hear you too sometimes. When you think things that you want to say out loud."

"You can?" asked Davis. "What about Zera and Warrick . . . and the others?"

Lucas shook his head. "They seem to know what I want them to do, but they don't hear my voice in their mind, and I don't hear them. The connection you and I have is much stronger and different." He saw Zera and Warrick come over, and Zera handed him a piece of the dry meat before sitting down on the other side of him. "What are you making?" she asked, pointing at the water canteen.

Lucas held it up to show her the magpie and trees he had already carved.

"Pretty good," said Warrick, standing before him and chewing the meat. "I didn't know you could do that."

"Hmm," answered Lucas. "I carved Amalia's leather ball one time with her name when I spent all those months recovering at the monastery. I thought I'd try something different this time."

Zera wanted to say something else but stopped when Lucas suddenly froze.

"What is it?" she asked.

Lucas put the canteen down and stood up. The other boys also got to their feet, but Lucas put his hand up. "It's all right," he said as a man came into view. Now clean-shaven, Dastan was only recognizable by his leather trousers and suede vest. "It's the person we've been expecting." When Dastan approached them, Lucas nodded in greeting. "It's good to see you again," he said, smiling.

"And you as well, Lucas," replied Dastan.

They shook hands, and then Lucas turned halfway to Davis, who had come to stand behind him. "This is Davis," he said. Lucas had told him how Dastan had saved his life twice but also that he had been the one who had stopped him from crossing the river. Seeing Davis eyeing Dastan from head to toe, Lucas could only assume he was questioning his intentions.

"You are one of the chosen twins," said Dastan, extending his hand to Davis and glancing over to Zera. "Lucas spoke of you. It is a pleasure to meet you finally."

Davis took a moment before accepting it. "Likewise," he said and shook his hand.

Zera and Warrick gave Dastan a nod when Lucas pointed them out, as did the rest of the chosen as he said each of their names.

Leaving his friends behind, Lucas followed Dastan to the top of the rocks. From there, they could see far over the countryside.

"I heard you were sent here by Itan himself?" asked Dastan after a moment of silence between them. "May I assume he knows who you are then?"

"Yes," answered Lucas. "I told him after we fought the battle against Lord Killeand."

"How did he take it?"

"It didn't come as a surprise to him. There had always been the dispute that I was not a true chosen, and his brother is a firm believer of the prophecy." Lucas stared into the distance before speaking again. "I lost a chosen during the battle," he said. "I didn't expect anything like that to happen, though that was foolish, of course, and I now know better. Tanner's death has been a big loss to us."

"I'm sorry to hear it," said Dastan. "It's never easy."

"I should have been able to prevent it," said Lucas. "My connection with the chosen is getting stronger every day, as if their blood runs through my veins."

"But you did not feel Tanner's at the time?"

Lucas shook his head. "No, I didn't," he answered.

Dastan looked at Lucas, but when he didn't say anything else, he pointed to the snowcapped mountains in the far distance. "That's where we have to get to," he said. "It'll take us a few days, and we will need your skills to get us there safely. King Boran knows you are here and has deployed many soldiers to find you."

Lucas nodded. "I can get us past them."

"Have your powers gotten stronger since we last met?"

"Yes," answered Lucas, recalling the conversation he and Davis had that morning.

Lucas noticed Dastan look at him. "Well," Lucas said. "We best get going then. It looks like we have a long way to go."

They made slow progress as they traveled over open grasslands and forests and the occasional sprawling farm. They went around villages to avoid all the patrols looking out for them on the roads. On one of these occasions, as they made their way past the outskirts of a town, they noticed a burned ruin. Dastan turned back twice to look at the ruins of the house that once stood there.

"Did you know the woman who lived there?" asked Lucas, without looking at the ruin himself.

Dastan turned around in his saddle and stared at him. "How did you know it was a woman? And yes, I knew her."

"I no longer need the stone to show me the past or future," explained Lucas. "If an event directly affects me, then I can see it."

"Then she was the one who gave up the location of the hunter's village?" asked Dastan. Lucas nodded.

"I thought she might have been," continued Dastan. "Her child's father was a hunter I used to meet regularly until a year ago when he was killed by Boran's men on his way back to the forest." He paused as if waiting for Lucas's response but, when he remained quiet, Dastan continued. "Did they suffer?" he asked.

"It was quick enough," answered Lucas, who tried to push away the grim images flooding his mind. He was glad knowing Byram had not escaped the hunters' arrows and that he had watched him go down with the last of Boran's soldiers.

They continued to ride on in silence, the thought of what happened to the women and child at the cottage weighing on Lucas's mind. When Lucas knew patrols were getting close or when he sensed danger, he would have them change direction, and Dastan assisted in directing them around the farms and villages he was familiar with.

"We should avoid being seen by anyone," said Dastan. "The people here in the lower lands love their king and will not hesitate to point us out to the soldiers."

"Why is that?" asked Zera. "From the way I have heard people talk about him, I thought he was a bit of a villain."

"To some, he is," answered Dastan. "Like the hunters, and my people, but not to those living near him. Unlike his father and his grandfather before him, Boran stopped demanding taxes. He only accepts gifts and donations from those who can afford it, hands bread out to the poor. He also makes himself often seen by the people."

"For what purpose?" asked Lucas.

"Yes," added Davis. "Why would he give food away and get nothing in return?"

"Ah," said Dastan, "but he does want something in return. He requires the firstborn son of each family to join his army at the age of fifteen. Most boys are never heard of again, and no one knows for sure what happens to them."

"And the people simply accept that?" asked Zera.

"Unfortunately, yes, they do," answered Dastan. "They see it as a small price to pay for living in peace, especially for those who still remember the tyranny under his father's rule. They also make it a point to overlook that the prison in Ulmer—a big town near Boran's castle—is strangely empty, and not because there is no crime. People accused of any wrongdoing simply vanish there."

"He is clouding the people's minds then?" asked Zera.

"Yes," answered Dastan. "Boran comes from a long line of greedy, heartless ancestors, and we don't believe he is any different from them."

"But he might be," said Lucas.

Dastan turned around in his saddle and looked at him as if he thought he was joking. "Yes, he might," he answered before returning his gaze to the path ahead of them.

When they reached the foot of the mountains, Dastan led them through a forest and up to a cave where they stopped and dismounted so that they could all rest for a few hours before making the difficult ascent. Lucas was thankful to finally be able to put his head down in a place where he felt protected by the distance they put between them and Boran's patrols. Before he fell asleep, he heard Dastan make a bird call, which was answered in the far distance, from somewhere farther up the mountain.

Lucas woke up when he sensed someone else coming to the cave and joined Dastan, who was standing at the entrance. He heard a bird call, unlike the one he'd heard earlier, and Dastan replied to it.

A moment later, a dark-skinned man with graying black hair was coming down the mountain path—he was on horseback and leading a mule laden with fur coats. When he reached Lucas and Dastan, he dismounted and started to offload the coats.

"What are the coats for?" asked Archer, exiting the cave.

"Best put that on," said the man as he handed Archer one. "It's mighty cold where you are going."

"How cold?" asked Archer, staring at the heavy bundle of fur in his hands that resembled a thick, hooded blanket more than it did an article of clothing.

"Ice cold," replied the man with a grin and handed coats out to the rest of the chosen.

After each of the chosen had joined them outside and put a coat on, Dastan had them mount up, and they were soon on their way again. The temperature dropped as they climbed, and Lucas was thankful for the extra layer of protection.

When they reached the tree line, the rough sandy earth was replaced by slippery rocks, and the horses had a hard time finding stable ground. Then the ice appeared on the ground, and they dismounted.

"I thought he was joking when he said 'ice cold,'" said Archer from the back of the line. "I can't feel my fingers."

"I have never felt this cold in my life," added Warrick, "and I don't think the coats will stop us from freezing to death."

"Blow warm air into your cold hands," said Dastan, "or tuck them inside your coat. And don't worry—it won't be cold where we are going."

They walked until they came to a plateau covered with snow and a dense fog that prevented them from seeing more than forty feet in front of them.

"Welcome home!" smiled Dastan to Lucas.

"I remember this place," said Lucas, looking around. "This is where I was given to Einar as a baby. I remember the snow on the ground. There were people dressed in fur coats, and the fog was behind them."

Dastan nodded. "The fog followed you and our last people to safety, and it has been here ever since. It used to be much denser and covered the entire plateau after you were handed over to Einar. Then, a few years ago, it started to retract and thin out. The elders say it is a sign, and they are anxious to meet you. Come," he said and started walking towards the fog, disappearing within it. Pulling the hoods of their coats more snugly around their faces, the chosen pulled on their horses to follow.

They could see nothing for a long time as they made their way through the fog and had to stay close together not to get lost. Only when Dastan stopped to make the call of an eagle could they vaguely see the outline of a rock wall in front of them. After the call was answered, they turned towards the left until a crevice became visible in the rock face. The crevice soon became larger—like a narrow canyon opening—and revealed a path just wide enough for a horse to pass through. They all mounted up, and Dastan warned them not to make a lot of noise. In case it was ever discovered, the passage had been rigged with large boulders, and they could dislodge with too much vibration.

The path became wider after they entered, and looking up, Lucas noticed several mountain people watching them from a ridge above as they silently moved through. They stared at him, and some nodded their heads to greet him. He nodded back in return.

After a while, they started to descend and eventually came to the opening of what looked to be a cave or tunnel. Dastan dismounted, and the chosen followed suit. The temperature had become milder, and they shrugged off the fur coats and handed them back to be strapped down on the mule. Dastan lit a couple of torches that had been placed in a barrel by the entrance and handed them down the line. Their purpose was clear—to light their way into the cave. "Not far now," he said when everyone was ready to move again.

"Why did they ever take you away from here?" asked Davis as he marveled at the impressiveness of the cavern they found themselves in. "Looks to me, you would have been safe here."

"I wasn't supposed to be hidden away, apparently," answered Lucas. He marveled at the height of the cavern's ceiling, which had to be two stories high and was equally as wide. "Dastan's brother had a vision of the warrior monks, and the elders decided that was where I was supposed to be."

"We were also not this prepared and organized at the time," added Dastan. "That evolved when it became clear we could never leave the mountains without being hunted down by Boran."

They followed a narrow path on a ridge along the edge of a deeper part of the cavern, where they were met by the deafening sound of water cascading from an opening higher up. The water collected in a pool at the bottom and was carried off by a river running parallel to the path. As the cave passage narrowed, the river veered off to the left and disappeared underground, only to reappear when Lucas could see light ahead of him, indicating the end of the cavern.

They doused their torches into a barrel of sand and had to shield their eyes from the bright sunlight when they exited the cavern. Their horses stepped off the rocky ground onto soft soil, and the chosen looked around in amazement. Before them lay a valley surrounded by towering rock formations protecting everything within—the expansive lake, lush green grazing fields, and orchards as far as their eyes could see. Forests lined the rocky perimeter.

Dastan answered a call that came from below, and they soon met five riders who stood waiting for them at the bottom.

"Nolan," greeted Dastan when he stopped his horse. "Lucas, do you remember meeting my brother at the monastery? He's the leader of our people here."

Lucas could immediately see the resemblance between the two brothers and tried to recall the image he had of the stranger in the courtyard. Both brothers were tall and lean with dark eyes that could pierce through you. He remembered Nolan with a stubble beard, but he was cleanly shaven now, and his hair was shorter than Dastan's. The most significant difference between the brothers was the way they carried themselves. Lucas met the same stern look Nolan had given him as a boy. He nodded to greet him.

"It's been a long time," said Nolan. "We have been eagerly awaiting your arrival." He then turned his horse around, and they followed him down the road to what looked like a settlement that could accommodate hundreds of people.

"Was there not an elite born once by the name of Nolan?" asked Warrick quietly of Davis.

"There was," answered Davis. "He was one of the boys who died in the stable fire. Same fire Egon rescued Lord Meloc from when he was a chosen one."

"I heard Egon was friends with him," said Zera. "I mean, as much as a chosen is allowed to be friends with an elite born."

They had spoken softly, and Lucas did not think anyone had heard them, but Dastan turned around and looked at them. "That fire was unfortunate," he remarked, "and very tragic for the two boys who did die that day."

The air was filled with the smell of blossoms when they followed the road through an apple orchard. The trees were planted in a natural fashion, rather than in rows as was typical, but each tree was given enough space and, therefore, light to grow in. After the orchard, they passed crop fields and pastures for horses, cows, and sheep. The people working in them paused to look at them as they went by. They could see houses and other structures built in clusters throughout the landscape, and these looked to be small villages.

"I guess they are," said Dastan when Lucas asked about them, "but they are also part of one big community." Dastan pointed to the houses by the lake. "That's where the fishermen live and, over there by the fields, the crop farmers. By the forest, we have the woodsmen and the carpenters."

"So, every village has a specific role?" asked Lucas.

Dastan nodded. "Precisely. All goods are brought to a central market and traded fairly and honestly. Rarely has there been a dispute that could not be handled with a civil discussion."

They rode towards the lake and stopped by a large rectangular building that was raised on pillars and had a large porch in the front. They dismounted and Lucas followed Nolan and Dastan up the steps. The chosen came in behind him. The five riders who had accompanied Nolan took all the horses and continued on.

"We thought you might be hungry," said Nolan. He gestured to a large round table where food was laid out. "Please sit down and help yourself. There is plenty."

"That's very kind of you," said Lucas and walked to the table. He waited until Nolan and Dastan took their seats before sitting down and viewing the food spread out before him. There were platters with slices of wheat bread, fish, cheeses, and fruit. Jugs of milk stood in between. All of it looked fresh, and the bread still felt warm when he took a slice of it to put on his plate.

Dastan talked to Nolan at the far end of the table while they ate, and Lucas watched them closely. Dastan was informing his brother about the death of the waitress and told him how Boran's soldiers had entered the hunter's forest. Nolan listened and occasionally glanced in Lucas's direction.

"Do you recall seeing Nolan at the monastery?" asked Davis softly next to him as he looked in the direction of the brothers.

"I do now," answered Lucas. Feeling Nolan's deep penetrating eyes on him brought his memory back. "Nolan came to watch me practice with the warrior monks after my father was killed. It was also the day I became Father Ansan's student."

"Was that a coincidence?" asked Zera while pouring milk into her cup from an earthenware jug. "Or did he have something to do with that?"

"He told Father Ansan that I had to stay at the monastery, and that I needed to be taught the ways of the warrior monks," answered Lucas. "That was after he snuck up on me during practice and tried to take my sword from me."

"Which probably wasn't possible even when you were, what, ten years old?" asked Davis.

Lucas shook his head. "No," he answered. "I felt his presence behind me and before he grabbed my arm to take the sword, I had switched it to my other hand." He noticed Nolan cast another glance in his direction and suddenly interrupt his brother by holding up his hand. He kept his eyes on Lucas.

"I see you are wary about being here, Lucas," remarked Nolan. "Are you wondering what you mean to us and what I want from you?"

The chosen at the table paused and looked at Lucas. Dastan, too, sat up straight and turned away from Nolan to face Lucas.

"I have learned that the events happening in my life are happening for a reason," answered Lucas. "I'm not wary of being here, but I do wonder if I can fulfill the expectations you have of me."

"I am the one who had the vision of the warrior monks when you were an infant," explained Nolan. "I have been guiding our people with visions for a long time, but since the fog has started to retract, I have had none. The last vision I had was of seeing you here with us, so we all believe you can provide us with answers as to what is to come."

"And before that," said Lucas, "you had a vision of a battle?"

Nolan nodded. "Yes."

"Then we have experienced the same vision, and you probably know as much as I do," said Lucas. He recalled the image of himself sitting on a black horse, with king's banners flapping in the wind around him and an army in the distance. When he was younger, he had thought it to be a mere dream, linked to his desire to become a soldier for the king. "Boran is preparing for a battle," he continued, "but I don't know when, where, or how he is going to do it. The hunters believe he is building a new mountain pass, within the mountains to the west, to get his army across."

"I've had the same thought, and it makes sense," said Dastan. "His father built a wall on either side of his castle, spanning the valley and connecting with the mountain ranges on either side— preventing anyone from seeing what is beyond the castle, further down the valley. Rumor has it that an opening in the mountain on one side—the mountainside facing us—has been created. Over the years, some of our people infiltrated Boran's army in order to find out what he is planning or preparing, but they have all disappeared, with none returning to us."

Nolan folded his hands in front of him on the table. "I know a battle is to be fought," he started, "and I am sure in due time we will find out when and where that battle will take place. I did not bring you here to discuss that, however." He paused, looking Lucas directly in the eye. "What I, and the people here in the valley, expect from you," he said sternly, "is for you to lead our people in this battle when that time comes. I wish you to give our people a life free of fear, either here or in the lowlands. We all know it is up to the gods to decide which king is to rule, and we will accept either, as long as our people can live free of persecution. I've been training young fighters for years, and they are yours to lead. That is the true reason why I brought you here."

Nolan's direct words should have made Lucas feel uncomfortable, but they didn't. He was relieved to know his purpose, even though he felt an enormous weight had just been placed on his shoulders.

It was Dastan who broke the silence. "We can show you our resources to give you a better understanding of the task ahead of you, but that can wait until the morning." He stood up and stepped away from the table. "I know you are all tired," he said. "I certainly am after our journey here, so if you follow me, I'll show you to your quarters."

Lucas and the chosen followed Dastan out of the building, and were shown to a log cabin with bunk beds. It was here where they would spend the night.

"When was the last time we slept on a proper mattress?" asked Warrick as he climbed on the bed above Lucas's. "It's filled with wool, by the feel of it."

"Not since we left King Itan's castle," answered Archer, climbing on another. He threw himself onto the mattress and let out a long sigh. "This feels so good," he said. "I have a feeling I'm going to sleep well tonight."

"Hopefully, we all will," said Lucas, sitting on the edge of his bed. He took his boots off and placed them underneath the wood frame. All the chosen were unusually quiet, and most were already lying down. Feeling his fatigue, Lucas put his head on his pillow. He was already drifting off when he watched Zera fluff her pillow and organize her bed covers, a content smile playing on her face.

Lucas was still lying on his bed after everyone else had already gotten up. He had his arms folded behind his head and was staring up at the slats of the bed above him. He was thinking about everything he had seen and learned the day before when a sudden sense of urgency pulled him from his restful pose. He got up and walked out onto the porch. Most of the boys were relaxing in the early morning sun on chairs or railings and turned to him when he appeared.

Zera stood up and went to stand next to her brother, who was leaning against a post.

"Who is that?" asked Warrick, who was sitting on the railing.

A figure was walking along the lake towards them, and Lucas started down the steps without a word. He knew that firm and self-assured stride very well.

"Time has not been unkind to you, Father," said Lucas when his old teacher came closer. "I did not expect to see you here."

"It just means our paths are meant to cross again," answered Father Ansan, holding his arms out to embrace him. "How have you been since we last met?"

"I've been well. Thank you."

"Then you have accepted who you are?"

"I have."

Father Ansan held him by the shoulders to take a good look at him and smiled. "I am pleased," he said and then gestured towards the chosen, who had all stepped off the porch. "I hope you have managed to pass your teachings over to them?"

Lucas looked over his shoulders and nodded. "Yes. They are with me."

"Good," said Father Ansan, placing a hand on his shoulder. "Then let's go and show me. You have an entire army to train, and hopefully, your friends here can help you."

Lucas followed Father Ansan to a large open field at the base of the rock face that surrounded the valley, where Nolan and Dastan were already waiting with a group of warriors. Trees flanked the field on both sides while the front faced the lake.

"We are still awaiting the arrival of other warriors from the settlements," said Nolan when they walked up to him. "They should be here shortly."

"That's all right," said Father Ansan. "It will give us a chance to see how well they have been trained."

The group of older boys and men had gathered with swords and other weapons. They stood organized in groups, and on Nolan's command, they stepped forward to be introduced and took turns demonstrating their skill set. There were archers, close combat fighters, long-distance spear throwers, and cavalry. Each group also showed their skill with the sword. When the warriors' demonstration was over, Father Ansan turned to Lucas. "Do you mind showing us what you and the chosen are capable of?"

"Not at all," answered Lucas. He walked some distance away, and the chosen followed him. He took his place in front of the chosen as Father Ansan had done with the warrior monks when he was a young boy and concentrated. He connected with each of the chosen until he became one with the entire group behind him. He led, and they followed in perfect unison, as if he was moving their swords for them through the different stances. He saw Father Ansan nod approvingly when he finished. Lucas walked up to him, and Ansan placed a hand upon his shoulder. His eyes glistened with emotion.

"You have come a long way since that day I saw you at the door of the monastery," said Father Ansan, "to deliver the sword I had asked Einar to make."

"That was a long time ago," replied Lucas. "I am no longer that young boy whose only desire was to learn to fight and join the king."

"No, you are not," said Father Ansan. "It's a joy to see you calm and focused and as fluent in your movements as only highly trained monks can be. You have certainly become one with your sword." He gestured to the warriors who had arrived for training. "By the way they look at you, I can tell they feel the same thing I did so many years ago and each time I have seen you since. A connection stronger than words can describe."

Lucas looked at the warriors. He could feel a link with them, but it wasn't as strong as the one he had with the chosen. He watched as Nolan finished speaking to them and approached him.

"They are ready when you are, Lucas," said Nolan. "They are eager to learn from you."

Father Ansan put his hand on Lucas's shoulder. "Best not to leave them waiting, then," he said. "Show them everything they need to know."

"I will," replied Lucas. As he walked away, he heard Nolan speak to Father Ansan.

"I had to convince you once to take him on as your student," said Nolan. "Has he become what you expected him to become?"

"No," answered Father Ansan. "He has exceeded all the hopes I had for him. The gods have gifted him with powers far greater than I ever imagined."

"What does that mean, do you think?"

"That his journey to the end is not going to be an easy one."

Lucas wiped the sweat off his face with the sleeve of his shirt. He had spent all morning training the warriors that were entrusted to him, as he had done the previous few days. The chosen had settled into the structured community life. The people living in the valley rallied together to provide food and support for the warriors now training on the field every day. The chosen played their part, and especially Zera lent a helping hand whenever an occasion arose.

"It looks like the women are setting up the tables for lunch," said Warrick, resting his sword in the dirt. "Can we stop now, or do you want us to continue until they ring the bell?"

"I think we can break early," answered Lucas. He turned to Nolan, who was standing not far from him. "If that's all right with you, Nolan? To call an end to the morning session?"

"Fine with me," answered Nolan and let his voice bellow across the field to the warriors. "Everyone, our break commences now. We will resume in an hour."

Zera put her sword in the scabbard and turned to Lucas. "I'm going to see if they need help with getting food out," she said in a cheerful tone. "I'll see you at lunch."

"All right," said Lucas and watched her walk away. He was about to put his sword in the scabbard when he noticed Zera pause midfield. She swiped at her neck as if squashing a bug and looked at her hand. When a little girl dressed in a blue dress approached her, she stopped and then let the little girl take her by the hand.

"Where's Zera going?" asked Warrick, looking down the field as he picked up his sword.

"I don't know," answered Lucas as he watched Zera disappear down the road leading to the orchards. "She said she was going to help with lunch preparations, but she must have changed her mind."

Lucas sat down with the chosen at one of the long tables laid out with fresh bread, milk, fruits, and cheeses. He was hungry and took some of the bread and cheese, but while he ate, he couldn't keep his eyes off the empty seat next to Warrick, where Zera would typically sit.

"She'll come," said Davis next to him. "She likely went to the barn and ended up helping with the lamb born there yesterday. She told me this morning that one of them wasn't drinking the mother's milk."

"Lucas and I saw her walk towards the orchard with a little girl," replied Warrick. He picked up his cup to drink his milk and gestured behind Davis and Lucas. "That little girl, in fact," he said.

Lucas turned and saw a little girl in a blue dress running towards them. She stopped next to Nolan, sitting at the end of a table, and talked to him.

Nolan turned to face her and then jumped up. "Where, Lilly?" he asked, gripping her by the shoulder. Lilly started crying and pointed her finger down the road. "Where is she?"

Lucas jumped up from his seat. "She's in the orchard," he called. He had used his mind and seen her lying down in the grass. "By the third row of trees."

"What's happening?" asked Davis, standing up.

"It's Zera," answered Lucas. "We need to get to her. I think she got stung by an insect on the training field and has had a reaction to it."

Davis's eyes went wide—then he started running with Lucas and the chosen right behind him.

They found Zera with a swollen neck and gasping for air underneath a blossoming apple tree. Her eyes were wide with fear as she gripped her brother's arm. She tried to say something, but no words came out.

"Don't speak," said Davis. "Try and stay calm. We'll help you."

"We need to get her to Father Ansan," said Nolan, feeling her neck. "She was stung on her throat, and swelling is obstructing her airway."

"Will she be all right?" asked Lucas. He wished there was something he could do, but no gift he had could help her.

"There's time," answered Nolan. "We've dealt with bee stings before and know how to get the swelling down."

The wagon could not come fast enough, and Davis went from pacing to squatting beside Zera and pacing again. Lucas held him back as several warriors lifted Zera and placed her in the wagon when it finally arrived. "Let them help her," he said. "All we can do is wait."

"We cannot lose her to a stupid bee," said Davis as they watched the wagon drive off. "It's not right."

"She will make it," said Lucas. "Zera's tough, and Father Ansan is here. He knows how to heal."

The chosen walked back to the communal building where Zera was taken in a somber procession and waited on the porch for news. To Lucas, it seemed an eternity before Father Ansan stepped outside and told them she was going to live. "The ointment put over the affected area, and the oral medication has stopped the swelling," he told them.

"Can I see her?" asked Davis.

Father Ansan nodded. "She is resting."

Lucas watched Davis rush inside, and he followed Father Ansan when he stepped off the porch. "Thank you," he said as he walked beside his former teacher. "I don't know what I would have done if we'd lost Zera."

"You would have continued," said Father Ansan. "With sorrow in your heart, but you would have continued."

They walked to the lake and stopped by the edge of the water. Together, they gazed out over the lake and watched the fishermen pulling nets into their small rowing boats.

"It's peaceful here," said Lucas. He could hear nothing but the bees buzzing on the flowers in the grass, and the only ripples in the water were coming from the boats.

Father Ansan nodded. "It is."

"Is this your first time here?" asked Lucas.

"Yes," answered Father Ansan. "I came because Nolan asked me to come. He thought you needed more convincing of your destiny. But I'll be leaving soon. You don't need me anymore."

Lucas gave him a sideways glance and then returned his gaze to the fishermen. "When did you know for certain?" he asked. "About who I am?"

"For quite some time," Father Ansan answered. "But not when I first met you."

"Do you mean the day I nearly fell off the wall, or the day I saw you at the door when I delivered a sword?"

"No," sighed Father Ansan. "I met you before that."

"When? I know you were not there when Einar brought me to the monastery as a baby."

"That's right, I wasn't, but I heard about it when I returned. I took it upon myself to have a look when I was told about the agreement Einar had made. You must have been around the age of three when I asked Einar to forge me a special sword, and I saw you sitting on the floor, in the corner, drawing pictures in the sand."

Lucas smiled. He remembered he drew pictures for a long time. It was his way to distract himself from the chaos in his mind until he was able to do that with meditation and practicing the sword.

"You barely acknowledged me," continued Father Ansan. "Even when I sat down next to you one day and tried to engage with you. I returned a few weeks later and received the same response—you were stacking river pebbles that time. I did not get the feeling you were anything special, and I concluded that the decision to refuse you had been the right one."

"But you allowed me to watch from the wall," said Lucas. "You did not chase me away."

"No," answered Father Ansan, "but I did try to discourage you from climbing those walls, if you remember?"

Lucas nodded. The wall had been a challenge. He recalled the various ideas he had to come up with to climb the walls after the vines he had initially used were cut down. He had stacked branches instead, but they had disappeared as well, when he came the following day. In the end, he had brought a rope ladder from home. "I guess I was very persistent."

"Yes," said Father Ansan. "It roused my curiosity, but I wondered how much of that was because of what Einar had told you."

"He never gave me any indication that I was anything other than his son," said Lucas. "He always told me he wanted me to become a bladesmith, though I insisted that I wanted to join the king's army."

"That is what he told me when I asked him to come . . . right after you nearly fell off the wall. I was ready to give him a stern telling off for endangering your life by putting notions into your head. He assured me you knew nothing and then convinced me to allow you to come and learn the ways of the sword so I could find out for myself you were the one."

"That wasn't enough to convince you, was it?" asked Lucas. "I remember the conversation you had with Nolan when he came after my father died. You weren't thrilled to take me on as your student."

Father Ansan looked at him and smiled. "I was not ready to deal with a ten-year-old on a permanent basis. If you remember those first few days, they were not easy, and you tested my patience more than once."

Lucas smiled. He remembered running off more than once when Father Ansan tried to teach him to meditate. He had thought it to be a complete waste of time. All he wanted to do at that time was learn how to fight.

"But by then," continued Father Ansan, "I had already discovered that the stone had spoken to you, and I could no longer turn my back on you. I have often wondered if things would have been different if I had told you of the prophecy that was written about you. Perhaps on one of those nights when the two of us spent hours reading at the monastery? Or when you told me about your desire to go with the circus group? What if I'd sent you back to your people instead of watching you disappear down the path to join the circus? I came close to calling you back that day. How could I allow you to leave with people I knew nothing about?"

"Why didn't you?" asked Lucas. "I would have listened."

"I know you would have," said Father Ansan, "but you were so determined to find a way to get close to King Itan and thought the circus would make that possible. I didn't feel it was my place to stop you."

Lucas watched a fish break the surface of the water and jump back in. "What about the time when I was recovering at the monastery from my fall down the well?" he asked. "You could have told me about the prophecy then."

"I contemplated doing so," answered Father Ansan. "It broke my heart to see so badly hurt and lost. I wanted nothing more than to ease your suffering and provide you with answers, but I didn't think pity would be in your best interest, and so I chose to remain silent and to be tough on you instead. It was another decision I questioned many times in the months it took to help you find purpose again."

"I remember finding the crutches in my room and being told I had to look after myself instead of others doing everything for me," said Lucas. "I felt rage at first, but it became a turning point in my recovery. It forced me to use my legs again."

Father Ansan nodded. "As I watched you leave a second time, accompanied by king's soldiers, I still wasn't sure if I'd done the right thing by not telling you about the prophecy, but watching you today with the chosen and the warriors, I know I did. You have found your own way in securing your destiny, making a name for yourself through your actions and words, rather than by the name you were born with."

"I think I was meant to discover my own truth," concluded Lucas. "You made the right decisions."

The fishermen had finished pulling their nets and were rowing back to shore. Curious to see what their catch was, Lucas started walking in their direction. Father Ansan walked next to him in silence. When they reached the dock, they stopped and waited for the boats to get there.

The boats moored, and Lucas walked enthusiastically onto the dock to help unload the baskets of white fish. They were brought over to tables where the fish were gutted straight away, cut in strips, and sent to the smokehouse for drying. Lucas was happy to help. It felt good to do some hard work again, and he stayed until it was time for him to go back to training.

CHAPTER 30

Nolan lowered his sword, walked over to where he had hung a cloth over a branch, and picked it up to wipe the sweat off his face and neck. "You've worn me out," he said. "Yet you've been training the troops for days now, and you don't even look tired."

"Oh, I'm tired," said Lucas, who had followed him. "I've learned to hide it."

"To not show weakness," said Nolan. "Smart."

Lucas pointed to the back of Nolan's neck, where a burn scar was visible. He had noticed it before, and he had also seen how Davis and Warrick had been closely watching him ever since they heard his name. "When are you going to tell us where you got that?" asked Lucas.

Nolan finished wiping his face and looked at him. "I think you already know," he answered. "So do your comrades over there."

Lucas looked over at Davis and Warrick, who were close enough to hear. "They believe you're the elite born who was said to have died in the stable fire."

Nolan nodded. "I was."

"Why did you make everyone believe you died?"

Nolan hung the cloth back over a tree branch and sat down on a fallen tree where Zera was sitting. "Dastan told me that the scars on your back are Finton's doing," he said. Without waiting for Lucas to confirm this, Nolan continued. "My scar is due to him as well. He is only a few years older than me, and he was one of the older elite borns in the group at the time. He caused the fire in an attempt to kill me, so I chose the path of least resistance and gave him what he wanted."

"Why did he want you dead?"

"Jealousy, pure and simple. A dangerous thing." Nolan paused and waited—some of the chosen were gathering closer to hear his story. "I had been sent to the castle with the pretense of being an elite born. Our people already had someone there, a chosen one, who was supposed to keep the elders informed of what the king was up to."

"Egon?" asked Lucas.

"Yes," answered Nolan. "Egon was adopted and raised by our people on Itan's land with our beliefs, but it proved too difficult for him to get any information out. As you know, the chosen ones are under watch all the time. When no word was received for months, the elders sent me to help him. Meloc was twelve at that time and had just become obsessed with the prophecy after finding a book in their library that mentioned it. No one shared his beliefs, but Meloc had made it his mission to find the true king's protector, and then I showed up unconventionally. Meloc I could handle, but Finton was a different story."

Davis looked at Nolan in earnest. "So, he set fire to the stable because Meloc believed you were the one?"

"No," said Nolan. "He likely set the fire because no one was paying him any attention anymore. I had defeated him in multiple fights, and it wasn't sitting well with him."

"Much like Lucas and Eli's story then," remarked Zera.

"Like father, like son," said Warrick.

"How did you get out?" asked Lucas.

Nolan took a deep breath. "My horse's stall was in the back of the stable block. I wasn't aware of the fire until I heard the screaming, and by then, it was too late. I saw Egon rush into the stable, but a barrier of fire was already separating us. I had no way out—I could only go up and started climbing towards the roof. Two elite borns who were also trapped followed me, but they didn't make it. The smoke and the fire spread quickly. I had taken my shirt off and held it over my mouth and nose to prevent myself from inhaling all the smoke, and I managed to break through the roof just as the flames reached me."

"But didn't anybody see you?" asked Zera. "Didn't anyone notice?"

"It was always said that three boys died in that fire," said Davis. "I can imagine no one saw him because they would have been busy trying to get horses out."

"And Meloc was inside the stables as well, remember," added Warrick. "The focus was on him. That was when Egon saved him and was rewarded with the king's mark later."

"I'm aware of that," said Zera. "I'm simply asking if anyone saw him once he got out on the roof."

Davis shrugged. "Well, if anyone did, then they never told."

"What happened next?" asked Lucas when he saw Zera purse her lips and cross her arms in front of her chest.

"The only thing I could do," answered Nolan. "I jumped into the moat. The cold water took the burn out of my body, but I realized how much I had underestimated the danger I had been in."

"I always knew Eli was dangerous for Lucas," interjected Zera. She unfolded her arms and turned to her brother. "You never wanted to believe me."

"It's not that I didn't believe you," said Davis. "I may have played it down, but if I'd known Finton caused the fire . . ."

"Well," said Nolan, clearing his throat. "Egon had warned me about Finton. He'd known him longer, and they were of similar age, but I thought I had it under control. I didn't. Two boys died that night, and I wasn't going to be the next. I swam to the opening in the walls, to where the water from the underground river comes out to fill the moat. I had to swim upstream to make it through, then let the river take me away."

"Did you know where it was going to take you?" asked Lucas.

Nolan nodded. "Yes," he said. "There were scrolls with maps of the castle's layout—they were part of our studies as an elite. One of them showed the caving system on which the castle was built. I knew I would have to swim through an underground passage before the river finally surfaced. From there, I let myself float down. Miles from the castle, a farmer found me lying on the bank. He tended to me. I told him I had jumped in the river after the mill I worked at had caught fire. Fearing he would find out the truth, I stole a horse from his farm as soon as I was strong enough. I managed to get to the border and eventually made it back home." Nolan looked around at the group of chosen. "You know the rest of the story. Egon rescued Meloc and was given the king's mark for his bravery, securing a high-ranking position at court, which was precisely what the elders had wanted me to do."

The sound of the dinner bell rang just as he finished his story, and the chosen all got up to leave. Lucas was about to follow, but Nolan called him back.

"There's more," he said when Lucas sat back down next to him. "Something you should know." Nolan waited until other people had passed on their way to dinner before continuing. "I was able to get myself to the river border, but not home. I collapsed near the river's edge, unable to go any farther. It was a hunter who found me. Einar."

Lucas looked up at Nolan and then lowered his head to hear the rest of the story.

"Our people had not seen any hunters for decades," continued Nolan. He picked up a caterpillar crawling on the ground near his feet and put it down on the other side of a log. "As most of our people had fled to the safety of the mountains after the Great Battle, the hunters had fled deeper into the woods, but neither of us had forgotten how both our people once stood side by side. After I told Einar who I was and where I came from, he did not hesitate to put me on his raft to take me across."

"I'm not surprised by this," said Lucas. "Einar was a kind man. He wouldn't have left you."

"He was," said Nolan. "He brought me to his village, and after he made sure I was cared for, he set out to make contact with our people to let them know where I was. It was several weeks before I was strong enough to leave, and Einar accompanied me to the edge of the forest where my father and Dax, your true father, were waiting to take me back. Einar and Dax decided to stay in contact to reestablish the bond between our people, and they became friends. It's how Einar knew everything about you and why he was the one trusted to take you to the monastery. It was thought that only a hunter could evade the dark order."

"When I was young," said Lucas. "I used to have nightmares about drowning in the river. I know now that it was a memory from when I was an infant, from when Einar tried to get me across the river on a raft. I saw the dark order on the riverbank—they had arrived too late."

"I want you to know," continued Nolan, "that Einar raised you like his son out of respect for your father . . . not just because of who you are."

Lucas nodded. He understood that Einar's decision to raise him might have been because he felt it was his duty, but the love he had given him had felt sincere. He recalled the memory of his father lifting him from the table in the forge and the words he so often spoke. "He used to call me his little warrior," said Lucas. "I know he loved me, and

I have no doubt he came to see me as his son. As I will always see him as my father."

Nolan put a comforting hand on Lucas's shoulder. "Come," he said. "Let's go and see if there is any food left."

Lucas heard Father Ansan's voice and the laughter of children as he walked to the open-air pavilion that was used for gatherings. He could see Father Ansan sitting on a stool in front of a large unlit stone fireplace that covered the back wall. Swallows were sweeping by on their way to and from nests built in the rafters of the pitched roof. In front of him, children had gathered on benches and on the floor—they were listening to a story he was telling them. Zera was sitting between the children on one of the benches and was braiding Lilly's hair on her lap. The little girl was wearing the blue dress she had worn when Zera was stung.

Lucas leaned his shoulder against a pillar in the entrance opposite the fireplace and crossed his arms as he settled in to listen.

"And as the sun set behind the mountains," said Father Ansan, "the wolf turned his back to the village and disappeared from view, never to be seen again."

"Never, ever again?" asked a Lilly.

"No," answered Father Ansan. "Never again."

"Ah," responded several children simultaneously.

A young boy with long curly blond hair sat up straight and raised his hand in the air. When Father Ansan gave him a nod, he lowered his hand. "Can you tell us the story about the stone?" he asked.

"Oh, I don't know," responded Father Ansan. He lifted his head and looked directly at Lucas. "Maybe someone else would like to tell you that one?" The children all turned around, and some scrambled to their feet to run towards Lucas. A little girl grabbed his hand and led him to where the children were sitting.

"Can you?" asked the curly-haired boy. "Can you tell us the story about the stone?"

Lucas smiled as he sat down. "I think Father Ansan is the story-teller here," he said. "But I can stay and listen, just in case he tells it wrong."

Father Ansan waited for the children to all face him again before he leaned forward. "I will tell you the story," he said, "the way it was told for many generations before it was no longer passed on. Most people have since forgotten about the existence of the stone, and with it, its purpose. Only a few people still remember."

Lucas looked around the group of children, and, when they all remained quiet, Father Ansan asked, "Are you ready?"

The children all nodded, and Father Ansan began. "Our people have been skilled with the sword for a very long time," he said. "We were a small tribe at first and lived in peace, but after we suffered great losses from invasions, we started to practice the art of fighting, in order to defend ourselves. When our reputation and power grew, so did our numbers and our bloodthirst. Warriors started to challenge each other for leadership, which caused chaos and uncertainty for the future of our people.

"Then, one night, after a leader was killed by Yric, his own brother, the people witnessed a fire coming from the sky. It struck the earth where our people lived, causing it to shake. Terrified of what it could have been, they waited until daybreak before standing at the edge of the enormous crater the impact had created. The ground inside the crater was burned and bare, except for something in its center that they had never seen before. It was large and black, and they wanted Yric to go down into the depression to find out what it was. Fearless, Yric took on the challenge, and he started walking towards

319

it. His feet crunched on the scorched ground with each step he took while his people watched in silence. When he was close enough to see what it was, he smiled and turned around.

"'It's just a rock!' he shouted upwards to his people, and then eagerly walked forward to touch it. Other warriors wanted to walk down, but before they could, they watched in horror as Yric touched the stone with his sword."

Father Ansan had whispered his last words, and Lucas could tell that had put more excitement into the story. The children had their eyes glued on him and were eager to hear what happened next, though some put their hands over their eyes in anticipation. Father Ansan made a loud explosive sound by clapping his hands together and stamped his feet hard onto the floor to make it shake. Some kids screamed. Others ducked closer to their neighbor, and Lucas felt squashed by kids scrambling towards him for protection.

"What happened?" asked Lilly after all the children were calm again. Zera had finished braiding her hair, and she pulled one braid over her shoulder to look at it.

"Well," said Father Ansan. "When the stone was touched with the sword, the people heard a loud explosion and watched the sword burst into flames. It set Yric on fire."

"Did he die?" asked a little boy with jet-black hair and a baggy shirt.

"Of course he did, you fool," said an older boy next to him, giving him a hard nudge.

Ignoring the two boys, Father Ansan continued. "Fearing the same would happen to them, the people backed away from the edge of the crater and never returned. Over time, the grass around the stone sprouted up again and turned the black soil into a lush green field. People believed the stone was sent by the gods, who had been angered over the killing of yet another leader, and so the elders decided that no leader was ever to be killed again. Over time, our people were split into smaller groups, with elders in each clan to make decisions and one chosen leader to lead everyone in times of need."

"Like a king?" asked Zera.

Lucas saw that Lilly had jumped off her lap and was now sitting on the floor. Her two braids rested on her shoulders.

"No, like Nolan," answered the older boy. "He's not a king, but our leader."

"Or maybe more like Lucas," said another boy while looking at Lucas. "He will be leading everyone. Nolan only leads our people in the valley."

"Shh," said Father Ansan to stop the children when they started bickering. "Do you want me to continue or not?"

The children all nodded their heads and became quiet again.

"You could say, the chosen leader was like a king in some ways, but, whereas a king's crown gets passed down to the next of kin, our people did not do that. Instead, young warriors from the different clans who wanted to become the new leader would face each other in fights. The strongest would become the new leader. It was done that way for many years. When a leader was dying of old age, a call was sent out to all clans to send their most eligible warriors to try for leadership."

Father Ansan paused and picked up the cup that was next to him on the bench. The children waited while he took a sip from the water. "A young warrior named Arak," he continued, setting the cup down, "was put forward by his people to make the journey towards the meeting grounds. He was by no means the strongest warrior they had ever seen, but he was the most honest, just, and well respected. Arak had to travel from afar and was not familiar with the land he had to cross. The story of the stone had been told to him when he was a child and had been presented as mere legend. He had seen craters in the high mountains before—deep barren holes full of loose rock and not overgrown with green grass and flowers like the black stone's crater. That is why he did not recognize it as a crater when he came across it. He simply stood at the edge of it when he watched the sky turn dark above him.

"With nothing around him to act as shelter, he decided to press on, but as soon as he stepped down into the crater, the weather turned on him. It became windy, and he struggled to move forward. As the rain pelted him, he pulled his cloak in front of his face and pushed on, even when the wind and the rain worked together to create a white barrier that made it difficult to walk and even more challenging to see. Undeterred, Arak moved slowly, step by step, down the crater until he reached the bottom. Something dark loomed up in front of him. He was out of breath when he came to the stone and leaned against it to get a break from the wind. At the bottom of the stone he saw a small overhang, and crawled under it to hide from the rain. With his back against the rock, he pulled his legs in and put his fur cloak in front of him to cover himself from the cold. He thought maybe it was his fatigue causing him to imagine things, as he could have sworn that the rock was warming his cold body. He was tired and soon closed his eyes."

"The stone did not burn him like it had that leader?"

"No," answered Father Ansan, sounding surprised himself. "It didn't. Instead, Arak's mind filled with images of forgotten times and occurrences yet to come as he slept through the night. When he woke, Arak felt he was a different person. The storm had passed, and the sun shone brightly. He crawled out of his shelter and laid his hand on the smooth surface of the rock and then gathered his things to continue his journey. When he made it to the gathering grounds, he told the people about the stone that was smooth to touch, that had provided him with warmth and had filled him with dreams that seemed more like visions. The people realized he was talking about the black stone and did not take him seriously. They laughed when he told them that the stone had shown him a future where he was the new leader. Arak was half the size of some warriors that had arrived, and they told him he stood no chance of making it past the first round."

"Did he?" the children asked.

Father Ansan nodded. "He did, and the rounds after that, until he had won every fight."

"How? If he was not as strong as the other warriors?" asked the older boy.

"Because he had spoken the truth about the stone," answered Father Ansan. "Not only had the stone shown him the past and the future, but he had been given powers that no one else possessed, which helped him defeat even the strongest of warriors."

"Why did the stone give him powers? Did it want him to be the leader?"

"I suppose it did," answered Father Ansan. "You see, Arak was different from Yric. His heart was pure. He cared for all living things, and not just for himself as Yric did."

"So, he became the new leader?"

"He did, but not before he led all the warriors into the crater and told them that the stone would show them what he had seen. It was not to be feared, and yes, it had been sent by the gods, not to punish them but to show them a different way of life.

"One by one, the people touched the stone, each of them realizing he had spoken the truth. It would be the only day that the stone would speak to everyone. After that, it only spoke to Arak and priests, who worshipped it as a gift from the gods. For many years, Arak remained the leader, and, under his rule, our people changed back to a peaceful clan once more.

"We maintained our art of fighting but no longer used our skills for our greed. We acknowledged a king in the east and started to trade with other people. They came to settle in our land, and as they built villages to live, Arak ordered the stone moved to higher ground. He told the people that upon his death, every young and eligible warrior would have to take his place on the stone. Only one would be given the knowledge and power to lead the people. That leader would be vital to the survival of the people. Without the right leaders, chaos and corruption would once more grip the lands. Arak ordered a monastery be built with the stone at its center—he created the order of the warrior monks to ensure its protection.

"By the time the sixth leader was chosen, many of our people had adopted a new way of life. They had become farmers, tradesmen, fishermen, and merchants, and no longer saw the need to maintain warrior skills. They stopped telling the story of the stone to their children. Those who remained warriors moved east and were employed by the king to keep order. They kept their traditions alive and still sent young warriors to the stone to be selected as leaders. When the twelfth leader, Toroun, was chosen by the stone, our people had been loyal servants to kings for many years, yet our warriors were still both admired and feared.

"Did the stone choose another leader after Toroun?" asked Zera.

"No," answered Father Ansan. "After Toroun's death and with the land now divided by two kings after the Great Battle, our people became separated from the stone and the monks who protect it. No other young warrior was ever sent again."

"What happened to it?" asked the curly-haired boy.

"It remains at the monastery, and monks still guard it."

"Have you seen the stone, Father?" asked a little girl. When Father Ansan nodded, she looked up to Lucas. "Have you?"

Lucas looked at Father Ansan first and then nodded. "I have, yes," he said. "The first time when I was a young boy living at the monastery, and twice since then."

"What does it look like?"

"As Father Ansan told in the story. Smooth . . . and as black as the night sky."

Father Ansan put his hands on his knees and stood up, which signaled to all the children that it was time to go. They muttered and argued but stood up and left when they saw Davis at the entrance, waving Lucas over.

"Nolan canceled practice for everyone this afternoon," said Davis as they walked out of the pavilion.

"Why?" asked Lucas.

"Not sure," answered Davis. "He left in a hurry after he received a message and told all the warriors to go home. Having time off, the boys now want to ride to the back of the valley. Dastan told Warrick about a rock formation from where you can view the entire valley, and you can jump into the lake below. Do you want to come?"

"Sure," answered Lucas. He wondered what the reason for canceling practice could be, but he was ready for a break and had been keen to see the rest of the valley himself.

When they neared the corral, he saw that the other chosen were already saddling the horses. Most of them were engaged in cheerful chatter, and Warrick whistled a tune.

They rode past the fishing and tradesman settlements through the forest towards the high cliffs, where the road continued through a narrow canyon. Still wide enough for a wagon, the chosen rode three abreast, and Lucas rode next to Davis and Zera. He felt relaxed and looked upward at the towering, orange-tinted rock formations.

"How far does this road go?" Davis called out to Warrick, who was at the front. His voice echoed off the rock walls.

"To the other side of the lake," Warrick called back, "but we don't go that far. Dastan said to look out for a small group of trees on the left side of the road. That's where we will find a trail we need to follow on foot."

"That shouldn't be too difficult," said Zera.

"Maybe not for us," said Archer, looking over his shoulder with a grin on his face, "but how many times did you walk right past your rake at the stables when you were looking for it?"

Lucas was happy to see Archer smile. He had not seen Archer smile since Tanner's death, and it was a relief to finally see him do just that.

"Are you implying I will not be able to find a small group of trees on this otherwise barren road?" replied Zera. "I am sure I can find it before any of you."

"I accept that challenge," said Archer and spurred his horse forward into a gallop.

Zera did the same, and the other chosen immediately followed. They were leaving Lucas and Davis behind in a cloud of dirt.

Davis turned to look at Lucas. "What do you think?" he asked, reining his horse in.

"I think we'd better go after them," smiled Lucas and let his horse go.

With the wind rushing through his hair, Lucas could hear the playful cheers from the others up ahead. He caught up with them when they were dismounting by the trees and running up the path between the rocks. Lucas secured his horse and waited for Davis before following them. The trail first went in the direction of the lake but then split in two, continuing to the water's edge and the other way going upward along the cliff face that stretched out into the lake. The chosens' pace and chatter diminished as they climbed higher. Finally, they reached the plateau overlooking the valley. Lucas joined Zera and a few boys near the edge as they stood in silence, taking in the breathtaking view. He could see the entire lake and the settlements that dotted its edge.

"This is beautiful," said Zera as she took in the scenery.

"It makes you never want to leave this place," remarked Warrick.

"So peaceful," said Davis.

The other boys muttered in agreement.

"Hey, Zera?" asked Warrick. He was standing close to the edge and was peering over the rock to the water below. "Didn't Dastan tell you we could jump into the lake from here?"

Zera nodded, "He did."

"Awesome," said Warrick and started taking off his boots and shirt. "Anyone with me? Lucas, Davis?"

Lucas took a step forward and looked at the water below. They were at least thirty feet high, and it would be a risky jump. "All right," he said. "I'll do it."

"I'll have to pass on this one," said Davis. "I can't swim."

"Same here," said Zera.

Two other boys couldn't swim either and settled themselves away from the edge. After taking his shirt and boots off, Lucas went to stand next to Warrick.

"Have you ever done this before?" asked Warrick.

"No," answered Lucas. "You?"

"Never," said Warrick, "but there's a first for everything." He took a few steps back and then ran towards the edge. Without hesitation, he jumped. Lucas watched him hit the water feet first and disappear underneath for a few seconds. When he resurfaced, he let out a cry of excitement. "Hurry up!" he yelled. "What are you waiting for?"

Lucas let out a deep sigh as he stepped back and then ran forward to jump. He entered the water before he had time to think about it and let himself sink deep down in the lake, where the sun's reach lost its strength, and the water became dark . . . almost black. Above, he could hear the other boys hit the water one after the other. He looked up and could see their feet treading water. Running out of air, he pushed himself to the surface, where he was greeted by the beaming faces of his friends—some of whom were already climbing out to do it again.

They all jumped until the thrill of it wore of, and they were tired from climbing up to the rock plateau each time. Lucas laid down on the plateau to let the sun warm his body and dry his clothes. He closed his eyes and listened to the cry of an eagle in the distance. He had no idea how long he slept before the sensation of movement nearby woke him. Davis was getting up and walking towards the edge.

"What's wrong?" Lucas asked, pushing himself up on his elbows. Davis had a puzzled look on his face.

"I don't know," answered Davis, "but all of a sudden, there's a great deal of movement in the settlements."

Lucas quickly jumped up to look for himself. He was right. There had been barely any activity in that direction when he had looked earlier, but now tiny dots were on the move everywhere.

"What do you think it means?" asked Davis.

"I think something's wrong," answered Lucas, grabbing his shirt. "We have to go."

Riding back, Lucas saw several groups of people ahead of them on the road heading in the direction of the communal buildings. He noticed the worried faces of the people in the first group he passed as they looked up at him and halted his horse. "What happened?" he asked a man carrying a small child in his arms.

"I'm not sure," answered the man. "We were told to come to the pavilion right away, and not waste any time doing it."

A feeling of unease came over Lucas. Why was everyone called to gather? He was glad when he saw Dastan ride towards them and hoped he could put his mind at rest, but he looked just as worried.

"I was just coming to get you," said Dastan, pulling his horse alongside. "There is something you and I need to see."

"Outside the valley?" asked Lucas. He noticed a couple of fur coats tied to the back of Dastan's saddle.

"Yes," answered Dastan, riding off without waiting for a reply.

Leaving the chosen behind, Lucas followed him past the communal building and the fields towards the orchards and the path leading to the valley entrance.

They rode in silence through the cave, abandoning the horses for fur coats when they came out on the other side. They climbed up a set of steps cut into the ice, which terminated at what looked to Lucas to be a narrow path that followed the main path, only higher up. When they reached the edge of the high cliff, which marked the beginning of the secret valley's mountain barrier, they were met by Nolan and a small group of senior warriors who were already there. Dastan walked past them to see for himself what he had heard. He shook his head solemnly. The fog that had previously hung high and thick had thinned significantly. Anyone who would reach the mountain plateau would now be able to find the entrance to the valley with ease—if they knew it was there to find.

"Anything you can do about this?" asked Nolan when he turned to Lucas.

Lucas looked upward and saw the sun's rays breaking through gaps in the thinning fog. When the light hit the snow, it reflected, causing the ice crystals to sparkle in a magical way. He didn't know how to bring the fog back, but even if he could, he didn't think he was supposed to. "No," he answered. "There is nothing I can do. I'm sorry."

Nolan nodded reluctantly and let out a deep sigh. "Then we better inform the people to get ready."

"What do you mean, there is nothing he can do?" called out a man from the group gathered in front of the communal building. Lucas was standing next to Nolan on the porch. He determined that the man who had spoken was from the fishing community by the smock of rough cloth he was wearing. A farmer wearing a knee-length linen tunic stood next to him, alongside a woman with an apron over her blue dress, her hair swept up away from her face and tied in a knot at the top of her head. Nolan had just told them that the fog would soon be gone completely, and Lucas could see that with panic already in the air, tempers were flaring. They spoke of Lucas as though he wasn't there, and it reminded him that, though he was one of them, he was still a newcomer in some ways.

"He was the one who put the fog there," said the fisherman.

"He was an infant then," the woman called out.

"We had a need for it then," said the farmer.

"And there is no need for it now?" said the fisherman. "Without the fog, it will not be long before Boran learns where we are."

A mutter rose from the crowd, with people nodding and shaking their heads.

Nolan raised his arms. Lucas watched as he gestured, trying to calm the people down. "People, be still!" he called out. "It is not like we have not seen this coming. We have been preparing for a possible invasion for years. Our warriors are better trained than ever before, and we have Baelan here to lead them when the time comes. In the meantime, we will be building more and better defenses."

Lucas looked at Father Ansan, who was standing quietly, and at the

330

chosen, some of whom looked sullen. The joy and happiness from that afternoon at the lake was all but a distant memory. Lucas had felt the peace the valley radiated across the people and feared it could be lost soon. He didn't know how to bring the fog back, but there was something else he could do. His eyes met Father Ansan's briefly before he placed a hand on Nolan's arm to get his attention.

"May I speak?" he asked softly.

Nolan turned to him, a confused look on his face, but then nodded.

Lucas walked forward until he stood at the top of the steps and looked at the people before him. He took a deep breath and tried to swallow the lump in his throat. He waited until the assembled crowd grew quiet before speaking. "I know you had expectations for my arrival here," he began. "Expectations you fear that I am unable to fulfill. I understand that is causing great concern, but even if I was able to bring the fog back, it could not guarantee that it would protect you forever."

"Then what do we do?" yelled the fisherman. "Just stay here and wait until our women and children get slaughtered by Boran's army?"

"That will not happen," called Lucas before the crowd got too noisy for them to hear. "Not if Boran doesn't come."

"Oh, yes?" asked the farmer. "And how are we going to stop him? He has been waiting for this moment all his life and now it is upon us."

"What Boran wants most right now is me," called Lucas. "And I am going to hand myself over to him. That way, perhaps I can have some sway over him."

An unexpected silence came over all that were present. Dastan began to pace, stopping occasionally and shaking his head. Those people that had been on the porch began to settle onto benches—they looked to Lucas as if they had resigned.

"You can't go to him," Dastan finally said. "Boran will have you in chains the minute he lays eyes on you."

"If Lucas feels that he has to go to Boran, then he has to go," said Nolan. "We all have our role to play in this prophecy and have made sacrifices in doing so. He can be no different."

Dastan stared at his older brother with wide eyes. "I cannot believe what I am hearing," he said. "You really think that sending him to what would essentially be his death now, after all that we have done to keep him safe, is in everyone's best interest?"

"You are forgetting the vision I saw," said Nolan, "of Lucas leading a battle."

Dastan stopped and rubbed both hands through his hair. "You haven't had that vision for a long time," he said with a raised voice. "You told me yourself that you didn't know why it stopped repeating in your dreams and feared the prophecy had shifted. None of us know what is to happen when Lucas faces Boran, and I, for one, would rather fight than sacrifice one of our own."

Other people began voicing their opinions, some of them standing with renewed vigor. All were talking at the same time until Father Ansan's voice interrupted. He had stepped to the front of the porch, his hands raised to quell the crowd before him. "Please. All of you. Quiet down and give Lucas a moment to explain himself."

Dastan turned his back to his brother and leaned his arms behind him on the railing of the porch.

Lucas hated to see the two brothers argue. He had never seen Dastan angry and, as the older brother and the leader of the people, Nolan would not appreciate his brother disagreeing with him. Lucas stepped into the space between them. "Dastan," he started. "I'm grateful for your commitment to my safety, but your brother is right. We all have our role to play, and I believe I know mine. The fog has served its purpose for many years, but for reasons unknown to us, it can no longer protect the people. Boran knows I am here. He knows who I am, and I know he wants to see me."

"Boran is not like Itan," interjected Dastan while peering over his shoulder. "He's ruthless, and if he doesn't kill you, he'll torture you . . . imprison you indefinitely."

"Dastan," scolded Nolan, "let him finish."

"I don't think he will," said Lucas, looking Dastan in the eye. "He believes in the prophecy—and that the rightful ruler has not yet been chosen. If I can convince him that he might be the last king standing, he will keep me close, and I may be able to discover his motivations. Perhaps even influence his choices."

"How are you going to do that?" asked Dastan sternly. "That man has hunted you all his life, with the sole intention to stop you from fulfilling your destiny. How do you think you can convince him now that he has been wrong and that you will not follow in Toroun's footsteps and betray him?"

"I will have to save his life," answered Lucas calmly, "like I did for Itan."

The people around him became quiet, and they all stared at him.

Nolan sighed and broke the silence. "That will require a cunning plan and for you to be in a position to carry it out," he said, "which may not be easy."

"No," answered Lucas. "But unlike you, I still see the vision of a battle, and I feel it is what I must do."

Nolan looked to Dastan, who had turned around and was facing them. "Do you still have your contacts in Ulmer?" he asked.

Though Lucas was still uncertain about the details of his plan, what he did know was that things needed to happen quickly. He packed his things and prepared to say goodbye. A large crowd of people had gathered, and warriors were assembled on the training field. Lucas sighed. He knew it would possibly be the last time he would be seeing them assembled together. He turned to Father Ansan, who was holding his sword.

"Be careful," said Ansan, holding the blade out to him. "There is a darkness coming."

Lucas saw the worry in the monk's eyes as he took the sword and put it in its sheath. "I know," he said. "I can feel it as well, but you know I have no choice but to face what comes." He looked out over the warriors.

"You have gained the power to connect with them, as you have with the chosen," said Father Ansan, following his gaze. "They understand you, respect you, and are ready to follow you everywhere."

"And they will," said Lucas. "One day." He turned away and walked over to Archer, who had brought him his horse.

Archer held the reins while Lucas checked the tightness of the girth on his saddle. "I wish you would take all of us with you," he said. "I hate being left behind like this."

"I understand," said Lucas, "but I only need a few chosen to get me close enough to Boran's castle. And I will travel the last part of the journey alone. Besides, I need some of you here to lead the warriors out of the valley when the time is right." He took the reins from Archer and brought them over his horse's head and onto its neck. "You'll be fine," he said as he put his left foot in the stirrup and heaved himself into the saddle. "As far as I'm concerned, this isn't farewell."

Archer stepped back and nodded. "I'll see you, then?" he asked.

"Count on it," answered Lucas, taking both reins in his hands. He wished he could say more to ease Archer's mind, but in truth, he had no idea what he was about to get himself into. He turned around in his saddle and looked at Zera, Davis, and Warrick sitting on their horses behind him. "Are you ready?" he asked.

ABOUT THE AUTHOR

L. Waithman lives in Texas with her husband and three children. When not writing, she is an avocational archaeologist and volunteers her time at a state historic site educating students about the Texas Revolution.